Praise for Richard Taylor
The Haunting of

...catnip for Stephen King fans... An incredible first novel. Highly recommended!

— Jay Bonansinga,
author of *The Black Mariah*,
The Sinking of the Eastland,
and *The Killer's Game*

... a damn good book to soak up during the long winter nights...
— Justine Warwick
Rue Morgue Magazine

The Haunting of Cambria is... a treat...

— Marilis Hornidge
Main Coast NOW Magazine

...will scare your pants off... reminiscent of... Jack Finney's "Invasion of the Body Snatchers... Richard Taylor's debut novel is a gem...

— Heather Eileen
Romancejunkies.com

If you read this on a late stormy night, you are inviting some frightening dreams. (You will have to trust me on that one.) Fantastic! *****

— Detra Fitch
Huntress Reviews

...haunting and beautiful... Refreshing characters, laugh-out-loud comedy, and spine-tingling suspense. I highly recommend this book.
— Wendy Hines
armchair interviews

...really freaked me out... that scary! I haven't had the pleasure of being frightened by a book in a long, long time... you get to the end of a chapter and can't wait to read the next... Don't miss out on this one, it's a real treat.

— Jen Thorpe
Book Sandwich

...a typical haunted house ghost tale... changes into something much deeper and more satisfying... Recommended.

— Harriet Klausner
reviewcentre

Red Mist

a novel

by Richard Taylor

RG A Ransom Greene Book

Other Books by Richard Taylor:

The Haunting of Cambria

*Dark Reflection
and Other Tales*

The Richard Taylor Screenplay Series:

American Mythic
A Boy's Adventure with the U.S. Cavalry in India
Steel Eyes
Dystopia in the Time of the Triple Helix
Pistoleer
A Tale of the Boy Gunfighter
Naked in the Roses
A Nakedly Romantic Comedy
Country Life, Inc.
A Romantic Comedy
Asphalt John
Careful Who You Screw With

Author's Web sites:
www.richardtaylorwriter.com
www.hauntingofcambria.com

Second Printing: August, 2009
Published by Ransom Greene

ISBN: 1441486054
EAN-13: 9781441486059

Parts of this book
Copyright © 1995 and later
by Richard Taylor

Red Mist Copyright © 2009
by Richard Taylor

for Jeff
My Oldest and Best Friend

Acknowledgments

Special thanks to Bill Goergens, whose flash of brilliant insight changed this book, and guided the editing process. Novelist Peter Delacorte took a meat tenderizer to the book, and it is more tender because of it. Moana Re, who then lived in Dallas, provided much needed long-distance research years after I'd walked Dealey Plaza. Tom Merino dedicated a month of lunchtimes to read this book and his help and dedication are appreciated. Thanks to Karen Stoeckel and Sherri Bell, sticklers for truth both, who provided excellent commentary. Bob Sfarzo helped with line edits. And last but certainly not least, thank you Jacqueline Ward, whose advice is always sterling.

I'm sure I'm leaving someone out, which occurs when a book has been stewing for more than a decade. For you, many thanks for your kind indulgence.

Red Mist is a work of fiction. It occurs in what must be considered a fictional parallel universe. Even though historical figures play a role in the story, they are not *our* factual historical figures, even if some of the same things happen to them in both worlds. Historical people are portrayed because the story could not legitimately be told without them, but the story is fiction.

The characters, places and events portrayed in this book are fictitious and any resemblance to persons living or dead is purely coincidental.

16/5/23

Red Mist

Starting during World War II, United States Army military intelligence students were required to undergo a field exercise in order to graduate. They were dispatched individually to an unfamiliar city and ordered to create a dossier on a specific 'public person' ('public persons' having little legal recourse if their privacy was invaded). This practice continued until the early 1970s when the arrest of a soldier stalking a motion picture star uncovered extensive surveillance of American citizens. The greater historical impact of this program is unknown.
              — *Encyclopedia Cognitio*

Red Mist: A term dating from the introduction of explosives in war capable of rendering a soldier's body down to its constituent liquids. Example: "He was standing right next to me, and then he was gone — there was nothing left of him but red mist."
              — *'Terms of War' Column*
                 War Quarterly
                 Summer 1962

- 1 -

Wednesday, August 1, 1962

Brentwood, California

The first time David Dengler saw Marilyn Monroe, she was sitting on her haunches on the front step of her concrete house in Brentwood, California, sweeping leaves away from the stone walk with a hose. She wore faded pink pedal pushers, a gray Jamaican blouse that left her stomach exposed, and cheap Mexican sandals. Her bleached hair was a gaggle of strands, leaderless and unkempt which caught the light like cotton candy, a swirl of sugar and white gold.

She was ordinary.

She was beautiful.

Dengler had no chance but to think these two apparently contradictory thoughts before returning his attention to driving. He was heading for the end of a cul-de-sac named 5th Helena Drive. It was a narrow blacktop road no wider than an alley, all of a hundred yards deep and providing access to a handful of exclusive homes hidden behind walls or fences, each with its own style and identity. Dengler braked the Ford Falcon at 5th Helena Drive's end, a curbless brick wall, backed the car up enough to turn it around, and returned the way he came, proceeding slowly enough to catch another glimpse of the film goddess as he went by.

She was now facing the opposite direction, pointing the hose along the angle of her hips, wiping hair back out of her face with a free hand. She might have been a housewife, although her husband would have been, in the parlance of men, "one lucky son-of-a-bitch."

Dengler braked. It was an involuntary act. The car slowed to a crawl. Marilyn Monroe didn't look up, her mind seemingly far away, lost in thoughts he could never know. She appeared half-immortal, a creature greater than he or anyone who wasn't a star, and half-mortal, wearing clothes which were not perfect, with a roll of flesh at her midriff that wouldn't have been there ten years before, a divine creature in descent.

Like a child who has seen the same person looking down at him from a crib's edge every day, Dengler was thrilled by Monroe's face. He wanted to stop and engage her in conversation, make her laugh at some silly thing he said, beckon to touch her, even, in the way of a toddler whose arms can't quite reach the adult above him. Nonetheless he was aware he was in the presence of the most desired woman of the age, a goddess of the neon world, more famous even than Helen of Troy. Yet here she was, spraying leaves from her walk, guiding a rainbow of water droplets with the shake of a wrist, as human, and ordinary as any hometown girl.

Dengler accelerated suddenly as she began to look up.

Three days before, Dengler had attended a graduation ceremony at Fort Lee, Virginia. In the company of fellow students he opened his orders and read, in part: *You are to proceed to Los Angeles California, arriving on or about August 1, 1962, there to locate the person of Marilyn Monroe, motion picture celebrity. By means of surveillance, while remaining inconspicuous and unidentified, you are to determine the location of her residence, places of frequency, associates, incidentals, and details relating to her. You are to prepare a dossier, which may be compared to and contrasted with existing documentation from prior surveillance, for the purpose of evaluating your field operative ability, both learned and native. These orders are to be signed, dated and returned to Commanding Officer, United States Army Military Intelligence Training School (USAMITS), Fort Lee, Virginia, prior to execution.*

From that instant to this, from the Virginia birches and clapboard barracks of Fort Lee, Virginia, to the white-washed concrete of Monroe's Brentwood house with its red, Spanish tile roof and gaping driveway gate, Dengler had tingled with the knowledge of his extraordinary good fortune.

Dengler expected far less for his graduation exercise, the assignment to follow a small town politician, possibly, or a local television personality. Almost any 'public person' would do. Few undergraduates were assigned to someone really famous. Still, here Dengler was, in Los Angeles, California, having steered down the same tiny street Monroe drove home on each day, tires in the same ruts, with the same cul-de-sac wall her eyes saw daily framed in the windshield before him. Finally, there was the woman herself, mortally near, watering her lawn with a garden hose, private in her thoughts and Dengler closer to her than any other human being on earth.

David Dengler knew very well what the assignment to surveil Marilyn Monroe was. Add something new to the dossier of a small town politician and the yawns of his instructors would combine to blow him out of the classroom. Discover something new about Monroe, something the scores of trainees before him missed, and

Dengler's enterprise might eventually lead to an invitation to join the CIA or the FBI once his Army enlistment was up. Dengler knew very well what Monroe was — she was opportunity.

The man Marilyn Monroe failed to look up and see that morning was twenty-four years old, old for an Army Military Intelligence recruit, a muscular six-footer with gray eyes and bland brown hair. His expression was almost always taciturn in appearance — more than once in his life he'd needed to tell people this was the way he always looked, in order to explain to them he wasn't angry or depressed. As counter-balance, there was his accent, a mild southern twang whose more gruesome nuances he controlled visibly and without grace. He strove for a mid-west delivery, and occasionally achieved it. Still, the twang had the effect of rendering his persona harmless, as Southern accents so often do.

He arrived that morning from Fort Lee, Virginia by way of National Airport, Washington D.C., on a Boeing 707. He'd never flown before.

It took Dengler two hours to find Monroe's address. It was part of the challenge. He arrived in Los Angeles with her name, simply that, with no other knowledge about her except what he could distill from fan magazines and the like. Still, two hours later he drove by her house on 5th Helena Drive for the first time, having tricked a Pacific Bell office manager into divulging where one of his most famous clients lived. Dengler used one of his phony IDs — he and a friend at Fort Lee had concocted three of them — to convince the Pacific Bell manager Dengler was a postal inspector who needed to review Monroe's telephone bill. There was an issue of Monroe having received some threatening calls and mail, Dengler told the Pacific Bell manager, and he was working to link the two.

12305 5th Helena Drive was located below Sunset Boulevard in Brentwood, which Dengler found described in *Los Angeles: Introduction To The City* as, "a Bentley compared to Beverly Hills' Rolls Royce. Brentwood is greener, more wooded, more Bohemian, and very ritzy. It is the sort of place where bachelors go to live before marriage takes them away to more sedate neighborhoods."

Earlier Dengler drove by 5th Helena Drive several times. There were actually over thirty Helena Drives, each flowing into or out of Carmelina Avenue, a wide north-south artery that fed the east-west city jugular known as Sunset Boulevard. On his first pass by the open gate of Monroe's house Dengler saw a two-tone cream-and-green 1956 Ford parked just inside the driveway. *Cleaning lady,* he'd guessed. It was on this earlier go-round that Dengler noted the yard was shouldered by trees, two of them close enough to the wall to provide quick access to the ground.

Dengler then drove to nearby Westwood Village, a college town which lay at the feet of UCLA, and rented a second car, a Chevrolet Corvair convertible. He parked the Corvair on Hilgarde Street near Sorority Row. He would revolve the two cars through the surveillance area to avoid detection.

It was then Dengler drove the Falcon past Monroe's driveway a second time and caught the film star watering her lawn. The 1955 Ford was gone.

Dengler made a right on Carmelina Avenue and pulled the Falcon to the curb. For a long moment, he sat completely still. It was an effort to be motionless. It was an effort not to step from the vehicle and shout. It was as if someone had pulled open a giant door, like one of those Hollywood sound stage doors, and he'd walked onto the world's set. He was a player now, a cast member, not a star certainly, but a performer as much as Monroe herself.

For the first time, it all seemed real.

Later, how much later Dengler couldn't recall, he placed the Falcon in drive and took the car to Sunset Boulevard and right. He drove east until he found a motel near the San Diego Freeway (called that not because it was located anywhere near San Diego, but because it went there, eventually). He rented a room for the week and paid in advance.

At a quarter after six he took a shower, and then wearing only a towel sat down at the writing desk and opened a composition book he'd brought from Virginia. At the top of the first page he wrote:

Dossier:

Monroe, Marilyn
Address: 12305 5th Helena Drive, Brentwood, California
Description: House is Spanish or Mediterranean style; of concrete construction; relatively small, one or two bedrooms; surrounded by brick wall painted white which creates a compound when wood gate is closed.
Observation: Drive-by at 4:35 P.M. 8/1/62 witnessed a cream/green (over/under) 1956 Ford Crown Victoria parked in driveway, Cal. License HYM 726. Housekeeper?
5:19 P.M.: Saw Monroe.

- 2 -

1950s

Chartersville, West Virginia

David Lawrence Dengler wanted to be somebody important, somebody who mattered. Which is to say, he wanted to be what he wasn't. He was born country; he wanted to be cultured. He was born poor; he wanted to be classless. He was born into a family twisted by poverty and wrenched by the inhospitable hills of West Virginia. He wanted to be a citizen of 'the city' and a member of a family whose children were a delight and the hope of the future. He imagined this family to be the sort where money was incidental, and it was idealism and ambition that mattered.

Adam Dengler, David's father, laughed at the pretensions of his son. Dengler thought it was because his father clung to the lowest rung in a society where even the well-to-do had dirt under their fingernails. David Dengler wanted to go to college, and his father laughed. David Dengler wanted to work for the federal government someday, maybe as an FBI agent or a CIA agent or a Secret Service agent, and his father laughed.

"Hell, boy, you ain't bright enough to do any of them things. Put a suit on you and your cuffs'll curl up, your sleeves'll glisten with snot, there'll be jelly and ketchup and drool all down the front of your shirt. You're like your mama, boy, pretty but stupid."

"I am not, old man," Dengler told him.

"Don't tell me what you are," his father said. "I seen you come squirtin' into this life. I know what you are."

Dengler's mother left when he was five. There was a man he vaguely remembered coming into the house while his father was working in the mine. He wore clean shirts, this man, and spoke gently to his mother, although he treated Dengler with a cool disregard at best, and hostility at worst, particularly if his mother were in another room. Once he saw them together in his parents' bedroom, naked and sweaty and entwined in a way that made his young mind reel. The man threw a shoe at him. The boy squealed in fear and ran from the room.

Then a day came when his mother was gone.

David Dengler and his father were not always antagonists. There were the times when his father worked two shifts in the mines. There were the times when the older man was sober, or ill. There were the times when he left for days and wouldn't tell his son where he went. All these were silent times. Liquor would open his mouth, but the words of anger and hatred were there always, spoken or not.

When he was twelve, David Dengler tried to contact his mother's sister Carolyn, her only living relative, but she hung up when he identified himself. Once, seven or eight years before, she'd come to visit him and his father attacked her, slapping her and bloodying her mouth when she wouldn't provide the whereabouts of her sister. David Dengler vaguely remembered the incident, although he did recall he'd grabbed onto his father's pants leg begging him to stop and was kicked across the room for his trouble.

When he was fourteen his father came into his room at the rear of the house and said, "You're quittin' school. I got you a job in the mine."

"I'm too young," the boy protested. "They won't hire me."

"I told 'em you was sixteen. They'll hire you."

"No. If I can't finish high school, I can't go to college."

"You're not going to college, boy. You're goin' to work. I ain't payin' to fill your belly any longer."

They yelled at each other for hours — Dengler was big enough by this time to be immune from physical attack by his father — but it came down to this: The senior Dengler would buy no more food for his son. He wouldn't throw him out — that would require a struggle, and the old man, stooped now from a lifetime of mine work and dissipated by liquor, wouldn't challenge the boy physically. He'd bought his last loaf of bread for this household.

Dengler spent a few hungry weeks until he secured several part time jobs to feed and clothe himself. His schoolwork suffered — he had an A average before the incident and his grades dropped considerably — but at least he could continue. He worked three nights a week in a convenience market, *Junior Walker's*, located three miles away, across town. Another four nights a week he worked at the railroad yard where he did anything that needed doing, sweeping up or hefting and moving things. He worked 30 hours a week. By the time he was sixteen he'd saved enough to buy a 1951 Chevy, a car newer than his father's '49 Ford, although he had to forge his father's signature on the license application. The forgery was so good that later, when challenged by his father about the license, the old man couldn't remember not signing it.

Dengler bought an Admiral 16-inch black-and-white television set and placed it in his bedroom. It was the first television set he had regular access to, although he rarely had time to watch it except late on Saturday and Sunday nights.

He grew up eating Twinkies and Snowballs and drinking Cokes and Pepsis bought at *Junior Walker's*. He was always careful to buy the food he ate, not just take it, because he knew how lucky he was to have this job and he wanted to protect it. He brought lunch meat home and kept it in a cooler beneath his bed with mayonnaise and ice. He kept bread in the sock drawer of his mother's oak chest along with mustard. Every now and again he bought himself a meal, real cooked food, at a truck stop not far from the railroad yard. At these times he always ordered extra vegetables, for which he would often get an uncontrollable urge.

Except for beer, which Dengler didn't drink, their refrigerator remained empty. His father worked ten hours in the mines and spent the rest of his time at a bar, *The Blue Bell*, which was located two hundred yards from the house. He came home each night in a stupor and collapsed into bed. They spoke with one another once a month or so, and then only to argue.

When Dengler was seventeen he found his father still in bed at seven-thirty in the morning. Drool had run down one side of his father's mouth and dried like cold lava on the slope of a dormant volcano. He was in a coma. Dengler called an ambulance from the public phone in *The Blue Bell*, watched as they took his father away, and then went to school. That afternoon he called the hospital and talked with his father's doctor. The old man had suffered a stroke.

"Is he going to die?" Dengler heard himself ask.

"There are no guarantees, David," Dr. Leeson, the hospital doctor, told him. "But I do think he's past the critical stage. He is paralyzed on his left side. That may clear up, or it may not. The truth about stroke victims, David, is we can't predict what will happen. There is no way to gauge cerebral damage accurately."

"What if he doesn't recover?"

"Then he will need a lot of care, and a lot of love."

A shiver shot down David Dengler's spine.

- 3 -

Thursday, August 2, 1962, 1:36 A.M.

Brentwood, California

Dengler woke with a start. He saw the car too late to identify its owner. A Mercedes sedan was parked near the Monroe driveway. Someone had slammed one of its doors and then disappeared inside the yard before Dengler was fully awake.

"Damn it," Dengler said as he pulled himself up and realized that at some point while asleep he'd wrenched his lap and up-ended a large bag of corn chips. He now attempted to scoop them back into the package. Salt caked his pants. He brushed the crystals off, then found his theme book dossier, which he opened. He wrote:

8/2/62 1:37 A.M.: Silver Mercedes 4-door sedan parked near Monroe house. California license ZZI 127.

Dengler was tempted to get out of the car, but resisted. If he got out of the car and approached the driveway to look in at the house and yard, he'd expose himself if the Mercedes's owner walked out unexpectedly. Also, neighbors were certain to question a strange man skulking about.

Still, missing the identification unnerved him. He needed to act. "To hell with it," he whispered to himself.

Earlier he'd rigged the piston controlling the Falcon's dome light not to work when he opened the door. He remained in darkness as he stepped from the Falcon and allowed the door to close. A Walther PPK, Dengler's single prized possession, flopped against his rib cage as he straightened his blue windbreaker, tugging it down around his waist, and casually stepped to the sidewalk.

It was cool now, August heat having surrendered to the night. Dengler stifled a yawn, then stiffly walked down the street toward the driveway. As he approached the angle point providing a view into the yard, he saw the wooden gate was ajar and the house porch light was on. The car he'd witnessed earlier, the 1956 Ford, was parked in the driveway, as well as a 1962 Thunderbird convertible he suspected was Marilyn's.

That's why the Mercedes is on the street, Dengler thought. *No room for it in the driveway*. From this angle, he could just make out the ripples of light reflecting from the surface of an unseen pool onto the side of the house. He heard the ghosts of voices, a man's, and a woman's. He stopped at the tree delineating the southern boundary of the driveway, merged into shadow, and listened.

The man's voice asked, "You have your keys, right?"

"Yes, I have my keys." Woman's voice.

Then another man's voice, one strangely familiar. "What's keeping her? Mrs. Ketchum, go in and get her."

"Don't rush her. This is traumatic enough already." Woman. Presumably Ketchum.

"I've got a full (unintelligible) tomorrow." Maybe *schedule*. Maybe *day*. "Let's move this along." Man's voice. The familiar one.

The door opened, and a man wearing a sweater stepped out. He was possibly six feet tall, lean, youthful looking but obviously at least 40 and slightly graying. He looked familiar but Dengler couldn't place him. He stepped to the center of the driveway and glanced straight up at the night sky, assaying the field of stars, and then turned and looked directly at Dengler.

He's seen me. The thought shot up Dengler's spine, but he remained totally still, and in a moment the man's lack of reaction meant he was looking in Dengler's direction, but seeing things elsewhere, possibly in his own mind.

The second man exited the Monroe house. He wore a suit and projected a ministerial air. *Doctor*, Dengler thought. *Lawyer. Cop, maybe. Professional.* He walked up to Sweater, hands thrust into his pockets. "So... how's your tennis game?" Suit asked him.

"Lousy," Sweater said. "How's yours?" Sweater had an English accent, Dengler realized. He was more familiar now. There was something about him that begged labeling.

"We should get together for a set," Suit said.

Sweater looked at Suit. It was clear from his expression this wasn't going to happen *again*. "Sure," he said finally, making the words mean, *No fucking way, pal*.

"I really enjoyed..." Suit started, but Sweater anxiously left him standing alone and trotted to the door. In a voice slightly louder than before he said, "Hey, can we get this thing on the road?"

A woman's voice answered from inside, "She's almost ready."

Sweater paced past Suit with, "I'll warm up the car." In a matter of seconds Sweater passed Dengler who remained hidden in the shadow of the tree and rounded the Mercedes to the driver's door, which he unlocked. A moment later the engine sounded.

Dengler was in the shadow, and nonetheless standing in the direct course the people leaving the house might take. If they bunched up as a group and one passed west of the tree, rather than east of it, he would be discovered. *Hell*, he thought, *I might be tripped over*. Still, there was Sweater to think of. If Dengler abandoned his position, Sweater might see him in the rear view mirror. At this point he was merely a pedestrian, but they might remember him and later, when he really needed anonymity, and identify him. *Move or stay?*

Dengler heard the house door close. Someone was sobbing. A feminine voice, sobbing pitiably. The group walked closer. Dengler moved slowly toward the base of the tree and then swung out the opposite side.

"It's going to be okay, dear. You'll see," said the woman Dengler heard earlier.

Suit agreed. "It's really a very simple (unintelligible). You'll see."

He saw them clearly now. Three people. Suit, seen earlier, then a woman in her fifties wearing a work shift, and a blond woman wearing a man's raincoat and what was called 'flip-flops' in West Virginia, but in California were known as 'thongs.' They made a distinctive *flap-flap* noise with each step. As she walked, the blond woman's legs caused the bottom of the raincoat to swing open. Dengler saw she was naked beneath it.

Marilyn Monroe.

It was she who was sobbing, but as they neared the sidewalk, the older woman on her left, the suited man on her right, Marilyn stopped crying and straightened herself, pulling her emotions together.

"I know what to expect," she said, almost defiantly, to the suited man. "You don't have to treat me like this."

"I just wanted to comfort you," he told her.

"I'm okay," she stated. "Really, I'm going to be okay."

"I know you are."

They might have bunched up around Dengler's tree. There was no room for all three of them to pass between it and Sweater's Mercedes. Sweater chose to pull the car out from the wall. They waited until the rear passenger door was facing the driveway before venturing past the tree, saving Dengler from discovery.

Suit opened the passenger door and assisted Marilyn inside, then opened the front passenger door for himself. The woman circled the car and got in opposite Marilyn.

Marilyn looked out of the rear passenger window then and saw Dengler, who had allowed himself an instant too long before shifting back into shadow. Fascinated, as if looking into the eyes of a new lover, Dengler's eyes locked onto Marilyn's. For the second it took Sweater to put the car into gear a silent, mysterious communication passed between them.

Who are you? What are you doing there?
I'm just passing by.
Liar.
Are you really Marilyn Monroe?
Yes. Whoever she is.
You're beautiful.
Yes, but only when your eyes are on me.

The car accelerated away. Dengler stood and watched for some sign — movement within the car, any of the passengers turning around to look at him, anything suggesting Marilyn Monroe had given his presence away. There was nothing. Even she didn't turn around and look back.

Dengler was numb.

He burst down 5th Helena Drive and across Carmelina to the parked Falcon and threw himself inside. He had to catch that car.

- 4 -

1959

Chartersville, West Virginia

They brought Adam Dengler home four weeks after the stroke and placed him in his bed. Dengler had gone to the trouble of cleaning up the place, washing the sheets and pillowcases, sweeping the floor. The house still smelled of rot, of human sweat and anger.

The elder Dengler remained paralyzed and unable to speak. The left side of his face drooped as if an avalanche had taken it. The eyes remained alive. They were terrified. David Dengler listened to the nurse's instructions regarding the care and feeding of a stroke victim. Once she was gone, he went into the bedroom and looked down at his father. For a long time — minutes, tens of minutes maybe — he stared down at the wrenched flesh of the man who had given him life but little else. The eyes looked back. They were living eyes, understanding eyes.

"You bastard," Dengler said. "You've done it now."

Dengler came to realize there wasn't enough money coming in.

If his father had stashed any money away, he couldn't find it. He placed a tablet and pen beside his father's good hand. "Tell me where you've hidden the money, old man." The hand didn't move. The old man's eyes didn't move.

Dengler had saved eight hundred dollars by this time. He spent it on rent and food. He sold his father's car. He tried to get more hours at either of his jobs, but found, to the contrary, he had to accept fewer hours. The recession was taking its toll on the local economy.

Dengler continued going to school. He came home for lunch each day and cleaned his father's bedpan. The old man didn't try to rehabilitate himself. He wouldn't even try to get up and walk or even crawl to the porch or the bathroom. He did have a few visitors from *The Blue Bell* now and again and very often was given whiskey to drink. He would eat if a plate were left for him. He would use the bedpan rather than defecate all over himself. He managed to clean himself afterward. It ended there.

Once Leonard Pevey, his father's supervisor from the mine, stopped by to see how he was doing. Dengler guessed this was an assessment trip to see whether the old man would ever return to work, and when Pevey exited the bedroom he looked pale and shaken, stunned by what he saw in there. He was a big man, full at shoulder and throat, with a face made up of rivulets of flesh, each ponderous layer blemished and pockmarked. "Listen, boy," Pevey said to Dengler, his breath smelling of tobacco and whiskey, "you ever want to work, you can have your old man's job. That's a contract. You just come see me." Pevey looked at the bedroom door before whispering, "God, he should be dead, shouldn't he?" Then he shuffled out, wrinkled hat in his huge callused hands, and never returned.

Even though his father's life was over, David Dengler tried to go on with his own. There had been petty dalliances with girls in grade school and later, but nothing since his life took an abrupt right turn at age fourteen. He simply didn't have the free time after school to socialize, and he knew few girls would be interested in the desperation and anger that made up so much of his life. Late in his junior year this changed.

He'd known Etta Mae Warren since they were in Kindergarten together. Then she'd been merely one of the skinny Warren girls, redheads all, four of them, each a year apart, Etta third. They were as poor as Dengler's family, although their father worked the land and stayed clear of the mines. The two older Warren girls had left school one and two years before; both pregnant and neither married. Etta was rumored to be just as wild as her older sisters, but barren (so it was said) and so likely to finish school unmarried, or at least not pregnant.

Dengler was headed for the school gate to go home for lunch and care for his father when Etta stopped him. "Davey," she called. "Davey Dengler, wait for me, will ya?" Dengler turned and saw Etta trotting toward him. Her figure was ample without being fat, her large breasts protruding through the cashmere sweater she wore like a pair of matched cannon shells. Her skin was as white and pale as cream and provided a clear view of nearly every vein not clothed. She had green eyes, naturally red lips, and red hair of a color than can only occur in nature.

She'd never shown any interest in Dengler, so he said, "Look, I've got to get home. Take care of my father."

She was breathing hard by the time she reached him. Her chest rose and fell in quick starts. She just looked into his eyes for a moment, smiling that smile of young women whose juices are flowing and only they know it. "Davey," she said after a thoughtful moment, "the other boys don't like you much, do they?"

"Etta, I got to go..."

"I saw what you done to Earl Calloway," she told him, resting the palm of her left hand between his pectorals to hold him there. "I saw what you done to him, and I saw that the only person not impressed by it was you."

A week before Earl Calloway, who was a senior, a defensive end on the football team, and a longtime big man on campus, decided to make himself look bigger by picking on Dengler. Calloway didn't have to move crates half the night to make a living. Beneath Dengler's clothes, which made him look somewhat pudgy, he was all muscle. Calloway tripped him and Dengler's books went flying. Everyone in the hallway laughed until Dengler jumped up and hit Calloway four times, three blows to the stomach and one to the face, causing blood to spurt from Calloway's split lip. While Calloway's friends hustled him off to the nurse's office, Dengler picked up his books and walked on.

"Fuck Earl Calloway," Dengler whispered.

"I'll leave that to someone else, Davey," Etta told him. Her hand slipped down to his flat stomach.

"Look, Etta, I'm not what you think I am. I work every night. I take care of my old man. I study. I'm broke. I can't afford to take you out, and I can't afford to take the time to socialize, so..."

Her hand slipped down below his belt. She leaned close so no one behind her could see she had the outline of his cock between her fingers. Her green eyes remained locked with him. Her smile was constant.

"I don't know if you're a virgin or what, Davey. But, when I'm through with you, you'll..." She let the sentence drag out. Blood was gorging into his manhood, pushing her fingers farther apart. "Well, actually, darlin', I prefer to think about how things will be when you're done with me."

Dengler could think of nothing to say. It was wonderful to have this girl's fingers touching him as he became excited. It was far more wonderful than all the Playboys beneath his bed. It was... She released him when he reached maximum erection and stepped back. She looked at the bulge in his jeans with satisfaction. Her smile broadened. "Why Davey, I do think you like me."

Dengler was still mute. Etta laughed. "After school, darlin'," she told him. "I'd let that thing relax before I went anywhere if I was you. Don't want to give people ideas."

All the way home he thought about Etta Warren. He thought about her breasts, he thought about her face and he thought about her legs, which he'd seen in gym class when the girls were on the field at the same time as the boys. Her legs were thick but shapely and as pale as moonlight.

He changed his father's bedpan, washed, made a sandwich for lunch but couldn't eat it, drove back to school, attended each of his classes but remembered nothing said in them, and finally walked to the parking lot after school where he saw Etta sitting in his '51 Chevy.

Dengler slid behind the wheel and said nothing for moments. He was petrified. He didn't know what to say, or how to say it, or whether he should try to act like someone he wasn't, or...

"For a boy who's so concerned with time, you're certainly spending a lot of it in this parking lot," Etta said coyly. Dengler started the car.

Ten minutes later they pulled up in front of Dengler's house. He'd still said nothing to her. She got out of the car and looked the outside of the house over. It was as ordinary and as typical a West Virginia house as any could be, built high and narrow, one bedroom in front opposite a sitting room, one bedroom in back in what was once a porch. She looked at him, smiled sweetly, and then ascended the four steps and pulled back the screen door.

Inside, she almost turned left into the bedroom. "My father's in there," Dengler warned her.

"Where's your room?"

"In back."

She started toward the back, then turned to face him. "Oh, I forgot. I brought you something." She handed him a handkerchief. He unrolled it in his hand. It wasn't a handkerchief at all. It was her panties. "I took them off for you just after lunch. Wanted to think about you the rest of the day. Anyway, some things just got to breathe," she finished and laughed.

Dengler had never seen a woman naked before, at least not since he was five and he saw his mother and the man she ran away with making love not five feet from where he now stood. His body trembled as he caught up with Etta and spun her around. She was grinning so broadly it was a silent laugh, but he didn't give a damn about her at all. He lifted her skirt and its hem dangled higher and higher, above her knees and thighs, exposing ever larger sections of her creamy white skin, until finally the legs joined at an oasis of bushy red hair.

Etta held the skirt aloft as he kneeled and kissed her knees and followed her legs skyward, stopping to touch his lips to her here and there, each kiss causing a moan to erupt from her. When he reached her womanhood, the smell of it wafted to him. It was unlike any smell he'd experienced before, pungent and hot and alien and wonderful. He ran an index finger up between the lips and as they parted a white cream descended. When he stood he held his wet finger up and heard himself say, "Why Etta, I do think you like me." He didn't feel that confident. His manhood was as hard as blue steel and pulsed between his legs. The smile was now gone from Etta's face, her lips open, her eyes narrowed, and her complexion pale.

He stripped her. Only the brassiere gave him trouble. She said, "Here, let me do it." Etta's breasts freed from the bra were not shaped like cones at all, but were heavy, and round, and hung ponderously from her rib cage. Her skin was almost transparent, and he could see her veins, even the deep ones that threaded in from her chest to her nipples, which were quarter-sized and pink. Whenever she moved, even an inch, her breasts wriggled.

Standing naked in front of him, she was stunning, he thought. Her hips were round and her legs thick and muscled — she would be stout in later life like her older sisters and her mother were already becoming — but now, in youth, she was lean and round and shapely.

Etta let him look at her for a while. She was proud of the way she looked, but no amount of pride could suppress the need throbbing in her. She burst to him and kissed his face madly while her hands unbuttoned his shirt and removed it. As she kissed his nipples, her hands went to his jeans and unbuttoned them. She yanked them down. "Kick your shoes off," she commanded urgently, and he did. She kneeled and lifted each of his feet out of the pants, and then looked up at him. His manhood was erect in the jockeys and stuck out like a tree limb. She reached up and took the jockeys by the waistband and tugged them down, causing the blood-gorged member to work free. When it was, she kissed first the shaft, then each testicle.

Etta stood. They pressed into each other, kissing. Her breasts flattened against his chest while his manhood planed up her against her stomach.

Dengler took Etta on the kitchen table. He was carrying her back toward his bedroom, but she saw the table and said, "No, here. Do it here." He was already in her, her legs wrapped around his back, her hands clinging to his shoulders. He lowered her to the tabletop and immediately began to thrust rhythmically into her. With each thrust she called out, finally telling him, "Fuck me, Davey... Fuck me... Fuck me... Fuck me..."

The words excited him more. He couldn't believe he was here, in this beautiful girl, fucking her, and her words were too much. "Stop it. Don't say that. Don't say that." He burst into her.

When he was finished, he leaned close. "I'm sorry," he told her. She grinned, sweat peeling down from her. "Why Davey," she said in a sing-song voice. "You're a young man. There's more where that came from."

Indeed, there was. Twenty minutes later she straddled him in bed and soon came repeatedly, screeching her sexual victory like a cat in heat.

- 5 -

Wednesday, August 1, 1962

Brentwood, California

The Mercedes had gone three blocks before Dengler managed to get the Falcon's engine running and its wheels in motion. The car almost stalled twice from being too cold before he reached the end of the block and spun it around, but then the engine surged and held. After he completed the turn, he saw the Mercedes make a right turn onto Sunset Boulevard. Dengler gunned the Falcon, its tires squealing briefly, and accelerated down to Sunset, where he saw the Mercedes progressing east in the right lane. Dengler followed.

By the time he was on Sunset heading east, the Mercedes was a little more than three blocks ahead. He closed the gap quickly — the Mercedes' driver was in no hurry — and settled into the invisible vacuum trough the larger car made. He followed the Mercedes as it crossed over the San Diego Freeway, and minutes later, turned south onto Hilgarde and drove past UCLA's Sorority Row. Dengler made a mental note his rented Corvair was right where he left it.

The Mercedes turned onto Broxton, which led onto the UCLA campus. The streets were so devoid of traffic by this time Dengler allowed himself to fall back two blocks. He arrived at the Campus Police gatehouse just as the Mercedes, two blocks ahead and on the campus grounds, made a right turn into what appeared to be a newly constructed building complex. The Mercedes hadn't even stopped at the kiosk, but when Dengler attempted the same maneuver the gate arm sliced down onto the hood of his car. The Falcon screeched to a stop, and a Campus police officer stepped out. Dengler apologized and backed the Falcon out of the driveway.

Dengler pulled to the side of the street on Broxton. He remembered the Thomas Brother's street map he'd purchased with the other L.A. books had sections on USC and UCLA. He flipped to the back and thumbed through the pages until he found it, a not-to-scale map of the UCLA campus with legends. He quickly found the complex the Mercedes had entered. The Neuropsychiatric Institute.

Neuropsychiatric Institute? At 2:00 A.M.? Quickly Dengler ran through the obvious possibilities. They were meeting someone at the facility. No. Marilyn wasn't dressed to "meet" anyone. Marilyn or someone she knew was an inpatient. Dengler suspected the Institute had no inpatients. Even if it did, two o'clock in the morning wasn't the appropriate time to meet them, unless they were dying.

Dengler saw a public telephone one block up the street and left the Falcon idling at the curb. Information provided UCLA's 24-hour number. It rang six times before a male voice answered, "UCLA Campus Police. May I help you?"

"Yes, can you give me the number of The Neuropsychiatric Institute? I think my cousin is a patient there, and I need to talk to her. It's a family emergency."

"Sir, the Institute is closed. They don't have inpatients. They do have outpatients, but you can reach them only during normal business hours."

Dengler hung up. Across the vacant streets of Westwood there was no one, nor any movement except the stoplights changing from red to green and back. The silence was so profound he could hear the stoplights blink on and off as their circuits connected, and beyond, the occasional and distant roar of an internal combustion engine or whine of a transmission. Dengler dismissed the outside world and applied what he knew to what he didn't. The former included a sobbing movie star going out with three unidentified people in the middle of the night to a university research center. She was wearing relatively little. They treated her like a patient. One of them had a faculty sticker on his car allowing him to pass unquestioned through campus security.

Now, what he didn't know. Why a medical facility after hours? Obviously, someone had need of medical equipment without what is normally attached to them. No people. No paper. No records.

He understood.

Marilyn Monroe was having an abortion.

- 6 -

1959

Chartersville, West Virginia

It was dark when Dengler got out of bed and left the room to find his pants and shirt. Naked, Etta lay on top of the covers looking like the famous picture of Marilyn Monroe posed on red silk sheets, twisted into a question mark and laughing as men's eyes devoured her. Etta liked that too, Dengler saw when he returned, a man's eyes devouring her.

"Where'ya goin'?" she asked languorously, running the fingers of one hand through her curly red hair. "Or have I drained every drop of you?"

"Got to call *Junior Walker's*," he told her. The shirt was already on and even partly buttoned, but the pants caught on his manhood. It flopped about like a just-hooked fish in the fly. "I'll tell 'em my car broke down, and I don't know when I can make it."

"Tell 'em you got yourself one bodacious piece of ass and you want to rest a spell in it." she said, and laughed at herself, body wrenching as she stretched. "Tell 'em you're a virgin no more. Tell 'em anything, but come back, darlin', 'cause I ain't done with that thing."

Dengler stopped at the door to look at her. He tried to remember her from when they were children together, the flat-chested little girl who sat next to him in Kindergarten, or when she was just one of the Warren girls, four little redheads most people thought of as children of white trash. She laughed again, a shared secret, this fornicating between people who had looked at one another for most of their lives, and yet had never seen one another clearly.

"You're a mystery to me," he said. "You're a goddamn mystery."

Dengler bolted out the front screen door and heard it slam behind him. He trotted down the hill and across the road where semis roared day and night, sometimes minutes apart, sometimes hours, and a moment later crossed the gravel parking lot of *The Blue Bell*. Inside the dark bar a Patsy Cline song dripped from the speakers, honey and gristle. There were a few patrons splattered about at tables, and vast pools of shadow punctuated here and there by red and purple ceiling lights. He found the telephone outside the doors to the men's and women's bathrooms. He gave a good accounting of himself to Otis Vincent, the *Junior Walker's* head clerk, and was on his way back to Etta in two minutes.

He took his shirt off before he closed the door, and the pants were flopping at his naked feet before he crossed the threshold into the bedroom, but Etta was gone. "Etta." he called out, afraid she'd left him already, but he heard, "In here," and knew the *here* was his father's bedroom at the front of the house. He pulled on a green plaid robe from the bathroom door and bolted to the front, fear rising into his throat. He didn't want his father to see Etta, didn't want him to know about her, as irrational as he knew this was. His father couldn't even move. He had no say about anything anymore.

Dengler entered the bedroom and froze. Etta stood at the end of the bed, naked and leaning on the bed footboard. She was staring at Adam Dengler's prone form in the bed, and the gaze of the old man's eyes was moving slowly from her breasts to her hips to her face.

"Etta, goddamn it, what are you doing?" Dengler yelled.

He surged toward her and grabbed her arms. She let him, but said, "It's okay," in a manner that caused him to release her. "It's okay. He likes what he's looking at."

"That's not the point."

"I thought he was out of it," she said to him softly. "I thought he was unconscious, like. You know, not there anymore."

"He's there."

"— so I didn't bother to cover up. I mean I didn't do it intentionally, Davey. But, when he saw me, it was done, and I could see he likes it; he likes looking at me."

Dengler glanced at his father. There was no change of expression there, but the eyes, the eyes, moving here, moving there... said Adam Dengler was alive.

"Anyway," Etta continued, "he's your father. It's important for a father to know his son has become a man. Not only in the biblical sense, you know, but in every way. That he's become an adult."

"You don't know my father," Dengler said. "You don't know the way it is between us."

"Doesn't matter," Etta said. "It doesn't matter. He's your father. You're his son. You have to love him."

"It matters."

"Does he ever talk, Davey?"

"No."

"Does he move? Does he try and walk?"

"No," Dengler said softly. "He can move the bedpan. He can take a drink. He can swallow. That's it."

"He's mostly dead to the outside world, then?"

"Mostly."

"He's alive inside, Davey." It was dark within the room now even with Etta's pale skin reflecting residual light. She opened a matchbook on the dresser and lighted a small candle. Its flame danced across her naked, sweaty flesh. When she returned to stand with her back to Dengler, he barely noticed. He watched his father's eyes follow her. She pulled Dengler to her, opened his robe and cinched him to her with its tie, holding the two ends in her fists before her. He felt his manhood lodge between her buttocks.

"I don't want to be in here like this," he told her. "I don't want to share you with him."

"You're not sharing me," she whispered. She leaned over the bed. Her breasts brushed against the bedspread. "He can't have me. He can only watch." Her nipples hardened. Dengler felt himself responding to her movement. Her buttocks massaged him. He felt himself rising. He'd never possessed a woman before this night. He'd never been possessed before, either. This woman, this perfect female animal whose skin was transparent and whose flesh undulated against him, he could deny nothing.

The old man's gaze swept across her body. His life was the sight of this naked woman. His life was the instant of this moment, watching.

"Give him this," she panted. "Give it to him."

"I don't want to," Dengler heard himself say. He didn't turn and walk out. Almost without realizing it he was in her. He felt the moist heat of her surrounding himself. He was ashamed and angry, but far more emotions wrenched him. He was hard as steel made with West Virginia coal, and he was a man taking a beautiful woman from behind for the first time, and he couldn't stop himself. He watched her buttocks and back as she writhed and pumped, and the sides of her breasts as they hung to the bed like ripe fruit from a tree, shimmying as if in a wind.

"This will be the last time," she whispered, working now, in control of his body as well as her own, her eyes riveted to Adam Dengler's eyes. "The last time he will ever look into a woman's face... as she comes."

The last time.

It was years later before Dengler discovered why she did this.

It was after Midnight when he returned to the house from dropping Etta off. He stepped inside and closed the door behind him.

Silence. Usually, he could hear his father's snoring by this time. He saw from the light beneath the door that he had left the candle burning. He stepped into the bedroom to snuff it out and saw his father was awake. For a while, they stared at one another. Then the old man closed his eyes leaving Dengler alone in the room.

For hours afterward Dengler lay in bed and thought about his father, the man he'd hated his entire life, and the wreck of a human being he'd become. He knew much of his father's anger came from the close similarity Dengler bore to his mother. That the old man had loved her was a startling realization to him; that he should hate his son, then, because the son reminded him of the woman he couldn't keep, was for the first time comprehensible.

He thought about making love to Etta standing at the foot of his father's bed. He dismissed the shame he felt and focused on the expression in his father's eyes as they drank in Etta.

"There ain't much to a man but spit and dust," he'd heard his father say many times, "and my spit is dryin' up."

It was just about dry.

Dengler moved his television into his father's room the next day, placing it near enough to the bed so his father's one good hand could switch between the town's two local channels.

All that semester David Dengler spent every moment he could with Etta Warren. They made love in every manner and place imaginable. She came to sleep as often as to fornicate, and made dinner for him and the old man several times in the kitchen that first he had to restore to operable condition. At Etta's insistence he also kept the house cleaner, although her insistence was more of a warm *please* spoken softly. The Warren household wasn't pristine, either.

He started missing work, and school, regularly. There was nothing more important than Etta, nothing greater than holding her as he made her moan or cry out in a sharp voice any passerby would surely identify as the shriek of a cat in heat. She meant more to him than anything or anyone. He couldn't understand how he'd ever lived without touching her soft, pale skin, or looking into her emerald eyes, hearing the sound of her voice, basking in the light of her presence, and especially possessing her voluptuous body.

It ended the day the generator went out on his '51 Chevy. He had to replace it. Getting the part and putting it in took most of the day. When he was finished, Dengler cleaned up and drove to school to pick Etta up. He stepped out of the Chevy into the school parking lot and saw her with her hand on the chest of another boy, Theodore Petty, who was known for his bookishness and lame sense of humor. Dengler understood immediately the language her body spoke, her legs wide beneath the pleated skirt, the way her hand pushed against his heart as if reaching inside. It was the same way she'd approached him. Dengler knew he wouldn't let this bookworm take his woman. He raced across the parking lot, shoved her out of the way and hit Petty so hard blood sprayed from his nose. They were both on the ground in an instant. Dengler would have killed Petty had Etta not put a stranglehold on him and pulled Dengler from Petty's prone body.

By this time several students and a teacher were running for the scene. Dengler stood up and grabbed Etta and pulled her to his car. She didn't resist. An instant later the Chevy was squealing from the parking lot spewing dust behind.

Dengler drove for an hour before pulling to the side of a country road beside nowhere. Cow patties and weeds decayed together in the nearby pastures.

"We've had each other, Davey," Etta said, filling the silence. "We've made love upside-down and inside out. You've had me and I've had you. Standing up against walls and floating in the lake. Once in the middle of Victory Park at two in the morning. Once at the Fourth of July picnic under a blanket with hundreds of people milling about and pretending it was cold when it wasn't. We've had each other."

"What do you see in him?"

"Someone new, that's all."

"You're a whore."

"You don't think that. You're hurt, that's all."

"You're a whore."

"Have it your own way."

Dengler was crumbling inside, collapsing within the compressing hands of love and anger. "I love you, Etta," he said finally. His voice cracked. "I love you so much I could..."

"No you don't," she replied softly. "You don't love me, Davey."

"I love you," he said firmly, a challenge.

"What you love is my body. What you love is what you've never had before. But Davey, when we're done making love, we don't have anything else to talk about. When we laugh, it's because we're excited, not happy."

"I don't want to lose you," he told her.

"You already have. And I lost you. And that's the way it is."

He took her home without saying another word.

He was suspended from school for a week for fighting, but that wasn't the worst of it. His grades had slipped steadily for months, and the suspension meant he would have to repeat the latter part of his junior year.

Junior Walker's replaced him with someone more dependable.

Desperate for money, he called Leonard Pevey. At first, the mine foreman didn't recognize him.

"Who are you?" he growled. "What?"

"David Dengler," he said into the phone. It was late evening, just after what was traditionally the dinner hour, and Pevey was obviously hard of hearing. "Adam Dengler's son," Dengler completed.

"Oh," Pevey said. There was a moment's silence before, "Did he die?"

"No, not yet," Dengler told him. *Did he die?* They might have been talking about steaks on the grill. *Is the meat done?*

"Oh," Pevey said. "I thought he might have died. He looked pretty bad."

"Yes sir."

"You need some money? Your dad's got friends, you know." He said this with some hesitation, as if he weren't quite sure the elder Dengler actually had any friends left.

"I need that job, Mr. Pevey. The job you talked about. I need it."

"Your dad's job, you mean?"

"Yes sir."

"That was six months ago," Pevey said. "Hell, I already hired two men since then."

"You said it was a contract, sir," Dengler reminded him. "I had to get things sorted out, see if I could finish school. I can't, sir. At least not without a full-time job."

"It's hard work."

"These are hard times," Dengler said, knowing full well the language of 'The Depression' his father's generation spoke so easily.

"Come in Monday. Be ready to work."

A cold chill went up Dengler's spine. He wanted this less than anything except starvation. "I'll be ready, sir," he heard himself say.

"Monday morning."

- 7 -

Wednesday, August 1, 1962

Brentwood, California

As he drove back to Brentwood Dengler reviewed what he'd seen. There were some glaring irregularities. First, there was the Mercedes driver. Of the two men, Sweater and Suit, Sweater was an unlikely pick for college faculty member. Suit looked like a professional and acted like a doctor when he and the woman escorted Marilyn out to the car. Sweater seemed annoyed by the whole proceeding. There was more. Sweater was somebody he knew, someone famous, like Marilyn but less prominent. He racked his mind trying to find the correlation, but...

Then he remembered. Sweater was Nick Charles, or played Nick Charles, *The Thin Man*, on television... *Peter Lawford*. So he couldn't be the owner of the Mercedes. The Mercedes belonged to the UCLA faculty member, the doctor. And his nurse? *Let's not leap too far*. Actually, it all made sense. The doctor and possible nurse attend a distraught Marilyn while Lawford drives the car.

Being famous himself, Lawford had a lot to lose if he were caught driving Marilyn Monroe to an abortionist. Other possibilities were few. One, he was Marilyn's good friend, there was that. He hadn't acted like Marilyn's good friend earlier. Or two, he was the father of the child she was aborting.

Dengler chose the latter. Marilyn Monroe was aborting Peter Lawford's child, and Lawford was a reluctant participant.

Dengler was very, very lucky, and he knew it. He'd far exceeded his assignment. Anything he found more than what his predecessors reported would count for a higher evaluation. Here was something none of his predecessors could possibly have discovered because it was happening before his eyes, right now. He could document Marilyn Monroe was having an affair with Peter Lawford, and she was aborting his child with his assistance tonight. Military intelligence careers were started with less. Much less.

For this reason, David Dengler, United States Army military intelligence operative, would exceed his orders, what the intelligence community termed 'exceed his purview.' If he ever hoped to get out of the Army one day and join the CIA, FBI, DIA or Treasury, he would need more than a three-year tour with Army M.I. and a college degree. Each of those agencies had been known to turn down former Army M.I. and Naval Intelligence guys just for having been members of the intelligence community's lowest echelon organizations. He needed a break, something that would set him apart from the average uniformed spook, and this was it.

He was going inside the house on 5th Helena Drive.

- 8 -

1959

Chartersville, West Virginia

The first months in the mine were difficult for David Dengler. Though he'd worked hard in his life, he had never felt like a pack animal before. Although there were pneumatic tools and other kinds of mechanical automation, a miner still worked with his hands, muscles, and sweat. *No wonder my father thought he was a beast of burden,* Dengler considered.

He found no energy left to think when his ten-hour shift in the mine was done. When the whistle blew, he walked blackened, and bent from the mine's elevator shaft into the daylight thinking he was never this tired before in his life. He returned home costumed by dust and unable to remove it completely from his body. It hid beneath nails and in cracks and folds of skin that, even when scrubbed, released coal dust later. Without school, there was no hope.

He occasionally saw Etta from a distance, more often one of her sisters, and the sight of any of them, Etta especially, sent him reeling into a dark pit. There were other women, paid-for women, and he had them, but it was only a temporary respite from hunger. He wanted Etta. He wanted her body and he wanted her laughter. More than anything else he wanted to be near her.

He would not plead for her.

When Etta's little sister Sela became pregnant, father unknown, Etta left Chartersville. She just disappeared. It was the year Dengler turned 18. He asked around about her, but no one seemed to know where she went, except possibly the Warren family, who weren't talking. Dengler ran into the oldest Warren girl, Greta, shopping in the Corliss Market. Greta had been two years ahead of him in school and Dengler couldn't remember ever talking to her. He approached her in the canned goods aisle.

"Hi, Greta," Dengler said, surprised he was reticent to speak. "You remember me. David Dengler. We went to school together."

"Sure, David," Greta replied with a rueful smile. "Etta told me all about you, nice boy and all." Greta was pregnant again and her girth was barely covered by a maternity dress that had suited her quite well the last time. Now in her eighth month, the dress was tight. This child would be big. Although no one had ever seen him,

Greta's husband was said to be in the Army serving somewhere in Germany. Greta's hair and skin and eyes were almost identical to Etta's, but there was something common to her personality, a small town sameness that was a vital contrast to the persona of her younger sister.

"I haven't seen Etta around, Greta," Dengler said. "I heard she left town."

"Three weeks ago," Greta confirmed. "We have relatives in Baltimore, of all places. She went there to finish her school. Etta wants a career, you know."

"I didn't know," Dengler mumbled.

"Really? She led me to believe you two were very close." The words were intended to be mischievous, but Dengler's pained expression must have made an impression on Greta, for she offered, "I can give you her address and telephone number, David, if you want. I'm sure she won't mind if you call her."

He took the address and telephone number, but didn't use them.

After three months his body hardened, and he came home from the mine unbent and possessing enough energy to think. He bought a larger television for his room, but instead returned to reading books and thoughts of getting out of West Virginia. His father wouldn't live forever, and although there was no way for him to leave now, someday the opportunity would come.

He signed up for a G.E.D. correspondence course and began assigning one night a week to each subject. He found history, English, geography, and social studies easy; mathematics, particularly abstract mathematics, and any other technical sciences drudgery. There was no one to ask questions of, no friendly teacher from whom he might extract an understanding of the alien ideas in the books. He failed Algebra twice.

Meanwhile, he began checking into the minimum requirements for a job with the CIA, FBI, or the Treasury Department, which managed Alcohol, Tobacco & Firearms as well as the Secret Service. All required a college degree; several mandated street experience with a police force. One recruiter suggested he join the army or navy. Naval Intelligence or Army M.I. might not be what he was looking for, he was told, but at least it would be a move in the right direction. He could easily get a degree during a three-year stint in the armed services. Transfer into another, higher echelon government agency, such as the FBI, or CIA, would be easier afterward.

Dengler's father's condition didn't improve, and there were moments when Dengler wished the old man would die. Since the night he and Etta made love in front of him, Dengler saw something different in his father's eyes. He wondered if his father's animal heart found kinship with the beast in his son. Dengler didn't find the prospect appealing. He didn't like the animal his father had been; he didn't trust the beast in him that occasionally roared and struggled to get out.

Dengler continued to care for his father, feeding him four times a day, changing his bedpan, washing his clothes and bed linen. The old man watched television constantly now, something he'd had disdain for before his stroke. He was still without speech, his left side motionless. His skin was distinctly cold and appeared a deathlike shade of gray. None of the old man's friends came anymore. His father's gruesome face was too scary.

Dengler felt he was less than half-alive himself. Each night after his work was done, he returned to his room and stretched out in bed. The walls smelled of years of humidity and human sweat, the sounds of the night outside seeming to crawl through pores in the wallpaper. His books were small rugged mountains that spread near the bedside. He hardly read Ian Fleming anymore. He lay on his side until sleep overtook him, thinking of Etta, thinking of freedom.

- 9 -

Wednesday, August 1, 1962

Brentwood, California

Dengler parked the Falcon in the same exact spot as before, making small adjustments forward and reverse to achieve it. When Monroe and her associates returned, it would appear the vehicle hadn't been moved.

For a moment Dengler sat in the darkened car and looked at the wood gate of 12305 down the street, which remained open half a foot. He wished he had bugging equipment, but he didn't. He'd brought his camera from Fort Lee, but it was back at the motel room. He didn't have time to retrieve it.

What he had was himself. That and nothing more. He got out of the car.

Dengler pushed the wood gate open far enough to allow him to sidle through. Inside were the two parked cars, the 1956 Ford Crown Victoria and the 1962 T-Bird, whose license he now jotted down in a notebook. To his left was a lawn, and right of that, around one corner of the house, the pool surrounded by a flagstone surface. The front door to the Spanish-style house was curved at the top and appeared to be made of four planks secured together by miniature wrought iron braces. There was a small leaded glass peephole at the top covered by an iron grill. He tried the door. Locked.

Dengler walked around the side of the house facing the pool carefully avoiding the grass, because it was a surprisingly damp night and the grass would retain his footprints for some time. He couldn't be identified by them, of course, but he didn't want Monroe's group to know someone had been in the yard.

The double French doors leading off the master bedroom didn't fit the style of the house and probably had been added with the pool, which looked as though it was a recent addition. There were four pool chairs and an umbrella table near the side of the house, and several lounges around the pool. A large tree blocked the view of the pool from the front of the house, or conversely the driveway area from the pool. At the seven-foot level it split into two massive branches, one toward the street, the second toward the house. The street branch overhung the wall.

Dengler tried the French doors. They were unlocked.

They had left most of the lights on. This first room was a living area. It was sparsely decorated in the popular California Spanish style. There was a painting of Marilyn over the mantle. In the painting, she wore a red evening gown and sat alone at a nightclub booth. There was a Martini glass between her open hands on the table. She was laughing. It was a good likeness and for a moment Dengler was transfixed within its gaze. He forced himself to turn away.

The kitchen and dining area were off one side of the living room, and a short hallway reaching the two bedrooms off the other side. There was also a door at the end of the hall that Dengler quickly learned led to the garage, which was full of *Bekins Van and Storage* shipping boxes. Altogether, the house was even smaller inside than it looked from the outside, a 1930s relic that seemed as far beneath the standards of a Hollywood movie star as he could imagine. Dengler made a mental note: *Monroe in financial bind?*

The bedroom farthest from the front of the house seemed neat and orderly, with a made-up bed and clothes hanging in an orderly fashion in the closet. The front bedroom, however, was quite different. There were sheets but not blankets or a bedspread on the bed, and papers strewn about in piles. The closet was almost bare, a few pairs of slacks, jeans, and sweaters hanging in abject loneliness. Dengler recalled some of the boxes in the garage were wardrobes. The light in this bedroom, as in the other, was off, so he left it off. Using a penlight he perused the stacks of papers, several of which turned out to be screenplays. One title read *Something's Got To Give* and had the *20th-Century Fox* logo at the bottom of the title page.

Other papers were unsigned contracts, mortgage papers under the name Norma Jean Baker, and paperback books, plays mostly. Shakespeare. Eugene O'Neill. Another novel, *Look Homeward, Angel*, by Thomas Wolfe.

On the bed stand he found two large bottles of pills, Nembutal and chloral hydrate. There were also two bottles of aspirin, one unopened, and a gooseneck lamp that looked to have been wrenched recently, possibly by a fall. Wedged between the bed stand and the bed Dengler saw a fat personal telephone book stuffed with pages from other telephone books that, judging by their well-worn look, dated back years, as well as sheets from tablets and notebooks. The whole thing was held together by a thick rubber band.

Dengler wanted to open it, but he wasn't wearing gloves. He didn't want to leave fingerprints. He would have to come back, he knew, and chided himself for not being prepared. He should have had the camera loaded and with him. He should have brought gloves. He vowed not to make the same mistakes again.

Beside the personal telephone book was a drinking glass, a tall tumbler with a happy flower design. There was a milk stain at an angle at the bottom, indicating the glass had been dropped while there was still some liquid left in it.

Dengler lowered himself to his knees and looked under the bed. There were several garments, the closest being a pair of women's pants, and several old newspaper sections. *Los Angeles Times*, the banner read.

As Dengler was starting to stand he saw it. It was wedged between the mattress and box springs and had been pushed far enough back so that at first only a slightly bulging slit in fabric was visible. Using a pen to widen the slit between box springs and mattress and aiming his penlight into the crevice, Dengler could see it was a book with a spiral spine. *Another phone book? No.* Anything valuable enough to hide was worthy of a look.

Dengler didn't carry a handkerchief and made a mental note to do so in the future. *Handkerchief. Gloves. Little things,* he thought. A handkerchief would have allowed him to pull the book out then and there. Instead, he was forced to search the nearby vicinity for something to use. There was nothing immediately visible. He opened the nearest clothes chest using his knuckles to grip the handles — there were two small chest-of-drawers, both antique-white, at opposite ends of the room from one another — and found himself staring down into Marilyn Monroe's panty drawer. As much as the idea of stealing a pair of her panties for this purpose appealed to him, rationality prevailed and he found another drawer filled with scarves; none of them folded terribly neatly. He took one.

The book slid easily from between the mattress and box springs and rested in his hand. A flowery print on the front stated *Diary*. Dengler's spine was being assaulted by frozen needles. He felt his breath catch. He opened the book to a middle page and was surprised to find it filled in with a quirky, jerky handwriting.

June 19. Jack called. He was very considerate. He said he missed me and thought of me always. He said he never felt the way I make him feel before...

He turned a page. Two. Three.

June 22. Zanuck called again. He was nice at first, but then he started telling me how it was all my fault <u>again</u> and how I let everybody down, and I should get some help. <u>He</u> should get some help.

Dengler flipped through pages.

July 9. Bobby stopped by after making a speech at the L.A. Press Club. He was excited because the speech went over well. We made love in the limo on the way to Peter's place in Malibu. He held me afterward and told me he loves me. He asked me to marry him. I said yes.

Peter Lawford wasn't the father of Marilyn's baby. At least probably not, Dengler realized. A man named Bobby was. Bobby who? He had to be someone prominent enough to be asked to give a speech at the Los Angeles Press Club. Dengler considered that. Los Angeles Press Club. Maybe "Bobby" was a big-time journalist, someone who wrote for *Time, Newsweek,* or one of the nationally known newspapers, like the *Washington Post* or *New York Times.*

If Bobby were the father, why was Peter Lawford placing himself and his reputation in jeopardy by being present during a very illegal abortion? Dengler retreated to his earlier assessment of Lawford. He had to be a close friend, someone who cared a great deal about Marilyn, though he didn't act like it.

The sound of a car engine idling outside on 5th Helena Drive pulled Dengler out of his thoughts. He didn't know how long he'd been aware of the sounds. There were voices and a car door slamming and for moments after the noises crept into his reality Dengler didn't respond. The sounds seemed so far away, so... distant. He snapped the diary closed then, realizing what the voices and sounds might mean. He almost shoved it back between the mattress and box spring, but then calmed himself and took care to return it to as close to its original position as he could remember. He leaped up, found the dresser, folded the scarf as neatly as he could and dropped it in, shoving the drawer home.

Dengler was in the living room area when he realized he'd originally found the door to Marilyn's bedroom closed, and he'd left it open. He doubled back quickly and pulled the door closed.

Dengler stood and listened just outside the French double doors. The voices continued, and then there was a woman's laugh. It was light, youthful, almost childlike, and Dengler realized it couldn't have emitted from the throat of either Marilyn Monroe or the woman who cared for her.

"'Night," a man said. His voice was deep, throaty, and nonetheless as youthful as the woman's. Teenagers. Listening now to the idling engine of the car stopped in the street, Dengler realized this was a big V8 with a 4-barrel carburetor and fiberglass mufflers.

"See you next week." she called. The car door slammed. A moment later the engine revved and the car squealed down the street. The sound of her heels clicking on pavement diminished into the distance.

Dengler considered returning to Monroe's bedroom, but did he have time? *How long does an abortion take, anyway?* He would have to come back into this house anyhow. He knew taking the time to read the diary might cause him to be caught. It was unnecessary and foolish. Even so, he considered it for a long moment in the cool shadows of night. A breeze rose up and jostled the tree limbs. He heard the leaves rustling together. The moment was singular and sweet, as clear, and crystalline as any he'd ever experienced. He was alive, and he was creating a dossier of a world-famous person and he was somebody doing important things. For the first time since Etta left him, he felt happy.

Dengler was sitting in the Falcon and almost asleep when the Mercedes pulled up to the Monroe driveway. He quickly checked his wristwatch. It was 4:52 A.M. Lawford slipped out from behind the wheel and trotted to the gate, which he pushed wide open. Suit, meanwhile, stepped from the passenger side, crossed in front of the headlights and slid behind the wheel of the Mercedes. A moment later the Thunderbird's engine roared in the driveway, and its big taillights flashed. It backed out into the street and accelerated away. The Mercedes replaced it in the driveway.

It took Dengler a minute to catch up to the T-Bird, and ten minutes afterward he followed Lawford onto the Santa Monica Freeway heading west toward the Pacific Coast Highway.

- 10 -

1961

Chartersville, West Virginia

A month before his second 'event', Adam Dengler drew something on the tablet left beside his good hand. He no longer had the power of speech, or writing, and for years the tablet went unused. David Dengler left it there just in case, of what he wasn't really sure. When Dengler came home from work that night, the old man made a guttural noise from his throat and motioned for Dengler to come close and read the tablet.

Adam Dengler had drawn three half circles on the yellow foolscap page, two circles with the opening down, the third on top of the other two. Above the third circle he'd drawn a simple cross.

"You want me to bury you here?" Dengler said. "Where is here?"

Adam Dengler shook his head no and struck the tablet with his good hand, forefinger digging into the flesh of the page. The effort drained him. He collapsed into sleep.

Over the ensuing weeks Adam Dengler drew the same symbols, three hills, sometimes with one cross, sometimes with two. Dengler didn't understand what the old man was trying to say.

Then one morning Dengler came into his father's bedroom to turn him in bed, a procedure to prevent bed sores, and his father wouldn't wake up.

Dr. Leeson came out into the waiting room and called his name.

"Here," Dengler piped up.

They conferred by the coffee machine. "Well, Mr. Dengler, your father has been stabilized. We've stopped much of the hemorrhaging in the frontal lobe of his brain. He's unconscious. His vital signs are steady. The problem with stroke victims is there's no adequate way to predict what's going to happen. He may recover, at least to the level of his first stroke. He may not."

"When will you know?" Dengler said.

"Hour-to-hour, day-to-day," Leeson replied tiredly. "This is your father's second major incident. My advice is to get his affairs in order and hope for the best. My opinion regarding his condition is," and Leeson considered this a moment before he said it, "he will probably not come out of the coma, but may live indefinitely. In that case he will need around-the-clock care. Having read your case file, I understand he won't be able to get that at home."

"I can't take care of him around the clock."

"I didn't think so. There are rest homes that provide this kind of care, but unfortunately not very many in West Virginia. You could move out of state."

Out of state. The thought of moving out of state never occurred to Dengler. Or that he could turn the care and feeding of his father over to strangers and go on with his life.

"You mean, like in New York or somewhere?" he heard himself ask.

"New York, certainly. Or closer, if you like. Your father's social security check would pay for most of it, from what I understand. He is drawing Social Security?"

"Yes, he is."

"And you are his conservator?"

"Yes," Dengler responded, still numb from the realization he could be free.

"There is a federal agency that handles referrals for these kinds of cases. It's possible they can make the arrangements, I don't know. I'll have our admin look into it for you, if you want."

Throat dry, Dengler said, "Yes," hoarsely.

"Good," Leeson said, already dismissing this problem and preparing to move on to the next. "We'll be moving your father out of ICU in a few days. If there's a change, I'll give you a call."

For some minutes after Leeson left, Dengler stood beside the coffee machine and considered he was now free. Until very recently Chartersville didn't even have its own hospital, not to mention a specialized one to care for invalids. The old man had no other family, and no friends, so it didn't really matter where he slept until the day he died.

It really didn't matter.

Dengler called Pevey at the mine and quit.

Eight months later, after having graduated from Army Basic Training, Infantry School, and Ranger School, Pfc. David Dengler arrived at Fort Lee, Virginia to receive training in military intelligence.

- 11 -

Thursday, August 2, 1962, 5:00 A.M.

Brentwood, California

Dengler trailed the T-Bird as it followed the Santa Monica Freeway to its end, and was dumped onto the northbound Pacific Coast Highway. Lawford drove steadily, maintaining his speed at around the limit or just below, and several times Dengler had to slow down and fall back. It was his habit to exceed the speed limit. Lawford's habit was to obey it, or at least to obey it whenever he didn't want to be stopped or have his identity or location at a given time noted in some report somewhere.

Traffic on the Pacific Coast Highway soon diminished to just Lawford and Dengler. Lawford took the fast lane. Dengler, so as not to appear to be following him, moved up in the slow lane until the two cars paralleled each other. Dengler checked his speedometer. Fifty-nine miles-per-hour.

Using peripheral vision, Dengler spied on Lawford to his left. Lawford was smoking a cigarette and playing radio station roulette, punching buttons on the dash periodically. He looked older and softer than Dengler remembered him, although the television series he was identified with, *The Thin Man*, had ended half-a-decade before. Dimly, there were other memories of this man, more recent ones, from television too but from the news, not from old movies or TV series. *Rat Pack*. Dengler tried to assemble the related thoughts in his mind. *Rat Pack*. Other entertainment personalities leaped into his mind. Dean Martin. Sammy Davis Jr. Joey Bishop. Peter Lawford. And Frank Sinatra.

While these images formed in his mind Lawford's T-Bird slowed down, and then made a left turn and stopped before a bank of four garage doors obviously belonging to the same beach-front estate. With no traffic ahead, and afraid to brake or his taillights would beacon attention, Dengler turned around in the seat and watched as one of the garage doors opened automatically. The T-Bird pulled inside, and the door closed behind it.

Dengler braked, executed a quick U-turn, and stopped the Falcon before the four garage doors. He quickly jotted down the address, 27233 Pacific Coast Highway, before accelerating back toward Santa Monica and Brentwood beyond.

After returning to his motel room, Dengler spent an hour filling in his dossier with the events of the evening. Then, so sleepy he could hardly hold himself upright, Dengler collapsed into bed.

Dengler woke on his own at 1:38 P.M. He was groggy and stiff but exhilarated. He showered quickly, dressed in casual clothes, and then made sure he added his camera to his equipment bag. The last thing he pulled on was the Walther PPK harness. Realizing he would have to wear a jacket to cover it, and it would probably be hot again today, he removed the harness and shoved it into the bag. The PPK he placed on top in the bag and closed it.

At the Department of Motor Vehicles office in West L.A., Dengler presented the three automobile license numbers he'd collected, paid a $1 fee for each, and received background information regarding the registered owner of each car.

The first number he knew. The T-Bird belonged to Peter Lawford of 27233 Pacific Coast Highway, Santa Monica, California. The Mercedes belonged to Dr. Fred Bauer of Beverly Hills, and the Ford Crown Victoria to Mrs. Agnes Ketchum of West Los Angeles. He now had the cast of characters from last night's performance.

Because it was almost five, Dengler didn't return to his motel room to make the call. Instead, he went to a Denny's Restaurant located two blocks from the Department of Motor Vehicles office and looked up Bauer's office in the public phone vestibule. He found it in West L.A. and dialed the number.

"Dr. Bauer's office," a woman's voice answered.

"Ah, yes, I was referred to a Dr. Bauer by Dr. Shapiro. But the problem is, I lost the slip with Dr. Bauer's number on it. Can you tell me, is this Dr. Bauer a dermatologist?"

"No, I'm sorry. This is the office of Dr. Fred Bauer. Dr. Bauer is a psychiatrist."

"I'll keep looking. Thanks." Dengler hung up. Bauer was Marilyn Monroe's psychiatrist. *That relationship should generate a few referrals,* Dengler thought cynically.

This time Dengler chose to park at the 'T' where the cul-de-sac and the major thoroughfare, Carmelina Avenue, joined, but on the east side of the road. It was almost seven o'clock, but it was still daylight, with long shadows drifting lazily across the street from trees on the west side of the road. Overhead a silver needle winged across the sky toward Los Angeles International Airport.

From here Dengler could observe the comings and goings at the

Monroe house without endangering his cover. If he had the resources — at least three other agents and several weeks time, instead of one — he would have done a first-class job of placing the house under observation. He was one man, and he had to settle for establishing patterns within the household, repeating episodes, rather than a moment-to-moment event sequence. Tonight he would record the comings and goings between eight and midnight.

If opportunity presented itself, he would go in and photograph Monroe's diary.

Dengler glanced at his watch. He had approximately an hour. He slipped out of the Corvair, rolled up the window, and then strolled west toward the next intersection. It was already beginning to cool down, the hot Santa Ana wind succumbing to an onshore breeze. Days like this often gave way to foggy nights, he'd heard on the radio, and a foggy night would be welcomed.

He was crossing the third intersection when he saw the car. It was a cream-colored Bentley. Its fenders were a light shade of brown and its 'B' hood ornament reflected the last flashes of sunlight from the west. None of this impressed Dengler much. It was the driver who caught his attention: *Frank Sinatra*. He remembered his thoughts of this morning. *Rat Pack. Peter Lawford. Sammy Davis Jr. Joey Bishop. And Frank Sinatra.*

Dengler pivoted as if on parade and crossed the street at a martial clip. Even so, he saw the Bentley turn onto 5th Helena Drive before he reached the curb.

Before reaching the Corvair Dengler made himself slow down and assume a casual gait. He slipped behind the wheel, opened a copy of the Los Angeles Herald-Examiner he'd bought at *Denny's*, and watched the Monroe house out of the corner of his eye.

The Bentley was parked in front, empty. The gate was open several feet. Dengler checked his watch, estimated the actual time of arrival of the Bentley, 7:18 P.M., and jotted it down in the dossier.

At 7:39 P.M. the 1955 Ford Crown Victoria backed out of the driveway and accelerated up to the corner. He saw Mrs. Ketchum at the wheel. She executed a right and diminished down Carmelina to Sunset, and then East. *Heading for Sepulveda Boulevard*, Dengler thought, *and probably home.*

Dengler waited. At 8:09 a pickup truck backed out of the driveway. Jotting down the license plate number, Dengler made a mental ID of the man driving the truck. *Twenty to twenty-five, sandy blond hair, with a light complexion, wearing a T-shirt. Handyman*, Dengler guessed, *or a job-specific repair person. Electrician.*

Plumber. The pickup didn't look as if it belonged to a plumber. He wrote, *Maybe the pool boy.*

More time passed. Half an hour. Forty minutes. Then he saw Sinatra and Monroe walk out the driveway. She was wearing a black cocktail dress with what appeared to be sequins across the bodice. Sinatra was smiling and Monroe was laughing at something he said. Dengler contrasted this Marilyn, full of laughter and smiles for Sinatra, with the woman he'd seen the night before, sobbing and being sustained between the arms of two attendants. Either this man made her this happy, or she wanted him to think so. Dengler assessed the body language. Good friends. Maybe lovers. They moved like two people who knew each other well, were completely at ease with one another, and whose pretenses were laid aside in one another's company. At least, once they were lovers, Dengler guessed. Sinatra opened the passenger door for her, closed it when she was inside, then circled the car to get in himself.

Prince Charming, he thought. *White Knight.*

Well, that's okay, he considered after a moment, surprised at his own cynicism. *Here's a woman who needs a White Knight.*

Dengler assessed that neither of them had seen him, so before the Bentley reached the opening of the cul-de-sac he slipped down in the seat. The Bentley made a right turn, moving for Sunset, and Dengler guessed, an exclusive private restaurant somewhere in Beverly Hills where their celebrity was easily hidden.

Worth — oh, two hours, easy.

Just to be sure, Dengler waited twenty minutes before getting out of the car and strolling north on Carmelina. In the interim, he pulled on the harness and placed his Walther PPK in its holster, covered it with a windbreaker, found the *Leica* camera, and loaded it with super-fast film. He locked the Corvair behind him and pretended to walk with ease, but even so he entered the driveway of 12305 5th Helena less than twelve minutes later. It was 9:14 P.M.

The porch light was again on, although the driveway was empty. Dengler tried the front door first, found it locked as before, and then circled the house to the double French doors, which were again unlocked. He stepped inside. All the lights were off. He withdrew his penlight and followed it into the hallway, then into Marilyn's bedroom.

He found the diary unmoved from the previous night, wedged beneath the bed. He was prepared this time and wore gloves, so he merely reached between the mattress and box springs and withdrew the red book.

Dengler decided the best place to photograph the diary would be in the kitchen, beneath the big lamp that hung over the kitchen table. Of course, this necessitated turning it on, increasing the possibility of being discovered from outside, but it was a chance he would take.

He had to work quickly, so he read very little of the text as he snapped the pictures. He caught phrases, snippets of sentences, names such as *Jack, Bobby, Darryl, Hoffa*. Occasionally a sentence would make an impact on his mind, such as *'put him in jail if it's the last thing he ever does.'* Mostly it was gibberish going by at a terrific pace. Dengler finished one 36-exposure roll, went to the second, then the third. He feared he didn't have enough film to complete the project.

That fear was superseded by another when the beams of two headlights cut across the wall of the kitchen. A car had just pulled into the Monroe driveway. Dengler knelt beside the sink and looked out the window, his brow barely breaking the surface of the window. The car was — a pickup truck, possibly the one he'd seen leave earlier. The engine died, and the lights faded. A form got out of the car and stepped from shadow into near-light. *A man. Tall. Thin. Young.* He walked toward the house, leaned under a birdhouse, slid open something unseen, and withdrew what Dengler knew instantly was a key.

A key. To the house. To the goddamn house. To the goddamn kitchen door of the house.

-12-

Dengler moved to the door where the second of two light switches was located. He'd switch off the light the moment the intruder entered the kitchen, use the darkness as a cover, hit the man, and then make his getaway down the driveway.

Then he saw the Leica camera where he left it sitting on the kitchen table, and Marilyn's red diary. *Shit*, he cursed. *Shit-shit-shit.* He dove across the kitchen floor, knocked over one of the chairs, grabbed the Leica camera and the diary, leaped back across the floor and again positioned himself behind the door, and waited.

Two minutes went by before Dengler could bring himself to look out, and then it was through the window in the door. There was a light on across the driveway. *A guesthouse.* He'd never realized there was a *guesthouse*.

When his breathing settled, Dengler stood up and looked out through the kitchen window. Obviously, the handyman — the man he saw leaving earlier in the pickup — had returned to do some work on, or in, the guesthouse.

Dengler quickly set the red diary back in place beneath the kitchen lamp and started snapping photos. He averted disaster once when a bead of sweat from his brow almost landed on a page. Somehow he was able to yank the diary out of its path, then he carefully wiped his face and brow with the dish towel. It was an effort not to allow his accelerated breathing to effect the stability of the camera. He half-completed the fourth roll of 36-exposure film when the writing stopped with yesterday's date and the entry: *Tomorrow 7:30 P.M. — FS.*

Dengler returned the diary to its place in Marilyn's bedroom. He checked to make sure everything was as he'd found it, and then ten seconds later stood again in the kitchen looking out the window at the guesthouse.

He now faced a dilemma. He could turn off the kitchen light, which might alarm the handyman. He could leave it on and take the chance Marilyn, when she returned, wouldn't remember whether she left it on or not. In either case, there was an element of risk. If either of them became suspicious, the police might be called. Cops might question a certain individual sitting in a car within sight of the Monroe house. Things could become untidy.

Waiting, however, might be worse. What if Dengler attempted to out-wait the handyman and Sinatra brought Monroe home? He might become trapped within the compound, find himself arrested and certainly kicked out of the academy. After all, he'd exceeded his instructions the moment he entered private property. He was supposed to observe and report. He was supposed to be a passive, rather than an active, agent.

Dengler struggled with the issue for minutes. It seemed like decades. The handyman drove into the compound at 9:22 P.M. It was now 9:29. Less than ten minutes had elapsed. He had to make a decision. *Fuck it*, he thought, and flipped the light switch. The kitchen sank into a pit of darkness where pools of gray bathed in, perfectly formed rectangles on the floor, from the kitchen windows.

Dengler secured each roll of film in its own tiny aluminum canister. He gave the entire room a quick scan in the dark to make sure he was leaving nothing, placed the camera back into his windbreaker pocket and left the kitchen.

When he exited the Monroe house, Dengler paced purposefully up the south sidewalk of the cul-de-sac to the waiting Corvair, shoved himself behind the wheel. He drove back to his motel and deposited the film with the desk clerk for safekeeping. On the way back to 5th Helena Drive he stopped for a hamburger and fries at a *McDonalds* in West Los Angeles.

It was 10:53 when the Corvair pulled up just outside the glow of the overhead street lamp on Carmelina. Dengler parked and waited.

The Bentley pulled into 5th Helena Drive at 11:52. Dengler dropped in the seat so his eyes were at dash level. The car rolled halfway into Monroe's driveway and then curved out so the passenger door was facing the house. Marilyn Monroe stepped out and closed the door, leaning down on its window frame to talk with Sinatra in the driver's seat. Dengler couldn't make out the conversation except for the tone of Marilyn's lilting voice. He did hear "'Night," spoken in a male voice, and the reciprocating, "'Night," by Marilyn. Then the Bentley powered past the Corvair and out toward the entrance to Carmelina.

For moments, Marilyn watched the Bentley. When it was gone, she looked across the street at the parked Chevy. Dengler saw by her manner she was considering something, weighing it in her mind. A chill ran up his spine and splashed over onto his shoulders, when he saw she was walking across the street, walking toward him, the sound of her heels clicking on the sidewalk.

In a moment, the angle would be such she could see into the car and would observe Dengler, no matter if he remained down or not, so he straightened in the seat and attempted to look disinterested.

Marilyn Monroe stopped ten feet from the car and looked at him. She was gorgeous, the black dress contrasting her lovely yellow hair, the sequins across her bodice twinkling with reflected light, the cleft between her breasts subtly visible. Dengler looked back and felt foolish. She recognized him from the previous night, not a revelation, but a confirmation. He nodded and smiled sheepishly.

She completed the distance to the car in seconds and tapped gently on the window of the driver's door. "Can I talk to you?" she said.

- 13 -

Thursday, August 2, 1962

Brentwood, California

"Can I talk to you?" Monroe said.

For moments while she stood beside his parked car, Dengler was frozen with indecision. He was compromised and that was that. Dengler cranked the window down. "Ah, sure," he told her. "Can I help you with something?"

She hesitated. Dengler sensed this was a chance taking for her. Finally, she smiled to release his tension, and hers, and asked, "Do you mind if I get in?"

"Sure." It sounded a lot more enthusiastic than he meant it to. Dengler reached across the bench seat and pulled the locking knob up. Marilyn crossed in front of the car, opened the door, smoothed her dress out as any lady would, and sat down. She tugged three times on the door to get it to swing all the way closed.

For a long moment David Dengler and Marilyn Monroe looked at one another. The silence was tangible. Needing something — anything. — to break the silence, Dengler reached into the McDonalds bag on the floor and withdrew a smaller bag of fries. "Care for one?" he asked.

"I just had dinner," she said with a smile, taking a short fry from the pack. "But I guess one won't hurt, will it?" She had no desire for a French fry at all, Dengler could see that, but this was her way of breaking the silence, too.

"No," Dengler heard himself say. "Won't hurt."

The Seven Year Itch. Dengler had seen the movie twice, not so much because he liked *it* as he liked *her*. He remembered how lovely her eyes were, the intonation of her voice, the shape of her exquisite body, and the wholly intangible *something* that made Marilyn Monroe unlike anyone else. Now here she was, sitting in the same car with him, looking at him as he looked at her. He smelled her perfume and heard the rustle of her dress and had he wanted — *he wanted* — had he been *free to*, he could have reached over and touched her soft flesh with his hands.

"You're Marilyn Monroe," he said.

She grinned. It was a small grin, one tired of recognition, and celebrity, but dutiful. "Of course I am," she said.

That was it for a moment. Dengler could think of nothing else to say. Then it was her turn. "I know who you are, too," she told him.

"You do?" A glacier of ice calved from his back and fell into the seat behind him.

"Yes. I do." Dengler watched her manner change. She strengthened herself, visibly toughened herself to say, "And you can help me. I have to get in touch with Jack."

Dengler had no idea who Jack was and, sensibly, said nothing.

"I know, technically, you work for Bobby," she continued. "I understand that. And I wouldn't want to put you in an awkward position or anything, but it's very important I talk with Jack. Everything depends on it."

"Like what 'everything'?" Dengler said gently.

Frustrated, she burst out, "Damn it! You goddamn well know what 'everything' I mean!" She regretted the explosion the moment it happened and reached out to Dengler as if to take it back, or to quiet his reciprocal anger. Finally she said, "I'm sorry. I shouldn't have yelled at you."

"It's okay," Dengler told her.

After a moment she looked up at him, and Dengler knew the image of this face would remain with him forever. Her eyes were soft and searching.

"Look, I don't know your name..."

"Danny," he lied.

"Danny, I don't want to hurt Jack and I don't want to hurt Bobby. You can understand that, can't you?"

"Sure."

"I know about the phones being tapped. I know about my home being under surveillance."

Dengler shifted in the seat and tried to hide his disbelief. He realized she had to be delusional. Why would anyone tap her phones, or place her home under surveillance? Certainly, she was a major Hollywood star, possibly the biggest female star in Hollywood, but still, why would anyone do it? There was himself, of course, he was there and he had her house under surveillance. His presence was a fluke, a training exercise. Who else would do it? Gossip mongers? Was that what she was saying? She was being pursued by gossip mongers?

"I... don't want to hurt them, but they lied to me. Jack lied to me and Bobby lied to me, and I'm not just some bimbo they can do that to, you know what I mean?"

Dengler gestured he did. Obviously, she thought he was a private investigator hired by this Bobby to surveil her, and Jack was Bobby's boss. "You don't want me to tell Bobby first," he said. "Just go straight to Jack."

"Yes. I mean, I like Jack a lot. You might even say I loved him. But with Bobby it's different. He told me he loved me and wanted to marry me, and then he stopped taking my calls. He had our private line disconnected. I've tried to call Jack, but he won't take my calls either."

"What exactly do you want me to tell Jack?"

"You tell him I won't be treated like this anymore. If I don't get answers personally from him or from Bobby, then I'm going to call a press conference and blow the lid off the entire affair. With both of them."

They sat in silence a moment before Marilyn's anger subsided. When she looked at him again, he saw tears were welling in her eyes. "I don't want to do this. I don't. But... I won't be treated like trash. I've worked hard all my life for everything I've achieved, and I won't be treated like this. You tell Jack that, too, Danny, so he'll know I don't want to hurt him or anyone else."

After a silent time she used to wipe tears from her eyes with her fingers, she said, "I've got to go now." She got out of the car and bent over to look in before closing the door. "I want to thank you," she told him. "Really. You're a great guy, and I know you'll do your best to contact Jack."

"I will," Dengler told her. "I'll do my best."

He watched her walk slowly across the street and up the driveway to her house. He wanted to go after her and knew in his heart if he offered her any commiseration at all, she would leap to take it.

He didn't move.

He offered nothing.

He was compromised.

- 14 -

Friday, August 3, 1962, 1:15 A.M.

Brentwood, California

David Dengler sat in the Corvair for an hour after Marilyn left. He could still smell her perfume, almost hear the rustle of her dress, wanted to reach out and comfort the phantom she'd become in his car, and in his mind. Obviously, she was having a bad love affair with a man named Bobby and hoped to make contact with him through his boss, this guy named Jack. Dengler knew the whole thing was futile. Love doesn't come from referrals.

It was 2:15 A.M. when he arrived back at the motel. He took a shower immediately and crawled naked and still damp into bed. He slept like death.

Dengler woke at 10:22 A.M. By 11:00 A.M. he'd picked up the film and was on his way to a *Norm's Restaurant* on Sepulveda Boulevard. He found a booth with a view of the rift between the hills and ordered breakfast.

Quickly he considered his objectives for the day. At some point, he would have to run the license plates he wrote down the day before through the Department of Motor Vehicles. Of particular interest was the plate of the man who drove the pickup onto the Monroe property while he was in the kitchen photographing Marilyn's diary. He would also have to trade in the two rental cars for new models again. As well, he would have to find some way to get the Leica film developed, not an easy task as he had no developing equipment with him and he wouldn't — couldn't, really — turn the film over to a lab.

While he considered these problems and ate his breakfast, Dengler jotted down new entries into his dossier. He was sure he broke new ground here, that no one had ever compiled as complete and revelatory a dossier on Marilyn Monroe as his. He had the names of a lover, his boss, two world-famous friends who visited her, a maid and handyman, all compiled during his time on site. Plus he ascertained other new data, such as the probable abortion she underwent the day before. He had a car identification for each person, addresses, and specific times for comings and goings. He also successfully entered the objective's home, photographed her diary, and exited without being caught.

Dengler wouldn't mention being 'made' by the objective, partly because it would spoil everything he'd achieved thus far, and partly because her identification was mistaken. She thought he was a private detective hired by a former lover to surveil her and bug her phone. Why she thought a former lover would do this when he wouldn't accept her phone calls Dengler couldn't fathom.

Dengler called the photography department of West Los Angeles City College and, using one of his phony IDs, arranged to borrow one of their student photo labs for an hour. He calculated there were nearly 120 exposures. He didn't have time to print each one. He would have to be satisfied with contact prints until he returned to Fort Lee. A roll of thirty-six exposures could be squeezed onto one $8^{1/2}$x11" page by printing directly from the film at its native size.

An hour and fifteen minutes after starting Dengler had four prints, each one containing as many as thirty-six exposures. The quality was good but, as he expected, the lettering was very small. He would need to use a photographer's loupe to read them.

An hour later Dengler exchanged first the Corvair and then the Falcon for a Ford Galaxy and a Dodge Fury II. He found a parking spot for the Galaxy on Gaily Street at the west end of Westwood Boulevard, and drove the Fury to the Department of Motor Vehicles in West L.A. He again stood in line for almost half an hour before paying $1 for each request and getting the names of the registered owners of the Bentley and the pickup truck he saw the previous night. As he expected, the Bentley was registered to Frank Sinatra with a Palm Springs address, while the pickup truck was owned by Lester Goodwin of West Los Angeles.

In the late afternoon Dengler returned to his motel room with a bag of fast food. He ate while watching a rerun episode of Amos'N'Andy on KNXT. Afterward, he washed his hands to clean them of grease, then drew the drapes and sat down at the all-purpose table and removed the contact prints from an envelope.

One item Dengler brought with him from Virginia was a photographer's loupe, a small magnifying glass used for reviewing prints and slides. Now, with the bright light of a hanging lamp arranged directly above him, Dengler took the device, which looked like a hard-boiled egg stand with a glass bottom, and began to study the contact prints.

Less than five minutes after he began, Dengler shouted, "Jesus fucking Christ!" and leaped back from the table, toppling the chair behind him.

For a long time, several minutes at least, he looked at the contact prints without the aid of the loupe. Then he righted the chair, sat down and again placed the loupe over a contact print, lowered an eye, and reread the text.

- 15 -

June 5, 1962: I don't want to be just a bed-partner to Bobby. He always has so much to say, so many things to talk about, and most of it doesn't mean anything to me. It was different with Jack. Even though he is the President of the United States...

Even though he is the President of the United States... Dengler swallowed. Hard. He was beginning to sense there was something very strange going on, an event to which he'd received no invitation and possessed none of the appropriate credentials, and something that very possibly might land him in jail, or worse.

John Fitzgerald Kennedy, thirty-fifth President of the United States, and his brother, Robert Francis Kennedy, his Attorney General, had in the past or currently were romantically involved with Marilyn Monroe. Dengler was sent by the United States Army Military Intelligence School to surveil her, in theory the subject a randomly-picked public person whose celebrity guaranteed no sticky legal problems if he were caught. However, in his zeal to succeed, Dengler exceeded his orders. He invaded the privacy of her home. He photographed her diary. He allowed himself to be 'made' by the subject herself, and her delusions about her phones being tapped and her house being watched didn't seem delusional at all now. A shiver sliced down Dengler's spine as he wondered who else might have 'made' him. Obviously, Monroe didn't think he was a private investigator, as he earlier assumed. When she asked him to contact 'Jack' for her, she meant *the President of the United States.* When she said she knew that 'technically' he worked for 'Bobby,' she meant he must work for the Justice Department, probably as an FBI agent.

Then there was the threat. Marilyn Monroe threatened to call a news conference and, in her words, "...blow the lid off the entire affair. With both of them."

David Dengler now stood squarely on the track with the express train barreling down on him.

Dengler considered his options. He could stop the operation now, return to Fort Lee and report everything he witnessed from the street, omitting the diary, and the presumed abortion trip, and hope the FBI didn't have the house under surveillance.

Is the house under surveillance? Dengler wondered. *Would the President of the United States want the Federal Bureau of Investigation surveilling his ex-mistress, and the mistress of his younger brother and Attorney General?*

The answer is no. Probably.

Then who is surveilling her?

The answer is no one. Maybe. If Marilyn Monroe is having an affair with either of the Kennedy brothers, she might presume they are keeping an eye on her when...

Dengler stopped cold. Peter Lawford. He accompanied Marilyn to UCLA that night along with her psychiatrist and her housekeeper. Lawford was married to Pat Kennedy, Jack Kennedy's sister. Dengler wondered at the time why Lawford would risk his celebrity by accompanying Marilyn to have an abortion. Dengler's first take on it was that Lawford was the baby's father. Now he understood clearly — Lawford was the father's brother-in-law, and he was along to make sure Marilyn Monroe went ahead with the abortion. He was making certain there wasn't a Kennedy-Monroe bastard to use as leverage, political and otherwise.

Dengler couldn't know the extent of his involvement without reading more of the diary. He continued.

June 5, 1962: I don't want to be just a bed-partner to Bobby. He always has so much to say, so many things to talk about, and most of it doesn't mean anything to me. It was different with Jack. Even though he's the President of the United States, Jack didn't like to talk business in bed. I don't want Bobby to think I'm dumb, or naive. I want him to know he can come to me and share his life, and I will know what he's talking about, so I'm starting this diary which I will use to record things Bobby tells me so I can study and become knowledgeable about world and national affairs...

June 15: Peter called and invited me to Santa Monica. He said there would be a surprise waiting for me when I got there, and there was! Bobby flew in this morning from Washington. He's going to be in town for several days. Bobby took my hand and said to Peter, "Excuse me, but we have business," and led me into 'our' room. We made love for hours. Bobby makes love so differently from Jack, who doesn't have time for foreplay because he's the President. Today Bobby is very playful, and we laugh a lot. Bobby told me he loves me.

June 16: Bobby called and said he'd like to spend the night here. I sent Agnes home early. Bobby arrived about six thirty, and we went right to bed. Bobby was angry about something else and distracted, so it wasn't very good. I told him it was okay and everything, and then he admitted to me his mind was on 'Jimmy Hoffa that bastard,' as Bobby always refers to him. Bobby told me he is going to put 'that bastard' in jail if it's the last thing he does. Bobby's official reason for coming to California is to attempt to convince a syndicate man to give state's evidence, and it's not working.

Bobby also apologized to me for having to be the messenger from Jack. It's the first time he brought this up. He said Jack didn't have a choice in the matter, and I told him I understood. Jack never promised me anything and I know that. Bobby said J. Edgar Hoover called Jack and mentioned there were reports of him having an affair with a Hollywood star, and also associating with Frank Sinatra, who Hoover said is a known associate of Sam Giancana. A word from Hoover was a warning, and he had to stop seeing me, as well as Frank. I don't think it's fair. Knowing somebody isn't the same as being in business with them. Well, okay, Frank is in business with Giancana with the Cal-Neva Lodge, but it's a real business, not some Mob place. If it isn't a real business, let them prove that. Anyway, Bobby told me Jack didn't have a choice. He is, after all, President of the United States and married, too, and he's got a lot more people to think of than just us. I told Bobby I was hurt, but I understood. When Jack sent his brother to tell me our affair was over, I got angry, I admit it, but I understood. Being famous isn't always easy. But at least he could have come himself instead of sending his little brother. Then again, I would never have met Bobby if he hadn't come, and I told Bobby that.

June 17: Beach party in Santa Monica. Pretended I know Bobby casually. Lots of people there. Tony Curtis. John Cassavettes. Dean Martin, who I love. Great guy. Frank Sinatra, who talked with Bobby privately for half an hour and then left right after. Bob Mitchum. Some women, too. Stars, I mean. Natalie Wood with RJ Wagner. Anne Margaret. Peter funny. Pretending to be the loyal husband while Pat's in Europe. Saw him making it with a teenager from the beach later. Peter is sweet, but he is such a deceiver, too.

Bobby and I made it on the beach, too. Bobby said it was such a turn-on, to make it with the most famous and beautiful woman in the world on one of the world's most famous beaches. Later he went to get me a blanket and returned with swimming trunks on, the coward. We lay on the sand and talked for hours afterward. Bobby told me he has a lot of pressure on him, and sometimes he has to help his brother, who if the world knew he was this ill, probably couldn't be President. Bobby gave me an example, the Bay of Pigs thing. He said Jack was in terrible pain that day and had taken a strong sedative and couldn't be awakened. Bobby made the decision not to send in our planes, not Jack, and he stands by that decision even if the administration took a lot of heat for it. Bobby says Jack probably would have given into the CIA and the Joint Chiefs and released the planes, even though he feels he was being manipulated. Bobby says the CIA knew there weren't enough soldiers in the invasion force to fight Castro — 1500 men against tens of thousands — the plan's failure would force Jack into ordering an American invasion. Those bastards think they're so smart, Bobby says. He doesn't regret not falling into their trap one bit. 'Fuck those sons-of-bitches,' Bobby said, 'Cuba or no Cuba.'

June 28: Bobby's back on the Coast for two days. We spent last night together and made love twice. Afterwards Bobby told me about his plans, about how when Jack's presidency is done he's going to run for the White House. We spent hours in each other's arms. I've never known a man as loving as Bobby. He told me he loves me and wants me to be First Lady in the Robert Kennedy Administration...

Dengler dropped the contact print onto the table and sat back. If any of this information reached the American public, it would mean the end of the Kennedy Administration. It would certainly mean the end of the careers of JFK, RFK, and J. Edgar Hoover. Hoover already knew of the President's dalliance with Marilyn because Bobby told her the reason for Jack ending the affair— a phone call from Hoover. This was probably the source for Marilyn's belief the FBI had the place watched, and the phone bugged. However, RFK certainly had no concerns in that regard, so possibly he shut down the FBI surveillance himself. Would the FBI comply? Or would they continue the surveillance under the pretext it was a matter of national security? It was pretty obvious Bobby Kennedy felt no jeopardy in telling Marilyn what could only be described as state secrets. The FBI might continue surveillance based on that alone.

Dengler assessed his involvement. If the place were under surveillance by the FBI, then he was probably 'made,' simple as that. As well as Dengler covered his tracks by switching cars every time he appeared at the house, a real agent would pick him out in a minute. Marilyn herself had done that, although it was really the result of a lucky meeting at curbside in the middle of the night.

Dengler thought back. Had he seen anything or anyone who

might be considered suspicious? Well, there was the handyman, but it was unlikely the FBI had placed a mole in Marilyn's employ. Otherwise, no, he could think of no one. No suspicious cars, trucks, or events. Which meant if the FBI were maintaining a surveillance, it was either by electronic means, or they had a perch from a nearby house. He could check to see whether anyone had moved out of the 5th Helena Drive area by asking a few misdirected questions of the mail carrier the following day. As for the electronic surveillance, it was probably beyond him and he knew it. He could drive around the neighborhood and look for a van with an unusual aerial which might be connected to a short-termination radio transmitter/receiver, but if they rented a house from which to operate their listening post it would be impossible to 'make' them with just a visual search.

Dengler picked up the fourth contact print and read the last two entries.

August 1st: I tried to call Bobby again. His private line into the Justice Department has been disconnected, and no one there will put me through. Peter's coming tonight and we're going to have the abortion. He's convinced it's Bobby's, although I'm not sure. It could be Jack's.

Abortion or no abortion, I'm going through with the press conference. I called Lois and told her to go ahead and set it up for Monday. Let Bobby or Jack call me then. Maybe MY line will be disconnected.

August 1st: I saw one of the agents last night. He was standing beside the tree outside the driveway as I got into Dr. Bauer's Mercedes. He looked at me with an expression... Oh, I don't know what the expression was, but he knows something, so he has to be one of the FBI agents. If I see him again, I'm going to ask him to contact Jack or Bobby and tell them what I'm going to do unless they stop me.

Unless they stop me... The words resounded in his mind.

Dengler gathered up all the contact prints and negatives and put them back into the envelope, along with the loupe. He sat in the room for hours, fingering the envelope's closing flap, just thinking, running it over and over in his mind, trying to convince himself it wasn't true. Every answer was the same. Every addition of two and two resulted in four.

If so, someone's going to die, Dengler thought. *Maybe me.*

He didn't have proof. Was Marilyn Monroe being watched?

Dengler made sure his Walther PPK was loaded before slipping out of the room.

- 16 -

Fifteen minutes later Dengler executed a left turn from Sunset onto Carmelina. He slowed the Fury II to a crawl and proceeded down the small street peering into each of the Helenas looking for a van or a small truck. He passed 1st, 2nd, 3rd, 4th, 5th, 6th, and 7th Helena Drives before he saw a van parked halfway to the end of the cul-de-sac of 8th Helena Drive, a white Ford Econoline with a new temporary license taped to the back window. Dengler jotted the number down in his dossier: *1LG772922*. Behind the license and window was a curtain made of some heavy, light-blocking fabric. Dengler continued down the street until he was sure his engine couldn't be heard, pulled the Plymouth to the curb and switched it off. It was after one a.m. on a clear, windy August morning. Distantly there was the sound of a barking dog and overhead, the hiss of high-power lines and the gentle rustle of tree leaves caressing one another.

Dengler slipped out of the car and strolled up the street. For a moment, he wished he had a pellet gun with him. There were several targets on the cross-pole above that might be booster receiver/transmitters, or for that matter some other very innocent gizmo. The truth was, Dengler knew almost nothing about electronic surveillance, and even less about disabling surveillance devices.

Dengler stopped twenty feet from the van. *Someone was inside, or it was empty. Really, it was that simple.* Dengler considered rapping on the van and asking its occupant, if there were an occupant, what he was doing parked outside Dengler's house, and was this a matter for the police? If there were a person inside, and if he were involved in very illegal electronic surveillance, then the potential of police black-and-whites arriving might force him to retreat. However, if that person was an FBI agent, he would probably 'make' Dengler and doubt about Dengler being a neighbor would turn into certainty. No, not a good plan.

Dengler decided there was nothing he could do to determine if the person in the van, if he existed, was in fact bugging Marilyn Monroe's house. The best he could do would be to find out if there was someone actually inside and let it go at that. The presence of a real human being would suggest something was going on, although what that something was, well...

Dengler found three rocks about half the size of his palm and casually strolled back toward the point where 8th Helena Drive and Carmelina intersected. He paused at the street for several moments, enjoying the warm night breeze, before pivoting quickly and firing all three rocks at the van. Before the last one hit Dengler was running at top speed down the center of Carmelina Avenue. He dove onto the grass behind a car across the road and lay there panting until he saw the fat man trot to the center of 8th Helena Drive and look both ways, up and down Carmelina. He was forty years old, balding, and wore baggy pants and a pullover shirt. *Not exactly the FBI profile*, Dengler thought. He looked like a man who'd been rudely awakened. Or maybe just startled. After several moments while he suspiciously checked behind nearby bushes and cars, the fat man turned and disappeared down 8th Helena Drive. Moments later Dengler heard the metal van door close very gently.

The bugger, Dengler thought. *Marilyn is not paranoid.*

Dengler walked casually down Carmelina to 5th Helena Drive, and then to 12305. He was over the wall quickly without leaving a shoe trace, using his legs and upper body strength to almost leap it. At the top of the wall Dengler briefly surveyed the yard, and then swung down. In the instant of his visual survey at the top of the wall he saw all the lights were off in the house except one, and that one light was coming from Marilyn's bedroom.

Since the first time he saw the tree Dengler knew it would provide cover from two sides. He could sit in its hollow and not be seen from the street because of the back branch, and not be seen from the house because of the forward branch. By just leaning to one side, an observer could look straight down into Marilyn's room.

Dengler scaled the tree quickly. He secured his footing, checked backward — no one could see him this far in shadow, of that he was sure — and forward. Below was Marilyn's bedroom, the bed with its sea of loosened sheet directly beneath him. She wasn't there. Dengler adjusted himself for comfort and waited. He checked the time. It was 1:37 A.M.

At 1:41 A.M. Marilyn Monroe stepped into his angle of vision. She was nude, and she was crying. She held a telephone receiver in one hand, the telephone base in the other, and she flopped onto the bed like a teenager. She was as beautiful naked as he imagined she would be. She rolled over onto her back and looked out the window, but the lights in her room prevented her from seeing anything. Her tear-marred face told him this woman, this sex goddess, was madly in love with Robert F. Kennedy, who would not return her calls. He'd promised to marry her, Dengler remembered from one of the passages in the diary, and make her First Lady in the Robert F. Kennedy Administration that was to follow John Kennedy's. *First*

Lady.

That Robert Kennedy knew such a thing could never happen Dengler didn't doubt. He was amazed she didn't understand it couldn't happen. No divorced man had ever been elected President. Monroe represented something less than what the American people would accept as First Lady, it was obvious to anyone who knew anything about American politics. It was invisible to her.

Dengler pitied her, partly because she represented the gullible outsider he secretly felt was true about himself. He also pitied her because the little girl innocence she feigned so well in films was an extension of reality. It really was a part of her personality to be trusting and naive. She really was the kind of girl who might tell a lonely bachelor she kept her underwear in the fridge because the weather was hot, like in *The Seven Year Itch*, and wouldn't think anything of it.

Marilyn Monroe slowly hung up the phone and covered her face with her hands and sobbed. Dengler felt the urge to go comfort her. She had knowledge that could bring down a President, and while Dengler wasn't sure this President, John F. Kennedy, would use the power at his disposal to silence her, he knew by reputation J. Edgar Hoover was a man to be feared.

David Dengler wanted to get the hell out of there, but couldn't as long as he wasn't sure if the FBI knew about him. He had to find out.

Which meant he had to stay.

Dengler thought of the man in the Ford van parked on 8th Helena Drive. He was probably waiting for Marilyn to dial out again, waiting to record her conversations with friends that probably would extend far into the night. Or listen as Marilyn made another attempt to contact the man whose baby she aborted not two days ago and whose special telephone line, put in just for her, was ordered disconnected only recently by one of the most powerful men in the world, Robert Kennedy.

Dengler's brief campaign against the electronic surveillance van succeeded in no more than dinging its side.

He saw Marilyn dial another number. She waited while the phone rang and stared out a window that presented a view she couldn't see.

-17-

Saturday, August 4, 1962, Early A.M.

Dengler remained in the tree hours after Marilyn Monroe drifted off into a drug-induced oblivion, the telephone still in her hand, the bedroom light on. Dengler lingered partly because he enjoyed looking at her. Though she was a world-famous beauty whose nudity was his and his alone for this moment, his fascination with seeing her nude wasn't overtly sexual. Rather, perched in this tree and gazing down on a naked and vulnerable person, he felt like a guardian angel.

The final reason he remained was to continue thinking about his situation. In the darkness and silence of Marilyn Monroe's Brentwood yard, David Dengler could think about the forces arrayed against him.

He began to run possibilities through his mind.

Possibility One: He hadn't been sent to surveil Marilyn Monroe by accident. He knew Hollywood stars were well represented on Fort Lee's list of surveillance subjects, for a number of good reasons. For one thing, they were used to being followed by the press and wouldn't find it unusual having another body camped outside their door. Another reason Hollywood stars were good surveillance subjects was because they were relatively easy to find, and then equally easy to follow and document. Their lives were more than public — their professions were public, meaning their comings and goings were a matter of public record in gossip columns and the like. Dengler also knew certain celebrities were not on the Fort Lee list. At Lee he'd heard rumors about a surveillance of Rock Hudson the year before that had backfired, resulting in Hudson's name being removed from the list forever. It was said Hudson was a homosexual, and it wasn't Fort Lee's intention to reveal private information that would damage the subject and draw attention to its own training practices. The subjects were supposed to be innocuous, damage-proof, and thoroughly ordinary. Marilyn Monroe was anything but ordinary, and when the elements of a President and his attorney general were stirred in... Dengler feared he might have been sent to witness something, what he wasn't sure, and the ramifications frightened him.

Possibility Two: He was sent in blind, without anyone's knowledge Monroe was having an affair with the Attorney General of the United States. This scenario frightened Dengler even more. If it were discovered he had knowledge of what was going to happen — and Dengler was sure something would occur that would prevent Marilyn Monroe from having her press conference Monday morning — then he would be in extreme jeopardy.

Possibility Three: Robert Kennedy discovered the FBI had placed Marilyn's home under surveillance and ordered it stopped. If so, then the man in the Ford van probably worked for someone else, possibly a private investigator. If so, Dengler would be able to walk away free, although come Monday morning the Kennedy Administration would pay dearly for the sexual favors its leaders received from Marilyn Monroe. There was a lesser jeopardy here that his report, filed at Fort Lee, might attract scrutiny from the FBI and embroil him in unwanted controversy and attention. He could circumvent the entire matter by going to the FBI with the photos of Marilyn's diary and everything else he knew, thereby warning the administration and perhaps endearing himself to it. If the administration were already aware of what was happening, though, he could present himself as an unwanted witness to events best kept unwitnessed.

Of course, there was the worst case scenario — Robert Kennedy ordered the FBI to cease bugging, and they continued anyway, which meant David Dengler might find himself in the very awkward, perhaps life-threatening position of hostile witness against The Bureau. Dengler reassured himself such things didn't happen. Not the life-threatening part. Still, the reputation of J. Edgar Hoover scared the hell out of him.

There was Marilyn herself. Dengler looked down at her as she lay unconscious on the bed. Earlier he'd watched her take a handful of pills he thought would certainly choke her, but they didn't. For a brief moment he thought she was committing suicide, but then she returned some pills to their bottles. There was little doubt in his mind from the way she acted, both with him and later alone in this room, she was emotionally distraught and possibly unbalanced. He'd read one magazine article about Monroe in which she admitted attempting suicide on several occasions in the past. The standard way for a woman to take her own life was with pills, and Marilyn Monroe certainly had the means. Beyond that she also had the right kind of mentality, a person who saw herself as a victim — she'd referred to her childhood self as a 'waif' in the article — who now pined for the attentions of a man who was married and the father of — how many was it, seven children? To expect such a man to leave his wife and, in this society, lose his children just to share a bed with her was asking a great deal, more, apparently, than Robert Kennedy was willing to give. Therefore, Kennedy would be faced with three options: Convince her that her actions would hurt the country and ask her not to go public. Allow Monroe's public revelations and deny them — hard to do with so many witnesses who must have seen them together at one time or another, not to mention Marilyn's friends. Or arrange to discredit her, possibly by having her institutionalized. Marilyn Monroe's mental state and dependence on drugs would certainly assist such a maneuver.

Of course, there was a fourth possibility, one that was so disturbing he didn't allow himself to consider it.

Murder.

An hour before dawn Dengler dropped from the tree and approached the window. He stood less than three feet from Marilyn, separated only by glass. If she woke, she would see a man standing outside her window looking at her, naked and defenseless. Dengler was sure she wouldn't wake up for a while yet.

This close, Dengler could see she was just a woman, beautiful it was true, but a mere mortal. Her hair was matted and twisted, her fingernail polish chipped and scraped, and her body, while shapely, was certainly no more so than millions of other women. Dengler wondered how she got into this position, what Marilyn Monroe did that Norma Jean Baker couldn't do, to become Hollywood's biggest star and later mistress to a President and an attorney general. This waif, as she described her childhood self, had become royalty, and now she lay here naked and alone.

Dengler knew this woman would be dead in only a few years, if not sooner. The way she took pills earlier shot into his mind. It was with a skill born of repetition. Dengler was sure drugs were as much a part of her life as hair spray or cologne. She used Nembutal to deaden her reality, to dive deep into painless sleep, and one day she wouldn't rise to the surface.

Dengler suspected she sought relief from the everyday reality she created as Marilyn Monroe. This was Norma Jean Baker, a cute little brunette whose mama made repeated visits to psychiatric hospitals, a child who lived in foster care when she was lucky. She was as much the world-renowned Marilyn Monroe as David Dengler was James Bond. To the gentle soul, pretension and insecurity are ingredients for madness.

Dengler turned and walked away.

- 18 -

When Dengler woke, he was wrapped mummy-style in a sheet and the window air conditioner was rumbling on high. He turned the clock radio so he could see the face, which read 10:38 A.M. "Early," he mumbled to himself.

Dengler showered and shaved. He gathered up all notes, note pads, anything that might conceivably be tied to him and burned them in the bathroom sink, rinsing the ashes away. He then wiped clean the telephone, alarm clock, television dial, anywhere he might have left a print.

Dengler checked out, paying the bill in cash. He carried his bags to the parked Ford Galaxy and placed everything in the trunk. He would rent another motel room later that night, if necessary. If not, he would fly back to Virginia as soon as possible.

Dengler drove the Galaxy down Sepulveda Boulevard to the first fast food outlet he saw, a *Jack In the Box*, pulled in and ordered a bag of burgers and fries, and then drove east on Sunset toward Brentwood. He passed Carmelina and continued on to Hilgarde Street, where he took the bags and other personal items out of the Galaxy and placed them in the trunk of the Fury. He hid the contact prints, and the film taken of Monroe's diary in the side panel lining of the Fury's trunk. He then drove the Ford north to Sunset, and west toward Carmelina. He arrived at Carmelina Avenue at 1:49 P.M. and had to park south of where 5th Helena Drive and Carmelina intersected, giving him a less than ideal view of the cul-de-sac. Still, he could see almost the entire distance of the short street and it presented him with a less than obvious vantage point if someone were looking.

It was this possibility — that someone might be looking — that became the most important issue to him. He had to know if he was in danger, even if by gaining the knowledge he placed himself in greater danger.

Dengler took out the Leica camera and exchanged the standard lens with a telephoto. He loaded it with high-speed black-and-white film and placed the camera on the floorboard next to the passenger seat. He taped his wristwatch to the interior roof post on the driver's side so that 12 pointed up. He then rolled up his heavy jacket and shoved it against the passenger door so it would fill in beneath the armrest and turned himself, sliding across the seat so he faced out toward 5th Helena Drive. He removed the Walther PPK from its holster beneath his left armpit and rested it in his crotch, in open sight so he could get to it quickly. He then ate a *Jack In The Box* triple-decker burger and fries, spilling some of the sauce on his black-and-white striped shirt. The stain, he saw, would never come out.

An hour passed. Two. Several cars came out of 5th Helena Drive, neither of them from Marilyn's house. Being sedentary made Dengler sleepy; he rolled down the passenger window to provide better ventilation. He ate another burger. This one didn't taste nearly as good as the first because it had cooled, allowing the grease to congeal.

A green Chrysler pulled to the curb then, and a man wearing a gray suit got out. He was at least six feet tall with a rugged, scraggly face. He was a professional type that much was certain by his dress. The suit was impeccably tailored. He looked at Dengler across and down the street and Dengler, forced into it, glanced back indifferently. The man looked away.

Dengler made a show of eating some french fries, thinking anyone who would sit in a car and eat french fries would pose no threat to anyone. The suited man didn't look back and Dengler soon slowed his consumption of cold processed potato and grease. Instead, the man looked up Carmelina toward Sunset Boulevard, as if waiting for someone, and Dengler took the opportunity to snap several side-angle shots of him, balancing the camera on a knee so he could get a full-face shot when the man turned.

Click-Whrr-Click-Whrr. Got him. Dengler returned to feeding his face french fries with his unused hand and casually looked away when the suited man's attention swept past him.

Five minutes passed. Seven. The suited man checked his watch. Two more minutes passed. Again, the watch. Then another car pulled up behind the Chrysler. Dengler recognized the car. It was Peter Lawford's T-bird. Dengler brought the camera up. A man stepped out of the car. *Click-Whrr-Click-Whrr-Click-Whrr.* This man wasn't Peter Lawford. Dengler choked on a French fry, heaving forward and dropping the camera.

Robert Kennedy.

- 19 -

Saturday, August 4, 1962, 2:23 P.M.

As loud as Dengler's choking cough was, it wasn't heard by Kennedy, who greeted the man standing beside the green Chrysler. The suited man smiled. Robert Kennedy returned a more reserved smile. Then came an incomprehensible verbal exchange whose single identifying aspect was Kennedy's high, nasal Boston accent. Dengler forced the food up from his throat, coughing uncontrollably, as the two men shook hands. The suited man gestured toward 5th Helena Drive and Kennedy shrugged okay. The suited man removed a small black physician's case from the front seat of his car.

Dengler, still sucking air to keep from retching, brought the Leica up and into play. *Click-Whrr-Click-Whrr-Click-Whrr*, and as they were about to disappear into the mouth of 5th Helena Drive, Dengler refocused the camera on his wristwatch taped to the roof post in the foreground, catching the time, then focused outward in small increments until he reached infinity focus, establishing time as well as place.

It was a minute before Dengler stopped hacking, and another minute before he could say, "Jesus fucking Christ," several times between breaths.

Quickly, Dengler assessed the situation. Bobby Kennedy had arrived to reason with Marilyn. The man in the gray suit was a medical doctor, indicated by the physician's bag, and was here to provide medical support, probably sedatives, should Marilyn become hysterical, presuming she wasn't hysterical already. There was another possibility. The doctor might be a psychiatrist brought in to assess Marilyn's psychological competence before being committed.

Dengler kept the Leica propped on his knee and aimed at the driveway. Moments passed. He checked his watch. Five minutes. Ten. He bit into another french fry, a reflex action, then spat the morsel out the far window.

Dengler contemplated walking down 5th Helena Drive. It would be stupid, he knew. Unprofessional. On the other hand, it was the only way he could find out what was going on, and even then he would have to piece together the truth from inferences, an overheard voice or a... No. He wouldn't give into himself.

A truck stopped at the intersection. Dengler recognized it. It was Lester Goodwin, the handyman, and he executed a right turn and accelerated toward Sunset. Two minutes later Agnes Ketchum, driving the 1956 Ford Crown Victoria, stopped at the same point, and then followed the pickup up Carmelina toward Sunset.

Marilyn sent them away, Dengler guessed. Or Bobby had. Whichever the case, now Marilyn was alone with Bobby Kennedy and the doctor. Would Marilyn isolate herself with Kennedy? Of course she would. She would think of it as an opportunity to get him back. Alone, or nearly alone (Dengler imagined she had the doctor step outside) she could use the shorthand of intimacy, shared moments that would open his eyes and heart to what she really meant to him. Or give him the opportunity to express his anger and frustration at being penned in. Was Kennedy the sort of person who would strike a woman, possibly even beat her? Certainly, his public persona didn't suggest that. Dengler was beginning to distrust all public personas.

Thirty minutes passed. Dengler was becoming restless. There was no harm in getting out of the car and taking a stretch, was there? No. He put the camera down and slid out of the car. Traffic on Carmelina was light, a car a minute, and most of those cutting down from Sunset to Wilshire Boulevard below, or possibly neighborhoods to the south. No one would see him, he reasoned. Probably not, anyway. He was sure now no one had the house under visual surveillance, merely the electronic kind, so he could walk where he wished without paying the price of being 'made.'

He was lying to himself. He knew no such thing. He knew nothing. He was being drawn down 5th Helena Drive without reason, because he had no business down there, not any day, and certainly not today.

Dengler stopped at the corner of 5th Helena Drive and almost turned around. Almost. The Walther PPK rested six inches from his left nipple. He thought, *What a strange thing to be carrying on a nice day like today*. He shouldn't be doing this, and the knowledge he shouldn't made him giddy.

Dengler pivoted and started walking down 5th Helena Drive. It was more of an alley, really, than a street. There were no sidewalks, no lawns, no front doors. All the houses pointed in directions other than toward the street, or were hidden behind fences and walls. The two houses at the corner actually faced Carmelina rather than Helena. Except for trees at the end of the street, there were no places for him to duck away and hide. He might open a gate and enter a yard, presuming the gates were unlocked, but there were no bushes or walls delineating driveways. There were no driveways in the true sense of the word.

Dengler listened intently for the sound of voices. If Kennedy and Monroe were arguing, he would hear them from here. There was only the distant growl of traffic on Sunset, the crunch of sand and small rocks beneath his shoes, and his own breathing, which was heightened.

Dengler told himself to relax. He was merely walking down a street. *No harm in that.*

The gate to Marilyn's driveway swung open, and two men stepped out. A chill rocketed up Dengler's back. At first, the men didn't notice him, the doctor and Robert Kennedy, who looked grim and stared at the ground as if seeking guidance from the center of the earth. The doctor was talking, trying to convince Kennedy of something, and Kennedy was reluctant. *Reluctant to do what?* Dengler wondered. *To have her committed? To have her silenced?* The two men turned and started walking toward Dengler. In his haste to walk up this street Dengler made a tactical mistake and took the north side, where Kennedy and the doctor could be expected to walk when they left, and now he was on a collision course with them. To cross to the south side now would be to admit something was out of the ordinary, that he wasn't a local resident but an interloper.

Dengler looked at the ground himself and tried to appear as if he were thinking deep thoughts. *Got to get the lawn seeded. Got to get that toilet plunger replaced. Got to fix that screen in the patio. Got to... Shit.* It wasn't working. He looked up. Into the eyes of the doctor, who recognized him from the street when he sat in the car and ate french fries. Their eyes met, and locked. With every effort he could muster Dengler made his eyes ask a casual, *Yes?*

Bobby looked up, and he too locked eyes with Dengler.

"Afternoon," Dengler said.

- 20 -

Kennedy looked away. The doctor didn't. Dengler smiled and kept walking. After he passed them, forcing the two men to separate for an instant, Dengler resisted turning and looking back. He had no idea if they turned and watched him. Dengler walked to the end of 5th Helena Drive and stopped. Only then did he spin around.

5th Helena Drive was deserted. A second later Dengler saw the doctor's green Chrysler accelerate north on Carmelina toward Sunset. The doctor had turned around in some driveway to the south and doubled back. Peter Lawford's T-bird with Robert Kennedy at the wheel probably drove south.

Feeling foolish and very exposed, Dengler turned and paced down 5th Helena Drive toward Carmelina, and then across the small thoroughfare to his Ford Galaxy. He'd left the Leica camera sitting in plain sight on the seat. Any passerby could have stolen everything, including the film of the doctor and Robert Kennedy meeting outside Marilyn Monroe's house. To have left the camera where it could be stolen was stupid, and he knew it.

Dengler crawled back inside the car and mentally began scolding himself for the breech when the silver Mercedes sedan slowed as it neared 5th Helena Drive on Carmelina, then executed a left turn and rolled slowly down to Marilyn's gate. *Dr. Fred Bauer,* Dengler recalled. *Marilyn's psychiatrist.* Which meant Marilyn was probably distraught and had called him. Bauer slipped from behind the wheel and entered the grounds of Marilyn's house. As he went, David Dengler photographed him three times, and then pulled back to his watch to establish the time — 4:38 P.M.

Bauer's presence settled Dengler because he knew Marilyn's psychiatrist, more than any of her other associates he'd seen so far, was on her side. At least she wasn't alone.

Dengler thought back to the diary. Marilyn wrote extensively about her feelings in her diary, and while those passages were not as explosive as the ones about the Bay of Pigs invasion, or Bobby's struggle with Jimmy Hoffa, they were far more suggestive of the kind of person Marilyn was. She wrote haltingly of how she was afraid to appear ignorant to Bobby, of how she really started the diary as a way of taking notes so she would be prepared to talk about his life, rather than her own. She was sharply aware he was better educated than she, and somehow his education made him a better person. Marilyn was striving to rise above herself and her low-born past. There was no consideration in her self-analysis that she arrived where she was as an orphan without an inheritance or a friend. Kennedy, without the aid of his father's money and associates, might just as easily have become a Boston cop — or for that matter, an auto mechanic — as Attorney General of the United States. It angered Dengler, who was born poor and friendless himself. Dengler's anger turned to worry about the woman whose nakedness and isolation he watched the night before. He was beginning to realize his reasons for not running away were more complex, and unfathomable, than he knew.

As Dengler finished changing the film in the Leica, a black Lincoln passed the intersection of 5th Helena Drive and Carmelina at a crawl, then sped up negligibly. As it passed Dengler's Galaxy he sat up slightly, seeing all four men inside looking away from him. Dengler brought the Leica up, quickly focused and captured the license number, GBH 721. He then pulled back into a wider angle and shot the occupants, then back inside to his wristwatch taped to the post to establish the time, 5:12 P.M.

Dengler thought he recognized someone sitting in the back seat of the Lincoln.

The car came and was gone in less than a minute.

Dengler sat up completely, his heart hammering blood through his temple. Stafford. The man looked like Stafford. He couldn't be sure. He saw Stafford only once, when he made a speech at Fort Lee.

Stafford was a man in his mid-forties, with graying hair and a deeply accented face, pockmarked from youth. Even so, he was extremely self-confident and carried himself with an aristocratic air. He walked as effortlessly as an athlete. His clothes, Dengler remembered from that night at Fort Lee, were without flaw or wrinkle.

This isn't Stafford, Dengler told himself. *This can't be Stafford.*

He tried to recall what Stafford spoke about that night. The intelligence school attempted to get at least one "major hitter" to speak every class. Stafford was a coup. A high-ranking CIA operative during the Second World War, he earned his credentials behind Nazi lines, and later took the same Nazis and turned them against the Russians. He was reputed to be indestructible in personal combat and equally tough mentally.

What did Stafford say that night?

Stafford was Agent-In-Charge, European Theater, before accepting the job as Senior Aid to the National Security Advisor in March,

1961. Dengler remembered because it meant he was in Kennedy's favor, a personal appointment.

Of course, this wasn't Stafford.

The Greater Good, Dengler remembered. The theme of Stafford's speech that night had been *The Greater Good*. "In the intelligence business," Dengler remembered Stafford as saying, "things sometimes become muddy. Lies pile upon misinformation, and intentions can become cloudy, or suspect. It's vitally important to remember your single unfailing objective, to serve the greater good of the United States of America."

Dengler didn't see the Lincoln return until it pulled to the curb a block north of his Ford Galaxy. He saw it in the rear-view mirror. No one got out of the Lincoln. No one moved.

Dengler checked his watch. It was 5:29 P.M.

Dengler suspected what these men were here to do, even though it seemed crazy. He tried to think of a way Marilyn might be stopped from having her press conference Monday. She might be discredited. Marilyn was addicted to drugs, that much was certain. Her behavior was often erratic. A case might be made she was slipping into dementia, that she was mentally ill. Even so, someone would believe her assertions about the Kennedys. Someone might even launch an official investigation. It wouldn't be the first time an investigation was initiated for political reasons. No, these men were not here to take Marilyn into custody and spirit her away to a sanitarium where she could be made to appear crazy. Some people might later believe Marilyn Monroe, movie star. Enough people, perhaps, to swing an election.

Then there were the men in the Lincoln. They didn't look like the sort of men who would argue Marilyn Monroe was mad. These men looked capable of other things.

Dengler knew what these men were here to do.

- 21 -

Saturday, August 4, 1962

What are they waiting for? Dengler thought, but really he knew what they were waiting for.

They were waiting for Dr. Bauer to leave Marilyn's house.

The engine of Dr. Bauer's silver Mercedes turned over at 6:37 P.M. Dengler saw the flash of the car's taillights as it backed out of a driveway and up to the wall at the end of the cul-de-sac. A moment later Bauer executed a right turn onto Carmelina and proceeded north toward Sunset Boulevard, passing the Lincoln on the left. Bauer didn't even look at the car.

The moment the Mercedes disappeared, the Lincoln pulled from the curb. Dengler, a block away, was suddenly gripped by terror. What could he do? Nothing. They would kill him if he intervened. He would just disappear and never be heard from again. They had shown no interest in his presence. His cover hadn't been 'made.' He was free to walk. He was free to run, goddamn it. Who was Marilyn Monroe to him? Merely a face on a movie screen, a public personality, and nothing more.

Dengler watched the black Lincoln drive slowly up the street. It turned left onto 5th Helena Drive and continued nearly to its end. Dengler was transfixed. He observed the men exit the car and walk casually toward the gate. He was shaking by this time. He realized, the distant, pitiful noise he heard was coming from within himself. He was paralyzed and whining with pent-up energy.

Dead, he thought. *Dead-dead-dead-dead...*

What's she to you? he wondered. *What is she to you? No one. You want to live, don't you?*

The gate swung closed. The four men were inside. It was still light out, a warm August 4th, and dusk merely toying with the sky. It was a gloriously warm day with a breeze that licked seductively at the trees. It wasn't a day when someone could be murdered. It wasn't that kind of day.

Still, Dengler sat frozen behind the wheel of the Galaxy, fingers tightening, sweat extruding from his skin like hot metal from a die. The whine in his throat grew louder, so loud it seemed like a siren. *What's she to you?*

The door sprang open and Dengler spilled out of the car as if he'd been spat out of it. He rolled to the pavement, drew himself to his feet and fell into a frantic run that carried him across Carmelina and down 5th Helena Drive. In his hand was the Walther PPK.

The still rational part of his mind realized one of the men would be stationed beside the gate to keep out anyone who might happen inside. Dengler stopped thirty paces from the gate, re-holstered the PPK, and eased forward to get a better view of the gap between the gate and its hinges. He saw the dark cloth of a suit through the gap.

Dengler stepped back. The only way in was to go over the wall. He scaled it in one leap. At the summit he looked down on the yard, and the house beyond, and closer, the guard, whom he now saw was a beefy man of thirty-five standing inside the gate with his arms crossed.

Dengler drew the Walther PPK, held it by the barrel with the handgrip pointed out like a hammer, moved down the top of the wall and leapt out into the air in one quick, graceful motion. His shadow preceded him. By the time the bulk of his body and the handgrip of the Walther PPK was brought to bear on the guard, he'd turned and deflected the blow. He punched Dengler solidly in the jaw, reaching for his holstered automatic an instant afterward. Being struck enraged Dengler, who now attacked with every ounce of strength in his body. The guard stepped back, tripping over his own foot as he retreated. Dengler fell on him and began pounding his face with his fists until both were bloody.

When it was over Dengler lay on top of the sentry and sucked for oxygen, then rolled off the operative and disarmed him, pulling a bulky .45 from a shoulder holster. He threw it as far as he could and realized too late when he heard the splash, he'd thrown it into the pool. *Shit*, Dengler thought. He was up and searching for his own weapon which had gone flying in the melee. He found it ten paces away and noted with some satisfaction he must have hit the man when he jumped on him — one of the PPK's hand grips was shattered.

Dengler almost dropped the gun twice as he moved toward the house. The blood on his hands, both from the face of the man he'd just beaten, and himself, made the PPK slippery. He controlled it once his index finger slid into the trigger guard and the other three fingers and thumb closed around the grip. He moved for the side of the house.

The double doors were open an inch, although the drapes were pulled, and Dengler heard a woman's voice — it had to be Marilyn's voice, although it was higher-pitched than he recalled from the movies — call out, "Who are you? What are you doing here?"

A male voice said, "FBI, ma'am. Please remain calm." Dengler saw through his mind's eye Gray Stafford flashing an official-looking identification — hell, it might even be his real ID — and smiling confidently, as if to say, *Just one moment and we'll explain everything.*

Standing outside the doors, Dengler's paralyzing fear returned, like in the car. He knew if he didn't act now, he never would.

- 22 -

Dengler burst through the double doors and drew a bead on the first person he saw. It was Stafford holding his identification wallet in front of Marilyn Monroe. She turned at Dengler and almost screamed. Dengler's mouth was bloody, and his hands were covered in blood.

"Don't move." Dengler ordered, and then twisted himself around to bring a second suited man under the bead of his weapon. "You. Over there beside Stafford."

Stafford twitched when he heard his name. The second man looked at Stafford, and then slowly stepped to his side.

"Where is he?" Dengler said.

"Who?" It was Stafford. There was a faint smile waiting to form on his lips, but his eyes were deadly serious and looking at the weapon in Dengler's hand.

"The third man. Where is he?"

"Who are you people?" Marilyn screamed. She wrenched herself around Stafford and moved for the telephone, but Stafford's associate grabbed her arm.

Dengler brought the PPK up to bear. "Leave her alone." He ordered. The associate released her. Marilyn looked at Dengler strangely then, realizing for the first time he might be an ally. "Where's the third man?" he asked her.

"I've seen just these two," she told him. "They just walked in. They didn't even knock. I can use the phone?"

"Call anyone you want."

"I was going to call the police."

For the first time he noticed she was drugged, probably a combination of alcohol and Nembutal. "Fine," Dengler told her. "Call the police."

She picked up the receiver and began to dial.

"You two," Dengler told Stafford and his associate, "on the ground. Now." The two men exchanged looks, then lowered themselves to their knees. In a moment, they were flat on their stomachs. Dengler approached them and pulled two .45s from their suits. He tucked his 9mm into his belt in front, one of the two .45s into his belt in back, and then cocked the remaining weapon.

Marilyn stopped dialing. "Did Bobby send you?" she asked Dengler. Through the blood and mess, she remembered him from the previous night.

Where was the third man? Dengler tried to think. He was still reeling from the blow the sentry posted at the gate gave him, and he was so scared he thought he might just throw up right there. "I'm here to protect you," he told her. "Bobby sent *them*."

Her breath caught, and she turned to gape at the two men on the floor. Stafford looked up from the white carpeting and said, "As I told you a moment ago, Miss Monroe, we're FBI agents sent here to conduct a sweep for electronic devices that might have been planted in this house. The request originated in Washington."

"Yeah, sure," Dengler said. "That's why you didn't knock first. You just walked in."

"I knocked twice. No one answered the door. It was open." Stafford made it sound as ordinary as mail delivery.

"You're here to kill her," Dengler said, and Marilyn gasped. As easily as she found an ally, Dengler saw she now began to reassess her alliance.

"Who are you?" she asked him.

"My name is David Dengler," he told her. *Where is the third man? Where is he?* Dengler eyes darted from the double doors to the passage into the kitchen to the hall that led to the bedrooms. The house wasn't that large. "I came here by accident. I'm completing my field assignment so I can graduate from the Army Military Intelligence School in Fort Lee, Virginia."

Stafford laughed. Dengler jerked instinctively and the .45's barrel wavered before Stafford's face. "Calm down," Stafford told him. "Calm down and take a deep breath. Let's be reasonable here."

"Yeah. Reasonable," Dengler said sarcastically.

"I'm reasonable, and my partner is reasonable, so you be reasonable, too."

"Knock it off." Dengler shouted. "I know what you're doing. You're trying to make me look crazy. It doesn't matter whether she thinks I'm crazy or not, because I've got the gun. You'd better tell me where the third man is, or I'm going to start altering people's body parts."

"Look," Stafford said calmly, "consider this. Isn't it possible you've misjudged this situation? You say you're a student at this military intelligence school. You're here by chance, you say. So, what if what you think is happening isn't what's really happening at all? Consider that for a moment. You're not an experienced person. Isn't it possible you've misjudged this situation and we're really here to do what I said we're here to do?"

He's engaging me in a debate, Dengler realized, *and Monroe is the prize. Here are an immaculately dressed man and his associates, both of them with appropriate government IDs, who say they were dispatched to sweep Monroe's house free from electronic bugs. Then on the other hand, here is a young man, too young to be an FBI agent or anyone else credible, who's got blood on his face and hands and who is acting like a madman and aiming a gun at everyone. Who would you believe?* He looked to Marilyn and saw the doubt that was flowing into her expression.

"What's your name?" he asked Stafford, nearly shouting.

"Bristol. Roger Bristol."

"Wrong. You're Gray Stafford. You're not an FBI agent. You're a CIA operative and currently an assistant to the National Security Advisor."

"Are you sure? Isn't it possible —"

"NO." Dengler screamed. "I was THERE, you son-of-a-bitch. I heard your speech."

"What speech?"

Marilyn started dialing again. Dengler pivoted. "Who are you calling?"

"You said I could call," she said in a voice so soft it reminded him of the Marilyn Monroe little girl voice from all those movies. "You said I could call anyone I want."

"Yeah, I said that."

"So I thought I would call the police and let them sort everything out. Is that okay?"

Dengler's head was reeling. His mind was floating on a sea of confusion, and occasionally it dipped below the surface. "Yes," he said slowly, trying to keep everything simple, "that would be good. If you want. Call the police."

"That wouldn't be good," Stafford said. *Of course it wouldn't*, Dengler thought. *He still thinks he's got the edge. He's still got the third man and when he enters the equation, it's three-to-one, no matter how you count it.* "The President sent us here to make sure there are no bugs. For your safety and his safety. That makes sense, doesn't it?" He was talking to Marilyn, and she stopped dialing again.

"Yes, I suppose it does," she said.

"If you call out the police, there will be questions asked, questions which could embarrass —"

"THIS IS FUCKING CRAZY." Dengler yelled. "Don't you see, he's not afraid of me. He knows he's got at least one more guy out there.

You call in the police, he's got to prove he is who he isn't, and he can't do that. Listen to me, Marilyn, go ahead and call the police. Call anyone you want. Just do it soon because —"

Two men leaped through the double doors. Before Dengler could turn they were on him, the agent he'd beaten minutes before and the third man. Dengler kicked one and belted the other, but Stafford and his associate attacked him from the back. Dengler felt a sharp blow to the side of his head. Stunned, he dropped to the floor. They took the two .45s from him as well as the 9mm.

The sentry Dengler fought earlier started to hit him but Stafford stopped him with, "No. No blood in the house." The sentry lifted Dengler to his feet and guided him to a wall and leaned him against it. Dengler was still too dazed to resist. He heard Marilyn's anxious voice ask, "Who are you people? WHO ARE YOU PEOPLE?"

"Let's take her into the bedroom," Stafford ordered. "Bring him, too."

"There's no one on the gate," Bloody Mouth said.

"Never mind. Lock all the doors. Pull the curtains. We have too much to deal with here."

Dengler found himself being led into Marilyn Monroe's bedroom as the closing curtains draped him in darkness. In a moment, he heard Stafford say, "Put her on the bed," and then through a fog saw Marilyn being forced down onto the bed and held there, shoulder and ankle.

"Take her clothes off. Be careful not to bruise her."

"Is that all you want?" Dengler heard her ask, disdain commingling with terror. "Is that all you want?"

The two operatives — Dengler thought of them as Shoulders and Butch, because one had shoulders that extended straight out from his neck at a 90 degree angle, while the second had a butch haircut — removed Marilyn's clothes, twisting her onto a shoulder to unbutton the blouse, then returning her to her back to unzip the peddle-pushers and pull them off. True to her reputation, Marilyn wore no panties.

Dengler was beginning to rise out of the fog. He assessed his chances. Shoulders and Butch on Marilyn, Bloody Mouth on him, that left Stafford free...

Then he saw why Stafford was free. Stafford walked from the bathroom pulling a rubber surgical glove onto his right hand. Behind Stafford, on the bathroom counter top, was a small plastic kit, its lid open exposing a row of football-shaped pills wrapped in aluminum foil.

"No," Dengler said. His voice sounded twisted and vague, as if his tongue were having to make the words around stones someone had shoved into his mouth. "No, don't..."

Shoulders, who was pressing down on Marilyn's hips, turned her slightly and brought one leg up. When she saw Stafford unwrapping one of the pills, she started to struggle. Butch held his hands over her mouth and muffled her scream.

Shoulders forced her upper leg up until the knee pressed into her stomach, exposing her. Marilyn twisted, but the operatives held her firmly, Butch securing her wrists and mouth, and Shoulders her hips. As Marilyn twisted between her oppressors, her eyes sought out Dengler's and he saw the terror in them. *Help me!* the eyes begged. *Help me!* Dengler almost wrenched himself free from Bloody Mouth's grasp, but the beefy operative hit him once on the side of the head and all the strength in Dengler's body drained from him.

Stafford kneeled at the end of the bed and placed the first suppository against her anus. Gently, so as not to cause telltale bruising, Stafford pushed the small football-shaped suppository inside. When it first entered her, Marilyn's struggle intensified, but when the suppository penetrated the length of Stafford's middle finger, she began to relax. She was already dead, but in waiting. The drug went directly into her blood stream.

The second and third suppositories went in without struggle.

Dengler was breathing heavy, gulping air and wondering if his heart were going to burst. He saw the last suppository slide into Marilyn Monroe, saw the look of dying horror in her eyes, and made the last eye contact she would ever make with another human being.

- 23 -

"Hold her for five minutes," Stafford said. Marilyn's struggle had become an occasional twitch, and her eyes — those lost child eyes — were now turned toward the ceiling and what might wait for her there.

Stafford looked down at Dengler. "Okay, bring him in here."

"Fuck you." Dengler barked. Bloody Mouth lifted Dengler from the floor where he'd lain since his most recent attempt at resistance and guided him toward the bathroom.

"Face the counter," Stafford ordered. Dengler found himself looking at his reflection in the mirror, face pressed flush with the tile. Stafford's hand held his cheek there. "Shoe laces," Stafford ordered. "Tie his hands behind his back." Bloody Mouth removed Dengler's shoe laces and used them to tie Dengler's hands.

"Now then," Stafford said, allowing Dengler to straighten up. Dengler looked at himself in the mirror, and behind him, the reflection of Stafford and Bloody Mouth. Too close, the three of them. "I want to know who you are and what you're doing here," Stafford ordered.

Terrified, Dengler still managed another "Fuck you."

"You're going to tell me now," Stafford said. His voice showed not one ounce less patience than before, but Dengler's fingers in his grasp tightened in a sharply unnatural way.

"You're going to kill me anyway," Dengler heard himself say — he hoped it was a lie; he prayed it was a lie — "so kill me."

"Pants," Stafford ordered. Bloody Mouth unbuckled Dengler's belt, then unhooked his pants and yanked them down. His shorts soon followed. Naked from the waist down, Dengler's hips were shoved against the counter. Stafford gripped the back of his head and made him look down. His penis and testicles were flayed out on the countertop like pieces of meat on a butcher's block.

"Hand me one of the shoes," Stafford told Bloody Mouth, and a moment later Dengler saw one of his own shoes, now laceless, in Stafford's hand. He touched the heel against the tip of Dengler's penis.

"I don't have time for in-depth questioning. Understand?"

Tap-tap-tap.

Dengler said nothing. He was contemplating what was about to come next. Stafford would crush his cock and balls. If the first blow didn't kill him, the pain would make him wish it had. He thought about the shoe heel slamming against his soft flesh and about how excruciating that pain would be. He wondered for an instant if flesh so treated would ever act as it was intended again. Even if he lived — as unlikely as that seemed now — his limp manhood would be capable of urinating and nothing else.

An instant had gone by. "Now," Stafford said, "You are going to tell me who you are, who you work for, and why you are here."

"I'm telling you nothing," Dengler heard himself say. Was that just his breath catching, or was he holding back sobbing?

"Put a sock in his mouth," Stafford ordered. Bloody Mouth yanked a sock from Dengler's foot and shoved it into his mouth. Dengler wrenched himself, but not free.

Stafford slammed the shoe down. The pain was an explosion so intense Dengler passed out, and woke up seconds or minutes later supported between Stafford and Bloody Mouth. A sound washed across him like a sonic boom, his own voice screaming through the sock. The pain radiated out from his groin, stealing all strength from his limbs, stealing all thoughts from his mind. Dengler lived in the moment of the pain, a moment that was unending.

Dengler looked down. His penis was turning purple, the testicles blood red.

"Very well," Stafford said. His tone of voice hadn't changed since he'd reasoned with Dengler in the living room. "Consider that an object lesson. Tell me."

"David Dengler," Dengler said quickly, between sobs and gasping for air. "David Dengler. Army M.I. Training mission."

The shoe heel tapped against his flesh.

Dengler's back arched. He screamed. The pain was less. Even so the world became hazy like a television picture with a bad aerial.

"That's who I am, who I am, who I am..." Dengler sobbed through the sock.

"There are no training missions being conducted on Marilyn Monroe. I know that for a fact."

"... Fort Lee, Virginia. Training mission..."

Dengler saw the expression change in Stafford's face, a hardening, an anger. He saw the shoe rise in the air. *Oh dear god it's coming. Oh please god don't let him do this to me.* "Speech." Dengler screamed. "I heard your speech at Fort Lee. 'The greater good,' that's what you said. 'Blind trust. Freedoms in a blind trust' ..."

Stafford lowered the shoe. Recognition. He remembered. "He is who he says he is," he told Bloody Mouth, and then, realizing

Dengler must have kept records, "Where's your dossier?"

Bloody Mouth removed the sock. "In the car," Dengler said.

"Where's the car?"

"Ford Galaxy parked on Carmelina."

Stafford dropped the shoe.

"Do him," Bloody Mouth urged from behind Dengler. "Do him right here."

"Too much mess," Stafford said. "He's not going anywhere. You can drop him."

Dengler dropped to the floor. The pain was so intense he pulled himself up into a fetal position. The central joint of his body, his groin, hurt so much he whimpered as his legs moved.

"How is she?" Dengler heard Stafford ask.

"She's gone," another voice answered. Dengler made himself look outside the pain to see Marilyn Monroe lying on the bed, her eyes open, her naked body without her humanity to give it beauty.

"Okay, Marty, you go get this Ford Galaxy parked out on Carmelina. Bring it into the compound." Butch, now called Marty, took the keys from Dengler's pants which were still around his ankles, and walked from the room.

Of Shoulders Stafford asked, "You got the wire, right?"

"Yeah. I got 'em both."

"Both?"

"Two wires. Custom, both of them. Different maker. Within ten feet of each other in the attic."

"FBI?"

"Maybe. Who knows? It's all custom stuff. One was tapping into the other."

"Who?"

"DiMaggio, maybe."

"Maybe."

"I'm missing a gun," Bloody Mouth broke in.

"Ask him," Stafford said.

"Hey, cockless wonder, where's my gun?"

"Pool," Dengler replied. He was becoming the pain now. The pain was him. They were together.

"What?" Bloody Mouth kicked him to get his attention.

"Pool," Dengler said. "In the pool."

Laughter. He didn't know from whom.

"Care for a swim?" someone said.

"Okay, get him up. Pull his pants up."

They stood him up and jerked up his pants. The pressure on his genitals made Dengler cry out, which also elicited laughter.

Marty came back into the room.

"Find anything in the car?"

"A notebook, a camera, some other shit."

"Put all that in the Lincoln. Throw him in the trunk of his car, run him up to San Luis Obispo or somewhere like that, toss him into the ocean. No hands, no feet, no head. Understood?"

"Sure."

Dengler could no longer stand. He dropped, his groin exploding.

From the floor he looked directly into Marilyn's eyes, but they didn't look back.

- 24 -

Saturday P.M., August 4, 1962

Dengler woke in a dark, noisy place. He heard the hiss of automobile tires kneading the road below him. When g-force pulling on his body told him this vehicle was turning left or right, he heard the slosh of gasoline in the tank located somewhere below. There was a faint odor of carbon monoxide, from the exhaust pipe, and the feeling of cold steel and coarse blanket-like flooring material.

Whenever the car turned, slowed down or accelerated, pressure on his groin caused his mind to leap back to the moment the shoe struck his genitals and his breath caught. The pain was a constant throbbing when he was still, and a searing pain when he moved.

Dengler's hands were still tied behind him. The shoelaces resisted his tugging on them, because the cord was very narrow and dug into his flesh.

Dengler told himself to ignore the pain, forget the humiliation, and focus on the here and now. 12305 5th Helena Drive seemed very far away, a distant universe, Monroe's murder indelible but in the past.

"... *no hands, no feet, no head. Understood?*"

Dazed, Dengler considered how they would kill him. They wouldn't want to get themselves soiled with blood. They would shoot him first. No active blood pressure. Then they would open him up and drain some blood. No residual blood pressure. Then they would cut off the feet first, then the hands, then the head, in that order. Less blood spill.

God, his head was numb, his thoughts vague. *Concentrate.*

Dengler wondered if it were dark. He had no way of telling, of course, but it must be dark. The car was making very few stops, so they must be on an open road, probably on the Coast Highway somewhere above Malibu. San Luis Obispo was hours north of Los Angeles, he knew. Or did he? Was it near Santa Barbara? *God, I don't know anything.*

Think, damn it.

The whine of the transmission and the whoosh of the road were so relaxing. He could avoid the pain if he only fell back to sleep, if only he released his anxiety...

I should be trying to cut these shoelaces, Dengler forced himself to think. *Shoe laces. Bare metal. Friction. Heat? No, not heat. Well, yes, heat, friction, cutting. Where? Bare metal?*

He gently maneuvered his body, touching objects with his hands which were tied behind him. He felt the spare tire below him in an indentation in the floor, and across it, a jack and tire iron. *No help there.* He needed to find exposed metal, metal that was unimportant enough in the manufacturing process not to be ground down.

Dengler found the trunk hinge. When the trunk was closed, the hinge recessed toward the rear of the trunk area. He found it with his bare foot first, then felt it with his hands, pushing them up high enough by supporting himself on his chin. He told himself there was no pain between his legs. He lied. He began to move the shoelaces between his wrists back and forth on the trunk hinge.

His hands were free moments before he realized it. He cut himself, but not badly. Hands free now, Dengler turned and stretched himself out, allowing blood to flow back to places where it hadn't flowed recently. There was no pain between his legs, he lied. Moments later he reached beneath him and unscrewed the brace that held the jack and tire iron. He pulled the jack out, removed the tire iron, and allowed the jack to slowly slip back into place in the tire well.

He had a weapon. *Now what?* Dengler considered forcing the trunk lid and leaping from the car. That would accomplish nothing except possibly his death on the road hit by a car following closely behind. Or they would see him jump, pull to the side and finish him off with their .45s.

Dengler lay in the darkness of the trunk for minutes considering the dilemma. He could wait for them to stop and open the trunk, but there would be two of them then, and they would be preparing to kill him. They would have the advantage. As he lay and thought about it, Dengler's fingers nervously explored the darkness of the trunk. He discovered that forward of the lid was a fiberboard divider held in place by snaps at its corners. He pulled one free and reached behind it.

The rear seat. He felt the crisscross of wires and springs there. Dengler quickly, and as silently as he could manage, pulled the remaining three snaps loose and laid the divider down flat by rolling as far toward the back of the car as possible. When it was flat Dengler was able to move forward another foot, and now for the first time he could hear the sounds emanating from the passenger compartment. In particular Elvis singing *Blue Suede Shoes* over a radio.

Dengler's fingers raced around the edges of the seat back seeking snaps or some other kind of binder, but he found nothing. A voice said, "Turn that shit off, will you?"

"Helps keep me awake," a second voice retorted. Dengler recognized this voice. It belonged to Marty, the man he called *Butch* because of his short haircut.

"I'll keep you awake. Turn off that rock'n'roll shit."

Dengler heard the sound of the radio dial tuning through a dozen stations before stopping at a call-in talk show. "Maybe they got some news," the argumentative voice said, and Dengler finally placed it: *Bloody Mouth*.

"It's too early for news. The story probably won't be out for hours yet."

"I don't give a shit about that. I want the National League box scores. I got money on the Phillies."

"Fuck the Phillies. The Dodgers are going to take the pennant."

"Give a shit about the pennant. I got money on the Phillies. One game, you shit."

Dengler fell back away from the seat back and tried to think. How would they install the rear seat in the factory? They'd want it simple and quick, and nonetheless do the job adequately. All the pressure would be from the front when people sat on the seat, so there's not much chance of it coming loose. Probably some kind of pop-in studs. There would be no way to tell in the dark, particularly if the studs recessed into some kind of receptacle. He would have to apply pressure and hope the seat gave way gently, and without much noise.

Further, Dengler figured the seat might be hinged, with the hinges acting as guides for the upper part of the seat back when the worker installed it. He tested the corner next to him by placing the heel of his hand against it and applying force. Nothing. He tried again. Nothing. Then he struck it. The seat gave way.

"Hey, what's that?" It was Marty.

"He's waking up."

"You want to stop and check on him?"

"He's not going anywhere. Not with flat nuts." Bloody Mouth said. Both men laughed.

Dengler was quickly turning himself around in the trunk as this exchange occurred. His groin hurt. He thought, *Fuck it, my balls hurt. Live with it. Use it.* He'd been pointed in the direction of the passenger side of the car, and it was this side of the seat he loosened. He would have to strike Bloody Mouth first, he reasoned, then Marty who would be occupied with keeping the car under control and unable to come to Bloody Mouth's aid. His best shot would be from the left side swinging right. He wanted Bloody Mouth out cold while he dealt with Marty.

Dengler found the exact opposite spot of the first seat retainer, set the tire iron down in front of him and made sure he knew where it was — it was still dark and if he rolled through the seat without the tire iron they would subdue him quickly. Then Dengler brought both of his hands up and struck the seat back. It budged, but held. He hit it again, and when it snapped he grabbed the tire iron and rolled through the back of the seat into the passenger compartment. He was up in a kneeling position before Bloody Mouth could turn fully. Dengler hit him as hard as he could with the tire iron. He felt Bloody Mouth's bones crack — his jaw, probably — and then swung back and hit Marty in the same place. Back to Bloody Mouth, a lesser blow this time, and then back to Marty just as the car rolled.

The world spun. Dengler was a die in a dice cage being rattled before the throw. He was screaming and so were the others, screaming and striking the seat and roof with his body. The car rolled four times across the highway and into a ditch, where it finally settled and Dengler knew he had to ignore the pain, old pain, new pain, and get out of there. The passenger side door wouldn't open, but Dengler kicked the driver's side door open and fell out. Marty, the driver, lay beside the car. There was an unnatural bend in his neck.

Dengler stayed on all fours for minutes, gasping for air and afraid to assess the damage.

The two-lane highway was deserted. To one side of the road were fallow fields, and on the other side several hundred yards of Eucalyptus trees and, Dengler thought he could hear it, the sea beyond. *The Pacific Coast Highway*, he reasoned, *somewhere above Santa Barbara*. Fog wafted past him in banks, with moments of crystal clarity between.

The front passenger door opened and Dengler immediately pushed himself to his feet. He circled the car at what he thought was a run, but was actually a painful lope, and confronted Bloody Mouth standing beside the passenger door. Dengler hit him with his closed hands, the only weapon he had. Bloody Mouth was out before he got to him — he must have awakened just long enough to work the door handle and fell to the dirt, unconscious.

Dengler searched for his .45, discovered Bloody Mouth's shoulder holster was empty, and then found the automatic on the floor under the seat where it landed after the roll.

Holding the gun in his hand, Dengler staggered away from the car. He was surprised he had no pain now, adrenaline hiding the trauma brought to his groin by Stafford, and any injuries he picked up during the car's roll. Dengler lurched out of the shallow ditch to the edge of the road. A light mist still wafted by, a fog that glistened with the reflection of the headlights, which were still on, and from the glow of the amber dash lights. He leaned on his knees and gasped for breath, fighting nausea, and collapse.

A sound made him reel about to see Bloody Mouth was no longer lying beside the car. *He's after Marty's .45.* Dengler thought, and immediately burst forward. He was taught in the Army that in a fire fight aggression was the best defense, but Bloody Mouth's first round hit him in the head, and he dropped to his knees, then collapsed to the dirt, afraid that half of his skull was missing.

Dropping to the ground took him out of plain sight. The fog and the darkness were barriers to vision, but not bullets, Dengler realized, as he lay on the ground and ran his fingers over his scalp. He felt the blood there, but no wound. The bullet must have grazed him. He discovered, however, grazed or not, blood was flowing down his brow and into his eyes. He scraped it away with the flat of his spare hand, but felt the flow return.

Meanwhile, Dengler heard the sounds of Bloody Mouth over by the car. He was thrashing about in the foliage looking for something, probably Dengler. Below the surface of the ground mist Dengler was all but invisible. He knew he would have to act soon or take the chance of not retaining consciousness long enough to defend himself. He cocked the .45 and noted grimly Bloody Mouth's thrashing noise stopped immediately.

Dengler began to crawl. He was moving laterally toward the ditch thinking he might be able to gain enough distance to safely descend into the gully again. Then he saw Bloody Mouth rise up out of the mist behind him. He'd somehow circled Dengler and was now moving toward him from the highway. Dengler turned to face him just as blood cascaded into his eyes. He tripped and fell back into the fog, madly wiping blood from his eyes, as Bloody Mouth started to run forward. Dengler lost him almost immediately and twisted about, looking for the phantom that seemed to leap from mist to mist, and darkness to darkness.

Suddenly, headlight beams from an oncoming car bracketed Bloody Mouth in intense light and Dengler seized the moment to rise into a crouch. He used both of his hands to aim the .45 and emptied the clip. Seven rounds rang out and Bloody Mouth, distracted by the oncoming auto, didn't return fire before one of the bullets plowed into his brow. The last thing Dengler saw before the automobile lights took a curve and drew Bloody Mouth into darkness was the red mist that seemed to explode from the back of his head.

The red mist lingered, an apparition, three feet above the asphalt of the California highway.

- 25 -

It seemed like forever for the oncoming car to reach the crash site. In those moments Dengler hobbled to the road, took the .45 out of the dead man's hands, and then dragged him back to the wreck where he dropped him in front of the open passenger door. Dengler listened to the growing sound of the oncoming car as he took Bloody Mouth's wallet out of his pants, then circled to the other side of the car to retrieve Marty's wallet. He had no idea how much money or information was in either one, but he had no time to look now.

By the time the oncoming car completed the long curve and was back on the straightaway, Dengler staggered to the road and pulled Marty's shoes onto his own feet. They were tight.

Dengler stood and waved his hands in the air. Both guns were tucked out of sight, as were the wallets, and Dengler looked to be the bloody victim of a terrible automobile accident. The oncoming car, a Pontiac Safari station wagon, slowed thirty yards away. After a moment in which Dengler was sure the driver was assessing the situation, a man got out of the car and ran toward him.

"What happened here?" he said, looking first to Dengler, then at the car that lay twisted and dented in the ditch.

"Lost it," Dengler said, feigning a pained voice that almost approximated his real state. "My friends are dead, I think."

"Dear God."

"Need to get to the hospital."

"Well sure. I can..."

The .45, whose barrel kissed the Good Samaritan's belly, stopped his words cold.

"Listen, we can do this a couple of ways," Dengler said. "Me? I like the way you don't get hurt. What do you say?"

"Yes," the Good Samaritan said anxiously. "Sure. Whatever you want." He was a tall, thin, balding man of 35 wearing a suit shirt with rolled-up sleeves and a loosened tie.

"Do you have any money?"

The Good Samaritan pulled out his wallet and attempted to hand it to Dengler.

"Just give me the money," Dengler ordered.

The Good Samaritan took out eight or ten bills, denominations unseen in the darkness, and gave them to Dengler.

"There'll be another car along here soon," Dengler said, circling the Pontiac to the driver's side. "Sorry." He slipped behind the wheel of the Pontiac.

As he watched the Good Samaritan diminish in the rear view mirror, Dengler felt a twinge of guilt. He also knew he couldn't afford to answer any questions about the two dead men who lay beside the destroyed Ford, one of whom had a hole in his head. The Good Samaritan wouldn't be alone long — Dengler guessed another car would pass by within minutes, and just as he thought this the headlights of an oncoming car rose into view from behind a hill somewhere ahead. This car was no more than two minutes away from effecting a rescue of the stranded man.

Dengler turned to his immediate problems. He was still bleeding from the scalp, but less now than before. Adrenaline had dulled the pain in his groin, and now elsewhere, but that would subside soon. The car he was driving would be reported to the police as stolen within the hour.

First order of business was his physical condition. He saw a turn-off a hundred yards ahead and began slowing down, so by the time he made the turn he hadn't touched his brakes or activated their lights. Dengler followed the turn-off another quarter of a mile, then pulled the station wagon to a stop. He turned the rear-view mirror around and looked at his scalp. There was a cut on his brow above the hairline, a clean slice that was seeping blood down into his eyes. The wound was dramatic but not threatening. He probably wouldn't even need stitches.

Dengler exited the car, walked to the back and opened the station wagon's rear door. He found two racks holding suits and sport coats. The Good Samaritan was a salesman. There was a large cooler filled will melting ice and bottles of soda, and a suitcase.

Dengler opened the suitcase, found a T-shirt and dipped it into the cooler's ice water. He returned to the front seat and cleaned his wound using the rear-view mirror. The cold water was soothing. The T-shirt absorbed the caked blood. The bleeding had stopped.

Pain was returning. The head wound. His shoulder and opposite arm, from tumbling in the rolling car, probably. His genitals. Dengler found a flashlight in the glove compartment, stepped from the car, and pulled his pants down. The flashlight beam revealed that his penis was black and swollen, the testicles red and sore but otherwise okay. His penis had shielded the testicles from Stafford's shoe. Dengler touched himself. His breath caught as intense pain radiated out from the center of his body. He didn't want to, but decided he had to try to pee. If he couldn't, he would have to find a doctor. It would be possible for Stafford to track him by his injury by calling all of the hospitals and doctors in the area. If he couldn't pee, he might die. Dengler waited for the moment, felt the pressure build, felt a terrible, burning pain before urine trickled to the ground and he almost sobbed. He carefully pulled his pants up and sat back behind the steering wheel, sucking for breath.

He wondered if he would ever make love to a woman again.

Dengler relived the moment of his torture and humiliation. *I'm going to kill that son of a bitch*, Dengler thought of Gray Stafford.

Suddenly, he was tired. He stretched out on the seat of the Safari.

Dengler woke sometime before dawn when a passing semi roared by on the highway a quarter of a mile away. The darkness was serene. Dengler stepped from the car and looked up at a sky of velvet and gemstones. The mist that had rolled by earlier was now completely gone.

Dengler retrieved one of the bottles of soda from the cooler, noting that all the ice had melted, and drank the whole thing in one long gulp. The second one he nursed. He then slid back behind the wheel of the Pontiac and turned on the dome light. Marty, Dengler learned by going through his wallet and reading his driver's license, was William Crosswhyte of Trenton, New Jersey. Bloody Mouth was Victor Byrd of Brookhaven, Connecticut. Or they had been. Marty's wallet had seven hundred dollars in one hundred dollar bills, plus assorted change that added up to thirty-seven dollars more. Bloody Mouth's wallet contained nine crisp one hundred dollar bills, plus tens, twenties, and fifties adding up to another two hundred and twenty-three dollars. The money he stole from the Good Samaritan added another hundred and twenty dollars. All tolled, Dengler had over two thousand dollars.

I won't starve, he thought.

Neither wallet possessed documents that would shed light on who these two men were except they were authorized to drive a car in the states of New Jersey and Connecticut, respectively. Both wallets were new. No family photos, no laundry receipts, nothing. *Cover IDs*, Dengler decided, like his own bogus versions except more expertly produced. The cash was assignment issue. Dengler checked the serial numbers and found six bills were sequential.

Dengler had left his forged ID in the trunk of the Galaxy when he parked it on Carmelina Avenue. Later, when he was trapped in the trunk, he noticed it was gone. Stafford must have taken it, along with his camera and film of Kennedy and the doctor arriving and leaving, and his Walther PPK. Stafford wouldn't know about the second car parked on Sorority Row, nor Dengler's 'kit' in the trunk, which contained his real ID. His lost money was easily compensated for by the nearly two thousand dollars he took from Marty and Bloody Mouth.

He could live a long time on two thousand dollars. The question was — would he have to? The thing that kept running through his mind was Stafford's anxiety about Dengler's identity and what he was doing at the Monroe house just as Stafford was preparing to murder one of the more famous people on earth. It was almost panic — yes, *panic*, and Dengler enjoyed the realization — he saw in Stafford's eyes as Dengler identified him, panic at the thought there might be forces out there even more powerful than himself who might have an interest in this situation.

The question was who?

Dengler had little doubt John Kennedy and Robert Kennedy were behind the murder of Marilyn Monroe. Who else would have a reason to kill her? Still, men who have the President of the United States behind them aren't likely to show panic easily.

Was it possible the Kennedys were not aware of what happened? Was it possible Monroe's murder occurred for reasons other than the obvious? Dengler admitted to himself he could see no other reason to kill her. Except for her fame, Marilyn Monroe was an insignificant player on the world scene. Yet, the only reason someone would want to kill her in the 'executive committee' way she was murdered would be to remove her from the public stage. So far as Dengler knew, only the Kennedy brothers were jeopardized by her life. Each man had been her lover, and she was prepared to deliver unpleasant facts about him in a press conference scheduled for the week after her death.

The dark side of intelligence work was that rarely was anything obvious. Dengler knew this more from study than experience. In this world, friends were killed to make martyrs, and a motive for murder might be nothing more than the perception of an enemy's motive. *He had a reason to kill, so he probably did; we had no motive to kill, so we probably didn't.* Was Marilyn Monroe killed to embarrass the Kennedys? If so, details about her affairs with the brothers would come out soon.

If the Kennedys are behind it, Dengler reasoned, *then I'm a dead man.* He might leave the country, conceal his identity, somehow submerge himself beneath the surface of the world, but if they found him, they would kill him.

He had one asset: The diary. He would have to go back to Los Angeles, retrieve the contact sheets and film of Marilyn Monroe's diary from the parked Plymouth Fury, his clothes and what remained of his gear, and head east.

But where? He had no family, few acquaintances, and no friends. He had to go somewhere, he had to do something, and the west coast was too hot for him now.

Ninety minutes later Dengler parked the Pontiac Safari on a street in Santa Barbara three blocks from the bus depot. He left three hundred dollars in the glove compartment as penance for having stolen the car and the money he robbed from the Good Samaritan. He took a shirt from the suitcases in the back of the Pontiac and selected a suit that fit. He hemmed the pants with a sewing kit he found in the glove compartment. Dengler cleaned himself up as well as he could in the men's bathroom at the depot and changed into the clean clothes before boarding the bus to Los Angeles.

It was after 7:00 A.M. when the bus pulled out of the station. Dengler had a copy of the *Los Angeles Times*, Santa Barbara edition, which said nothing about the death of Marilyn Monroe. It was early yet.

The bus would take two hours to get to Los Angeles. He was asleep in twenty minutes.

- 26 -

Sunday Morning, August 5, 1962

The bus turned north at the San Diego Freeway and followed it up and over the Sepulveda Pass. Dengler saw the *Norm's Restaurant* where he ate breakfast several times. He watched Sunset Boulevard pass over him as a bridge, here no more than minutes from Marilyn's house. The bus got off the freeway at Wilshire and drove east. Three minutes later it pulled to a stop at the intersection of Broxton and Wilshire and Dengler got off.

It took fifteen minutes for Dengler to walk the distance to Sorority Row. The Plymouth Fury was parked where he left it. He found the hidden key under the front bumper. He checked to make sure the contact sheet and photos of Marilyn Monroe's diary were still in the trunk. They were. In a moment, he was in the car and its engine roared to life. Dengler turned on the radio immediately and twisted the dial until he found a news station. A male voice was reporting the Dodgers had defeated the San Francisco Giants the night before, then that the Phillies and Cubs had dueled to a 2-2 tie broken in the eleventh inning by an Ernie Banks single that drove in a run.

Dengler was on Sunset proceeding west when the news report about Marilyn came on. "This just in," the radio voice said. "Unconfirmed reports have it that Marilyn Monroe, who was found dead in her Brentwood home early this morning, is apparently the victim of an overdose of barbiturates. Los Angeles Coroner Thomas Noguchi stated today that while most cases of drug overdose are accidental, Marilyn Monroe might have committed suicide. Joe DiMaggio, Marilyn Monroe's former husband and a long-time friend, is reported to be in route to Los Angeles from San Francisco at this moment. Already eulogizing statements are coming in from the entertainment community. Dean Martin, who starred with Monroe in the ill-fated, shutdown Twentieth Century-Fox film *Something's Got To Give*, said..."

Dengler shut off the radio as he executed the left turn onto Carmelina. As he passed 5th Helena, he saw several police cars still drawn up in front of Marilyn's house. A blue van occupied the spot where his Ford Galaxy was parked the evening before.

Dengler turned around on 2nd Helena and drove back toward Sunset. He saw a motel, The Sunset Lodge, just two blocks from the intersection of Carmelina and Sunset, and pulled into its driveway and parked.

He rented a room, showered, was able to make himself urinate again, and then crawled between crisp sheets, turned the air conditioner up to high, and quickly fell asleep.

Dengler woke at 5:30 P.M. It was still light outside beyond the blackout curtains, and it was still warm. The wall unit air conditioner was straining to keep this little box of a room cool. Dengler quickly showered again, this time in cool water, and switched on the television. There was a news program on Channel 2. A newscaster was reporting the grief being expressed by the film 'colony,' as he called it, about the death of Marilyn Monroe. He saw filmed interviews with Groucho Marx, and Bob Hope, with whom Marilyn had toured Korea a decade before, and several people he didn't recognize.

Dengler dropped both .45s on the bed. They were big and unwieldy, although they packed far more power than his Walther PPK. The one he'd used to kill Bloody Mouth was empty; the second still had a full clip. He would need to buy several more clips, more ammunition, and a shoulder holster. He dressed as he made these plans, and listened to the news report.

Dengler stopped and sat at the end of the bed when they began to run film of Marilyn's body being taken out of the house earlier that morning. Two white-coated attendants guided a gurney out of the front door and into a waiting Chevrolet ambulance. He saw Agnes Ketchum being led to an unmarked police car. He saw LAPD detectives roaming about the yard and house. The reporter, again narrating this portion of the story, said, "While not official yet, authorities are leaning toward a report of suicide. Friends and associates of Marilyn Monroe say she was despondent over the cancellation of her recent 20th Century-Fox Film ironically titled *Something's Got To Give*, and she was under the daily care of a psychiatrist to combat depression."

So far at least, there was nothing on the news about the two men Dengler killed in central California.

Dengler shut off the television.

At 7:00 P.M. Dengler drove by 5th Helena Drive and saw there were no cars parked in front of 12305. The van was gone from 8th Helena Drive, as well. It was still too early for what Dengler wanted to do, so he drove to Westwood Village and watched the movie *Cape Fear* at the Fox Plaza Theater. Afterward he bought a copy of the evening Los Angeles Herald-Examiner, the local Hearst paper. Again, nothing about the deaths of Bloody Mouth and Marty.

It was past midnight when he drove back to Carmelina Avenue. He strolled down 5th Helena Drive until he came to the fence where, a little more than a day before, he scaled the wall and attacked Bloody Mouth. This time Dengler found climbing more difficult because of his groin wound.

He landed on the grass in transcendent silence. There wasn't even the distant bark of a dog, or any other sound. The house was dark.

There was no police investigation form on the door barring nonofficial entry, which surprised Dengler. Also surprisingly, the door to the living room wasn't locked. He merely turned the handle, and it swung open. Dengler entered and closed the door behind him, guided by the small beam of his penlight.

Dengler went into Marilyn's bedroom. Again, he was surprised, because it was far neater than he remembered. There were no piles of clothes and bric-a-brac on the floor, no disarray. Only the sheet on Marilyn's bed looked the same, twisted from where her body had been. Knowing the answer before he looked, Dengler checked to see whether her diary was still in place between the mattress and box spring, and of course it wasn't. He then looked under the bed, using the penlight to sweep light in front of him. He found nothing.

Dengler sat down on the end of the bed, where Marilyn's feet had last been, and asked himself why he came here. Was it on the chance he might meet Marilyn's ghost walking the house so he could tell her he was sorry, he wasn't strong enough and he wasn't smart enough to stop them from killing her? Or did he really expect to find something useful the police missed? Why was he taking this extraordinary chance of being caught in Marilyn Monroe's house the night after her murder when he didn't have to?

The only answer was he had unfinished business here. He would always have unfinished business here.

He sat in the darkness until almost dawn, and then left.

- 27 -

Dengler considered flying to the east coast, or driving. Flying would submit him to a bottleneck at the airport and increase his chances of being identified, if anyone were looking. If he drove he would have to get a car. Renting a car for a cross-country trip was out of the question, and buying one with his meager funds brought with it a number of problems; one being the California license plate would draw attention outside of the state. Finally, he chose to take a train.

First, he bought a hundred rounds of .45-caliber ammo, a .45 caliber cleaning kit, and a shoulder holster for his new weapons at a gun shop on Wilshire Boulevard, and a canvas satchel to carry everything.

He put the photos and contact sheets of Marilyn Monroe's diary in an envelope and mailed it to James Bond care of general delivery, the New York City post office, main branch. Then he returned the Plymouth Fury to the rental agency and took an RTD bus to Union Station.

Dengler purchased a ticket for a private compartment aboard the Atchison Topeka & Santa Fe *Super Chief*, the famous passenger train running between Los Angeles and Chicago. He locked himself inside his compartment, arranged to have his meals brought to the room, and passed the time reading day-old newspapers about the death of Marilyn Monroe. Hollywood was in mourning, the papers said. Stars were eager to speak of her, of Marilyn's simple kindnesses, of what a good person she really was, and a great star. Dengler thought of her eyes at the last. He thought of his failure to save her, or inability to even help her to protect her own life.

As he brooded about his inadequacy and shame, Dengler also thought about his own prospects. He had no idea what he was going to do next, although the germ of a plan was cultivating in the back of his mind. He thought he might make copies of the diary and send them to responsible journalists around the country. He might even contact a journalist and give him the exclusive. Which one? And when? Would it be better to wait?

Underlying all of these thoughts was the realization he'd killed two men. He'd never killed anything before, never even hunted or fished, and he felt strangely dulled by the experience. He thought his true feelings might not rise to the surface for a few days, or weeks, or possibly even years. He tried to convince himself it was shock that dulled his humanity, not something coarse and evil in his character. He was, he told himself, a rookie, someone so green at the field operative game he didn't know how he should feel.

When the *Super Chief* pulled into Las Vegas, Dengler paid the porter to bring him a newspaper. The porter returned with a copy of *The Los Angeles Times*. Dengler read one of the smaller headlines on the front page upside down as he searched for a silver dollar to tip the porter. *Federal Agents Murdered,* the headline read. Once the porter was tipped and gone, Dengler flipped the paper over and read the article.

(UPI) Two federal agents were killed while performing a routine background investigation of an undisclosed federal job applicant in central California Monday, a government representative announced today. The names of the deceased agents are being withheld pending notification of next of kin.

Missing is Army Military Intelligence trainee Private David Dengler of Chartersville, West Virginia, who accompanied the two veteran agents on a "ride along" training exercise. While not charged with the murders, evidence points to Dengler as the perpetrator.

"We believe Private Dengler may be mentally deranged," the government spokesman said.

"There is evidence Private Dengler might have brought a drug problem into the service with him," an Army spokesman concluded. "Private Dengler should be considered armed and dangerous."

Dengler collapsed onto one of the bench seats. *Well, there it is.* Dengler thought. *I'm a dead man.* He didn't really think Stafford would just let him go. He knew too much. Still, Dengler's dossier was confiscated by Stafford's men, and Stafford didn't know about Dengler photographing Monroe's diary, so as far as Stafford knew Dengler possessed no incriminating evidence. Even though he fantasized about doing to Gray Stafford what the CIA operative did to him, Dengler admitted to himself he hoped there was a chance he could just disappear, change his name and elude Gray Stafford altogether.

That idea was now dead.

Dengler recalled sitting for an Army portrait photo at the end of basic training, wearing his dress greens, his hair cut so close it was almost invisible, uniform crisp, and insignia polished brightly. He'd been proud of himself, proud of the uniform, proud to finally become something. Now they would use that photo to hound him.

Dengler looked at the photo of himself in the paper beside the article. It took him a moment to realize something was wrong with it, something subtle yet obvious if the photo were studied closely.

The photo wasn't of him.

The man depicted in the newspaper looked like Dengler. The resemblance was close. Dengler imagined he was approximately the same height, the same weight, with the same hair, skin, and eye color, the same shape of face with the same distance between the eyes, nose and mouth. The eyes, nose and mouth were all different, though. He wasn't David Dengler. He might have been Dengler's brother — *no, too close*. He might have been Dengler's cousin.

Dengler thought about it for minutes, running all of the possibilities and probabilities through his mind.

A mistake?

No. Had this photo been accidentally switched with the real one, to someone whose name was one letter ahead or behind Dengler in class, the chances of this man looking like him were astronomical. No, someone was purposely trying to lead law enforcement away from David Dengler, and simultaneously make the photo look close enough to the real thing to convince the casual observer it was him.

Like 'casual observer' Gray Stafford, for instance, who had seen him for no more than ten minutes and in a situation not conducive to dispassionate recall. Stafford would probably accept the photo as the real thing.

Why? Wrong question, Dengler decided. The correct question was, *Who?* Who had the power to switch out the pictures, and on a national scale?

The FBI.

The moment the two 'federal agents' were killed in Santa Barbara County the case became FBI property. *Fine*, Dengler thought, *the FBI*.

The FBI and the CIA were the two most feared agencies in Washington. It was common knowledge the FBI and CIA were in competition with one another. Indeed, in an organizational sense they hated one another. Whatever one wanted, the other wanted more.

Did the FBI plant a phony picture of him to ensure the CIA wouldn't get to him first? Or was there a greater, deeper reason? Dengler knew from what he'd read about espionage there were agencies within agencies, special interest groups whose actions sometimes ran in opposition to the 'official line.' If the FBI acted to save him from capture by the police, which might be expected to turn him over to anyone with appropriate FBI ID — something the

CIA could forge easily — then was the FBI's planting of a phony photograph representative of Bureau policy? Or was it the result of a splinter group that might not have the authority or power to protect him? The real question was, could he contact the FBI directly, right now, and have some guarantee he wouldn't be murdered before morning?

The answer was no.

- 28 -

The *Super Chief* Los Angeles-to-Chicago run was scheduled for thirty-nine hours and forty minutes. This particular trip it was late by seven minutes.

Dengler exited the *Chief* and immediately bought a ticket for identical accommodations aboard New York Central Railroad's *20th Century Limited*, a similar line that ran between Chicago and New York. It was this train that was featured in the movie *North by Northwest*. He had to wait ten hours between trains and spent the time in a nearby hotel room. Waiting in the main terminal was too dangerous.

Dengler had bought a tube of ointment in Los Angeles. It was an over-the-counter drug designed for muscle bruises and abrasions. He'd applied it religiously to himself. Now, more than two days after Stafford slammed a shoe on it, his manhood remained black and it still hurt to urinate. The pain seemed less, though, and it no longer hurt to walk as long as he didn't jostle himself. Looking at himself in the bureau mirror, Dengler's emotions ran from shame to anger to fear, each emotion rising and falling like a wave. As he had with pain, Dengler tried to control fear and shame. Anger gave him strength.

Dengler went straight from the hotel room to his train car. The porter directed him to his compartment. Dengler told him he was recovering from the flu and didn't want to spread it around. He would be taking his meals in his compartment and would be happy to pay more for the privilege. The porter seemed to think nothing of this.

As the *20th Century Limited* sped toward New York, Dengler considered his position. Only the FBI could have switched the photos, he decided. The FBI was trying to send him a message. He came to believe his chances for survival increased exponentially if he contacted them and used the Monroe diary as leverage. The question was, how should he make contact?

He needed a go-between, someone who couldn't be hurt by association with him, and someone he could trust.

Etta.

The *20th Century Limited* Chicago-to-New York run was scheduled to take fifteen and a half hours. The train pulled in to New York's Grand Central Terminal on schedule at nine A.M. Dengler disembarked, walked directly to the cab stand and caught a taxi to a car rental agency where he rented a 1962 Buick Elektra. Without having stood still for more than five minutes, Dengler drove out of New York City.

He still had Etta's Baltimore address which her sister had given him years before. He tried calling her when he arrived in Baltimore, but there was no listing for Etta Warren. He went to the address. The landlady directed him to an old woman who lived in back and who had befriended Etta when she'd moved out from her relatives' apartment after an argument. Eventually, the old woman told Dengler the truth, and the name of the street where Etta worked.

There was no reason to go to the street until business hours. Even so it was early when Dengler arrived. Only a few whores had wandered out into the new darkness, but as Dengler sat in the parked Buick and watched they seemed to emerge like cockroaches from beneath the curbs and up from the sewer grates to take their places on the corners. He waited for hours but saw no one who even remotely looked like Etta.

Dengler got out of the car at 9:00 P.M. and started walking the streets with the women. They called to him. He pushed past them, looking for Etta. Later he started asking for her, which garnered laughter. A john who was attached to one whore, and not anyone currently present, was an object of pity and scorn. "I got what you need, sweetheart," they would reply, "I got it in spades, and I got it right *here*." Dengler ignored them and continued looking.

Does she look the same? Dengler wondered. *Has she changed that much?* He saw a number of redheads, not one of them Etta, and told himself to look for the shape of her face and the way she carried herself and not her hair color. She could be a blond now. She could be anything.

Dengler saw her half a block down and made for her. When Etta saw him, she pivoted and crossed the street. Dengler crossed behind her and caught up with her as she was about to disappear down a side street.

"Etta." Dengler called, spinning her around.

"Let me go. Let me go." she screamed. "Let me go or I'll call my pimp and he'll cut you up."

Dengler almost released her. This wasn't the Etta he remembered. She'd dyed her hair black. Her skin was pale, but it was an unhealthy pale, no longer cream but sour milk. Bruises marked her face and shoulders like acne, and there were open sores at the corners of her lips. Trench mouth. As a whore, Etta Warren was approaching the end of her career. Few men would pay to have sex with a woman with this obvious infection, and those who would, would more likely give her a disease than the reverse.

"I SAID LET ME GO OR —"

"I'll pay you," Dengler said gently.

This touched her like a slap. The girl who had taken David Dengler's virginity sweetly and with love, now barked, "Go fuck yourself, David. You're trying to hurt me. You're trying to fuck with me and I —"

"How much?"

He saw her harden herself, as if to say, *All men are pigs.* David Dengler wasn't interested in her as a person. He just wanted another piece of her ass. He just wanted to screw her one last time, even if he had to do it in a cesspool with the excrement of society floating by.

"Fifty," she said.

"Fine."

She led him down the street to a hotel, and then up to the fourth floor. She didn't even bother to stop and pick up a room key. This was her place for the night. Once she closed and locked the door behind them, she said, "I'll take the fifty up front."

Dengler removed two twenties and a ten from his wallet and dropped them on the bed. Etta snatched them up and placed the money in her purse, which she kept beside her as she undressed. Dengler did nothing. In a moment, she was down to black panties and a bra.

"Like old times, isn't it, Davey?" she said with a seductive grin that any other man would have thought sincere.

"Don't call me that," he told her.

She unsnapped her bra and her breasts wriggled free from it. They were larger than he remembered and hung farther down, but the true difference was the bruises, which marked her, dark ones, light ones, new ones, old ones. Black and brown and purple. The more fair the skin, the easier to bruise, and Etta, who had been the fairest woman he'd ever known, had paid the price for the many hands that held her.

Needle tracks marked each arm, Dengler noted. Heroin.

She removed her panties and Dengler saw the familiar patch of red hair between her legs. She smiled in an exaggeration of coyness and lifted each of her large breasts and approached him. "Remember these, Davey?" she said, rubbing the lax nipples against his shirt. "Remember how we used to make love? Remember the day I took your cherry, Davey? Remember —"

"I told you not to call me that."

"Oh, Davey, what's the matter?" she said, lapsing into baby talk. "Is the big strong Davey afraid to fuck little Etta?"

"Stop it."

"'Cause I've got to tell you, I'm twice the woman I was when you knew me. Oh, the tricks, Davey, the tricks you learn turning tricks."

"Knock it off."

Seeing his pain, she grinned. Etta slid onto the bed and settled with her legs apart and her womanhood facing him. "I've learned so many things, Davey. I've learned things you wouldn't begin to believe. I've had Arabs and I've had niggers. I've had spiks and nips. I've had college boys who I've made into men. I've had old geezers who can't get it up anymore but with careful, careful work can get off anyway. I've taken it in the mouth, up the ass, in my ear, in my armpits, and between my toes. I've got one client, Davey, who just wants me to jerk him off on a public bus. I've got another client who made a wooden cock in his workshop and for a price — a very good price — I let him put it up me. I'm just a cunt for hire, Davey. Anyone can have me. Even you."

"SHUT UP."

She laughed, a loud, disdainful cackle, fell back on the bed and held her stomach, causing her breasts to writhe like hills in an earthquake. Finally, she stopped laughing and sat up. Dengler hadn't moved. Not an inch.

"You just take your clothes off, Davey," she said softly, sensing danger, "Let Etta take care of you."

"Why did you leave me?" he asked. His voice was a whisper, timid and beseeching.

The question floated between them for moments.

"That was so long ago," she said.

"For this?" he whispered. "You left me *for this*?"

"David —"

"I loved you," he said.

After a long moment, Etta rose from the bed and began to undress him. She was startled when she found the first .45 in his belt in back. Unfamiliar with guns, she held it between index finger and thumb and set it on the dresser and returned to pull off his sweatshirt. She found the second .45 in the shoulder holster and fumbled with the straps until it was unattached and she placed that weapon with the first.

When at last she lowered his pants and shorts, what she saw made her gasp.

"David," she asked, all disdain and guile gone from her voice, "were you in an accident?"

"No accident," Dengler said.

"Someone did this to you?"

Dengler didn't answer.

"Did you see a doctor?"

"No."

"David–"

"It doesn't matter."

Etta rose from her knees. She combed the hair out of his face with her fingers, gently stroking his brow, then hugged him. "I left," she said, "because you deserve better than me."

- 29 -

In the darkness Dengler found the old Etta. She didn't smell the same, and in truth she didn't feel the same, but this woman had been his first sexual encounter. She would be his yet, if she'd let him keep her.

Etta touched him. Dengler winced. She withdrew her hand and placed her cheek against his chest.

"What have you gotten yourself into?" she asked.

Dengler said nothing.

"All that talk," she continued. "All that day-dreaming about becoming a secret agent— Is that what you are, Davey? Are you a secret agent?"

Dengler barked a laugh, cynical and brittle. "Yeah," he said. "That's what I am, all right."

"I knew a man once," Etta said. "He was a regular, you know? Anyway, he was in a motorcycle accident. I went to visit him in the hospital, and he was lying there naked 'cause of the salve they had on him, I guess. Anyway, his dick was so bruised it was black, like yours is. He was afraid he'd... never do it again. They told him, maybe he wouldn't. Something about broken blood vessels in there. But, a month later he was visiting me on his regular day, just like before. So don't you worry, okay?"

Silence lay across them like ankle-high fog. Neither said anything for minutes.

"Tell me," Dengler said finally. "Tell me what happened between us."

"There's not much to tell, Davey."

"Tell me anyway."

"I knew I couldn't give you or anyone else what a decent man needs."

"Which is what?"

"Children." She almost choked on the word. "My mother used to say," she continued, "a family is born and lives in a woman's body. I could never give you that, Davey."

"I never wanted a family."

"You say that now —"

"I say it forever. I never wanted, and never will want, a family. I never had one. There was only my father, who hated me because my mother slept around."

"David. You never told me this before."

"Not something you talk about. What happened to you? Why can't you have children?"

She didn't answer for a long time. Dengler had almost forgotten the question and was lost in his own thoughts when she said, "When I was ten I had an illness. There was a cyst in me. They were able to remove it without surgery — you know, it was down far enough so they could do it in the doctor's office. Anyway, the doctor said I would never be able to bear children. The infection had spread and... ruined me."

Dengler instinctively laid the palm of his hand against her stomach.

"It's not so terrible," Dengler said. "So you can't make babies."

Etta shook her head, short, quick tremors. "That's not all," she whispered.

"What?"

She refused to tell him.

An hour later they heard a pounding at the door.

"Open up. Open up in there, goddamn it."

Dengler leapt from the bed to the dresser and took both of his .45s, then stepped behind the door.

"It's Guy," Etta whispered. "He's my pimp."

Dengler gestured for her to call to him, then quietly unlocked the door as Etta said, "The door's unlocked, Guy. You can come in."

The door burst open, and Guy marched in. He was a man of perfect proportion, six feet two inches tall, lean at the waist and hip, with powerful shoulders and a stride that was long and muscled and suggested he spent many hours at a gym perfecting his body. He was wearing an expensive suit and a hat that had gone out of style with Bugsy Siegel. Dengler disliked him immediately.

Etta retreated in bed and pulled the covers up over her chest. That angered Dengler too because he knew what it meant. Guy strode to the end of the bed and glared at her.

"What the fuck have you been doing up here, bitch? You've been gone over two hours. What have I told you about time? You give 'em half an hour, if it takes that long. Half an hour. Then you get that merchandise back on the street. I don't take care of you so you can lay your fat ass up in some hotel room after the john's shot his wad. Now get that thing cleaned up and move it out of here."

Dengler kicked the door. It slammed like a mortar round landing nearby. Guy spun around. For a second Dengler saw fear in his eyes. He enjoyed it.

What Guy was confronting was a naked man, smaller than himself, with two menacing .45 caliber pistols in his hands.

"Who the fuck are you?" Guy said.

"None the fuck your business," Dengler responded. "That's who the fuck I am."

"He wanted more time." Etta rushed in, briefly pulling Guy's attention from Dengler. "He wanted to spend a little more time, 'cause he likes me. And that's okay, that's okay, Guy, because he's willing to pay for more time, aren't you, David?"

"No."

The single syllable fell into the room and killed all sound. Guy stared at Dengler, and at the weapons in his hands, and Etta looked at Dengler too, shock and fear written into her face. "David, this isn't funny. Please don't do this to me."

"Where does he keep his piece?" Dengler said.

"Oh god, oh god, please don't do this to me, David. Please. He's my pimp. He'll kill me."

"Where?"

"David, David, you don't understand. He takes care of me."

"From now on, I'll take care of you."

"No, you don't understand. *He takes care of me.*"

Guy smiled.

"I know all about it, Etta. From now on I'll get you heroin."

"David, you don't understand. You think you do, but you don't." She was out of bed now, her bruised body naked and ugly in the white shadow of the room. She was pleading. "David, if you do this, he'll hurt me, David. He'll beat me. I'm not his top girl anymore, and he doesn't always treat me good, David, so I have to be nice or he won't take care of me."

Dengler pulled her to him and she sobbed against his chest, one of the .45s inches from her brow.

"Now isn't this sweet?" Guy said after a moment. "Two young people who've found each another. But David, the meter's running, because whether you want to recognize it or not, this is a taxi you've got, not a new Lincoln."

Dengler flicked his arm and a gun barrel appeared beneath Guy's nose. Dengler frisked him. He found a silver-plated .32 in a shoulder holster, and a switchblade in a calf sheath. He also pulled out Guy's wallet and discovered a small fortune of nine one hundred dollar bills, plus assorted tens and twenties.

"Well-well-well, what have we here?" Dengler said. "Hard-earned money, I see."

"That's exactly what it is, John. Now you put it back and walk out of here, I give you Etta's time for free. We'll call it a negotiated peace."

"Ooh, best kind. Negotiated peace. I like that."

"You got a free ride, John. That's not bad. You get a free ride and a long-timer at that. We'll call it even, okay?"

Dengler guided Etta back toward the bed and her clothes. "Get dressed," he ordered.

"Yes, okay, but —"

"This pimp carry any extra money?" Dengler asked her.

"David, please don't do this." It was a whine now, pleading and pitiful. "Please don't do this."

"Where?"

"He has a money belt."

"You bitch. You fucking bitch. I'm going to slice your face up so bad no man will ever want you again. Do you hear me?"

Dengler moved with professional dispassion. The gun barrel connected against Guy's face with steel gear precision. His nose was broken immediately, his cheek shattered, blood went flying and marred the pattern of the cheap wallpaper three feet away.

"I think you misread the situation, friend," Dengler told him after the fact, when Guy was on the floor and sucking for breath. "You've sown enough. It's time to reap."

Dengler quickly pulled on his own clothes as Etta stood at the end of the bed and looked at the man she'd thought invincible. Guy looked up at her once and was about to say something when he realized what it would cost him, and said nothing.

"Take off your clothes," Dengler ordered Guy. When he didn't respond, Dengler knelt on the floor before him, popped the blade on the switchblade, and dug it deep into the fabric of Guy's pants and yanked downward. Guy jumped. "Please. Please don't do this to me," he begged.

Etta stood behind Dengler, a look of amazement on her face. *Guy? Begging?*

"Take 'em off, or I cut 'em off, makes no difference to me," Dengler told him. "Might make a difference to you if I slip and cut your balls off, though."

Guy unhitched his pants and pulled the money belt free. Dengler handed it to Etta. "I said all your clothes," Dengler warned him.

Guy stood up. In a moment, he was naked. Blood cascaded down his face. Dengler ran the barrel of the .45 down his cheek to his chest, and then down to his manhood and back.

"Anything you want to say to this little man, Etta?" Dengler said softly.

"No."

"After all he's done to you?"

"I did it to myself, David. I did it to myself."

"NO." The shout startled Guy as much as Etta. Both jumped. "He got you addicted to heroin. He put you on the streets. He made a living off your body while beating the crap out of you. Now I ask you again, is there anything you want to say to this little man — *before I kill him.*"

Guy began to cry. "Please." he blubbered. "Please don't kill me. Please..."

"David, don't do this."

"Turn around." Dengler ordered Guy. Guy complied. "Now spread 'em."

"What?"

"I said spread 'em."

Guy pulled his buttocks apart. Dengler shoved Guy's chrome-plated .32 up him until the muzzle of the weapon was flush with his anus. Dengler then cocked the weapon.

"Oh god, please. Please don't do this. Please. Please. Make him stop, Etta. Make him stop."

Etta was stunned and looked at Dengler as if he were a stranger. This wasn't the David she'd known back home. "David, don't kill him. Please don't do this."

"Take the gun. Pull the trigger. For once let *him* take it up the ass."

"David —"

"TAKE IT."

Etta flinched at the sound of his voice and placed her hand around the butt of the weapon.

"Now pull the trigger," he said, his voice suddenly soft.

Guy's bladder gave out. He began to urinate on the floor before him. He was sobbing, his words no longer intelligible, blood, saliva, and tears mixing and flowing down his face.

"Pull the trigger, Etta," Dengler ordered again.

For moments, Etta stood behind Guy holding the weapon between his buttocks that would disembowel him were she to use it. Finally, she looked to Dengler and said, "I won't do this, David. He's a son-of-a-bitch, but he's still a human being, and I won't do this."

Dengler saw she wouldn't do it, not ever. "Fine," he said after a moment. "I guess Guy gets to keep all of his equipment."

Etta released the gun and it remained lodged between Guy's buttocks as he sagged and caught his breath. "Take the gun out," Dengler ordered her, but she gestured no. Dengler reached past her to remove the chrome-plated .32. He spun Guy around. "Where do you keep your kit?"

Guy wiped snot and blood from his bent nose. "Kit?" he said between sucks for air.

"Heroin."

Guy didn't hesitate. "In my car."

"Where is it?"

"In the alley beside the building."

"Find the keys," Dengler ordered Etta. While she rummaged through his pants, Dengler took Guy's face in his hands and focused him. "You're lucky I didn't kill you, you know that?"

"Yes," Guy said eagerly. "Yes. Thank you. Thank you for not killing me."

"If you tell the police about this, or anyone else, I will be very, very angry, Guy."

Guy began to tremble. It was a moment before Dengler realized it was laughter. "Tell anyone," he laughed. "Tell anyone you did this to me? I don't think so. I don't goddamn think so."

"And if you even speak to Etta again, I will castrate you. Do you understand?"

"Yes."

"We'll leave your car somewhere in town. Report it stolen tomorrow, but not by who. You'll get it back."

"Yes. Okay."

Etta was ready. The last either saw of Guy, he was standing naked in a pool of his own urine as they closed the door.

- 30 -

They found the Cadillac parked in the alley behind the hotel. "I've got to pick up some things from a rental car on the boulevard, then we can go by your place and pick up your stuff," Dengler told her as he started the big engine.

Etta, who sat as far from him as she could on the passenger side, said nothing.

"Etta?"

"David, I don't know you, what you did."

"I did to him what he's been doing to you for years, nothing more."

"Yes, David, but I consented to be his whore."

"You consented to shoot his heroin. The decision to be his whore was somewhat tainted by need, don't you think?"

"No one should be treated like you treated him."

"What's the matter with you? Did you love him? Did he treat you well?"

"No." Darkness. Her features were lost in the shadows of night.

"Did he beat you?"

"Yes."

"Did he take your money and make you fuck for a living?"

She turned to face him. "You haven't been listening, David. You haven't heard me. I did that. I chose to fuck for a living. I chose to be a whore. I did that."

"Bullshit."

"David, I was turning tricks in high school."

"You decided to give it up. You wanted to give it up."

"Wanting isn't doing. David. David —" she looked at him as if he were a child. "I knew who Guy was. I knew what he did for a living. I knew what I was doing."

"The heroin."

"The heroin. Jesus Christ, the heroin. You talk like it makes a different person out of you, and it doesn't. What it does is cut everything down to very simple terms. There's no foreplay on heroin, David. There's no romance. People say what they mean and do what they want and fill their needs and there's very little lying."

"Bullshit," Dengler said. "You don't deserve this, Etta. You don't deserve this and I'm not going to let it happen to you."

Dengler parked the Caddy beside the Buick. He left the lights on, but switched the motor off and, with a brief glance at Etta, took the keys. He quickly transferred his belongings to the trunk of the Caddy. Inside the Caddy trunk was a large leather case, and inside it a bag of white powder, a case of syringes, some pills of various colors, and a paper bag filled with green marijuana, as yet not dried and hence not ready for smoking. Dengler closed the trunk lid, and then slid back behind the wheel.

"Where do you live?" he asked.

"I'll direct you," she said. "Go down two blocks, then hang a left."

Dengler put the Caddy into motion.

Etta pressed her palms together and placed them between her knees. "I'm going to need a fix soon, David."

"Good. You can show me how."

She looked at him nervously. "I don't need to show you how. Turn the kit over to me. I'll do it myself."

"No."

"What do you mean, no?"

"I mean no. You'll show me how to do it, and then I'll do it. That's the way it's going to be."

"Jesus," she whispered. "You're giving me the cure."

"That's the way it's going to be."

Dengler allowed her to go upstairs to pack her own things. The way Guy was likely to treat her if he found her, and the fact he had the 'kit,' ensured she would return. Meanwhile, he sat behind the wheel and counted the money from Guy's money belt. All tolled, thirty-seven hundred dollars. Minus what he'd spent from his own cache, Dengler had over five thousand dollars.

Etta returned with two suitcases. Dengler got out of the car and took them from her, placing them in the trunk. When he slid back behind the wheel, she was waiting for him. "David," she said, "I need a fix. I need it now."

"It'll have to wait until we get a room."

"I need it now, David."

"No."

He found a Motel 6 on the interstate outside Baltimore and checked in. When he returned from the office he started to take her bags out of the trunk when she said, "The bags can wait."

A woman just leaving the room next to theirs overheard this and grinned. The subject wasn't sex, however. Dengler took the 'kit' from the trunk and followed Etta into their room. He watched her mix the heroin powder in a spoon with water, and then draw it into the needle. She tied off a vein using a rubber hose wrapped around her left arm and shot the heroin directly into the bloodstream. In a moment, she seemed calmer than she had since he first saw her that evening. She collapsed onto the bed and Dengler took the kit back out to the car and locked it in the trunk, then carried the rest of their bags inside. She was asleep when he returned.

Half an hour later Dengler was soaping himself in the shower when she entered the bathroom naked and joined him beneath the spay. She buried her face in his chest and began to cry softly. Dengler washed her, every part of her like a father cleaning his child, and then directed her out of the shower where he dried her, then himself.

As she brushed her teeth, Dengler pointed out the sores at the corners of her mouth.

"Do you know what those sores are?" he said.

"My mouth gets dry sometimes. The skin does, anyway. These sores come and go."

"It's trench mouth. It's a bacterial infection."

Embarrassed, she wrenched her shoulders from his hands and stood up, busying herself with folding her towel and placing it over the bar holder. "We can find a doctor tomorrow and I'll have myself checked out," she told him with an edge to her voice. "You don't — shouldn't touch me until then."

"I don't give a shit about that. This is just a bacterial infection, it's not the clap, and it's not V.D."

She pursed her lips and turned away from him. Dengler spun her around once more, and this time she was crying. He held her close and wrapped his arms around her. After a moment he asked, "What is it?"

"I've had the clap, David," she whispered. "I've had V.D. God, I may have it now, I don't know."

"All right."

"I was remembering the first time we made love. Dear god, I was brand-new, David. I was as fresh as a young girl can be."

"I never saw a woman as lovely as you were that day. Never."

"Now I'm a filthy old whore who has to be told how to clean her mouth and..."

"You're twenty-two years old, Etta. You're not an old whore."

"I look forty."

"You look tired. You look beaten down."

"I look old." She cupped her hand over her mouth and breathed out. "Can you smell it?" she said.

Dengler pushed her hand away and kissed her. Before their lips touched Etta tried to avert her lips from him, but he pressed forward. Their lips touched, their saliva mixed, their tongues caressed one another. When they parted she looked up into his eyes in wonder. "Now," he said, "This is how you treat trench mouth. Gargle with a disinfectant six times a day, once after every meal, and three times between meals. Put a disinfectant salve on the sores so they won't dry out and open up again. In four or five days, voilà, you're cured."

She buried her head in his chest again and cried.

- 31 -

Dengler woke after 4:00 A.M. He dressed and stepped outside. The air was crisp, and the sky clear. The sound of the ice machine motor kicking in three doors down competed with the whoosh of the highway, which was intermittent and distant beyond the parking lot and a grassy berm.

Dengler strolled back toward the car. Had it not been so late, he would have ditched the Cadillac and bought another car, but it was almost midnight by the time he got Etta into the room and gave her a fix. As it was, he'd become so emotionally involved with her, and so distrusting of her as well, he hadn't followed his standard protocol of parking the car a couple of blocks away so no one could identify it later. Here it was, parked just outside their room, a big purple convertible Cadillac El Dorado, fins and all. Dengler grinned at the look of the machine. Its appearance said, *I am the most successful pimp in Baltimore. Believe it, baby.*

Dengler hadn't told Etta why he came looking for her, that he needed her to act as go-between with the FBI. In her emotional and physical condition he knew she wasn't capable of doing that. She might not ever be capable of doing that.

He needed a private place where her pleas and later screams as she came off heroin wouldn't attract attention. A cabin. He would rent a cabin and slowly wean her off the drug. It would take weeks. After that, it would be up to her. He knew enough about human nature to understand you can't make someone do what they don't want to do.

Anxious to be active and not go back inside and sleep, Dengler pulled the Cadillac's keys from his pocket and opened the passenger door. Inside, he opened the glove compartment and went through the papers there.

The Cadillac was free and clear. He found a pink slip to prove it. There were insurance papers, the car manual, and receipts from scheduled maintenance. Dengler ran his hands under the seat. Nothing. Then the driver's side. Nothing. He felt under the dash. Wires, from the radio and air conditioner. The last thing Dengler checked in the front seat area was the registration, which was strapped to the column. Underneath the registration he found a crisp, new thousand-dollar bill. Dengler grinned as he replaced the registration holder and pocketed the bill. He imagined what Guy would think when he found the money missing.

Dengler moved to the back seat. He found nothing there. He then moved to the trunk. There was Guy's 'kit' on the trunk mat where he'd left it earlier. Dengler pushed it aside and lifted the mat. He found a tire recessed in the floor above the gas tank and felt around it. Nothing. He then ran his fingers into the recesses at either side of the trunk. There was a book on the right side. Dengler pulled it out.

Back in the front seat with the dome light on, Dengler opened the small spiral-bound address book. In it were all of Guy's regulars and which girls they liked. Guy apparently had five girls. Etta was listed third. Dengler counted the johns with a '3' beside their names who came regularly inside Etta Warren and it made him angry, even though he thought he was past that. After a few moments he slammed the book shut and dropped it on the floorboard. He went inside.

When he opened the door, he heard a rustling noise and knew Etta was awake. He flipped on the light and caught her rifling through his smaller bag. She looked at him like a feral animal whose eyes were transfixed by headlights. Dengler held up the car keys.

"David, please," she begged.

"Go to sleep," he said.

"David, no, you don't understand. I need a fix, David. Guy gave me a fix whenever I needed it, and I need one now."

"No."

"David, you don't understand." She stood naked before him, her breasts wriggling with every gesture, her too-plump stomach and thighs spotted with bruises and her eyes drawn deep in anxiety. She was ugly. *I've got to keep her from becoming ugly*, Dengler thought. *At least to me.*

He glanced past her at the bedside clock. It was almost 5:00 A.M. "Get dressed," he told her. "We'll get some breakfast."

"DAVID. If you don't help me, I'm going to stand here and yell my head off. I'll do it, David, I will."

"Then I'll flush the heroin," he said simply. "Now get dressed."

She got dressed.

Dengler had paid for the room in advance. They loaded their bags and drove off in search of a coffee shop. They found a *Howard Johnson's* two miles down the interstate. Dengler was surprised when he saw Etta eat a big breakfast. He'd always heard heroin addicts wouldn't eat, but then realized for most addicts it was a choice between a fix and food, and they always chose the fix. In any case, he was happy to see her eat, because he wanted as much nutrition in her as possible.

He bought a paper but could find nothing more on the fugitive David Dengler, although he read Marilyn Monroe had been buried in Westwood, California, in a very private ceremony that excluded many of her social peers. This had been arranged by Joe DiMaggio, who it was rumored still loved her.

Dengler tossed the paper down in disgust and Etta saw the story he'd been reading. "Oh, Marilyn Monroe died, huh?"

"Yeah."

"You a big fan of Marilyn Monroe, David?"

"Yeah, I guess so. Sure."

"I had a john once who said I reminded him of Monroe. Couple of johns said that, actually."

"You're both beautiful women."

She grinned. "Really?"

"Yes. Really."

"Although, who knows? Hollywood can do anything. Maybe Monroe was kind of plain looking in person."

"She was beautiful," Dengler stated. He threw some money down on the table. "Come on. Let's go."

Dengler drove back into Baltimore and had Etta direct him to the area where they could buy a car. They found an *OK Used Cars* lot and wandered from car to car, looking at the stickers and inspecting the interiors and tires and such even though the dealership was closed.

"You want to pick one out?" he asked her.

"Can I?"

"As long as it's roadworthy."

Etta picked out a tan 1959 Pontiac Catalina hardtop. The sticker said $2300. When the first salesman, the general manager, arrived at 8:00 A.M., Dengler negotiated the price down to $1950. Dengler had Etta buy the car in her name.

Etta was too nervous to drive, she told him, and as they drove back to the Cadillac, which Dengler had parked some blocks away, Etta said, "I got to have me a fix, Davey."

"How often Guy fix you up?" Dengler asked.

"Three — no, four times a day, counting bedtime. Four times a day."

"Bullshit."

"David, I need it."

"Here are the rules —" Dengler started.

"David, I don't like you doing this to me."

"— you get a shot in the morning and another at bedtime, so you can sleep. I'm going to start cutting you down, day by day —"

"No."

"— until I wean you off the stuff."

"Okay. OKAY." she growled. "Fine. Do any fucking thing you want. But get me a fix now, David. I need a fix now."

Dengler transferred all their bags and goods to the Pontiac. When he slid back behind the wheel he said, "Okay, now." Again, he watched her do it. She relaxed once the heroin was coursing through her veins. Dengler packed up the kit and placed it back in the trunk.

He was alone in the car for an hour.

By the time Etta returned to him, they were already into the mountains. "Where are we?" she said.

"Does it matter?"

"It matters," she snapped back.

"We're about fifty miles out of Baltimore."

"Where are we going?"

"We'll know when we get there."

Etta settled back into the seat, lit a cigarette, crossed her arms and watched him drive, as cool as a wife after a spat.

- 32 -

It was the nape of the summer season, but there was one cabin left at Smoke Lodge. It had rented early and come open early, and it was farthest from the others near a small lake and obscured by a stand of trees. There were four rooms, a bedroom, a living room, a bathroom, and a kitchen/dining room whose windows provided a panorama of the nearby wilderness. Etta was taken with it immediately, although she looked nervously at Dengler to see where he kept his keys. They dropped back into his pocket.

The manager, a wizened old coot by the name of Owen, showed them the place. There was a television, a phone, and the refrigerator looked to have been recently cleaned. "How do you want to take it?" Owen said.

"What do you mean?" Dengler had the refrigerator door open and was marveling that the freezer didn't need defrosting.

"Day, week, or month?"

"By the week at first," Dengler told him.

"I may get a reservation."

"Before you take it, let me know. If we want to stay, we'll match it."

"You folks up here for a late vacation, that it?"

Dengler didn't know whether he was a gossip or merely curious, but he had to take precautions. "I'm a writer," he said. "Doing a book."

"Fiction or non-fiction?"

"Novel."

"Historical or current day?"

"Murder mystery."

"Set in a cabin," Etta joined in. "The first victim is the guy who runs the place. Gets too nosy, you know. He becomes the *Man Who Knows Too Much*." She spoke these last words with a theatrical flair.

Silence was finally broken when Owen laughed. Dengler and Etta laughed too. "That's very funny," Owen said.

"Actually, it is set in a cabin just like this one. But that's pretty much where Etta's scenario ends."

"Well, you folks need anything, don't hesitate to call me. I got the bigger place there next to the driveway."

"Where can I buy some supplies?" Dengler said.

"Two miles down the road there's a store. They sell gas, groceries, sodas, and such."

"Thanks," Dengler told him as Owen disappeared outside. The screen door slammed shut and came to a quivering rest before Dengler turned and told Etta, "Don't do that again. He didn't know you were making a joke."

"Yeah, well, I'm a little on edge, Davey. I could use a fix."

"No. I'm going to run down to the store and pick up some things. I'll be right back."

Etta nodded and Dengler was about to leave when something stopped him. He followed her gaze to the phone. Dengler ripped it out from the wall and exited without another word.

He ran into Owen on the porch. "Forgot. I need the first week's rent."

"How much is it?"

"Thirty dollars."

Dengler peeled off a twenty and a ten and gave it to him.

When Dengler returned half an hour later, Etta had unpacked their things and placed them in the two dressers in the bedroom. He dropped the two bags of food on the kitchen table and went looking for her. "I'm still here," she told him, "and I still need a fix."

"Come help me put the food away."

He'd bought eggs, sandwich meat, cheese, wine, milk, various condiments, a bottle of whiskey, soft drinks, steaks, and the makings of a roast. Etta took over once she was in the kitchen and Dengler sat at one of the kitchen chairs and watched her.

"This hurts me, David," she told him after awhile.

"It's going to hurt more."

"I lied to you before when I said I was used to four times a day, but I am used to three. I'm not going to be able to stand this. I'm already crawling out of my skin."

Dengler studied her. It was true. She was so anxious she dropped the package of steaks and a bottle of soda. Finally he told her, "Your pal Guy's got some more stuff in his kit, pills, what looks like marijuana. You can have that during the day, if you want."

The pills were 'downers,' Etta told him, and the marijuana would have to be dried a few days before she could smoke it. He gave her one pill from the kit, and she said, "You just have no idea, do you?"

"What?"

"Have you ever been addicted to anything?"

"You," he said with a smile.

"I need more than one pill, David."

"People addicted to things always need more than one," he told her finally. "You get one."

Etta took the pill and swallowed it without water. Before Dengler closed the trunk she took the marijuana from the kit and spread it out on a newspaper on the porch at the back of the kitchen where it would take direct sunlight. Afterward, she went into the kitchen and poured a tumbler full of whiskey.

"Hey. Hey." Dengler protested and took the tumbler away from her. He poured half of it into another glass, and then emptied a bottle of Coca Cola into the two glasses.

"Jesus, David," she told him. "You're no fun at all."

There was a 'slider' bench on the front porch and Etta joined Dengler there after a moment in the bathroom. "Listerine," she said with a forced grin. She had the tube of medicated salve with her that she applied to each corner of her mouth.

"Feeling better?"

"A little. Is the bottle off-limits, too?"

"I bought the whiskey for me."

"So it's off limits."

"No, it's not off limits."

"Good, 'cause a girl's got to find some amusement wherever she goes."

An outboard motor sounded. They watched a small boat motor to the center of the lake. A father was taking his son and daughter out to fish. Etta slowly drew her gaze in from the lake and directed it at Dengler. "So what happens now? We stay here until you've reformed me, then you take me home to see Dad?"

"Not likely," Dengler said. "My father died a couple of months back."

"Sorry."

"I'm not."

"So what happens now?"

Dengler turned to look at her. Could he trust her with the information he was a fugitive? He could trust her, he decided, but he couldn't trust the addiction. "I've got a thirty day leave, then I have to go back to the army."

"You wear civilian clothes in the army and carry two guns on you?"

"I'm with Army Military Intelligence. One of the guns is issued.

The other one belongs to me. I was afraid to leave the extra one in the car because someone might take it."

Etta looked at him without an expression and asked, "You have three sets of ID, none of them with your real name on them."

"You were looking in my bag?"

"Yes."

"You shouldn't look in my things. Like a said, I'm with Army M.I. and —"

"Now you're the one who's lying."

Dengler took another swig of the whiskey and cola. Anxious, he swished the mix around in his mouth, buying time. Finally he told her, "I was on a mission and things went south."

"How far south?"

"All the way south."

"How far is that?"

"Some people got killed?"

"Jesus, Davey." Then, "You did that?"

"Yes."

"Jesus Christ."

"It was self-defense. They were trying to kill me, so I defended myself."

"Who was trying to kill you?"

"I'm not sure. People working for the federal government, I think. I'm not sure."

"You're not sure?"

"No."

"Tell me everything," she told him. "I've got to know everything."

"It would be better if you didn't know," he said. "The less you know, the less likely—"

"Everything," she said, "or I'll stand up here and yell rape, or do whatever I can do to get away from you. Because either I'm with you and with you all the way, or I'm gone."

Dengler told her everything; even what Gray Stafford did to him in Marilyn's bathroom. He told her about his surveillance of Monroe's house, the slow discovery she was going to be killed and by whom, his ill-fated and unprofessional attempt to save her, her murder and his getaway. He told her about the film and contact prints of Marilyn's diary he'd sent to the New York post office (but not the name it was listed under). He also told her about the phony photograph in the paper and what it meant.

She stood up. "I'll be right back," she told him and trotted across the dirt driveway toward the other cabins. She returned in several minutes with a newspaper in her hands. "Owen had yesterday's paper," she said, kneeling before him. "I saw it in the office when we checked in." Etta studied the photo on the front page, and then looked at Dengler. "It's not you," she said at last.

"No."

"But how could they expect this to work? I mean, I know from experience, the first thing they do when you're arrested is fingerprint you."

"I've never been arrested," Dengler told her, "but I was fingerprinted when I joined the Army. The FBI has access to those prints. They might have already substituted phony prints for mine."

"Jesus," Etta whispered, falling back onto her heels. "David, you came looking for me because you're in trouble?" She appeared surprised.

"Yes," he said. "I needed someone I could trust. You're the only person in the world I can trust."

That night as they prepared for bed, Dengler put salve on Etta's many bruises. He finished with two large, dark recent ones on her left arm. He looked up from them to realize she was staring at him with an expression of amused affection. He grinned.

"David," she said. "You're taking care of me, let me take care of you."

"I don't think that's a good idea—"

"I'll be gentle," she urged. Dengler gave her the salve. She made him sit on the edge of the bed, cupped his penis in her left palm and began applying the salve.

"Ow."

"Don't be a big baby," she rebuked him.

"Well, it hurts."

Etta grinned. "You just leave yourself in my hands," she told him, looking up. "I never touched one of these I couldn't make better."

As they lay naked together in bed an hour later, after Etta's fix, she began to kiss him. In the darkness it was easy for Dengler to imagine this was Etta the way she used to be, but he was thankful his body wouldn't respond. He feared it might explode. After a time she settled into the cusp of his right arm, and they slept.

- 33 -

When he woke the next morning, the sun was already in the sky and casting leaf-shadows through the nearby trees onto the bed. The wind was up, and the leaves were writhing, scraping the side of the cabin. Dengler listened to the symphony of wind and leaves a moment before he turned and found himself face to face with Etta, who had been watching him while he slept.

"You need your fix," he said automatically and started to get up.

She grinned, and it was the first time since he rediscovered her that she grinned like that, mouth opened wide and perfect teeth gleaming. "No, David, wait," she said.

"You don't need a fix?"

"Yes," she said. "Yes, I do, but I have to tell you something first." She lay naked across the top of the bed, her head, and shoulders, butt and legs visible down the length of her. Was it true? Some of that distinctive luster was returning to her skin? The oldest of the bruises seemed to be disappearing.

"What is it?"

"Thank you for coming to get me."

"I'm ashamed to say it, Etta," Dengler told her after a moment, "but I came to get you for me. I needed you."

"Yes. Thank you. You're the only person who ever has."

She stopped him as they walked naked toward the kitchen where he'd hidden his keys. She turned and flattened herself against him, her breasts spreading around his rib cage, and touched her lips to his skin, kissing his chest for an instant before pulling away. "I'll make myself beautiful for you again. You'll see. I'll work some of this fat off my butt. And the next time we're anywhere near civilization I'll have my hair stripped and dyed as close to my original color as possible, so when it grows out you won't notice, and..."

"And what?"

"And you'll love me again, like you used to."

Dengler picked her up with one arm and brought her up to his level and kissed her. When he finally lowered her to the ground she said, "Oh, my."

"I've always loved you," he told her.

While she started breakfast, Dengler dressed and went out to the car and took the kit from the trunk. This time, for the first time, he 'fixed' her. The solution was slightly less than the previous day. She was unable to finish breakfast, so Dengler took over and she wrapped a robe around herself and went out onto the front porch and sat on the rocker. Dengler joined her ten minutes later with two plates of bacon, eggs, and toast with raspberry jam. His plate was empty by the time she felt compelled to eat from hers. He watched her eat, the gentle contours of her hands as she brought food to her mouth, the way her arms were shaped, the set of her shoulders, and when he realized she was marveling at him for the attention he was giving her, he was embarrassed.

"I really hurt you when I left you, Davey," she said after awhile, "didn't I?"

"Would you like a glass of milk?"

In the months that followed, Dengler forgot about the FBI and the CIA. He forgot about John Fitzgerald Kennedy and Robert Francis Kennedy and Marilyn Monroe and Gray Stafford. It was easy to do. In the mornings they hiked. In the afternoons they swam in the lake. In the evenings he drove her to the nearest town and they had dinner, or he made her dinner, or she for him. They exercised twice a day so Dengler could keep his tone and Etta regain hers.

With each day her skin became as it had been. Her eyes cleared. The lines disappeared from her face. The bruises that marred her body slowly faded. She regressed in age from a sorrowful thirty-five to a decade younger, and Dengler knew she would be new again, as she'd been the first time she gave herself to him, the most beautiful woman he'd ever known.

They fought occasionally, usually when she needed a fix. The marijuana helped, the 'downers' helped, but each day the heroin dose was smaller and there was no blunting that. The fights were short, and he forgave her even when she couldn't forgive herself. In minutes the argument was gone and within hours they were in love again, and Dengler couldn't deny this was what it was, because every time she entered the room he noticed her. Every time he caught a whiff of the perfume he'd bought her, it made him think of her.

Dengler showered with her every night and washed her, and then dried her hair and brushed it. It was sensuous to do this, and it made him feel there was nothing in her life that didn't in some way connect with his. She took pleasure in this, even though it didn't lead to satisfaction in bed.

Twice a day Etta applied salve to him. The pain withdrew as over time the color of his member went from black to purple, to brown, and then his own skin color returned. The pain gradually subsided, then went away completely. No matter how Etta handled him, though, Dengler's penis remained flaccid.

As she'd promised, soon Etta Warren was beautiful again. She found a beautician and had her hair stripped of all color, and then re-dyed as close to her original red as possible. It was a good match. Her skin was cream again, her green eyes crisp and healthy, and her body exercised and returning to good shape. They hiked in the woods, high up onto hilltop ridges, across meadows, and around the small lake. It might have been their own West Virginia they walked. It might have been years ago.

Now when Etta laughed, it was with that old resonance from deep within her, womanly and full. When she talked, it was with self-confidence, certain her words would be appreciated.

Only the needle marks on her arms set her apart as a heroin addict. Each day less heroin was put into her veins. Each day.

Some mornings Dengler woke with Etta's hands stroking him. Every time an irrational fear would sweep over him, and his erection would fall. She made light of this, telling him it wasn't important. Still, Dengler avoided the sex act, avoided thinking about it, turned away from the suggestion. The humiliation of what happened to him, and what might happen to him if he tried to make love to Etta, was too great to face.

One morning Etta's voice brought him up from a deep sleep. Sweat glistened on her breasts and shoulders, and her chest and stomach rose and fell as she breathed. Etta had pulled back the covers to admire his naked body and was pleasuring herself. "Please, David," she said urgently, "I need this. Please."

Seeing Etta approach release, watching her body undulate, her eyes opening and closing with a rhythm only she perceived, Dengler started to become excited. Etta climaxed with a gasp before seeing Dengler's erect member. Without hesitation Etta straddled him, lowering herself onto him. He felt the hot wetness of her surround him. "Oh, Davey," she moaned, writhing her hips slightly. Fear raced into him, fear he couldn't keep himself stiff, fear he would be shamed in front of her, but the fear was inundated by the pleasure of this lovely human female straddling him.

Fear became anger, anger became strength. Dengler thrust into her with increasing intensity. Etta came. Dengler threw her onto her back, spread her legs wide, and entered her again. Etta came yet again, and again. Sweat bound them to each other, to the sheets, to the rhythm of their bodies moving in anguished extension. When the moment came, Dengler arched his back and thrust himself as deep into Etta as he could go, spat his seed into her, and then slowly lowered himself into her encircling arms and legs.

They laughed self-consciously, exhausted.

"Where are your keys?" Etta said ten minutes later. "Give me your keys. I'll get the kit, and you can do me. Then I'm going to fuck you like you've never been fucked before, lover."

Dengler told her, "In the couch. On the left side, under the cushion," and fell back onto the bed. In a second, he heard the screen door slam and shifted to the upper part of the bed where he had a vantage point of the car and the lake beyond. She ran to the car stark naked, her breasts jiggling as she trotted gingerly should a twig or rock hurt her feet, and opened the trunk. She was the most beautiful woman he'd ever seen and even though he'd just burst into her, he wanted more of her.

Far along the shore of the lake two people turned and looked at Etta, but Dengler couldn't find it in himself to care. One of them looked like Owen and the second a woman Etta's age. Etta was quick and in a second he heard the screen door slam again and she was beside him.

Dengler 'fixed' her. She slept for half an hour. He slept too. Then they made love again. Later he washed her hair in the shower, dried it and brushed it until it was smooth and fell in straight furrows.

That afternoon they slept instead of swam and did not leave their bed until early evening.

- 34 -

It was Fall before the outside world entered their lives again. Summer melted away. In its place leaves fell from the trees and the wind sweeping across the lake became cold and shivering. The cabins emptied until only theirs and Owen's were occupied. Their walks in the woods or by the lake were with sweaters and hats now.

The Cold War affair that would become known as the Cuban Missile Crisis was three days old before Dengler turned on the television and learned of it. "Jesus," he whispered when he saw footage first of the American naval vessels being sent to blockade Cuba, and then the Soviet vessels were said to contain medium-range nuclear missiles which were on their way to Havana.

"What is it?" Etta said. She'd just returned from the kitchen where she was trying her hand at frying chicken.

"Maybe the end of the world," he told her.

John Kennedy appeared at a news conference and Dengler marveled that this wasn't the Kennedy portrayed in Marilyn's diary, a playboy who cheated on his young wife and ultimately shared America's preeminent sex goddess with his younger brother, the Attorney General. He appeared to be a poised middle-aged man who knew what he was doing and had the wisdom and the experience to pull America through this crisis. Dengler idly wondered if anyone would believe Marilyn's diary, even if he released it. He suspected not.

"What are those ships about?" Etta said, referring to the archive footage being shown during the news broadcast.

"The Russians are sending nuclear missiles to Cuba," he said. "Kennedy says no."

"Good for him." Dengler's story about Marilyn's death seemed not to have changed Etta's opinion of the handsome, young president.

"He's placed a blockade around the island and says we're going to board any vessels trying to go through."

"What do the Russians say?"

"They say it's piracy. They say if Kennedy stops them, it could lead to nuclear war."

"It won't," Etta said.

"You're sure of that?"

"If I'm wrong, there won't be anyone around to argue about it."

That night as Dengler slept with Etta spooned against his body, the warm smell, and soft touch of her the most real things in the world to him, he hoped Kennedy knew what he was doing. Now that he'd found Etta, she was his most important reason for living. He had to find a way to resolve this mess that ensnared him. He had to find a way for them both to live. Otherwise, he hoped Kennedy erred and the whole damn world died with them.

There was a more immediate crisis brewing than the one occurring off the coast of Cuba, at least to Etta, anyway.

After a time she was down to half the dosage she'd been taking before, but it was apparent the supply Dengler had taken from Guy wouldn't suffice. He would have to buy more. "I could come with you," Etta said one evening.

"No."

"He knows me, David. He might get paranoid with somebody new. Anyway, he's liable to cheat you. Drug dealing isn't necessarily an honorable profession, you know."

"You can show me what to look for. I just want you to make the call."

After dinner they strolled down to Owen's cabin and used the public phone outside his door to call a man named Joseph who lived in Baltimore. "Joseph," Etta said into the receiver, "this is Etta W. I need to make a buy."

"You've been gone a long time," Dengler heard the man on the other end of the line say. He stood close to Etta, sharing the receiver with her.

"Yes, but I'm back now."

"How much?"

"A couple ounces."

"Ounces now?" The voice named Joseph remarked. "You used to buy fix-to-fix. Come into a little money?"

Etta looked worriedly to Dengler, who gestured go on.

"I'm sending my new pimp."

"Now it comes together. Who is this guy?"

"His name is Lawrence." They'd agreed to use Dengler's middle name. "Can he meet you somewhere?"

Joseph must have covered the phone with his hand for a moment. The sound of muffled noises drifted lazily through the lines before he returned. "Okay. You're in luck. On Carmody Street, between Balfour and Creighton, there's an alley on the north side. My car will be parked there tonight at nine."

"How much, Joseph?" Etta said. "Lawrence is bringing only the purchase price with him."

"Two hundred an ounce. I'll accommodate him." The line went dead.

Dengler left her enough for one fix at bedtime and another in the morning, should he be detained.

"You can leave me the whole kit, David. I'm not going to OD on the stuff. You can trust me that much."

Dengler kissed her instead of replying, slipped behind the wheel of the Pontiac Catalina and drove away from the cabin.

- 35 -

Almost three months had passed since Dengler left Baltimore. The entire Monroe field op and its aftermath seemed so distant to him it could have happened to someone else. He felt like just another husband on an errand to the city for his wife. The first nights in their cabin Dengler expected to see the place surrounded by federal agents. When that didn't happen he began to hope. This newest part of his life had gone so well now anything less seemed unlikely. It was partly Etta, he knew. Etta made him feel invincible.

He had other concerns. There were several potentialities to prepare himself for, all of them related to Guy, Etta's former pimp. Dengler knew if he'd been treated as Guy was treated, he wouldn't forgive and forget. He had been treated as Guy was treated, and he hadn't forgiven, or forgotten. This Joseph was Guy's drug connection too. Guy might try to arrange some kind of ambush.

The most likely scenario was that Guy and a couple of thugs would be waiting for him instead of Joseph. They would try to kill him, or make him wish he were dead. Dengler felt confident he could handle this. Men who made money off of women's bodies didn't impress him. When such men were violent, it was usually directed against women or at best some john who had no training or experience in personal combat. Dengler had a knack for personal combat.

The next most likely scenario was Guy would betray Dengler and Joseph by tipping off the police. Dengler thought this was possible only because it wouldn't require courage of Guy. When Dengler last saw Guy, courage was one of the things he lacked.

He arrived in Baltimore after 8:30 P.M. The city was oddly subdued owing, Dengler guessed, to the Cuban Missile Crisis. He imagined people were sitting before their television sets waiting for advance word on Armageddon. Traffic was sparse, there were almost no pedestrians on the sidewalks, and the neon signs glowed and flashed with funereal effect.

He drove the Pontiac to Carmody Street and parked it between Balfour and Creighton streets on the south side. He could see the alley clearly across the street on the north side. He turned on the car radio. Khrushchev was warning Americans what would happen if the U.S. Navy attempted to board one of the Soviet vessels.

At 8:55 P.M. a brand-new black Rolls motored down the street past Dengler's Pontiac and backed into the alley. Dengler listened to its engine reverberate against the brick walls for a minute, and then die. He guessed the car was halfway down the alley.

Dengler stepped from the Pontiac. He slipped the second .45 into his belt in back. The other .45 was already in his shoulder holster. Dengler left the keys in the car and didn't lock the driver's door. He paced to the south sidewalk, and then down so he could look directly into the alley.

There were two men in the car. He could see them clearly because of the light reflecting off the brick walls to either side and behind them. Somehow Dengler had expected Joseph to come alone. Seeing the operation, he understood that would have been foolish. Dengler coming alone also seemed foolish now. Maybe he should have brought Etta. She could have kept the Pontiac's engine running and provided an additional presence. The thought of Etta being caught up in all this ugliness disturbed him, though. He wanted to take her out of that.

Moments passed. The two men had seen him. They didn't move, either. Finally Dengler crossed the street. His motion was slow and careful. He looked past the Rolls at the alley beyond, and then pulled his gaze back and looked at the two men themselves, who still hadn't moved since seeing him. Dengler asked himself, *Why didn't Joseph park his Rolls on the street?* Dengler could have just slipped into the passenger seat, made the deal, and then just walked away.

Dengler reached the alley just as the thought entered his mind, *I can just turn and walk away, find some other drug connection.* He was feeling something, not fear, not even suspicion, but something that caused tiny hairs on the back of his neck to rise. He didn't have to go through with this deal. Momentum carried him into the alley. He stopped in front of the flashy Rolls grill and waited.

A skinny black man slipped from behind the wheel of the car and stood with his elbow on the doorframe. The interior light didn't come on when he opened the door, which comforted Dengler. Joseph had rigged it not to work, meaning he must do this sort of thing often. "Lawrence?" Joseph said.

"That's right."

"You got the money?"

"That's right."

"Come on back here," Joseph told him, and then closed the car door.

As Dengler angled around the driver's side, he kept his eyes on the man in the passenger seat. It was dark, but he saw the man was white and relatively young.

Joseph opened the trunk, which obscured Dengler's view of the man sitting in the front seat. Joseph switched on the trunk light, drawing his attention downward to a suitcase that was centered on the trunk floor.

"Let's see the money," Joseph ordered.

Dengler removed the four bills from his windbreaker pocket. He separated the corners of the bills with his thumb, exposing four $100 symbols.

"Okay," Joseph said, bending over to open the suitcase.

It was then Dengler felt the gun barrel in his back and the hand grasp his right arm. "If you move I'll kill you," a voice said softly, and then louder, "Okay, I've got him."

He didn't have him. Dengler pivoted, the gun went off, the bullet rifling past his spine and into the Rolls Royce trunk. Dengler's right elbow slammed into the man's jaw. He dropped, the gun spilling from his hand.

In the instant he did this, Dengler realized the man in the front seat had diverted his attention from the more logical threat, the darkness behind him. Dengler was already drawing the .45 from his belt in back when he stepped on the perpetrator's arm as he flailed about, searching for his dropped gun, breaking it between wrist and elbow.

The man from the front seat stepped out of the car with a shiny weapon in his hand. New. Disposable. Thoughts rorschached through Dengler's mind as he squatted below the light line and kicked the first gunman's loose pistol into the darkness.

Passengerman turned the barrel of his weapon toward Dengler, who replied with his .45. Before bullets could be fired a cold, hard force struck Dengler in the side of the head. Light flashed in the alley, or maybe it was just inside Dengler's mind. When the flash bulb light receded, Dengler was on the ground with a gun barrel kissing his brow.

"He broke my arm." the first gunman reported. "He broke my goddamn arm."

Dengler still had the second .45 in his shoulder holster. He could reach that weapon with his left hand. It would be easy, in fact, if there weren't a gun barrel aimed at the center of his head.

The man who had been sitting in the front seat of the Rolls arrived at the back of the car. The trunk light illuminated his features. He was big, with broad shoulders and strong arms. Dengler had seen the type before. In Brentwood. In Santa Barbara. This man intended to kill him and Dengler knew it. The moment this truth registered Dengler reached for the .45 and found Gunman #2's hand had reached it first.

"Jesus, this guy comes loaded for bear," the man behind him said. Dengler thought of him as Darkness, from the direction he came.

"Check for other weapons," the big man ordered. "Toss them in the trunk."

Joseph grinned. He emerged from the shadow at the side of the alley. "Why thank you, gentlemen. I can always use a little extra hardware."

Big Man's smile broadened for an instant.

"My arm's like it's got a goddamn hinge," Gunman reported from the asphalt.

"Give it a rest," Big Man told him. "We'll get to you in a minute."

"Now," Joseph continued, "I think that concludes our business."

"Yeah, it does," Big Man said as the two .45s were dropped into the trunk and Joseph slammed it shut. Meanwhile, Dengler was yanked to his feet, thrown against the wall and frisked. "We have your money back here," he heard Big Man say just as Darkness grabbed Dengler by the shoulders and shoved him toward the back of the alley.

Dengler found himself walking with Joseph. The alley led no more than twenty yards back from the Rolls. There were shapes back there that could be another car. As they walked Dengler turned to Joseph and said, "They're going to kill both of us."

This hadn't occurred to Joseph. "You're full of shit, man," he said with a toothy grin. "Maybe they going to shoot you, but me —" He twisted at this and looked toward Big Man and Darkness. Something in their manner made Joseph turn around completely. "Now what kind of shit is this?" he asked them.

Dengler spun around. Big Man and Darkness were poker faced.

"You heard me, man." Joseph yelled. "You heard me. What kind of shit is this?"

Big Man fired once. The round entered Joseph's head dead center. He dropped to the ground, so much fresh meat.

Dengler knew what he was going to do. *Wait until Big Man draws a bead, then jump.* He would hit Big Man on the run, spin him so he became a barrier between Dengler and Darkness. If he got by, he would keep on going and hope he could leap past the Rolls and out into the street before he took too many rounds.

"David," Big Man said. He used Dengler's first name, confirming his suspicions. Stafford's men.

Fear and adrenaline, his old friends, percolated in his chest and stomach. "Yeah," he heard himself reply.

"Stafford asked me to tell you, you've done well for a grunt from Army M.I."

"Uh-huh."

"One other thing."

"What's that?"

"Stafford said, 'Ask David how they're hanging.'"

"Tell Gray Stafford my last words were, 'Fuck you.'"

This amused Big Man. "Yeah, he said you'd say that."

Big Man brought the shiny pistol to bear. "Close your eyes and it'll be over in a second," he told him. Dengler tensed, but his eyes remained open. An eternity passed. Dengler leaped. A bullet sounded, then another, and another, amid flashes of light from the back of the alley. In the din he heard a round strike, a splat noise. The round shattered Big Man's head. His brains and blood splattered all over Dengler, who flew past the falling corpse and sucked for air — *God, what's happening?* He ran with every pound of energy his muscles could produce.

Dengler sprinted toward the back of the Rolls. The gunman whose arm Dengler broke was crawling away maniacally when a wayward bullet plowed through him. Dengler leaped him and kept running. He heard, "Stop him." and a moment later he was tackled. Dengler fell toward the pavement. He kicked free from his assailant and crawled toward the end of the alley.

A man approached him from out of the darkness. The man was pointing an automatic weapon toward the sky, just as Dengler was trained to do between firing. He was a lean, fit man of fifty wearing an impeccable suit, gloves and a homburg hat. He stopped beside Dengler and bent down so his face was a foot, no more, from Dengler's own. "I'll take it from here," he told the man who had tackled Dengler. "Greetings," he said, returning his attention to Dengler, "from J. Edgar Hoover."

- 36 -

When Dengler didn't respond for a moment the man told him, "Have the decency to allow us to rescue you without further pursuit." He then opened his coat and slid the automatic weapon into a holster waiting there.

A car screeched to a stop at the mouth of the alley, its lights dancing on the brick walls, and another one behind it. Men rushed in and past Dengler, several of them with ambulance gurneys, and seconds later other men moved out and past him carrying weapons. These men imposed security in the street.

Dengler pulled himself up into a sitting position, dazed.

"Get these stiffs out of here," a voice ordered and Dengler recognized it as belonging to his hero. "I want this alley cleaned up, and I want it done in half an hour."

"Right."

"Confiscate the car. There's heroin and guns in the trunk."

"Right."

"Wait a second," Dengler heard himself say. "That heroin is mine. I was in the process of buying it when —" The absurdity of what he was saying hit him and he shut up.

The agent stepped into nearby light and looked down at Dengler. Finally he kneeled. "Look, tell us where she is and we'll go get her. We'll put her in the hospital and bring her out of it slowly. Do a professional job."

"Bullshit. I'm not telling you anything."

"Wherever she is, David, she's very alone."

"No."

"Okay," he said finally, shrugging it off. "How much did you buy?"

"Two ounces."

"Stoval?" the agent called.

"Yeah."

"How much heroin there?"

"My guess — a couple of kilos."

"It belongs to our friend here. Bring it along."

One of the agents slipped behind the wheel of the Rolls. Its engine thundered, and the car pulled out of the alley. Four gurneys carrying the bodies rolled past Dengler just as a bakery truck pulled to a stop outside. The gurneys were loaded into it.

The agent offered Dengler a hand. He accepted it and was pulled to his feet. "We should leave," he said.

"Okay." Dengler wasn't sure about where, and how, but leaving here was okay with him.

The agent walked out to the street. Dengler followed him, amazed the man wasn't afraid to show Dengler his back. There were no less than twenty other operatives bouncing about from alley to street and back. A Lincoln limousine pulled up. The agent opened the door for him. Dengler got in.

The agent lowered himself in and closed the door. Dengler found the dome light control and turned it on so he could see him clearly. The agent saw what he was doing and smiled.

"Special Agent-In-Charge Robert Lowry," he said, extending a hand.

"You have a card or something?"

"Yes, I think I do."

He opened a rear seat glove compartment located under the bench and removed his wallet and his ID case. Lowry showed him his badge, his ID, and gave him an FBI business card.

Dengler looked at the card, feeling foolish as it meant nothing and he knew it meant nothing. None of this meant anything because Dengler could have reproduced all of it, given time. He peered over the card's edge at Lowry. In addition to Dengler's earlier observations, he saw Lowry had prominent lips, a nose broken at least once and not fixed properly, and large ears. His eyes were also large and recessed, and his chin possessed just the hint of a cleft. The image was one of a man who knew himself, knew his job, knew his limitations, and was at peace with the world.

"Have me memorized, do you?" Lowry said with a friendly smile. A buzzer sounded. Lowry depressed one of a series of buttons near his armrest. "Yes?"

"Peterson just reported in. They took the fourth man."

"Good. Thanks. Proceed to Point B." He released the button and returned his gaze to Dengler. "They had a fourth man positioned outside the alley just in case you got away. He was to kill you. When things turned nasty, the gunman retreated and we had to pursue him."

"Who were these people?"

"You don't know?"

"Who were they?"

Lowry sighed. "I'm not at liberty to brief you, Mr. Dengler. Briefing exceeds my orders. Why don't you tell me."

"That might not be healthy for me."

Lowry chuckled. "Now really, Mr. Dengler, if we wanted to kill you, we would have killed you."

"Maybe you want to know what I know first, then you'll kill me."

Lowry surveyed him for a moment. Then, "Can I offer you something to drink?"

"Whiskey?"

"Bourbon."

"God, yes."

Lowry poured two drinks from the bar, handed one to Dengler.

"The man who would have killed you was August Stefano. He was a local hood doing work for the Central Intelligence Agency. The CIA started doing that in recent years, using the Mob for dirty work. The two men in central California were named Picerni, I think, and Silvestri. Both Gambino Family soldiers. You have a talent for killing, Mr. Dengler."

"I defend myself," Dengler said simply.

"Everyone's been looking for you since Santa Barbara County. I don't know why, that information is being held close to the vest, and above me. We traced all your contacts, of course, and so did the CIA. They found Miss Warren's pimp a day ahead of us. We had them surveilled. They reasoned it was only a matter of time until you showed up to buy your girlfriend heroin. They set a trap; we expanded it a bit. Now here we are."

"Going where?" Dengler said.

"To see The Director," Lowry said matter-of-factly. "He wants to talk with you."

- 37 -

"J. Edgar Hoover wants to talk to me," Dengler replied with more than a tone of cynicism in his voice.

Lowry smiled and nodded, but offered nothing further.

Lowry and Dengler rode in silence after they finished their drinks, and the FBI agent offered no refill. He wanted to remain sharp for The Director, Dengler supposed, and while Dengler would have enjoyed another, he said nothing. He wanted to remain sharp, too.

Dengler kept explosive thoughts beneath a veneer of calm. His pulse was returning to normal. Sweat was evaporating from his skin. His near-death experience in the alley was diminishing. He had no doubt what Hoover wanted to talk to him about — Marilyn Monroe. How did Hoover find out about him? Did the head of the FBI know what Dengler witnessed, and if so, what did he want Dengler to do about it? Dengler promised himself he would offer nothing, certainly not mention Marilyn's diary or its whereabouts.

After ten minutes Lowry leaned forward and tapped on the glass partition between the passenger and driver compartments. It rolled down with a whine and Dengler realized there were two men in the front seat. The one sitting on the passenger side turned around to face them. He had a microphone in one hand and was wearing a radio headset. Dengler guessed he was thirty, with sandy blond hair, extremely blue eyes and the delicate features of a New England Brahmin. "Bowers located three houses, all without power," he reported. Dengler was surprised when the man's Southern accent turned out to be thicker than his own.

"Oh, Agent Strong," Lowry said, "let me introduce you to David Dengler, recently of Army M.I. David, Wesley Strong."

"David," Strong said with a grin, extending a hand. Dengler took it. "I've been tracing you for so long, I feel I already know you." Strong turned to Lowry, "Bowers wants to know which house, Bob."

"Tell him the one farthest away from everything. Then seal it off. No one in, no one out."

"Right."

"And for god's sakes test the generator and make sure the backup works, too."

"Right."

The partition whined back up, and again the view forward was as black as night. The view from the side told Dengler they were heading out of the city, however. "Where are you taking me?" he said.

"To the coast. It's just a short hop from Washington, and with our backs to the sea and the sparse population, it's an area that's easy to control."

"What do you need the generators for?"

"In case we can't get the power turned on. That happened once in Sarasota and the AIC, that's Agent In Charge — Well, I think he's scheduled to rotate out of Alaska sometime in '64." Lowry said this with a grin that suggested it was a joke, and true in spirit.

"Why isn't the power already on?" Dengler asked.

"You'll see."

They rode on in silence for another twenty minutes, then the vibration from the road changed and Dengler realized they'd left pavement behind. This too gave way to another sensation five minutes later, one of floating, and Dengler guessed this was sand. The car stopped within minutes. Dengler heard the front two doors open and close.

"Want to get out and stretch your legs?" Lowry said.

Dengler stepped out and was assaulted by sensations. There was sea spray, the sea's edge thirty feet from the side of the Lincoln. A wave rushed in, hissing as it came, just as Dengler stepped out. The wind gusted and whooshed around his ears. The noise of ten trillion gallons of water caressing the beach deafened him.

"It'll be a few minutes," Lowry told him, checking his watch.

Dengler looked up and down the beach. There were two four-wheel-drive Jeeps parked at either end, two more in immediate sight at either side of a large, two-story house that was dark, and the headlights of more vehicles behind it. Between them Dengler saw men wearing hunting outfits and carrying M-2 auto-carbines, the weapon used by paratroops during the Second World War.

The lights inside the house came on.

"Come inside," Lowry said above the din. Dengler followed him up the beach to the steps, and then inside the house.

The house was unfurnished, confirming Dengler's suspicion they had commandeered a place that was for sale. Just inside the door was a large atrium surrounded on three sides by leaded glass. This gave way to a large living room shouldered on each side by other rooms, by the look of the doors, kitchen and dining room on the north side, library, or den on the south. Stairs led up the wall Dengler guessed separated living room and den. Across from the stairs was a large fireplace.

Much of the house was dark.

Strong entered from the back room with two light bulbs in his hands. It was dark back there. "Where are we going to put the chairs?" he asked Lowry.

"There," Lowry pointed, near the center of the room.

The front door swung open, and two men entered, each carrying a wing chair. "There," Strong ordered, where Lowry had pointed a moment before. The two men dropped their chairs and exited for more furniture. Dengler noted one wing chair was taller than the other. Otherwise they were identical.

"Nice house," Strong said.

"Good summer place. How much are they asking?" Lowry sat down in the lower of the two chairs. Dengler moved toward the taller of the two and Lowry shook his head. No.

"I can find out for you," Strong said. He moved for the door just as the two agents entered again, this time each carrying a small table and a lamp. "Hold it," he ordered, and then looked down each lampshade to make sure the lamp was outfitted with a bulb. Neither was. Strong made use of the two bulbs.

While he was gone the two agents placed the tables beside the wing chairs, set the lamps on the tables, and then discovered they were too far from the wall to hook up to the wall socket. "Get an extension," Lowry told them. "Oh, and bring in a throw rug to cover the cord."

"Right."

"You guys are going to some effort here," Dengler said.

"Not really," Lowry replied. "Actually, ninety-nine percent of our manpower expenditure is to provide security. The rest is an afterthought."

Strong reentered. "Bowers said it listed for twenty-two thousand."

"That's too much."

"Take off ten percent. Offer them nineteen eight."

"Still too much."

"Four bedrooms, I think."

One of the agents who carried furniture earlier stuck his head in the door. "E.T.A. five minutes," he called, and then withdrew. The second one pushed past him with an extension cord and a throw rug.

Lowry stood up. "Want to go out and watch the landing?" he asked Dengler.

"Sure."

"Wesley, one last precaution."

"Yes?"

"Frisk him."

Lowry headed for the exit as Strong gestured for Dengler to turn around. He frisked him quickly but thoroughly, and then patted him on the shoulder to indicate he was through.

"You ever meet The Director?" Dengler asked him.

"Sure," Strong said. "We're a special group. Everyone here has met The Director at one time or another."

Somehow Dengler never thought he would meet The Director of the Federal Bureau of Investigation. It had been his hope to work for him, or the CIA, but he never thought his contact with J. Edgar Hoover would be up close and personal. Dengler stepped out the front door of the beach house and saw again all of the preparations were ongoing for The Director's arrival. The lights of the various vehicles beamed inward where The Director's chopper would land, briefly illuminating men scrambling back and forth.

Dengler considered why he was here and not dead at the hands of a CIA assassination team. There was only one answer. *I'm worth far more to the FBI alive than dead, and to the CIA far more dead than alive.*

- 38 -

When the helicopter became visible in the sky, Wesley Strong took Dengler by the arm and led him away from the boardwalk connecting the landing site to the house. When finally the chopper set down Dengler was standing beside the limo again, trying to understand what this meeting with The Director of the FBI would mean.

Dengler saw a man of small stature, stocky and a little wobbly on his feet, drop to the ground from the landed chopper and led up the boardwalk to the house. Another man jumped to the sand as well, and when Wesley saw him he groaned. "Shit, Clyde's with him. We'll have to get another chair." He left Dengler beside the limo and trotted to two agents who were standing by the helicopter. In a moment he returned.

"This will take a second," Wesley said. "The Director likes to be settled before he receives anyone."

"Okay."

"By the way, did you think it was cold in there?"

"Not particularly."

"Bob had them make a fire. It may get too warm."

"Who's Clyde?" Dengler said.

"Clyde Tolson. He's Deputy Director."

"Oh."

"Good friend of The Director's. It'll be a minute."

Actually, it was almost fifteen minutes before Bob and Wesley led Dengler up the boardwalk to the front door of the house and inside. All the lights except the two lamps beside the chairs had been turned off, but the living room was well illuminated because of the fire that raged in the fireplace. A single wing chair faced the hearth and in it was the man Strong identified as Clyde Tolson. He wasn't quite within listening distance of the other two wing chairs, one of which was occupied by J. Edgar Hoover. It was no surprise to Dengler that Hoover had chosen to sit in the taller of the two chairs.

"Mr. Director," Lowry said, "I'd like to introduce David Dengler, formerly of Army M.I."

"Actually, that's not quite accurate, sir," Dengler told him, reaching out to shake his hand. The Director's grip was curt, the texture of his flesh moist and cool. "Actually, I'm still in the Army."

"I think it's safe to say you've served your last day in uniform, Mr.

Dengler," Hoover said, "unless you count the one they issue at Leavenworth. Please be seated."

Dengler sat down. Lowry retreated to the door, about the same distance on one side of the wing chairs as Tolson on the other. The Director's hands were steepled. He was deep in thought. His eyes perused Dengler for a long moment. Then he said, "We found you because of this whore you associate with. Women are difficult enough in our business, Mr. Dengler, although there is a place for marriage. Associating with whores will ruin you."

"I wasn't..." Dengler started. He suppressed the anger that prompted him to finish. *Who is this fat little man to tell me whom I should associate with?* Dengler realized The Director was staring at him. He said, "Etta Warren and I grew up together. We're friends."

The Director's expression said what he thought of that. He snorted dismissively before asking, "You are aware of our efforts in your behalf?"

"Yes sir. The phony photograph that was released to the press."

"We also switched your fingerprints."

"Yes sir."

"And my bringing this issue up, what does that prove?"

Dengler wet his lips. "My support within the bureau is from the top."

"Yes, it proves you have my attention."

"Yes sir."

"Now, can you tell me what happened a little more than an hour ago?"

Dengler shifted in his seat. He disliked this 'show and tell' and, along with The Director's comments about Etta, it was starting to piss him off. "People working for the CIA tried to kill me."

"They also killed a man by the name of Guy Parré. Did you know him?"

Of course, Dengler thought, *they would have to kill Guy, too. And Etta.* The thought stunned him and for moments his mind followed the entire line of logic, from killing Guy to eventually killing Dengler himself, and anyone else who might be able to tell anyone the truth.

"Mr. Dengler?" The voice was impatient but not short, used to prompt an answer.

"No," he lied, and then amended, "Not really."

"We saved your life?"

"Yes."

"I'm going to share things with you, Mr. Dengler, because I have to. Why will become evident. What does this suggest to you?"

Dengler shifted again in the wing chair. Being placed on the spot was getting to him. He said, "Excuse me, Mr. Director, but why don't you tell me what it means."

The Director didn't like being talked to this way, Dengler could see. Hoover stepped past it. "We were aware hours before it was scheduled to happen," Hoover said finally, "that they intended to murder you, Mr. Dengler. We might have just assassinated the entire team and been waiting for you ourselves, without the incumbent risk to the lives of our own agents. Certainly that's what the CIA would have done in our place. Instead, we chose to wait and catch them in the act, when their guilt was established. In other words, the Federal Bureau of Investigation works within the spirit of the law. The letter of the law is a technicality everyone must break occasionally, but the spirit of the law is its very soul, and we are its last protector."

Dengler saw he was absolutely serious. Hoover stared at Dengler with that bulldog expression that reminded him of Winston Churchill.

"You may trust us, Mr. Dengler," Hoover continued. "We do not take human life unless it is to protect another human life. We are the highest law enforcement agency in this land, and we have the best interests of the American people at heart at all times, not because of love or patriotism — those things can make you do awful things. Just look at the Germans. We have America's best interests at heart because of honor. Patriotism is the flag, Mr. Dengler; honor is the Constitution."

"Yes sir."

"Goddamn it, don't agree with me unless you want to."

"Yes sir."

"Bob."

Special Agent Bob Lowry sprang forward. "Yes, Mr. Director?"

"Do we have anything to drink?"

"There's a bar in the unit, sir." By *unit* he meant *limo*.

"No, I mean something hot. Coffee or tea, possibly."

"I'll get on it, sir."

"What about you, Mr. Dengler?"

"Whatever you're having."

"See what you can do, would you, Bob?"

"Yes, Mr. Director." Bob paced to the door and exited. Another agent from outside entered and took his place at the door.

"You'll have to pardon me," Hoover said. "It's been a long day. This Cuban missile thing has everyone wrung out."

"Yes sir."

Hoover massaged his eyes for a moment, rotating thumb and forefinger in the sockets, and then returned his gaze to Dengler. "Let's move forward. When you witnessed Monroe's death and were almost killed by Gray Stafford's operatives, why didn't you come to us?"

"Excuse me, sir, but how do you know I witnessed anything?"

"I don't," he said. "Not for certain. But let's look at the facts. Monroe died. You were under orders to surveil Monroe's house as a graduation exercise. Gray Stafford was known to be in town that day with a CIA field team composed of contract agents. Two of its members were found dead in Santa Barbara County early in the morning of the day following Monroe's death. The CIA came to us with this wild story about two of their agents tailing a known Russian operative when, they said, you attacked and murdered them without provocation. It's pretty obvious the real facts are you were being taken north to be killed, and your body disposed of. They would only do that if you could place them at the Monroe house hours before, during the murder. That you witnessed her death is merely wish fulfillment on my part. Are you a witness?"

Dengler's mouth was so dry he knew he was going to have difficulty forming words. He refocused his gaze from Hoover's face to the wall, and then to the fireplace, all the time thinking if Hoover lied to him about the 'spirit of the law' and his real purpose was to protect the Kennedys, then he would die if his answer were yes. The thought he was a dead man anyway, something that had receded to the back of his mind since the FBI saved him, again fought its way to the front.

"I am aware that both the President and the Attorney General had recent affairs with Marilyn Monroe," Hoover said deliberately, "and that you probably believe my objective here is to protect them, even perhaps to the eradication of witnesses."

Dengler said nothing.

"Who do you think sent you there that night, Mr. Dengler?"

Dengler jerked about. Hoover was smiling. It was the hard, cynical smile of one tough son-of-a-bitch.

"Look," Hoover continued. "Monroe had been under electronic surveillance for years, in part because of her romantic ties to certain Hollywood entertainers who are known communist sympathizers. When the Attorney General learned of our interest, he ordered all electronic and human surveillance of her home stopped. We hadn't surveilled her with agents, but his written order precluded even that then."

Lowry returned with an agent carrying a tray with a teapot and two cups on it. The agent set it down and left. Lowry poured tea into the two cups. He resumed his position by the door, dispatching his replacement back outside.

"I felt the public good would be served if Monroe's house were surveilled," Hoover continued. "Naval Intelligence, Air Force Intelligence, and Army M.I. all send their trainees out for practice runs. I arranged for representatives from each service to be revolved through. We chose the best candidates from each class. We chose you."

Dengler could take it no more. "This is bullshit." he hissed. "This is crazy bullshit." As his voice rose, Lowry took one step toward the wing chairs. Dengler ignored him. "I saw Gray Stafford shove a Nembutal suppository up Marilyn Monroe's ass. And the best you could do was put a trainee outside her house?"

"Yes." Hoover's voice was a monotone.

"Gray Stafford is the Executive Assistant to the National Security Advisor. He works directly for the President of the United States. I suppose next you're going to tell me the President is innocent of killing Marilyn Monroe?"

"That's what we have to find out, isn't it?" The Director said softly.

- 39 -

There was silence between them for some minutes. Dengler's mind raced. The Director of the Federal Bureau of Investigation had just told him he didn't know if the President of the United States was a murderer. Finally Dengler asked, "What if he is?"

"What if he is what?"

"What if he ordered her killed?"

Dengler thought he saw a tremor run through The Director, who said after a moment, "No man is above the law, Mr. Dengler. I would arrest him, even though he would remain President of the United States until such time as he was impeached."

"He could fire you."

"Yes."

"And replace you with someone who would drop the charges."

"Yes, that might happen. One would hope Congress acted quickly."

"He could order Gray Stafford to kill you."

Hoover scowled. "Yes, he could do a number of things — if he were guilty."

"But you don't think he is."

"I'm not sure. Are you?"

"No." Dengler halted. Should he tell The Director everything he knew? Was all of this merely a ploy to find out how much he knew before he was killed? Dengler wanted to believe Hoover. Still, he was reluctant to bring full disclosure, maybe because the information was his, he owned it, he'd paid the price for it, and once he told the FBI about it, it would be theirs.

"Yes?" The Director said, seeing he was holding back. "You would like to say something?"

"I have information you don't have," he told him. "About motive. Relative to motive."

"Yes."

"Marilyn Monroe scheduled a press conference for the Monday following her death. She planned to tell the press everything about her affairs with Robert and John Kennedy. She was going to 'blow the lid off.' That's the phrase she used."

"You gleaned this from her diary?"

Dengler moved forward in the chair, commanding the chill that attacked his spine to subside. "Diary?"

"We have it."

"You do?"

"Yes. Stafford missed it," The Director reported, suppressing an emotion Dengler suspected was glee. "Well, he was in a hurry. The LAPD found it in a purse beneath a couch where, presumably, she kicked it. It was taken with her effects to the Coroner's lock-up, where we found it."

Dengler could say nothing more. He sank back into the wing chair. He thought there was only one copy of the diary left — his photocopy — after Stafford destroyed the original.

"As valuable as the diary is," The Director said, "you are, Mr. Dengler, far more important than any evidence we have gathered in this investigation. You witnessed her death. You tried to stop her murder and almost paid full measure for it. You identified the perpetrator."

More important than any evidence we have... Dengler realized he would live. He was too important to kill, and too important not to protect. A wave of relief swept across him. If he lived, Etta would live. They would have a life together.

"The only question remains," Hoover continued, "who sent Gray Stafford to kill Marilyn Monroe, and for what reason?"

"What other reason could there be?" Dengler said, drawn back from personal thoughts. "The Kennedy Administration protecting itself."

Hoover's hands steepled again, and he studied Dengler. Finally he said, "Mr. Dengler, I have served six Presidents to date. Of them all I dislike John Kennedy most. I don't agree with his politics at all. And his brother, the Attorney General, is a sniveling little prick."

Dengler returned his gaze to The Director. It had drifted to the fireplace, to the lonely man sitting beside it, Clyde Tolson, to the dark recesses at the back of the house. Now The Director had his complete attention.

"I must tell you they don't care for me at all. They would fire me, in fact, if they could. You may recall Monroe mentioned that fact in her diary, that Robert Kennedy told her he would fire me, if he could."

"Yes sir, I read that entry."

"President Kennedy *would* have fired me already, in fact, except for one thing. In the course of normal, everyday investigations I have come into possession of enough information about him and his father to ruin the Administration. However, much as I may despise the man, and he me, not for a moment do I believe he is capable of murder."

"Then who? And why?"

Dengler felt the smaller man's puffy eyes bore into him, as if assessing the impact of what he was about to say. "The CIA budget is appropriated through closed-door hearings," The Director told him. "In this way was it intended that the CIA be controlled, through the appropriations apparatus. The CIA has always chafed at the leash. The Agency began looking for outside means of funding its various secret dealings very early on in its existence." Dengler had almost swallowed a sip of tea when The Director said, "And it was this situation that left it open to being compromised by the Mob."

Dengler coughed and leaned forward a centimeter. The Mob's involvement with the CIA explained the gangsters who attempted to kill him. The word *compromise* suggested which was the tail, and which the dog.

Seeing Dengler's interest pique, The Director continued, "In order to raise money for its illegal operations world-wide, elements of the Central Intelligence Agency provide intelligence services to the Mob in exchange for a percentage of the profits."

"Intelligence about what?"

"Drug sweeps. Secret files on Mafia leaders. Eventually, for a larger percentage of the profits, they began to coordinate drug shipments into this country. Later, they themselves did the smuggling."

"Jesus," Dengler whispered. *Could this be possible? Is the CIA in bed with the Mob?*

"Later yet they placed moles in every law enforcement and non-CIA intelligence agency."

"In the FBI?" The question was so obvious Dengler had to ask it, and yet it caused the ghost of a smile to form briefly on The Director's face. *He's got moles in their organization, too*, Dengler realized.

"While all of this was happening," The Director continued, "the Mob was making most of its profits from gaming and prostitution in Nevada and Cuba. When Cuba fell to Fidel Castro, much of those profits disappeared. They appealed to their CIA partners for help. The CIA increased its operations against Castro, in part because the Eisenhower Administration desired it, but also in part to please their Mob allies. The Bay of Pigs invasion was meant to return the island to the Mob. The CIA couldn't get Eisenhower's commitment to send in American troops, should they be needed — and the CIA knew they would be needed — so they set up the invasion plan in such a way as to embarrass the President if he refused to commit

American troops. Kennedy inherited this plan. When Kennedy refused to commit American forces and the invasion failed, The President realized the CIA had set him up. Kennedy vowed to reform the CIA, and shortly thereafter fired Allen Dulles, its Executive Director." Hoover shifted in the chair and crossed his legs. He was on autopilot now, briefing Dengler as he might brief the President or Congress. "You see, Mr. Dengler, the CIA was angry its manipulation of the President didn't work. The Mob wanted to get Cuba back. Both groups sought leverage on the President, leverage which only the FBI possessed, and of course we would never use our secret files in that manner."

Dengler almost said, *Yes sir. I understand that*, but didn't. He didn't believe Hoover.

"Into this equation enters Robert F. Kennedy's War on Crime," The Director continued. "He orders the FBI to compile information on the Mob. In his capacity as Attorney General he orders the prosecution of Mob figures. I have no problem with this, mind you. These people are scum and should be prosecuted, convicted, and sentenced to long prison terms. I mention this merely to show you the motives these men might have to damage the Kennedy Administration."

"I don't think I understand, sir," Dengler told him, leaning forward so his eyes were on a line with Hoover's. "Are you saying Monroe was killed by the Mob and the Central Intelligence Agency working together to embarrass President Kennedy? To bring down the Kennedy Administration?"

"If that diary fell into the hands of the press... If a witness named David Dengler hadn't escaped, thus presenting the threat of the truth coming out..."

Their eyes remained on a plane and locked for a long moment, as Clyde Tolson behind them lit his pipe and Agent-In-Charge Lowry, still hovering, felt foolish and retreated to the door.

"Stafford is working from within the White House to bring down the President?" Even as he asked this question, Dengler realized it was absurd, that the man asking the question was absurdly unimportant — too unimportant even to ask it. Hoover responded as if it were the most common question anyone might ask, and the questioner as qualified as anyone to ask it.

"The truth is, I don't know," Hoover said slowly. "The other three men with him that night were soldiers from the Cleveland Mob hired to assist him. We haven't ascertained the background of the men you met with tonight, but I suspect they're from the same source."

Dengler said nothing during the moments it took for logs in the fire to pop and crackle several times. It had never occurred to him these men were not what the press had reported them to be — government agents. In retrospect, he recalled they hadn't acted as he imagined college educated federal agents would act. Bloody Mouth and Marty had talked like a couple of dock stevedores. He'd been able to surprise Bloody Mouth at the wall outside Marilyn's house with ease, and with surprise as an ally, defeat him. Finally, Dengler looked back to his host, J. Edgar Hoover, whose expression, when he was relaxed back in the wing chair, was hidden by shadow. Dengler leaned forward.

"That proves it, then, doesn't it?"

"No," Hoover said. "It proves nothing. Stafford is already in bed with the Mob. That he can call on their muscle goes without saying. Why he called on them, that's the question. And for whom?"

"Then you think the President may have asked him to use Mob hit men to kill her?"

"It's possible. Remember, Mr. Dengler, my personal opinion is, he isn't involved at all. He's a victim in this game. However, I have no proof. It's an opinion. We do have evidence suggesting others may be involved."

Dengler didn't ask the question. The vacuum not asking created sucked all of the air out of the room.

"Jimmy Hoffa," Hoover continued, "employs an electronic eavesdropping expert named Alex Seidel. We have Hoffa under court-mandated surveillance ourselves. In several conversations Hoffa talked about Seidel with associates. Apparently, at various times Seidel taped both the President and the Attorney General in bed with Monroe. It's believed Hoffa always intended the tapes to be used as his trump card. If Monroe had held her news conference, the Seidel tapes would be worthless now, except for the prurient interest they would arouse."

"Did the FBI record any of this?"

"At the Monroe house? No. Our court-approved wire was on the telephone. We don't bug bedrooms."

"So you don't know. You know who killed Monroe, but not why. If you took the evidence you currently have and arrested Gray Stafford, and the President is the real authority behind the murder, you would be replaced. The investigation would end."

"Many things might end," Hoover said with finality.

The question presented itself. "And that leaves what to do with me."

"Yes, it does. You're a witness to the murder. You're invaluable to an honest investigation; correspondingly, you're a great danger to a cover-up. The CIA is looking for you. If I'm to protect you until your testimony is called for in court, then I have to find a place to put you. I have to fund this effort. Money means paper, and paper means a trail. Not impossible, but difficult."

"A new identity," Dengler said.

"Yes, obviously." The Director sat up and leaned forward. "Mr. Dengler," he said, his eyes boring into the younger man, "these men you see around you, every one of them, is special. When I realized the FBI had been penetrated by CIA moles, I realized I needed to create a bureau within the Bureau, an organization that couldn't be penetrated. I created this group, Q Force. It's their job to infiltrate the CIA, to conduct investigations whose findings would otherwise find their way into CIA hands, and to seek out the CIA moles within our midst. Now they have a new mission: Investigate the murder of Marilyn Monroe and prove the President innocent, or guilty. Each of these men is above reproach. I can think of no better place for you than with them."

"You mean protective custody?"

"No. Mr. Dengler, your actions have proven you a capable man. Were it not for your attempt to save this... *friend*, what's her name—?"

"Etta," Dengler provided, remembering Hoover had called her a whore.

"Etta. If you hadn't attempted to save her, you would probably still be eluding us now. So you've shown great skill, a native talent, if you will. You've proven yourself capable. I'm offering you a job."

"With Q Force?"

"With the FBI. Special Agent."

Nothing in Dengler's life had ever seemed so important as becoming a federal agent of some kind. Now he was being offered the premier badge. He'd not only regained his life, he was in the same stroke achieving what he always wanted.

Hoover smiled. "Having read your file this afternoon, I was convinced you would jump for joy at being offered the position of Special Agent with the FBI."

"I'm stunned, sir."

"Do you accept?"

"Yes sir, I accept."

- 40 -

FBI Special Agent David Dengler watched as the helicopter lifted from the beach and veered over the house, whose lights just then winked out. In a moment, the chopper crossed the horizon. Up and down the beach jeeps were being shoved into low gear and driven away. Dengler watched this operation for a while, and then looked out to sea where wave caps glowed beneath the moon.

"This area is no longer secured," Lowry said as he approached from the house. "We should be going." Wesley Strong joined them. He'd been up the beach conferring with another, unidentified agent. He now stood at the front fender of the Lincoln looking at Lowry as if he were the only one who knew the route to Yankee Stadium.

"Where?" Dengler said.

"Well, in my case, home," Lowry replied. He checked his watch. "I should just make it before one o'clock."

"No, I meant me."

"We can drop you off at your car," Strong said.

"You mean it's still back in Baltimore?"

"We took the precaution of moving it out of that particular area," Strong told him.

"Let's get in," Lowry said. "It's turning cold."

This time Strong crawled into the back of the limo and sat opposite Dengler, while Lowry resumed his position beside him. "I could use a drink," Dengler told them as the limo lurched forward in the sand, sliding a moment before its tires caught.

"A little late for me." It was Lowry, already looking done in.

"So, what do you have in mind, David?"

"Bourbon. Is there any left?"

"Oh, sure." Strong poured them both a tall shot.

Lowry laid his head back on the bench seat and closed his eyes. Obviously, Dengler thought, he was a nine-to-fiver who was already up past his bedtime. Dengler realized Strong was studying him even as he studied Lowry. Embarrassed for reasons he couldn't fathom, Dengler returned his eyes front.

"You guys knew this was going to happen?"

"What?" Strong said with a smile.

"Yes, we knew," Lowry said, his eyes remaining closed. "After all, Agent Dengler, what could he do? You're a valuable witness whose testimony may prove vital some day. You have proven skills and even more, proven instincts. Once we create a new identity for you,

you will be a completely untraceable agent. Everyone in the Bureau, Q Force or not, attended the FBI Academy and so is a known quantity. You, however, have the qualities of a chameleon. You will carry a shield, but no one knows you or can identify you."

"Stafford," he said in a monotone.

"We must try to keep you away from Stafford."

"No protest from me on that one."

"Yes, we know Stafford's tactics very well," Lowry said in an even, unprepossessing voice. He opened his eyes and sat up long enough to give Dengler a look. "Tomorrow you will debrief us, particularly how Stafford 'made' you at the Monroe house."

"I told him who I was," Dengler said honestly.

"We figured that." Lowry collapsed back onto the bench seat and resumed his search of the dark side of his eyelids.

Strong finished his drink and wiped the glass clean with a towel and put it away. Dengler nursed his drink, watching the liquid swirl at the bottom of the crystal glass like sewer water. Finally, he downed it and handed the glass to Strong, who repeated the cleaning process.

The divider powered down and the man driving the car, a different person from the trip out, said, "E.T.A. ten minutes." The partition hummed as it rose back into place and Lowry sat up and rubbed his eyes.

"David," he said, "this is what we need you to do."

"Okay."

"We have arranged to put your friend into a hospital under an assumed name. She will be detoxed. It may take awhile. You don't want her cleaned up so quickly it hurts."

"What if she doesn't want to go?"

"Then you must leave her."

"I'm not sure I can do that."

"You'd better convince her, David," Strong put in. "Where you're going, and what you're going to be doing, you won't have time to care for her."

"Okay," Dengler decided. "I can convince her."

"There's another thing," Lowry said. "You can't tell her what occurred tonight. This is Top Secret as of this moment."

"What should I tell her?"

"Don't lie. Just tell her you can't tell her what happened tonight, but you will be safe and you'll come visit her. Do you love this girl?"

He didn't want to say it. He was ashamed of her. She'd been a whore, and each of them knew it. Finally he said, "Yeah," in an off-hand way.

"Does she love you?"

"I think so."

"Then tell her she'll have to wait until you're free to tell her everything. You must convince her she can't tell anyone who she is. If that information gets out, her life will be in jeopardy as well as yours."

"I'll make sure she understands."

They were slowing down now and Dengler saw from the passing scene outside they were in downtown Baltimore, near the financial district.

"Here," Strong said, handing Dengler a card. "There's an address on the back."

The limo pulled to a stop. Across the street Dengler saw the Pontiac parked at the curb. Strong opened a case secreted under the seat and removed a weapon Dengler recognized immediately. It was the Walther PPK he'd bought when he entered the Army. Someone had replaced the broken grip. "Thought you might like to have this back," Strong said with a smile.

"How did you get it?"

"Stafford turned it in for printing. It was found in what was left of the car in Santa Barbara after they towed it into the wrecking yard."

"He planted it," Dengler stated simply.

"Yeah, that's the way we figured it, too," Lowry said. "Otherwise someone would have found it that night. I had the grip fixed. Hope you don't mind?"

"No. I broke it at the Monroe house."

"Careful. It's loaded," Strong warned him.

"The items you requested," Lowry said. "From the alley. I had them put in your trunk."

The heroin, Dengler realized. He gestured a thanks. "Tomorrow," he said, starting to get out, and then stopped with the door open a crack. "One last thing," he said, "what does the 'Q' in Q Force stand for?"

"Quid pro quo," Lowry said. "Give and take. The Director created Q Force when he found out the CIA boys have their own special task force aimed at spying on us."

Strong grinned. "It means 'tit for tat.'" he said in his melodious southern accent.

Dengler stood by the Pontiac and watched the limo pull away. It was a crisp night, clear as infinity. He tried to make his mind as clear. He'd begun to think of himself as a dying man, desperate, trapped and doomed, and suddenly he was being thrown a line. Dengler took the line because he had to. He wasn't completely trusting, though. It wasn't his nature to trust too much.

What would he tell Etta? How would he do it? Would she agree to go into the institution to dry out? Doubts. He had many doubts.

- 41 -

Dengler slipped behind the wheel of the Pontiac Catalina and started the engine. He was out of the city in twenty minutes and climbing into the mountains forty minutes after that. The roads were so empty of traffic he couldn't miss the headlights that seemed to stay with him in the rear view mirror.

Dengler checked the Walther PPK, found it had a full clip, and surprised himself by wishing he was holding a bigger, heavier, clumsier .45. That weapon had proven itself a killer, while he'd never fired the PPK in anger. Still, it was a weapon, and it was his weapon. He loaded a round into the chamber and placed the pistol beside him on the seat.

At the first opportunity Dengler got off the interstate and pulled to the side of the road. The car following him would have to pass this point if its driver intended to continue on his trail. Dengler took the PPK in hand and crossed the road to a small stand of trees. He didn't have to move behind them — their shadow swallowed him whole.

A minute later the Chevrolet slowed as it neared the Pontiac. When it stopped the passenger strained to look out the window in both directions, forward and back on the highway. The engine thudded noisily, its pistons sending echoes to the pavement through the pan. Dengler waited until the man on the passenger side of the car got out, then stepped from the shadows and said, "'Night, Wesley."

Wesley Strong, both hands on the steering wheel, grinned and said, "'Night, David." He appeared not at all surprised to see David Dengler standing five feet from him with a weapon aimed in his direction.

"I didn't think I'd be seeing you so soon."

"Actually, I kind of expected to be seeing you, David. You see, Jerry Fisch here and I are acting as your bodyguards."

Fisch was one of the agents seen earlier at the alley, and later on the beach with Wes. He was possibly thirty, with thinning hair and a nose like a tomahawk. Dengler returned his gaze to Strong.

"Acting?"

"Well, we're sort of your bodyguards."

"I don't need to be guarded, Wesley."

"We think you do, David. Now why don't you be a 'good old boy' and just sort of forget we're here. We'll follow you on up to that little cabin where you've been hiding your girlfriend and we'll keep watch over you while you sleep."

Dengler looked at him a moment. *Cabin? A guess.* Where else would he be going on this road? A dog barked distantly. The sound was lonely and longing. "What really bothers me," Dengler said, "is you didn't mention anything about this when you dropped me off an hour ago."

"David, you're going to turn yourself over to us tomorrow, lock, stock, and barrel. We don't have to follow you to betray you. However, it is possible one of the CIA guys has a fix on you. We like to run surprises, even on each other, and we don't like to talk in confined spaces like a limo, even after they've been swept."

"That's a crock," Dengler said. "Let me translate that for you. You're still not sure I'm coming in, so you figured you'd keep an eye on me just to make sure I didn't get confused or scared and run away."

"Isn't that what I just said?" Strong said with a rueful smile. "Something like that, anyway?"

"What if I asked you not to do this?" Dengler said, squatting in front of the car and preparing to place the PPK back into its overlarge holster.

"Orders are orders, David."

Dengler stopped the slide of the weapon into the shoulder holster, pulled it out, aimed it lazily at the Chevy's front tire and fired. The front end of the car lurched downward.

"See you tomorrow," Dengler told Strong as he walked to the Pontiac. In a moment, Strong and his partner Fisch were two shrinking forms in the rear-view mirror, little men with big gestures.

Once he was back on the road, Dengler dismissed them from his mind and thought about Etta and how difficult it would be to talk her into committing herself to a hospital without him there to help. It was going to be hard enough without two FBI agents sitting guard outside the cabin. In truth, Dengler wasn't sure he could talk her into it. As much as he loved her, as much as he'd grown to know what motivated her, she remained a mystery to him, and there was no doubt Etta Warren had a mind of her own. He didn't think she needed him enough to do as he told her.

It was after 3:00 A.M. when Dengler pulled the Pontiac into the little cabin court near the lake and parked it beneath the big tree. A full moon had risen. It cast the cabin road in pearly light, and reflected from the lake's surface like quicksilver in sand. He lingered halfway to the porch for several moments, thinking about Etta and how long it took him to find her again. Then he ascended the creaking steps and went inside.

The house was totally dark. She was in bed asleep, the shades up and the room bathed in silver moonlight. She was naked and half out of the covers, her hair a red shock on the pillow and her shoulders and breasts pale and pure in the natural light. Dengler stripped and fell in beside her, her bottom to his groin, her back to his chest, and slid his arms around her so his wrist was beneath her breasts. Her smell was a passage to where his hopes lived, a dream odor that was hers and not from a bottle. As Dengler felt the rhythm of her body, the rise and fall of her rib cage and the beat of blood through her veins, he remembered how easily life was lost — he'd taken more than one himself recently, and seen others who lost theirs this very night. He knew holding her here in his arms, this life was the most important in the world to him. He also knew she could spend her life any way she wanted and there was nothing he could do about it.

She awakened slowly. "David?"

"Who do you think?" He regretted asking it. Too many 'Who do you thinks' had spooned behind this woman since he was forced to give her up.

"Hi, sweetheart," she said. Sleepy. Her voice was full of sleep, and her breath smelled of dreams hours old. "Did you get it?" she said.

"I got it."

"Oh, good. Any trouble?"

Dengler thought about it a moment. "Not really," he told her.

"Good."

She shifted her hips slightly, touching him, and it made Dengler think of the first time he took Etta from behind, against his father's bedpost. The thought aroused him. She shifted again, trapping his manhood between her buttocks. "I have something to tell you, Davey," she said, using the name she always used when they were naked together and about to make love. "But first..."

He was rigid in a minute, and she wet a few moments later. Etta pulled her legs up into her chest, exposing her womanhood, and took him inside her. When Dengler moved to caress her she pushed his hands away and told him, "No. Let me do this." In moments they were apart except for their loins, and ten exquisite minutes after she made him come with a gasp and a sigh.

Etta rolled over. Dengler saw she was wide awake now. She sat up, cupping her breasts in a forearm so they wouldn't bounce and ran for the bathroom. When she returned he started to get up, but she told him, "No. I brought a washcloth. I'll do it." She washed him and then laid the cloth aside.

He knew she was serious. He knew something was coming. Finally she said, "David, I love you."

"You know how I —" She stopped him with her hand, crossing his lips.

"David, I love you," she said again, "but you should try to forget about me, because I'm a whore and I'm a junkie. I've done too many things, too many awful things, for you to keep loving me."

"Okay," he said. The room thundered with silence. Then he continued. "I'll get the gun. We can both die."

She smiled at that. It was an incongruous smile and might have meant nothing like what it was supposed to mean. Her green eyes were filling with tears.

"Is that the way you feel?" she asked.

"That's the way I feel."

"You poor son-of-a-bitch."

"I could die right now, and I'd be lucky loving you."

"Why, David? Why? I don't understand." He watched the moonlight glisten from her tears as they fell toward the bed linen, creating tiny riverbeds on her cheeks and breasts and legs.

"I don't either."

"I can't give you babies, David. I told you that."

"I don't want children. I want you."

She sighed. He watched her shoulders sag. She wasn't looking forward to this, whatever 'this' was. She looked out the window at the lake, and beyond where the mountains jutted into the moonlight. "I've lied to you, David," she said.

"How?"

"The first night I took the car key down to Owen. I told him I needed a copy 'cause I lost our backup, but I was afraid to tell you. He went into the village the next morning and had a copy made, and left it on the porch for me, to keep me out of trouble, you know?"

"You had your own supply of heroin?"

"I cut it with talcum powder, but gave myself more when you weren't around, so you wouldn't know. That's why I've been doing so good, no withdrawal symptoms, no shakes or any of that. You wouldn't have liked me if I was withdrawing, because believe me it's not like what you got the last several months."

Dengler grinned. There was no humor in it. "I thought things had been going pretty smooth."

"I'm a liar, David. I'm a thief, too. I used to go through the pockets of my street johns and steal their money. I'm a liar, and a thief, and a whore, and I'm not good enough for you."

Her eyes were a swamp of tears now, and her breaths came in short gasps. Dengler pushed aside his anger about the heroin with the admission he'd never loved, or wanted, anyone this much in his life. He reached out and took her crimson hair into his hand, moving to cup the back of her head.

"I'm going to get help for you," he told her, emotion rising in his voice and shaming him. He fought it down. "I'm going to get help for you and get you off this drug. But, first —" He kissed her, tasting the salt of her tears on her lips, feeling the fullness of them, touching for a fleeting moment her tongue and smelling the sleep still lingering in her. "But first I'm going to marry you."

"Marry me?"

"Tomorrow morning," he told her.

- 42 -

Dengler woke shortly after nine. He was alone in the bed. He wrapped a towel around himself and wandered into the kitchen where he found Etta giving herself a fix. She looked up and said, "Sit down. I'll make you some breakfast," as if injecting heroin into one's veins was the normal morning pursuit of the American housewife. The drug reached her bloodstream and in a moment she had to sit down, so Dengler assumed her position in the kitchen and began breakfast.

"We have to hurry," he told her.

"Why?" She asked the question, but there was no imperative in her voice. He could answer it, or not, she wouldn't care.

"We have to get packed up. I want to buy you some clothes."

"Why?"

"Because I want you to look great when we get married," he said.

Etta grinned. "Oh, David, you didn't mean that last night, did you? I won't hold you to it."

Ice formed on his spine. "We're getting married," he told her. Dengler cracked eggs and emptied them into the bowl, poured milk on top, and started beating them.

"No, David," she said after a moment. "It's okay. You don't want to marry me. I'm a whore, David. Who would want to marry a whore?" She said these things with a lilting voice that dispelled their meaning, smiling all the while and swooning with ecstasy at what the drug was doing to her. Dengler realized what had happened. She'd found the new supply of heroin, the new, almost limitless supply.

"How much have you taken?" he demanded, grabbing her arms and forcing her to look up at him. "How much?"

"Now David, really —" she began, but Dengler slapped her and her head revolved on her shoulders like a roly-poly doll.

"How much?" he said again.

"I know what I'm doing."

"You don't know shit." he told her. "What you don't know would float the fucking navy. Now tell me — how much?"

"I poked it a little, David, that's all."

"You poked it?"

"Sure. Gave it a little nudge, you know? I treated myself, because really, David, there's enough out there to last forever. Look, look— I don't need to go into some hospital. You can, we can— just..."

"What? We can just what?" He was yelling at her now, screaming with anger and a fear he'd never known before. "We can just what?"

"Keep on going, David. The way we are. We can go anywhere, do anything, because, because— there's enough out there to last forever. For-fucking-ever. So I, we don't, don't, need to —"

Her eyes rolled back into her head and Dengler knew she'd overdosed, possibly on purpose, possibly to escape him because she didn't want to marry him, she wanted to leave him alive in the world and go to where the meaning of death was to escape him.

"GOD DAMN IT." Dengler shouted. Etta couldn't hear him. She was merely a rag doll held between his hands.

Dengler exploded into the living room, picked up the phone, tried to dial and then realized he'd disconnected it their first day in the cabin. Then he burst through the screen door screaming "Help. Help." and ran toward Owen's cabin.

Owen wasn't at his cabin — he was an early riser and was probably already out on the lake fishing — but Dengler burst inside and dialed for the operator. It rang long enough for Abraham Lincoln to die, long enough for Moses and Mozart and Alexander Graham Bell all to die, one after another, while the phone rang and it was all he could think of, death. Then a voice answered, "Operator. Can I help you?"

"I need an ambulance. It's an emergency."

It was twenty minutes before the ambulance arrived. She'd been in the coma for almost half an hour by then. When the ambulance attendants entered the kitchen Dengler spared no propriety. "Heroin," he said quietly as he kneeled above her. "She's overdosing on heroin."

"Out of the way," one of the attendants ordered. They had her out to the ambulance and loaded in two minutes, and were gone an instant later.

Dengler went into the bedroom and pulled on the same clothes he'd worn the previous day. He went outside and opened the Pontiac's trunk. He found the white powder, so much white powder he imagined it would have 'fixed' Etta for years, and brought it back into the kitchen, emptied the bag into the sink and washed its contents into the drain.

Dengler gathered up the few things he needed to take with him, dropped a hundred-dollar bill on the kitchen table, and left.

It was a small thirty-bed hospital. It didn't even have an emergency room. He had to stop two people on the street to find out where it was located, the second person because he was so panicked he couldn't remember the first one's directions. He parked in the small parking lot at the front and went inside. He was sure she was dead, but no, the nurse told him she was still being treated and asked him whether he would fill out a few papers. He agreed anxiously and began lying from the start, lying so badly it became obvious to the nurse who left the papers on the counter and went into a back room.

A man wearing a white tunic came out and stood behind the counter. "Hello," he said perfunctorily. "I'm the facility administrator, Phil Costanza. I'm afraid I have to ask this. Do you have insurance, sir?"

"Is she okay?"

"She's still receiving treatment," Phil told him. "I'll be able to tell you more in a little while. In the meantime, though, we've got to nail down a few things. Set the record straight, so to speak. Now, do you have insurance?"

Dengler opened his wallet and removed five crisp hundred-dollar bills and laid them on the counter. When Phil made no move for them, Dengler shoved them toward him and asked, "On account. Now could you please go in there and find out how my wife is doing?" He said this with an authority that made Phil go into the back on a mission for knowledge.

Dengler sat down.

Then he stood up. The intelligence operative alive and aware in him knew what all of this meant. As a matter of course, Stafford's people would be looking for an OD victim, particularly a woman. He had hours at most, possibly minutes, before one of Stafford's operatives walked in the front door.

Dengler went to the phone. Strong's card was still in his wallet, although the back contained only an address. The pre-printed legend said, *Adam Avorkian Oriental Carpets*, with an address in D.C. and a telephone number. Dengler got change from a clerk at the counter, taking the opportunity again to ask how Etta was and receiving the same answer as before, and then returned to the phone and dialed the number. A male voice answered.

"Avorkian Oriental Carpets," the voice said.

"Adam Avorkian, please."

"He's not here right now."

"I'm supposed to meet Adam at noon, but I'm afraid I can't now. There's been an accident."

"I can call Adam and have him call you. What's your number?"

Dengler told him the number, hung up and sat down as near the phone as the floor-bolted chairs would allow. The phone rang in three minutes.

"David?" It was Wesley Strong.

"Jesus. Look, Wesley, I can't meet you. There's an emergency. Etta's OD'd and I've taken her to a hospital —"

"Which one?"

Dengler had to go to the counter to get the name of the place and while there asked again about Etta, receiving no answer. He took a business card from the counter with the name and address of the clinic printed on it. He returned to the phone and read the address to Strong.

"Listen," Strong told him, "they're waiting for something like this, David. How long have you been there?"

"Ten minutes. Twenty."

"We'll be there within two hours. Go outside. Take a walk around the town. Buy a magazine and go sit in the park. We'll rendezvous at 11:30, okay?"

"I don't know if I can do that," Dengler said.

"Make yourself do it. They won't harm her, David, and they won't be able to get her out of there before we arrive."

"Okay," Dengler told him, "I'll take evasive action."

"You do that. An hour, David."

"Right."

Dengler hung up. He composed himself. He had enough sense to bring the Walther PPK along, but the other weapons were back at the cabin. The PPK had one clip, seven rounds, and that was it.

He saw Phil the facility administrator enter the reception area and Dengler sprang forward to meet him at the counter.

"How is she?" Dengler asked.

"She's stabilized. The resident said that as overdose cases go, this one isn't excessive. She's been using heroin for some time, hasn't she?" he said. "For years?"

"Yeah," Dengler responded, elated Etta would survive and return to him.

"I'm afraid we're obliged to inform the police whenever we find cases of this sort," Phil told him.

"Could you wait, say, two hours before you made the call? Get busy with something and forget?"

"I'm afraid I —"

"Shouldn't I put something on account here?" Dengler asked him.

"A couple of hundred dollars, just on account." He pulled out two more crisp hundred dollar bills and laid them on the counter. Phil looked at the money a long moment, and then said, "Let me write you a receipt for that."

"Okay."

Outside, the day was clear and warm and promising to become hot. The morning sun reflected off of every car bumper in the parking lot, and many of the windshields too, blinding him momentarily. The previous week the weather had been overcast and cold.

Even though there was a chance he would see action again soon, and a chance this entire affair damaged him with the FBI even before his career began, the only emotion he felt was elation Etta was going to be okay. He would have her back.

Dengler crossed the parking lot to the street and then looked up and down for somewhere to go. There were three bars within sight, but he didn't want to spend the next hour nursing a drink and being a magnet for every suspicion the locals might have about a stranger. Instead, he moved for the market two blocks south.

Dengler found a magazine rack just inside the market and was surprised the face of the man who was supposed to be David Dengler, but wasn't, looked back at him from the cover of the Police Gazette. *Agent Killer Still At Large*, the headline read. He quickly perused the story, found it was full of inaccuracies and outright lies, and replaced it on the stand. The Baltimore Sun reported Kennedy and Khrushchev had come to some kind of accord. *Missiles To Go*, the headline proclaimed. *Eyeball To Eyeball*, a sub-headline stated, *Khrushchev Blinked*. "Glad somebody did," Dengler said out loud.

- 43 -

At 11:30 A.M. Dengler crossed the street at a clip and walked back toward the clinic. When he arrived at the parking lot he saw several vehicles not parked there before, a GMC stepvan and two sedans. He stopped and considered his options. There was no way for him to know up front if these cars were driven here by Strong's men, Stafford's men, or just by people receiving medical care. The stepvan looked identical to the those he'd seen the FBI use on field missions before, but as far as he knew, it could have been a bakery truck.

Dengler walked toward the back of the clinic, which crossed another section of the building in a T. This was the hospital proper. He tried a back door, but it was locked. Another door located twenty yards farther back led into the hospital itself. It too was locked. He realized he would have to go in through the front door.

Dengler paused before entering and glanced in through the double glass doors, but saw no one because of the L-shape of the room. Before entering he drew the Walther PPK and slid it into the front pocket of his jeans.

Two men in suits sat in the waiting area. Dengler didn't recognize them from the previous night. He walked past them. At the counter he asked the clerk, "How's Mrs. Crandall doing?" Crandall was the name he gave when Etta was admitted.

"She's awake and alert now, Mr. Crandall."

"I'd like to see her."

"Let me talk with the doctor."

The clerk disappeared into the back. Dengler turned and looked at the two suited men. They looked back. No emotion. No recognition. He twisted back around just in time to see Phil Costanza, the facility administrator, reenter the back area with a look Dengler interpreted as trouble. His mind went to war readiness mode in an instant.

The counter stretched across the front of the waiting area and around its side, leading to two bathrooms and a door with a sign that said *Authorized Personnel Only*. *Okay*, Dengler thought, *I'll make for the bathrooms. I can draw the PPK there without raising anyone's concern, then make for the back area and get Etta.*

Even as he thought this, a voice asked, "David Lawrence Dengler?"

Dengler turned and found one of the two suited men standing beside him. He felt rather than saw the other one behind him. "I'm sorry, were you saying something?"

"Are you David Lawrence Dengler?"

"No, sorry, you've got the wrong guy," Dengler said with a voice so convincing he saw doubt creep into the man's expression. It was short-term, however.

"Put your hands on the counter," he ordered.

"Do what?"

"Put your hands on the counter." the man behind him ordered. Dengler felt a gun barrel pressed against his spine and the man's spare hand frisking him. He found the Walther PPK in seconds, long before Dengler's two palms were pressed to the counter against his will.

An ID was flashed before his eyes. "FBI. You are under arrest, David Lawrence Dengler, for murder."

"You have just arrested the wrong man," Dengler told them. The number of agents involved in the operation grew as two more suited men joined the first from the back of the clinic, and another two entered from the front door. *Six men*, Dengler thought quickly. *An operation.* They handcuffed him and moved him toward the door.

Outside they walked him toward the stepvan he saw earlier. Its rear door swung open. A man squatted on the truck deck and looked down at Dengler as the two agents held him. He was possibly forty, with brown hair prematurely streaked with gray and slightly bulging eyes. His mouth was straight and narrow with an imperfection at one end that looked like an exclamation point had been laid on its side. He surveyed Dengler for a moment before he said, "He doesn't look like much, does he?"

"Who are you people?" Dengler said. It was the only thing he could think to say without tipping what he knew.

"Is the girl ready to go?" the man in the stepvan asked.

"The doctor says she can be moved. She's still sedated." The answer came from one of Dengler's handlers.

"Is she going to be okay?" Dengler asked him.

"Shut up, asshole," he told Dengler, "or I'll do you right here."

"Okay," the stepvan man ordered, "get him up here."

With his handcuffs binding his wrists behind him, Dengler didn't navigate the stepvan easily. The two men who stood behind him took some pleasure in making the ascent painful. Once inside, they directed him down onto his knees in the corner. "Get the girl," the leader ordered.

While they were gone Dengler turned on the floor so he could see the leader clearly. The leader squatted at the end of the van and smoked, sending gray air reeling into the clear morning sky.

"Who are you people?" Dengler said again.

"Does it matter?" the leader said with a smile.

"You've made a mistake, pal," Dengler told him. "You've made a big mistake."

The leader stood and walked to Dengler and kicked him once in the face. Blood seeped from between his lips, but he said nothing. The leader squatted before Dengler and said, "That's a down payment for the men you murdered, David Lawrence Dengler."

Etta was brought to the van on a stretcher. Phil Costanza, the facility administrator, followed the two orderlies who carried the stretcher, giving instructions to one of the 'FBI agents' who walked beside him. When he saw Dengler sitting handcuffed at the far end of the stepvan with blood on his face and chest, he blanched. "What happened to that man?" he asked.

"He tripped when we were loading him," the leader reported. "Hit his head on the step."

"Let's get him treatment," Phil ordered. He was surprised when no one moved to follow the order.

"We'll treat him where we're going. It's not far."

"Really," Phil said. "I must protest —"

"Go away," the leader ordered as two agents leaped into the back of the van. The four remaining men closed the big doors.

Dengler paid none of this any concern. He cared only for Etta, who lay nude beneath a sheet. Her clothes were folded neatly on her stomach. She looked as if she were sleeping, pale but alive. They would have to kill her too, of course. He knew that. *Damn it, Wesley, where are you?*

The van's engine sounded and Dengler heard the whine of the differential and drive shaft as the vehicle was put into motion. The leader and the two other 'FBI agents' sat down at the opposite end of the box and looked at him.

"How far?" one asked.

"Five, ten miles," the leader said. "Somewhere private."

"What about the girl?"

"Her too."

Wesley!

Dengler lost himself in thoughts of death. Would Etta and Dengler survive the destruction of their bodies? Dengler thought of Marilyn Monroe. Did she exist somewhere, free from her mortal ties, free from pain and suffering and the occasional sinus headache? He didn't think so. Life was a light, and death a one-way switch. That's how he saw it. He was strangely comforted to know Etta wouldn't survive her murder to mourn its loss, or him to mourn her.

As they rode, Dengler began to inch closer to her until finally the side of his leg came into contact with her hand, which had fallen from the stretcher to the stepvan floor. He couldn't 'feel' her as he might have with his fingers, but he felt her closeness.

The man Dengler thought of as the leader of this group of operatives smiled when he saw Dengler straining to be in contact with Etta.

Dengler knew at that moment he hated him and, given the opportunity, would kill him.

- 44 -

Dengler lost count of the passing minutes. He guessed at least twenty had elapsed from the time the van started moving until he heard brakes squeal and it started to slow down. The team leader removed a small microphone from a canvas satchel. He extended the aerial of a device hidden in the bag. "What is it?" he said.

"Road block," a voice answered amid static noise. Dengler presumed it was the stepvan driver or his partner with a radio up front. "One County Sheriff's black-and-white and four unmarked sedans."

"Fake it," the team leader said. The van ground to a halt, its brakes squealing all the way. Dengler heard the thump sound of the clutch being released in the driver's compartment.

For a moment there was no sound. Then a conversation warbled through the thin metal skin of the van. "What's going on?" The driver.

"We have a fugitive on the run. Identify yourself and state your business."

"FBI," the driver said. "This is an official FBI operation. We've got our own fugitive we just captured up the road."

"You don't say?" Another voice. One Dengler knew. Wesley Strong. "Kind of curious, don't you think? You're FBI. I'm FBI."

Dengler watched as the team leader groaned and stood up. "One of you stay with him," he ordered, gesturing at Dengler. He opened the rear door of the van. "Special Agent Strong," he called out as one of the two doors swung completely open. "What brings you to podunk central?" He stepped out of the van as Strong and two real FBI agents carrying M2 auto-carbines stepped around the end of the vehicle.

"Agent Keller," Strong said, smiling with a cobra's friendliness. His look past Keller took in Dengler and Etta and the operative guarding them. "The last I heard, you were still with the CIA. Did you see the error of your ways and join the FBI?"

"An innocent subterfuge," Keller said with a professional grin.

"I must insist your man get out of the vehicle, Jim," Strong told him.

"He's guarding the fugitive."

"Not anymore."

"Out," Keller ordered. The CIA operative stood and betrayed a worried look before he stepped from the van.

"I presume this individual is David Lawrence Dengler?"

"You presume correctly," Keller said.

"And I presume as well that rather than contact the appropriate law enforcement agency, the FBI, when you learned of the whereabouts of the fugitive, instead you took it upon yourself to apprehend David Lawrence Dengler?"

"He didn't kill two of your agents, Wes."

"I'm sorry, Jim, but I'm going to have to make an issue out of this," Strong told him.

"We were going to turn him over to you," Keller protested. "But first we were going to —"

"*Interrogate* him. Judging by the blood on his face, that's already begun."

"He slipped and fell," one of the CIA agents offered. "Really. It was my fault. I was guiding him, and I slipped and —"

"Shut up," Keller ordered, seeing it was more than futile, it was embarrassing.

"I have to make an issue of this, Jim."

"Okay. You have to make an issue of it."

"It's a federal crime. You're not authorized to pursue or apprehend federal fugitives. Also, the use of falsified FBI ID is a federal crime."

"Okay, Wes, goddamn it, make the issue."

"I want your IDs, and I want your pieces."

"You're placing us under arrest?" Keller clearly couldn't believe it. "No. Fuck you, no."

"You don't have room to bargain here, Jim. I want your pieces, and I want your IDs. Now."

Dengler watched Keller as he surveyed the situation. His men were armed, but their weapons were not drawn. Strong's men were armed with automatic weapons, and they were drawn. He acquiesced to the inevitable. "Okay. Listen up. Turn over your pieces and your IDs. This is only a temporary situation, so don't make a big deal out of it."

Once the CIA operatives were all disarmed, Strong ordered, "Okay. Everyone turn around and face the van."

Keller understood the situation immediately. "Handcuffs? Jesus Christ, Strong, is this really necessary? Handcuffs?"

Strong said nothing in reply and once all of the CIA operatives were in handcuffs he jumped up onto the bed of the stepvan and released Dengler using keys taken from Keller. "The next time you shoot out one of my tires, asshole," he told Dengler in a tone barely above a whisper, "I'm going to let the wolves eat you. How do you feel?" Strong gave Dengler his kerchief to wipe the blood from his face.

"I'm fine. I want to get her to a hospital."

"Already set up. Come on out."

Dengler touched Etta. It was brief and told him no more about her condition than he knew before, but it was sweet to touch her again this side of death. He moved from the back of the van and stepped outside.

All seven CIA agents were lined up against the van facing it. Dengler finished wiping the blood from his mouth, which was sore and beginning to swell. Now that his side was in charge, he could dispense the justice. The team leader, the man Strong identified as Agent Jim Keller, was almost indistinguishable from the others with his back turned, but Dengler found him and spun him around. His fist was inches from striking Keller's face when he caught; Keller's expression stopped him from following through. At the moment Keller realized Dengler was free to hit him, Dengler saw a look of abject fear ignite there.

"What is this?" Keller asked Strong, who took no action to stop Dengler. "What is this? WHAT IS THIS, GOD DAMN IT?"

"What is what?" Strong said.

"Why have you released Dengler? Why have you released him? He's a killer. He's a goddamn murderer, Strong."

"Keep your voice down," Strong told him. "You'll scare the chickens and ducks and whatever other kind of animals they've got out here."

"Tell me why." It was a demand spoken by a man who was used to having his demands answered.

"You made a mistake, Jim. This man isn't David Lawrence Dengler. We've already apprehended David Lawrence Dengler. This man is FBI Special Agent Jack Fleming who, I must admit, bears a slight resemblance to Dengler."

Keller merely stared at Strong. There was nothing more he could say. Obviously, Keller didn't 'buy' the Fleming story, and more, realized immediately Dengler had made some kind of separate deal with the FBI. Dengler saw it in his expression. Dengler also guessed Agent Keller didn't know the men Dengler killed were Mafia hit men. He'd bought the cover story put out by Gray Stafford and the CIA, and now was being victimized by the lies of his own organization.

Etta was off-loaded into a smaller van, a Ford Econoline, and Dengler went to assist. She was still unconscious. Dengler held her limp hand during the transfer and asked one of the agents, "Where are you taking her?" before Wesley called for him.

"She'll be okay, Jack," he said, but Dengler didn't recognize his new name and ignored him until Strong came to get him. By this time the CIA men were being loaded into the van, and the black-and-white sheriff's car was disappearing down the road. "It's okay. I've made arrangements for her to go into a very private institution. She'll get the best of care. You can start visiting her this weekend, if you want."

Dengler allowed the back door of the Econoline to be closed and caught a last glimpse of her as it shut. Then the van was moving and Strong marshaled Dengler's attention to the events at hand.

"We've got to find a place to cool our heels for awhile," Strong told him as they walked back toward the stepvan, shoes crunching in gravel. The CIA chase car was being turned around by two of Strong's men and headed back toward town.

"Why?" Dengler was still numbed by events, but even so caught the look of incredulity on Strong's face.

"Jack, I've got to wait for instructions about what to do with them."

Dengler realized for the first time the problem these prisoners posed. They were sent to kill him. If released now, the CIA would learn David Dengler was alive and working for the FBI. The CIA would certainly make another attempt on Dengler's life, but that wasn't the worst of it, at least not from the FBI's point of view. The information that Dengler was a ward of the FBI would signal open warfare between the two agencies. It would tip the existence of Q Force, presuming the CIA wasn't already aware of its existence, and it would make common knowledge the secret investigation the FBI was conducting into the CIA's connection to organized crime. If the President were a part of that conspiracy, it would probably mean the death of every agent here, Dengler included, and possibly even The Director himself.

They would have to kill all of the CIA agents.

"No." Dengler told Strong, grabbing his arm. "We can't."

"Jack." Wesley protested, wrenching his arm free.

"We're not going to kill them!" Dengler said.

"Keep your voice down, goddamn it." The warning, as much as anything, told Dengler he was right, they would have to kill these men. "Get in the car and shut up."

"No." Dengler said again, but it was more of a plea now, rather than a declaration.

"Get in the car."

With two agents in the van, and Dengler with Strong, there were just enough men left to drive all of the cars. Strong's Ford Galaxy took the lead, followed by one sedan, the stepvan, and two more sedans.

Dengler sat in the passenger seat and said nothing for a long while. "I can't do this," Dengler told Strong after awhile. "I can't kill innocent men."

"It's not my decision," Strong said angrily, "and it sure as hell isn't yours."

"They could be jailed somewhere," Dengler said dully. "That would be —"

"Kidnapping," Strong supplied with a grimace. "What if one escaped? Forget that. What about their families? Forget even that. What if the entire goddamn CIA is in bed with the Mob, and the President, too? What if..."

They all have to die., Dengler thought, denying it to himself even as he thought it. Clearly, there was no other answer. Just as clearly David Dengler knew he couldn't kill someone in cold blood. He couldn't do it. He turned away from Strong and took refuge in silence.

- 45 -

There was a road several miles down the highway, barely a dirt path of ruts and narrow points between trees, a way that led to somewhere even more desolate. The lead sedan with two agents continued on the highway, while the rest of the caravan turned off onto the road and within minutes was swallowed by the countryside, becoming a part of it.

They passed an abandoned farmhouse and took an even smaller road, and when it ended in a small depression in the earth, they lined the convoy up beneath a copse of trees whose shade was cheery and very unreal. Before getting out of the sedan Strong turned Dengler's face toward him and assessed the damage from the earlier kick to his face. Dengler knew his lips were swelling, but he didn't know how badly until he said, "What?" and the words slurred.

"Come on," Strong said in a subdued tone. "I have something for you."

Outside, Dengler used the side-view mirror to look at his mouth and was startled by what he saw. He would have to eat out of a straw for a week or so.

The remaining six agents spread out in groups of two to smoke and talk, while the CIA operatives remained sequestered inside the stepvan. Strong opened the Ford's trunk. "Come here," he said. Dengler joined him. Strong opened a briefcase. Inside were a number of official IDs including a badge case with an FBI ID for one Jack Fleming, with a photograph of Dengler.

Dengler rummaged through the paperwork. He found a birth certificate and a social security card, both properly aged. He also found a D.C. driver's license, a Marine Corps honorable discharge, a bachelor of science degree from Rutgers, library cards from several jurisdictions including New York City, a health club membership card from a place called Manhassat Street, all made out to one Jack J. (for James) Fleming. According to the documents he was twenty-seven years old, was born in Falls Church, Va., and had been a member of the Federal Bureau of Investigation for eighteen months. To Dengler's eye, the documents were absolutely authentic.

"It will take awhile for the corroborating paperwork to be placed, of course. We have to get the library cards put in the appropriate files, and your transcripts and attendance records at Rutgers probably won't go in until next week. Your federal government identification won't be authentic until Friday, but after that you'll draw a regular paycheck from the FBI."

"Jesus," Dengler whispered, fingering the documents, in particular the leather badge case where his face and the shield of the FBI countered one another. The leather, he noted, looked as if it had been in someone's pocket for a while.

"There's more," Strong said, pushing the paperwork aside to remove a smaller case Dengler knew held a weapon. He opened it and Dengler removed an absolutely pristine .38 caliber snub nose revolver. "Standard bureau issue," he said. "Careful. It's loaded." Strong removed a shoulder holster from another box and handed it to him. "You might as well get used to the feel of the thing."

"I've been carrying around a .45 for weeks now. This I won't have to get used to."

"Yeah, the .45's a monster all right."

Strong leaned against the bumper and withdrew a cigarette from his coat pocket. "Smoke?" he said. Dengler declined. "You became a different person today," Strong told him, lighting the cigarette with a match. "Get that into your mind. David Dengler is a name from the past. From this moment on you're Jack Fleming. Respond to the name, convince yourself you are the name, because otherwise you jeopardize your life."

"I know."

One hour stretched into two as they waited for instructions.

Finally the two agents who left earlier returned. They reported directly to Strong, who reacted by throwing Dengler a look.

"Jack." Strong called and Dengler almost growled an obscenity back at him for using his new name, the name they gave him, the name they would have him use as a murderer of innocent men. "Over here, Jack." Strong insisted.

"Fuck you. No." Dengler retorted beneath his breath. He'd spent the entire time standing at the periphery of the tree canopy, not in sun, not in shade. He was thirty yards from the lead car, another twenty from the stepvan jailing Keller and his men.

Strong said, "Shit," loud enough to be heard by everyone and trotted across the open ground to Dengler. "Jesus Christ," he told Dengler as he arrived at his side, "do you think you live in a goddamn vacuum?"

"I won't do it."

"Fine," Strong said, his explosive demeanor suddenly replaced by an icy rage. "You listen to me — every man here has gone out on a limb for you. Every man here placed himself in jeopardy last night when we yanked you out of that alley. Every man. You can take your goddamn holier-than-thou posture if you want to, but it doesn't inspire confidence in any of us. It won't with The Director, either. We're the only friends you've got. In this organization we share the glory, and we share the shit. Today the menu says shit. I've got my orders. They're the only orders possible under these circumstances. Choose."

Strong turned and marched toward the parked vehicles. Dengler watched him go, the rational part of him knowing he was right, murdering these men was the only rational thing to do while his conscience protested that it was wrong.

Dengler watched Keller and his men led out of the stepvan, hands cuffed behind them. He saw Keller realize what was about to happen. "No. You can't do this." Keller protested. A part of Dengler wanted to scream, "He's right. Let them go." Dengler said nothing. If Keller were let go, Dengler would die. Etta would die.

Strong and his agents lined Keller and his men up along the road. Several of Keller's men were sobbing. Most faced mortality stoically. These were men who had dispensed their own justice on more than one occasion, had in fact planned much the same fate for Dengler. One man prayed. Another whispered something only he could hear.

Strong and his group stood five feet away from Keller and his men. There were seven CIA agents, and six FBI men, so it was clear one of the CIA operatives would live to see the others killed, and wait for his own murder in the interim. The last man was Keller. When Dengler saw the FBI men raise their weapons and take aim, a bellow erupted from him. He took off running across the open ground, drawing his new .38 caliber service revolver. "Stop." he yelled. Strong turned at the sound of his voice and Dengler saw him brace for an attack, bringing his own service revolver up in readiness.

Tears, sweat, saliva and snot ran from the various points of Dengler's face. His lips throbbed with pain, and his head echoed with his words as he continued to yell, "Stop. Stop." Keller looked at him with hope. Strong held his fire. "Stop." Dengler finished breathlessly as he arrived, as if just now emerging from a tank of gelatin. "Stop."

"Okay, David," Strong said softly. "We've stopped."

"No," Dengler said through gasping breaths. "No. Not David. Jack Fleming." Dengler steadied himself, squared his shoulders, and turned to face the condemned men. "Let's get this thing over with."

"Aim for the heart," Wes ordered.

The rounds sounded as if they had been fired from one weapon, not seven. Agent Jim Keller fell with a bullet from the weapon of FBI Special Agent Jack Fleming.

- 46 -

Even though Special Agent Jack Fleming participated in the execution, no one complained when he didn't help move the bodies to the back of the stepvan. Dengler walked ten paces away and leaned against the lead car, his legs weak, his hands shaking. He'd killed three people since that night almost three months before when he attempted to stop Marilyn Monroe's murder. The man newly christened Jack Fleming felt he deserved to die, deserved to pay for his sins, the biggest one to dream of being a secret agent, an operative in the James Bond mold.

He too had a license to kill.

Wesley Strong left the grunt work to the others and strolled to Dengler's side. "Your lips are going to split," Strong said matter-of-factly.

"Yeah."

"We should get some salve on them."

"Yeah, we should do that."

Strong took a position beside Dengler and both men watched the cleanup operation proceed. One agent removed a jacket from the body of one of the CIA operatives and began to scoop up blood-soaked sand and drop it into the coat.

"Keller knew you," Dengler said. It was a simple statement, and yet an extraordinary truth. There were thousands of agents in both agencies and the likelihood one would chance upon another he knew was infinitely remote.

"Seminar last year. In Paris, of all places. I was attending. He was covering. At least, I think he was. You know, writing up a service report for the Agency. We got drunk together."

"Good guy?"

"The best."

"How do you feel about killing him?" Dengler looked at Wesley Strong for the first time since the killing. He was pale.

"Awful," Strong said.

The convoy split up at the interstate with the stepvan heading in one direction with several of the sedans, and Strong's Ford Galaxy moving in the opposite direction.

"You have a place to stay tonight?" Strong said.

"No," Dengler replied. His thoughts were on Etta and how she must feel now, ensconced in an institution somewhere and beginning heroin withdrawal. More than anything he wanted to be in bed with her, wanted to feel her warm flesh against his, wanted to hold her, and be held in return.

"You can spend the night at my place," Strong told him. "Daisy won't mind. You might even luck out and get a home cooked meal, although Daisy's a full time student."

"Daisy?" Somehow the name Daisy didn't connect well with the name Wesley Strong.

"My wife, Daisy. Her mother met Scott Fitzgerald once at some college in Georgia. Made a big impression on her, meeting the greatest author of the age, so she named her daughter after Daisy in *The Great Gatsby*."

"You said something about dinner."

"When I'm home," Strong said with a grin, "which isn't often enough, Daisy makes an effort to cook."

"Kids?"

"Not 'till she gets her masters."

"I could use the company," Dengler said. "Jack Fleming doesn't know many people."

"No, I guess not."

Jack Fleming was less than an hour old, in fact, Dengler thought. They rode in silence for a time, the countryside slating by like a painted backdrop. Then Dengler said, "I need to know where Etta is," he said softly. "I need to know she's okay."

"Morningstar," Strong told him. "It's a small private clinic on the outskirts of Washington. There's a doctor there by the name of Grodin. She's his private patient. She was signed-in under the name of Talbert, or at least she should be by now. Etta Talbert. We used her real first name. You can see her whenever you want by identifying yourself as Ed Talbert."

"I'd like to see her this afternoon." It was already after 2:00 P.M. "Maybe we could stop by on the way in. You could drop me off, and I'll catch a cab to your place." Dengler could see it irritated Strong he was this devoted to a woman. He guessed Wesley Strong was one of those men who believed a woman should never hold such power over a man.

"Sure, if you want," Strong said after a moment. "Actually it won't be much out of the way at all. And I'll wait for you, supposing you don't take half the day."

"I just want to make sure she's okay," Dengler told him. "Let her know I haven't deserted her."

It was almost 4:00 P.M. when Strong's sedan pulled up in front of a tree-shaded clinic in a partially residential section of Washington. "I'll be back in half an hour," Dengler told him.

"Right."

Inside the ivy-faced entrance Dengler found a reception desk manned by a young woman of possibly twenty-two. "Yes, may I help you?"

"I'm Ed Talbert," Dengler told her. "My wife checked in earlier today."

Five minutes later Dr. Grodin stepped through the interior reception door and presented his hand. "Mr. Talbert." Dengler shook it.

"About my wife—" Dengler started.

"She's doing fine, Mr. Talbert," Grodin said, ushering him through the interior reception door into the clinic proper. "She's resting comfortably. She hasn't fully recovered from her earlier 'sedation,' but she is awake and she's suffering no discomfort."

The interior of the clinic was surprisingly low-key, with prints of famous paintings on the peach-colored walls and plants dividing spaces here and there. The actual treatment area was small with the living areas taking up most of the building's space. Love seats and overstuffed chairs near beds, drapes, and homey furnishings suggested anything but the sterile environment of a hospital. Farther back toward the rear of the building living spaces became locked rooms. Through wire-reinforced windows Dengler saw desperate faces, anger and madness.

Dengler realized Grodin had said nothing more after they left the proximity of the receptionist. He wondered how much he knew. Was he 'in' on the 'joke?' Or was he merely a doctor treating a patient and leaving the ugly details to family, friends, and the FBI?

"Doctor, at times my wife may say things that are... not true."

Grodin smiled before unlocking a door that led to a private wing. A sign stated, *No Admittance — Authorized Personnel Only*. They entered the next level of security from the locked rooms Dengler saw a moment before. Here were locked rooms *within* a locked room. "Mr. Talbert," Grodin said, waving him through the door, "Mrs. Talbert's condition has been carefully explained to me by her previous physician." Inside the enclosed area, Grodin again locked the door, this time from the inside. "Mrs. Talbert will be kept in a private wing, in a private room, that one there." He gestured at a locked door twenty paces away.

"My concern is—"

"We won't allow her to socialize with the other patients," Grodin continued, "even the ones in this wing. We don't want to impugn her reputation when she returns to public life." The words were spoken with utmost sincerity, and yet the small smile Dengler discerned at the ends of his mouth told him all he needed to know.

"Let me get something for your mouth," Grodin said. "I have a salve on hand."

- 47 -

The door was locked even though Etta was strapped into the bed. The room was spacious, with a living room area off to one side, flower print wallpaper, a television set, and a shelf of books. There was a reading lamp beside the overstuffed chair. All in all, it didn't look bad to Dengler. Etta would think it a prison.

She was sleeping, her red hair a tumble of curls and strands, her pale skin almost as white as the sheets. The straps were to keep her from falling out of bed, because her arms were free. She could unstrap herself at any time. The door, however, was locked.

He kissed her, and she woke instantly. For a long moment after Dengler's swollen lips pulled back from kissing her she looked at the ceiling, disoriented. Then she became aware of his presence and turned suddenly to look at him. "David."

"It's okay," Dengler told her. "You're going to be all right."

"Your face — what happened?"

"I was kicked in the teeth," he said matter-of-factly. "I'll be okay in a day or two."

"How?"

"Never mind. Doesn't matter."

"Oh," she said. "I was wondering what..."

"You over-dosed. You're going to be all right."

"Oh, yeah, I did," she said, and Dengler's heart sank. If she knew she'd over-dosed, then she must have done it on purpose. *Suicide?* "Where am I?" she asked.

"Morningstar. It's a hospital in Washington."

"This doesn't look like a hospital," she told him, quickly taking in the room.

"It isn't a regular hospital. It's a private—" He searched for the word and finally settled on 'institution' rather than 'sanitarium.' "It's an institution, a private facility. They'll be able to take care of you here, wean you off heroin and help you to get your health back."

Fear ran madly through her eyes. She knew what this meant. It meant pain. "David, I —"

"You can't call me David anymore," he told her.

"What?"

"I have a new name now. You have to learn it and use it. Forget David Dengler forever."

Even though she wasn't entirely coherent, Etta Warren knew what this meant — David Dengler had made a deal with the FBI.

He saw the realization creep into her eyes. "David—?"

"It's Jack," he told her. He took out the ID case and opened it. On one side the FBI ID card said he was Jack Fleming, FBI, Department of Justice; on the other wing of the folder, his new FBI shield.

"Jesus," she whispered.

"You were admitted here under the name Etta Talbert. When I visit you, I'll sign in as Ed Talbert. All of this will be untraceable later."

"David—"

"When you're well, I'm going to take you out of here and marry you, just like I said."

She turned away from him and looked out the window, which was barred on the outside but provided a view of a small courtyard. Dengler touched her shoulder trying to bring her back, but she refused to acknowledge him. Finally he said, "You don't have to marry me, if you don't want to, Etta. Once you get out of here you can do what you want. They're going to wean you off heroin so you can start a new life."

"Or go back to Guy?" she said. Her voice had an edge to it. Dengler hadn't told her Guy was dead. Now was not the time to tell her, he decided. "You can do what you want," he said softly.

"I can't do what I want right now, can I?" she said.

"No."

"And when I become Mrs. David Dengler or whatever your name will be by then, will I have anything to talk about with the other FBI wives? I mean, they can give me recipes and I can run down the 'do's and don'ts' of john management, what to do when one gets nasty, or how to 'pop' 'em quick so you can get back out on the street and catch another one, useful things like that."

"You'll learn new things," he said.

"And so will they," she spat at him. "So will they. How will you feel about that? What if it should come out, David—"

"I'm not David."

"Ed? Jack? What if one of your fellow agents lets it slip your wife used to be a whore but now she's a Presbyterian? How will I fit in then?"

Dengler's hands exploded to her shoulders and pinned her down to the bed. He looked directly into her eyes. "Listen, neither one of us will ever fit in. Ever. Except with each other. That's it. That's all we have. It's all that matters."

She accepted his angry gaze and returned it. "Do you know what you are, David? You're a john who got his rocks off in me for the first time, and now you can't give me up. That's all it is. Shit, David, I've had guys like you before. They bring their cherries to me, and I make a man out of them and they can't let go. That's all it is. I was your first time. That's all."

"Bullshit."

"No bullshit. Listen, a real man wouldn't even wipe his dick with me. You saw where I was. You saw what I was doing. A real man wouldn't even bother, but you've got this fixation on me because of something we had in high school."

"Etta," Dengler said evenly, "I love you."

"You can't love me, David. I'm a whore. And I've got a little secret for you — I've always been a whore. I was born a whore. When my daddy didn't love me, I went out and I sold my ass for him and I gave him every penny, and he knew I was a whore, David, he knew it. He took the money, but he called me a whore and he wouldn't love me — *he wouldn't love me* — but he took the money. All of you cock suckers take the money but you don't love me. How can I have any respect for you, David, if you say you love me?"

Dengler didn't know Etta sold herself for her father when she was in high school. Even when she told him about her awful past, she didn't tell him that. Now her angry, tearing eyes revealed her shame and hatred, shame she should have to seek the attention of men, and hatred because she would never really feel wanted by them.

"I love you," he said again. "If you can't respect me for loving you, then you'll have to find the answer in yourself."

"David, I can't love you," she said. "I WON'T LOVE YOU," she screamed.

"I'll be back," he said, trying to kiss her cheek. She turned away. He released her.

Dengler pressed the buzzer by the door. The orderly came a minute later.

- 48 -

Wesley Strong's Georgetown house was a beautiful two-and-a-half-story affair as narrow as a tie and as quaint as a cover of *Town & Country*. Dengler's second thought was, *How can he afford this place?* He realized he hadn't asked Strong how much FBI agents make.

Strong parked the sedan at the curb in front. There were only half a dozen cars on the street for two blocks in either direction. Trees accented the boulevard, and their shade cast the scene in twirling, shifting, sparkling patterns of shadow and light brought by the late afternoon sun and filtered through living fans of leaves.

"Some place," Dengler said.

"Actually, it's my wife's. She inherited it from a maiden aunt," Strong told him. "Although I guess it's part mine, too. I've spent the last two years restoring the interior. Come inside."

Up the steps and past the oak door was a hallway that led to a staircase to the second floor, and to one side of the staircase, the kitchen in back. There was what once would have been called a drawing room to the right of the staircase with a sliding door. Inside, a large fireplace and hearth centered the far wall. There was a cello supported in a stand beside a straight-back chair at the far end of the room. "My wife's a cellist, did I mention?" Strong said. "Should have been a professional musician, but everyone in her family thinks of music as an avocation. To be enjoyed, but not profited from. She's going for her Masters in English so she can teach."

Behind the stairs, and before the kitchen, was the entrance to the formal dining room. It was an oblong room with two doors, an oak china hutch and oak wall runners. "Come upstairs," Strong directed.

He led Dengler up the stairs to the second floor balcony, which almost encircled the house. There were three bedrooms, a smaller room Strong identified as a sitting room containing an overstuffed couch and chairs and the family television set. A second set of stairs led up to the attic.

"Very impressive," Dengler heard himself say, even though it was beyond his experience to be in a house like this or to comment on its relative merits.

"I stained all the wood, put up the wallpaper myself, and painted the ceiling. We were thinking of putting in wall-to-wall carpeting, but it seems kind of out of place in a house like this, doesn't it? Hard wood floors," Strong noted, pointing down.

Dengler realized he must have looked awful, because Wesley asked, "Are you okay?"

Dengler gestured at his face and lips and said, "A headache. Blood feels like it's throbbing through my head."

"Would you like to lie down for awhile?"

"That might be good," Dengler told him.

Strong took him to the guest room, down the hall and across from the master bedroom. Unlike the master bedroom, which was outfitted in early American furniture, this room's decor ran more to current style. There was a small television on a movable stand, a sewing machine cabinet doubling as a desk, and two straight-backed chairs with arms.

"Daisy won't be home until after six," Strong told him. "I'll go down and see if the housekeeper's returned. Light a fire under her to cook some dinner. Any preferences?"

"Soft," Dengler said, touching his lips for confirmation.

"Right," Strong said with a sympathetic smile. "Soft."

When Strong descended the stairs below Dengler's line of sight, Dengler sat down at the end of the bed. His head throbbed menacingly and he felt like it was a ripe melon about to split down its middle. Without removing his shoes or even pulling his legs up onto the bed, Dengler fell back and rubbed his eyes and brow as if he could knead the pain away.

He lost track of time after that. The sound of a door slamming brought him around, and in a moment he heard light footsteps sounding on the stairs. Daisy Strong's brown hair bounced into sight, followed by her body, as she topped the steps and entered her bedroom, leaving the door open. She was a woman of twenty-five, a brunette with an olive complexion, with long legs and a relatively short waist. From where Dengler lay he could see all the way into the bedroom as far as the window on the back wall. He lost Daisy for a moment, but she returned to the bed in seconds with a pair of slacks and a sweatshirt in her hands, which she dropped onto the bed.

Dengler turned away while she changed. When he looked back she was out of the room and moving down the stairs as quickly as she came. The after-image of the woman was one of physical quickness, health, an intelligence of movement, and character rather than beauty.

In a moment Dengler heard her cello sound. He fell asleep an instant later, but not before thinking Wesley Strong was a fortunate man.

When he woke, Dengler still lay on his back. He experienced a brief moment of disorientation panic, pushing himself up on one elbow and looking around. The .38 revolver swung in the shoulder holster below his arm, a reassuring feeling. Momentarily he remembered he was in Wesley Strong's Georgetown home.

He'd slept for more than a few minutes, he knew. Possibly hours. The house was dark now. The curtains over the bedroom window showed no light at all.

Dengler rose and stepped toward the door. The Strong's bedroom was dark, the door slightly ajar. Light rose from the floor below, casting an impression of the stairway handrails against the wall and its paper design. Dengler paced to the landing and almost started down before catching himself, his head dizzy and his lips pounding with blood. He stood for a long moment before he began to descend, taking each step carefully.

The foyer light was on, while the study was dark, as was the dining room. A light showed from beneath the kitchen door and Dengler headed for it. The door swung open easily and he found himself looking at the woman he'd seen earlier, Daisy Strong. She'd changed into a robe and slippers and was now sitting at the kitchen table reading a book and sipping steaming tea from a porcelain mug. For a moment they said nothing to one another and Dengler wondered if she knew who he was. He found it awkward to present himself. Then she said, "You must be Jack Fleming."

"Must be," Dengler said.

"I'm Daisy. Ooh, that lip looks awful. Let me get something for it."

"Actually, I've got something." Dengler fished the tube of salve Dr. Grodin gave him earlier from his pocket. He'd used it once.

"Here, let me see," Daisy ordered. She directed Dengler into a chair. It was very easy to give himself over to this attentive woman. "Wesley told me you guys were on prisoner duty today and you got yourself kicked in the face. Really, Jack — You don't mind if I call you Jack?"

"Uhm-Mmm," Dengler said.

"Really, Jack, you're going to have to be more careful. You can't take any chances in the kind of job you have." She tilted his head back and assessed the wound. "I'll be right back," she said. He heard her feet pound up the staircase in main room. Medicine cabinet, he thought.

Daisy returned with disinfectant and cotton swabs. She gently cleaned the wound and applied more of Grodin's salve with a Q-tip.

Every time she touched him, blood throbbed in his lips and in his mind.

"What time is it?" Dengler managed finally as she released him for a moment to assay her work.

"Oh, you don't know, do you?" she said. "You were so tired, Wes didn't have the heart to wake you, so we let you sleep. It's after ten."

"Thanks. I think I needed the sleep more than food."

"I've got some soup I can heat up for you. Eliza made rack of lamb for dinner, but I don't suppose you want any of that?"

"My stomach is willing but my mouth is weak."

"Really, Jack, you've got to be more careful."

"My sentiments exactly."

"Soup?"

"Please."

As Dengler watched Daisy opened the door to the adjacent pantry and he saw row upon row of canned goods and cooking basics. It was the sort of room Dengler had seen only in magazines. "What kind of soup would you like?" she said from the pantry. "Cream of tomato?"

"Sure."

Daisy found the can and closed the door. The can opener whined and an instant later she emptied the soup into a saucepan.

"Where's Wes?" Dengler asked.

"Where else?" she said. "Bob Lowry called and he had to go out. You wouldn't think Lowry could zip his pants without my husband," she said sourly. Dengler wondered if Wesley's absence had something to do with the *"We'll think of something,"* statement he'd made earlier about getting rid of the bodies. That thought segued into the realization Daisy actually knew almost nothing about what her husband did, or how dangerous his life really was. To her he was just another young FBI agent whose job was mundane. She had no idea he was a member of J. Edgar Hoover's hand-chosen elite group, Q Force.

"Wes said you just moved back into town and you'll be looking for a new apartment."

"Yeah." This wasn't firm ground and Dengler didn't want to be drawn into it.

"Where are you going to look?"

Where indeed? "May I have some tea?" Dengler asked. It wasn't all subterfuge; the idea of a hot, soothing liquid passing across his lips was most inviting.

"The water's hot. The tea bags are just inside the pantry door, on the left."

Dengler found the tea bags and returned to receive a cup from Daisy, who was standing by the stove gently stirring his soup. He poured water over the bag and then returned to his seat.

"So, where?" she said again.

"Haven't thought about it much," Dengler replied.

"Wes said your old place was near here. Bet you wish you hadn't given it up."

"Not really. I'm not home much, so it really doesn't matter."

"You know," she said with an odd smile, "your accent doesn't sound right. You're a Virginian, right?"

West Virginian, he almost corrected her, but remembered the carefully crafted new identity the FBI had made for him. "Yeah, Falls Church," he said.

"You sound more like West Virginia to me."

"I spent a little time there. Relatives, on my mother's side."

"That's probably it, then."

"Do you have any straws?" he said when he realized he wouldn't be able to bring this hot cup to his lips.

"Oh, sure," she said, seeing his difficulty. She reentered the pantry and returned with two flexible straws. "For the soup," she told him, setting the second straw down beside his cup of tea.

"Thanks."

She returned to the stove and finished stirring the soup. Steam rose from the saucepan and wafted toward the ceiling like a portentous volcano. She shut off the stove and poured the red soup into a bowl, where steam also billowed, then placed the bowl in front of him before taking her seat across the table. Dengler, meanwhile, noticed the title of the book she was reading when he came in: Michener's *Hawaii*.

"I appreciate this," he told her.

"Heavens, it's nothing," she said. "It's the least thing I can do for a man who was injured today in the service of his country."

Dengler briefly thought of the men who died today while in the service of their country, but let it go and took the unused straw and slipped it into the hot, red soup.

"I'd let it cool for awhile," she warned.

Dengler removed the straw and laid it across the top of the bowl. He sipped his tea through the first straw and gestured at Daisy's book. "Michener," he said.

"Yes, I like James Michener a lot. Some people think his writing is common because it's unpretentious, but that's exactly the reason why I like him."

"You read a lot, Daisy?"

"Oh, yes. More now than ever, what with Wesley's hours. Are you married, Jack?"

Dengler didn't know if the persona he'd adopted was married or not, and decided it didn't matter, he would have to make it up as he went. "No. Close once, though."

"What's the matter? Develop cold feet?" she said with a grin that was penetrating and sweet. When Daisy wasn't smiling she was as plain as unvarnished wood, handsome but not special. When she smiled a light ignited. "Well, what was it?" she prodded him. "You can tell me — you hardly know me."

"I didn't get cold feet," Dengler said, thinking of Etta. "More like she came to her senses."

"I'm prying," she said softly, realizing she might be entering painful territory.

"No, you're not, Daisy Strong. Not at all."

"Well, I'll give you fair warning, Jack. The FBI asks a lot of a marriage. It asks too much. It asks that I sit here all hours of the night, sometimes for days, occasionally weeks, for the return of a man I sometimes wonder if I know any better now than when we first married four years ago. It asks a lot."

"I know," he said.

"I've got a friend, another FBI wife, who tells me it gets better later because with rank goes stability. Choice of duty assignments and choice of hours. Not so many night details. Sometimes I wonder what we'll be like by then."

"Two days after his last night job, you'll forget he ever had one," Dengler told her.

"Two days after his last night job, I'll still remember I didn't see my husband for two days before and five days after my last birthday, and when I did see him, he was so tired he slept for eighteen hours and then woke up in the middle of the night and wanted to go out to have something to eat — this when I had a class in the morning."

"It's painful, Daisy," Dengler said, knowing even as he said it he had no idea how painful it might be, "but it's worth it. You're husband is a patriot. He gives his country a gift of sacrifice. You do too."

Daisy Strong smiled again. It wasn't a smile of humor, but of cynicism. "You talk like a Democrat, Jack," she said in the mocking, sing-song voice of a southern belle. "'Ask not what your country can do for you; ask what you can do for your country.' Why, if I didn't know better, I'd take you for a Kennedy man."

"I am," Dengler said. *Maybe.*

"You poor thing."

- 49 -

Wesley Strong arrived home half an hour later. By that time Dengler and Daisy had exchanged facts about their favorite authors, football teams and parades — both favored the Rose Parade. They'd become fast friends.

They heard Strong open the front door and take his first few steps up the stairs before Daisy called, "We're in here." Wesley Strong strode into the kitchen and set his briefcase down in a chair before he kissed his wife. "Hello, Sweets," he told her. Daisy patted his back as if to say, *It's okay*. "So, Jack, did she tell you about how I'm never home and she hates the FBI?"

"She hates the FBI, Wes," Dengler said

"Oh, the FBI's not so bad," Daisy said in a long, languorous voice as she pulled Wes closer to her. "It's the hours that drive women to howling at the moon. By the way, where were you?"

"I had to run in to the Egg Company and put a few things to rest," Wesley said. "Plans for an operation I have to run tomorrow. But, the good news is after that I can take the rest of the week off — to help Jack here get settled. The AIC wants him to hit the ground running."

"Hear that, Jack? Better put on your running shoes."

"Look, Sweets, why don't you run upstairs?" Strong said in a way that wasn't asking. "I have to talk to Jack for a moment."

"FBI business?" she asked.

"I'm afraid so."

"To hell with the FBI," she said in not-so-mock anger. "Jack, welcome to our home. Please feel free to stay as long as you like," she told him as she gently pulled away from Strong and moved toward the kitchen door. "Although, after a month, we change the lock on the pool."

"There's a pool?" Dengler said with a smile.

Daisy threw them both a wave and exited. Strong waited to hear her footfall on the stairs. When it diminished to nothing, Strong turned a kitchen chair around and straddled it.

Dengler picked up the soup straw and tested the soup, which was cool enough now for him to swallow. "How's your mouth?" Strong asked.

"Could be worse," Dengler said. "He could have ripped it off."

Strong barked a laugh and rose to retrieve a glass of milk from the refrigerator. As he filled a tumbler he told Dengler, "The AIC wants you settled in before you report to the Egg Factory."

"What's the Egg Factory?"

"That's what we like to call home. We operate an office under the guise of an accounting firm — you know, so all the suits coming and going won't raise a fuss. Somebody got the idea of calling it the Egg Factory. The AIC wants you settled in, Apartment rented, clothes bought, car, everything."

"What about the Pontiac?"

"Gone." On Dengler's sour look, Strong told him, "Lowry said the money to pay for that car probably came from the wallets of the two dead CIA guys in Santa Barbara."

"Yeah, it did. Tell him to forget it."

"He already has. Lowry's also concerned your split lip might not fit in with the Egg Factory's image."

"It should be down in a couple of days."

"More like a week," Strong said during a break in guzzling the milk. "Any case, you've got to look the part before you go in. That means clean lip, new clothes and a briefcase that says 'auditor' all over it. Brooks Brothers with a single flap in the back."

"Okay."

"Give you a chance to recover, too."

"Recover from what?"

Strong grinned. "Jesus, Fleming, you've had a pretty tense three months. Take a break, will ya?"

"Okay, I'll take a break."

"There's one last reason," Strong said. "We've still got to 'place' all of your corroborating paperwork. And you've got to establish a banking account, get approved for credit with the gas company and the electric company and all that. Paper trail."

"I'm not alive until someone tells me I'm alive."

"That's the idea."

"Okay."

"Make yourself at home," Strong told him as he moved for the kitchen door. "Me? It's past my bedtime."

Dengler sat in the kitchen alone for five minutes, then washed out his dishes and followed Strong upstairs.

Later, as he lay in bed and thought about the practicality of establishing a whole knew life, he began to doubt Etta could join him in it. What if she failed? What if she couldn't stop being Etta Mae Warren to become whomever the FBI and Jack Fleming wanted her to be? Would they — could he — kill her as he'd killed Jim Keller and the CIA crew?

No.

Dengler had left the door open and was nearly asleep when he heard them arguing. Daisy said, "No, no, not tonight. I'm not in the mood for this," while Strong tried to coax her in a gentle and humorous voice that suddenly became viciously angry with words like "Bitch" and "Cunt." They were arguing about sex, Dengler knew. He wanted it; she didn't. Their voices rose with each rejoinder. Dengler thought the door might burst open any minute and Daisy stride out in anger, but it didn't, and she didn't. Finally, he heard the sound of a slap and long minutes of silence. Dengler knew the next sounds with great intimacy — they were the noises a woman makes as a man moves inside her. He considered going out for a walk.

Strong called out, "Daisy-DAISY-DAISY."

The door opened a moment later. Daisy stepped out and slammed it behind her. She was nude, and sweat glistened from her body, accented by the glow from the baseboard night light that guided the way to this floor's only bathroom. She turned to walk down the hall when her eyes met Dengler's and for a time they stared at one another, or at least she stared into the darkness where his eyes were. She did nothing to hide her nudity. She was motionless except for the hurried rise and fall of her chest. He felt her eyes pierce him. If he'd been close enough, she would have disemboweled him with the sharp edges of her eyes. Wesley's semen must have started to run from her because she reached down to feel something, and then walked quickly to the bathroom.

Dengler turned over and faced the wall. After a time he heard their bedroom door open and close again, and no more words were said. His thoughts turned to Etta. His last conscious thought was he was as uncertain about his life as ever.

- 50 -

The following day Jack Fleming rented a small, furnished two-bedroom apartment on Carlisle Street, eight blocks from Wesley and Daisy.

Later he went shopping at a store suggested by Wes. He bought suits, sports jackets, shoes, socks, shorts, T-shirts, sweaters, coats, a raincoat, and hats. He became Jack Fleming, an FBI Special Agent on the rise who had to dress for success. It was an image of success nurtured in the eyes of a boy who'd seen movies, magazine ads, and television spots about successful people and how they dressed and acted, what they drank, and wore, and what they laughed at and didn't laugh at. David Dengler's difficulty getting coal dust from between body crevices after a day's work related in no way to Jack Fleming, whose clothing and demeanor said he was unflappable.

Dengler was surprised to learn he made the astonishing sum of eighteen thousand dollars a year, more than twenty times what David Dengler earned as a private first class in the United States Army. Additionally, he was allowed to keep the money he'd acquired during his cross-country chase, a sum of six thousand dollars.

Visits to Etta often became angry and bitter. She told him she was being held against her will. She didn't want to be detoxed off heroin. She never loved him because he was "no fucking good in bed." At first, he was amazed by her anger. He'd taken her off the streets of Baltimore and offered her a future in which she didn't have to screw every stranger holding a twenty-dollar bill.

"I'll tell people who you are," she said. "I'll have you arrested for kidnapping."

"Sweetheart, if you can get someone to believe you, do it," Dengler told her.

Etta's reaction angered and hurt Dengler. He didn't know how to respond. It was true she wasn't free to come and go as she pleased. It was also true, once free, she would get a fix of heroin within an hour and sell her body to pay for it.

Dengler teased her and tried to make her laugh. When the strain became too much, he retreated from her, sometimes for days. He inevitably returned and Etta tried to be nicer to him, even suggesting they make love in the privacy of her room. Dengler wasn't in the mood to make love to her. This wasn't the Etta of his hometown, or even the same Etta he'd spent months with at the cabin. This was a desperate woman who wasn't receiving enough heroin to satisfy her. Dengler suspected she wanted to make love to him to influence him to get the drug for her, an amazing idea in light of the fact he'd put her there.

His first weeks as Jack Fleming slipped away. His face regained its previous proportion. He discovered not only could he afford a good meal, he could eat it. Wesley and Daisy invited him over for dinner, and again to join in a 'company' get-together at their place in which he met several of the Q Force agents. They talked about their jobs only when their women were not in the immediate vicinity.

Dengler pressed Wesley about work. Initially, he was told he would start 'orientation' a week after the CIA incident. Strong then informed him it wasn't possible, there were obstacles in the way, such as getting Fleming's background put in place and other things he couldn't go into. Dengler knew something was wrong. Strong advised him to be patient. He was.

Finally, Strong called him on Saturday night of his third week and told him he would pick him up early the following Monday morning.

At the beginning of Jack Fleming's fourth week in his own Georgetown apartment, Wesley Strong stopped by at eight fifteen in the morning. Dengler was ready for him. He was dressed in a conservative three-piece suit. "Good," Strong said, inspecting him. "You'll fit in nicely."

Dengler discovered the Egg Factory — E.G. Factor & Sons, Accountants — was the sole occupant of a four-story brick building located in the less prestigious section of Washington. E.G. Factor & Sons, a real accounting firm owned and operated by Q Force, occupied the Second Floor, just above the garage, which was located on the first floor. Floors Three and Four were the sole domain of the FBI.

Dengler was assigned to the Black Room, the library where research files and agent reports were maintained. Some of these files were mirrors of files maintained at FBI headquarters; others were originals created and maintained by and for Q Force. Dengler was made assistant to the librarian. He had access to the research materials when he wasn't pulling files for agents or doing media research. Media research was an activity that required little more of him than the skills he learned in kindergarten — using scissors and glue to attach clipped articles to standard-sized paper, and then filing the paper away.

Dengler suspected this assignment constituted 'make work.' He was assigned to it, he thought, because he failed to live up to his part of the bargain with The Director. By stealing away to be with Etta that final night, Dengler had set in motion events that led to the execution of the CIA detail. Guilt often drifted through his mind, the faces of seven men about to die, but there was nothing he could do about it. He focused on accomplishing the tasks given him.

At four o'clock one January afternoon, a secretary entered the Black Room with a message. "Agent Fleming?" she said.

"Yes."

"Agent Strong asked me to tell you he's been called away. He won't be able to give you a ride home. He asked me to remind you to keep track of your taxi fare and to be sure to get a receipt."

"Thanks." He and Wes had been ride-sharing because The Director thought it might be dangerous for Dengler to drive a car. There remained a possibility a cop might stop him for some minor traffic violation and then tie him to the bogus photo of Dengler that was still in circulation with the police. Dengler rode with Wes to and from work, or took taxis, which were paid for by the FBI.

At 4:30 Dengler wrapped it up for the day. He didn't return to his office and had the receptionist call a cab, which pulled to the curb just as he stepped out the main entrance of the Egg Factory.

He told the driver to take him to the clinic, but halfway there he changed his mind and gave the driver Wes Strong's address. Dr. Grodin had given him a piece of information about Etta the previous week which had sickened and angered him — she attempted to bribe an orderly to sneak street clothes in for her and arrange for her to break out of the clinic. She offered him sexual favors in exchange. Dengler hadn't been back to see her since, and didn't know when he would go see her.

He told himself he wanted to catch Wesley before he left — wherever it was he was going — but the real reason he was stopping by Strong's house was Daisy.

- 51 -

December — May, 1963

Dengler was released from the Black Room periodically to perform mundane tasks. He assisted doing background checks on prospective federal employees, two in Seattle, one in Denver, and two in Albuquerque, New Mexico, ironic considering what he was alleged to have done to two men said to be on similar missions in Central California in August of 1962. Dengler was merely personnel filler, a pick-up agent to carry a clipboard. He wasn't even allowed to ask questions.

Dengler was also added to a rampage killer task force in Iowa in February and March. Again, he was a filler agent paired with a senior man who didn't care enough to ask about him. He spent much of his time preparing comparison suspect reports, trawling thousands of files for similar modus operandi. He found none.

Etta made progress physically, but she was deemed in no shape to assume the role of Mrs. Jack Fleming, FBI Agent. She was emotionally unstable and angry at being institutionalized. Dr. Grodin extended her stay at Morningside again and again. Dengler was relieved of having a say in these matters, but Etta didn't see it that way.

Over the preceding months, Dengler and Daisy had become good friends. Dengler spent Christmas with the Strongs, or more precisely with Daisy as Strong was called away at the last minute to handle some detail or other of an operation in New Orleans. Daisy decorated their home with a mixture of old and new, some of the tree ornaments having been in her family three generations. It was the first time in his life Dengler experienced Christmas the way it was depicted in films. Christmas morning they drank eggnog with brandy while it snowed outside. Daisy arranged a date for Dengler with her cousin Sally, who was prettier than Daisy, but somehow not as alive. While Daisy would never compete with Etta in looks, she was easily the most intelligent and involving woman he'd ever known, and Dengler admitted to himself he was attracted to her. She never mentioned the night Dengler saw her in the hallway, naked and humiliated. From that night on Dengler saw Wes Strong as a different man.

Christmas dinner was memorable. They ate a roast duck with all the trimmings. They opened presents beneath a tree that touched the ceiling and sparkled with every Christmas color. They sang carols beside the piano as Daisy played, and a fire blazed in the hearth. It was the best Christmas gift he'd ever received, Christmas with Daisy.

Dengler dismissed the cab and trotted up the steps to the Strong home. It was a spring day, late in April now. The air was filled with potential, cold, wet, and blustery for the season. He rapped on the door and waited, listening to the sound of the wind as it whistled through the tree limbs behind him. Strong would probably still be here and Dengler might be able to find out what was going on.

"Jack." Daisy wore a black, long-sleeved turtleneck sweater and red ski pants whose stirrups hooked over feet that were covered with thick white socks. Barrettes held her hair out of her eyes, and she had no makeup on. She looked wonderful, natural, and feminine. She grabbed him by the arm and pulled him inside. "Quick," she told him, "before we freeze to death."

Dengler removed his coat and hat and placed them on hooks in the foyer. Daisy's sock-shod feet padded across the hardwood floors toward the kitchen. "I was just going to have some tea," she called back. "Would you like a cup?"

"I'd love some," he said. "Where's Wes? I stopped by to catch him before he left."

Daisy entered the kitchen and Dengler followed her. She was at the stove just as the kettle began to complain noisily. "What did you say about Wes?"

"I stopped by to see him before he left."

"Oh, he isn't here, Jack. He didn't call about a trip. But then, Wes keeps a suitcase at the office just in case he gets called away on a moment's notice. Don't you?"

"No." He was looking at her bottom, which the ski pants clung to, accentuating every contour.

"What do you do if you have to go out of town on short-notice?"

"I just buy what I need when I get there."

Daisy smiled knowingly. "Just like a bachelor. I'll bet you throw away your dirty clothes, too." She said this as she poured the hot kettle water into another pot, this one with a strainer filled with tea leaves suspended at its top. The hot water filtered through the strainer slowly, and Daisy rose to her tiptoes to look down, making sure no tea leaves rose to the surface. Dengler watched the movement of her body, the lanky grace of it, and he knew that instant without lying to himself he wanted her.

Daisy turned in time to catch him looking at her, and checked herself to see whether she'd dropped something on her clothes that would attract attention. Then she realized what he was doing, and her manner changed immediately. She stepped back nervously and almost teetered into the stove.

"Do you take sugar in your tea?" she asked nervously.

"Yeah."

"Cream?"

"No."

She took the cream pitcher out of the refrigerator anyway and placed it on the kitchen table. "Have a seat," she told him as she stepped past and Dengler reached out and wrapped his arm around her waist. She didn't look at him. She wouldn't look at him. Her breath caught, and then she gasped for air, causing her chest to rise. Dengler said nothing. Finally she told him, "I'm married, Jack."

"I know," he replied. He pulled her to him, and then twisted her around so her eyes bore into his chest.

"You're my friend," she said softly.

"I know," he replied again.

She still wouldn't look at him. He kissed her. She pulled away as his lips approached, expecting the kiss to be hard and to hurt, he imagined; but instead Dengler's lips lingered for long seconds less than an inch from hers. When they touched, it was with such a gentleness she was surprised. For long moments Daisy allowed her lips to remain in contact with his, then she pulled away and looked into his eyes. There were no words spoken, no gates unlocked, no rivers crossed, but he understood.

They held one another for what seemed like an hour, sitting in the kitchen chair and silently feeling their embrace, before they went upstairs.

In the hours that followed Dengler explored Daisy's body, and she his. Their forefingers traced curves and planes, climbed nipples, and descended ribs, followed muscles across shoulder and back, and caressed lips. The way she touched him reminded Dengler of her fingers playing the cello, gentle strokes and measures that drew him taut and fluttering. Daisy's body was the opposite of Etta's. Where Etta was overtly beautiful, Daisy was a woman of minimalist proportions. Her torso was lean and free from unnecessary fat. Her small breasts disappeared when she lay back, her curves subtle and sinewy. Daisy's skin was the color of cream and almonds, her nipples slightly darker and the size of dimes, her eyes brown and large. Dengler finally entered her. It was so slow she seemed to open like a flower. In complete union they moved together in such minute gestures Dengler marveled at the exquisite instant of the act, ecstasy in still life. When she reached climax, moments passed before he was sure of it. He remained in her, hard and still, listening to her breathing, watching her chest rise and fall.

"You've had me, Jack," Daisy whispered. "Are we still friends?"

Dengler could think of nothing to say. He kissed her, soft and wet on the lips, lingering there until she could take it no more and responded. After a moment she whispered, "Oh boy..." She shivered and arched her back involuntarily. Dengler waited for the arch to flatten. He was sure Daisy was blushing. "I... I..." she began. He shifted his weight, found a more comfortable position. He kissed her again, this time just a little more urgently. "Oh, Jack," she said, her back arching once more.

Later, as they lay in the darkness together, he told her, "You always teach me things, Daisy."

She sat up on an elbow and looked at him. "*I* teach *you?*" she asked him, grinning.

"Someday I'll tell you how much you've taught me. Someday I will."

He slipped out of bed shortly before one A.M. and was almost dressed when Daisy said, "Was it just for this once?" He turned. Daisy was a greater darkness in the shadows. She hadn't even risen from the pillow to ask it.

"God, no."

"Then what are we going to do about Wes, Jack? Are we going to sneak around behind his back, like thieves?"

"You'd do that?" It was like asking, *Do you love me?*

"Yes," she said softly after a moment's thought. "But if you care for me, you won't ask."

He kissed her and left the room.

- 52 -

Dengler called a taxi and waited on the stoop for it to arrive. He stood in the cold for more than twenty minutes thinking about Daisy. She was right. Turning an incident into an affair would diminish her. Daisy was the sort of woman who would stay loyal to a man even if he mistreated her.

Wesley Strong, on the other hand, would remain married to Daisy until she began to show a little age, and then would find someone younger.

In the interim, he would beat her.

Daisy was the first true friend Jack Fleming had made. He enjoyed her company. Maybe he just ruined that. If he turned her into a liar, wasn't that mistreatment too?

During the 10-minute cab ride home Dengler brooded about how alone he felt. A year before he'd worked in a mine and cared for an old man he hated, but at least he had a home. He pushed the thoughts out of his mind. He needed a distraction.

"Stop. I want to get a paper."

The cabby found a corner where there were two newspaper racks and Dengler bought both dailies, the *Washington Post* and the *Washington Times*. He slipped back into the cab. "Could you turn on the dome light, please?"

"Sure."

He saw the picture again. It was on the front page of the Washington Post, the Dengler *familiar* who was so similar to him, and nonetheless clearly wasn't him. The headline read, *Fugitive Killed In Shoot-Out*. Dengler quickly perused the story.

(AP) David Dengler, the alleged killer and federal fugitive who has successfully eluded capture for over six months, died this afternoon in a fiery shootout with agents of the Federal Bureau of Investigation. Dengler had been living in a trailer park in Dalton City, a small town in upstate New York, when federal authorities received a tip about his whereabouts from an undisclosed source. When federal agents arrived on the scene, Dengler barricaded himself inside a World War II-vintage trailer and refused to come out. As agents maneuvered into place around the trailer, they received gunfire from Dengler, and while returning fire the FBI agents accidentally struck an adjacent LPG tank, which exploded and set the trailer ablaze. Dengler died in the inferno. Authorities hope to make a positive identification from the remains. However, witnesses at the scene have positively identified the man inside the trailer as having been

David Dengler.

The rest of the story dealt with Dengler's history, including the murder of two CIA agents in Santa Barbara in August. It was also suggested two bank robberies that occurred in the Rochester, New York area, might be related to Dengler.

Dengler's apartment was dark and cold. He set two logs in the fireplace and used the back sections of the newspapers as kindling, then went into the bedroom to change. When he returned to pour himself a brandy the logs caught and the room was bathed in undulating shadows. He sat on the floor with his back to the couch and watched the flames dance on the walls, thinking briefly of Daisy before dismissing what happened. There were worse things to consider.

David Dengler was dead.

The brandy was half-gone when he fell asleep.

David Dengler woke to the sound of pounding on his front door. He'd been in a deep sleep and being yanked from that depth left him groggy and disoriented. He recognized the voice beyond the door. "Jack. Open up. It's Wes."

Wesley Strong. Dengler's first thought was, *He knows.* How could he have found out? Daisy must have told him. He knew Wes Strong — he would have to kill him, or be killed. He reached for his Walther PPK and realized he'd taken off the holster before he went to sleep. Where did he leave it? Meanwhile the pounding continued.

"Jack. Wake up. It's an emergency."

Dengler staggered to his feet. "Yeah, what is it?" Dengler pulled the door open and Strong surged inside.

"Get dressed. Now."

"What? Why?"

Strong shut the door. He was wearing a thick coat, gloves and a hat that had seen snow not too long before, judging by the crystals that still clung to it. "Just do it, Jack. I'll explain on the way."

Apparently, Strong knew nothing about Jack and Daisy.

Strong followed Dengler into the bedroom and the adjacent bathroom and watched as he splashed water into his face. "What time is it?" Dengler asked.

"Almost three. I've made reservations for you on the next flight out of National Airport."

"Plane reservations?"

"Yes. Pack an overnight bag. We'll supply you with everything you'll need at the scene."

Dengler gave up all protests and got dressed.

Strong had a Lincoln limo waiting. He and Dengler climbed into the back. Dengler didn't recognize the man driving the car.

Before Wes could say anything, Dengler said, "I was killed last night. Tell me how I was killed last night."

"Oh, yeah, I wondered when you'd hear about that. Lowry's been working on it."

"Who's sleeping in my grave?"

"We've been searching for a John Doe match for months. Lowry picked up the body from some morgue in Arizona. Had it flown in."

"How did you fake it with all those witnesses?" he said.

"We evacuated the place. There was a siege situation, remember? We cleared everyone out, then replaced our operative with the corpse and set the whole thing on fire. Real blaze. Nothing left of you. Just in time, too."

"Just in time for what?"

"We were prepping you for an assignment in New Orleans, but things are happening fast," Strong said. "Plans change."

"New Orleans?"

"Something happened. Tonight. Something we picked up on one of our wires." When Dengler gestured he didn't understand, Wes continued, "There's a mobster in New Orleans we've got a bug on. Carlos Marcello. You were going to join his surveillance group. Marcello is the capo of the oldest Mob family in America. It's been in place for well over a hundred years."

Dengler watched the out-of-doors slate by. The windows were frosted at the corners from the heater, which even now was piping warm air from the engine compartment to the back where they sat.

"We've had Marcello wired for some time," Strong continued, "because of his cooperative relationship with the CIA, and his involvement with Cuban drug smugglers, some of whose members are associates of Alpha 66, the Cuban anti-Castro organization. Before the revolution the Marcello family was the major connection between the Mob and Cuban interests, like dope smuggling and money laundering through the Battista government. There's still some dope coming out of Cuba, but now most of that action has moved elsewhere. But that's not the important part. Through our wire of Marcello we learned the Mob is planning a hit. A big hit."

"On who?" Dengler said.

"The President."

- 53 -

Silence was a wake that followed Strong's revelation. Dengler's mind raced. *The Mob? Does that mean the CIA? Does the CIA mean Stafford? Was Monroe's murder a covert move on the Kennedys?*

"Marcello was talking about a coming meeting of the Mob's Executive Committee," Wes continued. "The meeting had been called to discuss a proposal made by The White House to enlist the Mob in putting a hit on Fidel Castro. This proposal was carried to Sam Giancana by a woman named Judith Campbell. We know it's real because we saw her deliver a manila envelope to Giancana that she received at the White House. Campbell is one of Kennedy's mistresses; as a matter of course, we now surveil all the women who go to the White House when the First Lady isn't present. In any case, the Executive Committee is pretending to be considering this proposal."

"Executive committee?" Dengler said. His mind was nowhere near the question, but stalking others.

"Carlos Marcello, of New Orleans, Santos Traficante, who heads the Tampa family, Johnny Roselli from the West Coast, Sam Giancana, the Boss of Bosses, from Chicago, the capos of the Five New York Families, and other assorted Mob luminaries. Marcello let it slip out over the wire — the meeting would be about the hit on Kennedy."

Dengler was stunned. He could say nothing. There were no words to be said. The whole thing seemed preposterous. They wouldn't dare. They couldn't. This was the President of the United States. He commanded armies. It was his finger poised on *the button*.

Dengler thought of the men who helped Gray Stafford kill Monroe. It was possible. He said, "Is the CIA involved?"

"There are CIA people all over the place," Wes said evenly, not giving the words any more weight than the alphabet should have. "So far, none tied to this."

"Why would the Mob want to kill a sitting American President?"

"You might be angry too if the President's father asked for your help to get his son elected, and after the election his other son the Attorney General had you deported, or tried to put you in prison for the rest of your natural life. Robert Kennedy had Marcello deported, you know; Marcello returned from Guatemala wearing peasant clothes. He hadn't bathed in days. To say the least, he's fighting re-deportation in court. Hell, Sam Giancana's second home is court."

Dengler knew about Joe Kennedy sending Sam Giancana's men into West Virginia to buy votes during the Democratic Primary before the 1960 Presidential Election. It was one of the most thumbed files in the Black Room. Still, he wasn't sure he believed it. "Jesus, Wes, that doesn't make any sense. How could the President be involved with the Mob and at the same time allow his brother to go after them? It doesn't figure, not on any level."

"I don't know," Wes said. "Maybe Joe Kennedy never told them. Maybe they don't know. Maybe they think they're sons of an upstanding former Ambassador to the Court of Saint James, not a bootlegger with Mob ties."

"It's hard to believe the Mob would dare," Jack said. "Not against the President of the United States."

"Alone, maybe not," Wes replied soberly, and left it at that. "You'll fly to New Orleans tonight," Strong continued. "You'll establish a residence there, create a local identity for yourself. It's vital no one knows who you really are, or who you work for. I will act as your controller. I will give you instructions and provide you with information and equipment as needed. Jack, this is important. If there's a plot brewing to assassinate the President, we've got to stop it."

The limo pulled to the curb at the National Airport Eastern Airlines Terminal. Strong followed Jack out of the limo. It was a crisp morning. Their breaths hung like garlands in the air. "How long do you think I'll be down there?" Dengler said.

Wes inspected his ticket, and then handed it to him.

"I don't know. There's no way of telling. It could be months."

"Then I'll need to arrange to transfer Etta down to a New Orleans hospital."

Dengler knew by Strong's expression something was wrong. Finally he said, "Tell me."

"I was hoping we'd find her," Strong told him. "I was hoping she'd just show up, but..."

"What happened?"

"She bribed an orderly to let her out. She's been gone since this afternoon."

Dengler thought of Etta back on the street, hooked on smack, and selling herself in order to buy it. He felt his body caving inward, the pit of his stomach shriveling, and pulling the man who had become Jack Fleming inside with it. What was left was David Dengler, a little man who dug coal for a living and who had just lost his girl.

"Bribed," Dengler said, knowing the only legal tender she possessed was herself.

"She'll turn up," Strong said.

Dengler really wasn't standing in front of the terminal with Strong anymore.

He really wasn't anywhere at all.

- 54 -

October, 1962 — April, 1963

She was sedated when they brought her into the hospital, floating in a dreamy near-sleep in which she saw colors and images slide past her cloud-like, swirling and quickly lost. Etta tried to remember who she was and what she was doing lying on her back as the world passed over her. She heard voices.

"What have we got here?"

"Overdose. Heroin. She's stabilized."

She felt the sheet lift briefly from her body.

"Whew. This one's nice."

"Don't let Grodin find you doing that."

"Fuck Grodin, the Jew bastard. Would you look at this bitch? She's hot."

"Grodin will have your ass."

"It might be worth it."

Etta floated as light bulbs as brilliant as suns passed overhead and walls swung open and closed to reveal more corridors and more lights and more walls. Then she was in a bed, and a sheet was being taken from beneath her. She remembered this sheet had been used to move her from the gurney. She was naked and one of the two men was talking about how she looked, and then she felt his hands on her breasts and briefly tugging her pubic hair. Then the men were gone and Etta was alone in the room. Alone and not dead.

David came in then, or maybe it was later, and told her his name wasn't David anymore, it was Jack, like the President's name, and she should always call him Jack from now on. They fought. Or maybe she dreamed it.

When she woke the second time, a female nurse was giving her a sponge bath. "Who are you?" Etta said, never having had another woman except her mother touch her before.

"I'm your nurse," the woman said. She was forty years old, beginning to gray, and smelled of disinfectant. Her breasts were larger than Etta's and bound in a brassier beneath the white starch of her uniform. She was cleaning Etta's armpits, then her shoulders and neck.

"How long?" Etta asked.

"You've been asleep for three days," the nurse answered.

"Three days..."

"Yes. Before we changed your bedclothes, we thought it might be a good idea to give you a sponge bath."

Etta shrank from the woman's touch. She felt dirty. "I can clean myself," she offered, but the nurse reassured her.

"Listen, I do this sort of thing all the time. It goes with the territory. It's okay."

"I'm not a dirty person, really."

"Yes, I know that."

"They told you I'm a junkie, didn't they?"

"No one called you a junkie."

"They told you."

"Of course I know," the nurse said. "I have to know. But it's all right, because I'm here to help you." She washed beneath her breasts and then down the length of her body and Etta felt humiliated at being so dirty that a nurse had to clean her.

"Can I..." Etta tried to read her name from the black plastic tag on her chest, finally stopping the woman's work with her hand so she could make it out. Betty Stitz, R.N. "Nurse Stitz, can I leave here?"

"It's a closed ward, Mrs. Talbert."

"Talbert?"

Nurse Stitz didn't even blanch at Etta not knowing her own name. "It's a closed ward," she said, continuing her work, "but I think Dr. Grodin will allow a stroll around the grounds once a day, supervised, of course. And you'll find we provide all the comforts of home. Television, radio, newspapers, books, and magazines."

"Telephone?"

Nurse Stitz cleaned Etta's feet and then put hospital shoes on them. "Mr. Talbert asked that the phone be removed."

"So I'm a prisoner?"

"No, you're a patient," Nurse Stitz told her, making eye contact so Etta could see she was serious. "You're a patient who needs care. When you're healthy, in a few months, you'll walk out of here addicted to nothing more than kindness. That's our goal."

"I would like to make a phone call."

"Are you hungry?"

"No. I want to make a phone call."

"I can bring you some tea. How about that?"

"No. I know my rights. I want to make a phone call."

Nurse Stitz dropped the sponges into a tub and walked to the door. "I'll be back before dinner," she said, and left.

She intended to take stock of herself and her new environment, but before she could the need overtook her. She paced the room until almost four o'clock and had begun to throw books into the center of the floor when Dr. Grodin and two male orderlies arrived.

Grodin went immediately to the bed and retrieved a white robe and placed it over her while, behind his back, one of the orderlies smirked and drank in her nakedness. He was a small man, possibly of Puerto Rican ancestry, with a name tag that read Ramirez. The other man, who was shoulder and head taller, was blond, and pimple-faced. Both men were in their early twenties, half Grodin's age.

"Now, Mrs. Talbert," Grodin began.

"My name isn't Talbert. My name is Warren."

"Mrs. Talbert," Grodin said, "there is a room next door. It is padded and its only source of light is a single light bulb. There are no books there, no couches, and no bed. If you become destructive, I will put you there and leave you until you convince me you are sorry and will do no more harm. Is that understood?"

"I need a fix."

"Yes, so I understand. You will pick up all of these books and place them back on the shelves. Is that understood?"

"Fuck you," Etta hissed. "I need a fix, and I need it now."

The tantrum didn't really hit full-force until Etta was alone in the padded room. She threw herself against the padded walls and flailed as best she could inside the straightjacket they'd placed on her. When frustration took over, she began to sob. Afterward, she slept until six o'clock, when they brought the hypo and fixed her. Then she slept more.

Etta woke in the bed. Nurse Stitz had brought clean sheets, but she was standing at the foot of the bed observing Etta with a smile. Betty Stitz reminded Etta of her Aunt Myrtle, not real family but a good friend to the Warrens, who had been the kindest person in her life. She liked Betty Stitz.

"I thought he was going to leave me in there," Etta said, "until I asked him to let me out."

"You asked him."

"I didn't."

"I was there."

"I would never give in to that son-of-a-bitch."

"You were medicated. That kind of medication will make people do anything."

"I didn't do it."

Nurse Stitz grinned. "Come on. Get up. I've got to change that bed."

Etta rolled out of bed and slipped on the cloth robe the hospital provided. It was white with a blue insignia sewn over the left breast. "I'm starting to get anxious," she said at last, feeling the need in the distance, but closing. "Is... Are you going to...?"

"There are rules, Mrs. Talbert," Nurse Stitz said, looking up from squaring one corner of the sheet.

"Call me Etta."

"Rules, Etta. And by the way, you can call me Betty."

"Okay. Rules, Betty. I understand."

"One rule is you don't throw tantrums. No one likes tantrums, Etta, because they scare people. No one knows what you're going to do."

Etta suppressed her anger. It won't do any good to get angry, she thought. No good. Just make them more paranoid. It was a bitter thing to swallow, because they were holding her here against her will, and she'd have to beg for what she needed to stay alive.

"No more tantrums," Etta heard herself say as her mind considered other, angrier thoughts. "I'll be a good girl."

"Another one of the rules is you do what the doctor says. The doctor believes in exercise, so every afternoon one of the orderlies will walk you around the complex, inside and out. If you create a scene, Dr. Grodin will put you back in the padded room until your treatment is completed. Do you understand?"

"Sure. I'll need something to wear."

"They'll provide you with clothes, but they'll take them back every day. No one in this ward is allowed to have anything other than a hospital robe to wear."

"Why is that?" Etta said.

Betty ignored the question. "Another rule is food," she said. "Dr. Grodin expects you to eat everything the dietitian provides for you. He expects you to eat before you are medicated."

"I'll clean my plate," Etta promised. "I'll cooperate, Betty. Really. I didn't mean to cause a scene yesterday. I was angry because I shouldn't be here, you know? I mean, I didn't volunteer..."

"Etta, your husband put you here so you can get well."

"He's not my husband."

"You're here to get well. We can agree on that, can't we?"

For a long moment Etta's eyes were locked on Betty's. For all her kindness expressed toward Etta, Etta saw the calm professionalism that was the substance of the woman. She would do all she could to help cure Etta Talbert, as she knew her, and Etta had no chance at all to turn this woman into an ally.

"I'm a heroin addict," Etta said finally. "I guess if I had a choice, I wouldn't be."

"In two months you won't be."

Etta made herself smile. "Good," she said.

The routine of the hospital slowly became Etta's routine. She ate breakfast at eight, received an injection of heroin immediately after, then slept for an hour or so. Then she was taken for tests, or if none were scheduled, whiled away the morning reading or watching daytime television, which consisted of reruns of *My Little Margie* and *Amos'N'Andy*. At noon she was brought a light lunch, and then at two was taken on a fast walk through the complex with one of the orderlies. They brought her pants and a sweatshirt, again emblazoned with the hospital insignia, and afterward waited outside as she removed everything and passed them through the door. The clothes were new every day. She wondered how they could afford to do that, and realized this hospital must be contracted out to the government, probably the FBI. It was, after all, David Dengler's new profession, FBI Agent.

Etta's relationship with David had changed. The change was subtle at first, but gradually she realized he was responsible for putting her in this place. The last night they shared in the cabin he'd told her she would have to be hospitalized for a time, but he never suggested the hospital was to be a prison. David's dream to marry her was a fantasy, Etta knew, because men lost interest in her once their lust was extinguished. With David, it was just taking a while longer because somehow he confused love with sex.

For a time just after she reunited with David she thought he might be right, they were in love. Certainly, she felt something for David — Jack, now — that she never felt before. His rescue of her from the street, the way he nurtured her, the way he cared for her even after her looks were marred by drugs and beatings and too many nights selling her ass on the street, drew a great feeling of gratitude from Etta. Finally, she came to realize that was all it was, gratitude. She realized it the night David came to visit her, and she tried to get him to make love to her. He refused. At that moment she knew he really didn't 'love' her, and her feelings for him were nothing more than gratitude for getting her out of a bad situation. She began searching for a way out of the hospital, searching for a means of taking control of her life again.

Of the four male orderlies who took turns accompanying her on her fast-walks, three were as ordinary as any of the johns she'd ever serviced. They told her how pretty she was and complimented her on her beauty and one even compared her with Marilyn Monroe. "You're even prettier than her," he said in the shy way of men who lust but will not admit it even to themselves.

There was also Ramirez. He wanted Etta Warren and made no apologies for it.

"I'll bet you're one sweet fuck," he said one day when they were out on their walk. Ramirez had fallen back to watch the flex and release of her butt as she paced and he whistled almost silently at what he saw. Etta knew then the power she'd always had over some men hadn't waned. Ramirez was her tool to get out of this place, and she intended to use him.

When he returned her to her room, this time she invited him in. He said, "We're not supposed to come inside. I'll wait for you here." Etta laughed and pulled off the sweatshirt before she was fully inside. Ramirez looked anxiously up and down the hall before entering her room and closing the door behind him.

By this time Etta had shimmied out of the pants. She was sweating profusely and wiped the sweat from her shoulders and breasts and groin with the pants and shirt and threw them at him. Ramirez caught them and held them for a long moment, taking in her nakedness, before he buried his head into the mass of cloth and smelled.

When he looked up again, she was before him, the nipples of her breasts rising and falling at his shoulders. He tried to touch them, but she said, "Don't touch me, or I'll call the doctor." His hands lowered.

Etta touched his chest with the flat of her palm, first the great rift between pectorals, then his nipples, then the flat of his stomach. He was reaching for her again when she ordered, "Don't," and then shoved her right hand down the front of his pants. Her hand pushed past his manhood and took the balls. When she'd secured them in her hand, she said, "Unbuckle your belt. Push your pants down." Ramirez quickly complied, shoving the white hospital pants down. He was wearing boxer shorts. "There. Good," Etta told him.

"Now the shorts."

Ramirez was enjoying this, and wishing he wasn't enjoying this, as she stepped back to look at the testicles, and above them the quickly growing penis, gripped in her hand. "Good," Etta told him. "This won't take long."

She closed with him again so that her breasts were almost in his face, but not touching. When he tried to suck one, she squeezed on the testicles and he moaned, "No. Stop. Ah." Then she began to massage him, not gently working up to the rhythm of ejaculation but starting there and staying there, like a dynamo. It was less than thirty seconds when she heard the first, "Ah. Ah. AH." He spat his seed into her hand. She released him then, almost shoved him away, and carefully holding his ejaculate in the cupped palm of her right hand, strolled to the bed.

Ramirez stood where she left him, stripped from the waist down, breathing hard, satisfied and ashamed of himself simultaneously. Etta waited for him to look up at her before she dipped her left forefinger into Ramirez's seed and sucked it clean, as if testing the flavor of a sauce.

"I want to get out of here," she said.

"Jesus, lady..." he protested.

"You're right. I'm one sweet fuck. I know how to do it very well, Ramon, isn't it?"

"Yeah." She could see Ramirez knew he'd come out less than the victor in this exchange, but couldn't quite comprehend how. His manhood was already shriveling, drawing up into his groin, and the appearance of this strutting little man standing before her with his pants down around his ankles and his privates exposed for her to see was almost funny. Etta kept herself from smiling and said, "I want to get out of here, Ramon, and you can help me."

"Fuck me," Ramirez said as a curse.

"I'm going to need clothes. I'm going to need help getting past the locked doors."

Realizing the moment of sexual contact was gone, Ramirez yanked up his boxer shorts, then the white pants, and buckled his belt.

"They'll fire me," he said simply. It was true. They both knew it.

"If you get caught," she purred. "You're not going to get caught."

"I'm supposed to put my livelihood on the line for a piece of ass?" He said it as if he couldn't believe she would ask such a ridiculous thing of him.

Etta wiped his ejaculate from her hand onto a towel and strolled languorously toward him, allowing him to see every muscle, every contour, every gently quaking piece of her flesh. When again her breasts were inches from his face, she said, "Yes, but what a piece of ass."

This time she allowed him to touch her left nipple, to tweak it so it drew up and became hard and square. "No, don't," she whispered finally, "you're getting me wet."

"Jesus," he uttered.

"Tomorrow you're going to bring me something to wear," Etta told him, gently pushing his fingers from her breast. "A blouse and skirt."

"Okay."

"Tomorrow I'm going to give you something, Ramon."

"You are?"

"Yes. Something you'll like very much."

- 55 -

1958

Etta Mae Warren knew the power of sex from a young age. Even from her earliest memories, she knew men wanted what women had. She also knew men possessed something they would never willingly give up — power — and the only way a woman could get it was to use her sex.

Etta's earliest memory of her father was sitting naked in the crook of his arm. George Warren liked to hold his girls when they were naked and didn't mind the occasional accident. He held them all, from Greta and Marla at the top, to Etta and Sela at the bottom. He didn't start taking his girls until they started to menstruate. He wasn't a molester of children, but he liked to hold them. Naked. In the crook of his arm.

So old was this memory Etta couldn't remember not sitting on her father's arm, bouncing there sometimes as he walked around the house. Etta's mother never protested. She acted as if this was the most ordinary thing imaginable. Etta came to think it was, too. Fathers did this with their daughters, and later slept with them as a man sleeps with a woman. What could be more natural?

Problems didn't begin to rise until later, until school and accepted social beliefs began to invade their home. Guilt entered their lives, the knowledge of sin, the sure truth their father had broken the most basic of human laws by sleeping with his children. By then Etta accepted this life as being ordinary. By then she learned to compete with her sisters for the affections of their father. Even as first Greta, and then Marla was taken into their father's bedroom — it was never their parents' bedroom, always his — and the other sisters and their mother would sit in the parlor, Etta knew her time would come. She was secretly aware her father loved her best. She waited for the moment when she would menstruate, and be taken into that bedroom and given the one sure token of his love for her.

Etta was the prettiest. Her father often told her so, when they were alone.

Then she got sick. The doctor told her parents that even though she would one day mature, she could never have children. From that day forward George Warren paid no attention to her at all. He put her aside in favor of her younger sister Sela, even though Sela wasn't as pretty as Etta. He put her aside and never touched her again.

As she grew older Etta tried various means of gaining her father's appreciation and affection, but none of them worked. She eventually saw it was her ability to create children that defined her sexuality to her father, and not the way she looked or acted. Her talents as a person were insignificant beside this one function, and lacking it, Etta lacked everything that might gain his love.

She was fourteen when she went to her mother and spoke about her father for the first time. Etta rarely thought about how her mother must feel seeing each of her daughters, each but Etta, taken into the bedroom where they were conceived, to now be possessed by their father. Etta never thought of her mother's feelings because her mother rarely allowed her feelings to be known. Josephine Warren treated George as if he were a conqueror and she the daughter of a conquered peasant. She was submissive, obedient, and spoke of him with respect. If she hadn't been like this, her children surely would have known much earlier that what their father did wasn't acceptable to society, Etta later thought. Because her mother acted as if it were the most normal thing in the world for a man to possess his daughters from an early age, each of them took it to be ordinary, and more, took it to be something desirable. The four redheaded girls competed for their father's desire.

When Etta went to her mother, the older woman sat in the parlor and listened as patiently as any mother might to a child's minor problem. "He doesn't want me, Mama," she told the woman who looked enough like Etta to be an older sister. "He treats me like I'm dirty. Am I ugly?"

"No, child. You are most pretty." Etta's mother stroked her hair. It was long and hung down to her waist. "You are as pretty as any of my children."

"Then why doesn't he —?"

"We shouldn't be talking about this," her mother said with a quiet voice. "This belongs to him, and him alone. Who knows the mysteries of men?"

Etta never thought of her mother as a person before. Etta realized she was just Josephine Warren — Josie — wife of George Warren, a person who was once young and who knew nothing of life until it was lived. Now in her eyes Etta's mother was less a mother than a woman, and less a woman than George Warren's wife.

If she couldn't compete with her sisters at home, Etta found no difficulty taking their boyfriends away from them at school. If their father had known the Warren girls were the most popular sisters in school, with many admirers, he would have beaten every one of them. They were not allowed to have boyfriends. They were supposed to come home promptly every afternoon when school was out. They were allowed no extracurricular activities. At the time Etta thought it was because her father didn't want to share his daughters with anyone — and that was true enough — but later she realized his iron hand upon them was to protect himself. George Warren knew what he did to his daughters wasn't right, and he must have been afraid of disclosure.

It didn't matter. Etta found time during school to flirt with boys, and later, to have them. She lost her virginity to Greta's boyfriend Steven Coats the year she entered high school. Her sister was two years older and two grades ahead of her, as was Steven, but Etta paid him particular attention and took his virginity, and gave him her own, beneath the bleachers. She demanded he strip because she wanted to see him naked. He was tall and well muscled with a member so big she feared it might hurt her. She discovered it grew very little bigger when it became hard and hurt her not at all. Afterward, she had no use for him.

The following week Etta told her father she had been with a man. He was in the barn, which doubled for a garage, working on the family pickup. "Papa," she said from the entrance, "I was with a boy at school."

George Warren knew what "with" meant. Finally, he scowled and said, "So you're a whore, too."

"He liked me, Papa," she said softly, suddenly not so sure of herself.

"If you see him again, Etta," George told her, already returning his attention to the engine, "tell him he's welcome to what's there."

She was gone before he finished saying it.

Etta didn't go home for a week afterward, staying across town at Aunt Myrtle's house. When finally she returned she learned her father really didn't care what she did, or with whom she did it, or why, or what time it was done. He didn't even notice her return.

Greta wasn't as angry or spiteful as Etta expected her to be. Later Etta found out why, when Greta made a scene of announcing to the family that she was pregnant.

Steven Coats had never touched her, Etta knew, nor any other local boy.

Well, Etta thought at the time, *I guess you won't be needing Steven Coats after all.*

Less than a month later Marla announced that she too was "with child."

Once Marla's announcement sank in, Etta found herself even more isolated around the house. Their mother treated these pregnancies as if they were her own, and Josephine and her daughters Greta and Marla were often found at the kitchen table making plans for the children that were to come. Etta wasn't invited into these discussions. Nor was Sela, but at least Sela had the attentions of her father, who now spent every night with the fourteen-year old, trying to conceive another child.

Etta tried one last time to get across to her father. He was shoring up a fence out in the north field. She took a pitcher of cool water out to him. He grunted when he saw her and allowed the fence post to sag on his shoulder before shifting out from beneath it. She poured the cool water into a tin cup. He swallowed its contents whole before holding it out for her to refill. It was emptied twice more before she said, "Papa, I love you. You know that, don't you?"

George Warren stared into her eyes for a time. His eyes were gray and cool and as hard as a pewter mug. "Say what you've got to say, Etta," he told her.

A hawk flew overhead, its black wings snapping against the wind. They both turned to look at it before it soared past a thicket of trees east of the field and was gone.

"Papa, why can't you..." she began. The words caught in her before she could say them. They stuttered out of her mouth and were lost. She composed herself, and waited until there were no tears to fall across her voice.

"You don't love me," Etta said. "Not since I was sick four summers ago."

"I love every child I got. I guess I can say that."

"But Sela, Papa. *Sela*. She's fourteen months younger than me and you..."

He slapped her. Hard. Blood marked her lips. Her ears rang.

He sat against the leaning fence post and sucked for air to replace what he lost striking her. Etta wiped the blood from her lip and finally pulled up the apron she was wearing to stem the flow.

For a time they sat in the sun. Then George stood and moved to the shade of a nearby pepper tree. She followed. He took the water with him and poured most of it over his head, almost emptying the pitcher.

"I never meant to hurt you, Etta," he said at last.

"I know, Papa."

"I love you girls as a father loves his children. *As a father loves his children*, do you hear me?"

"Yes," she said.

"It was God," he wheezed at last. "God told me to do it."

"Papa?"

"Sacred, you see? Not like what you think."

"Sacred, Papa?"

"Sacred, goddamn it. Sacred. Don't you understand the word sacred?"

"Yes," she told him. "I do."

"God told me to take Josie and leave our home, our family, and come here. He told me to work hard and make babies with Josie, and when they come, make more babies with the babies, so a pure race could live again once the world nearly kills itself."

"Papa?"

"It's going to kill itself, Etta. And if I was to lie with you, knowing as I do you are barren of womb, then it would no longer be sacred. It would be blasphemy. Do you see?"

Etta saw.

- 56 -

January — April, 1963

Ramirez didn't come to escort Etta on her walk. Another orderly, a man by the name of Seton, accompanied her instead. Etta wanted to ask him about Ramirez, but she didn't want to seem interested. Seton said nothing during the outing. When they returned Seton locked the door behind her, forgetting the sweatshirt and pants she wore. She stripped them off and left them on a chair to go take a shower. When she stepped back into the room ten minutes later, the pants and shirt were gone.

Each day the dose of heroin they plunged into her veins was reduced a fraction, and each day she was drawn into anxiety and desire for the drug. At first, she made a scene, throwing whatever was nearby and threatening to kill herself if they didn't fix her. This inevitably resulted in being straightjacketed and placed in the padded room, where anger was gradually overwhelmed by desire for a fix. Eventually, she begged Dr. Grodin for forgiveness and was allowed back into her luxurious room. If she were in the padded room during mealtime, the staff hand-fed her. If she were there when she needed to void herself, they helped her. It was humiliating. Throwing tantrums was futile. She gave it up.

Thereafter her withdrawal ritual was to pace the room and hum, and later sing. She hummed and sang anything that came to mind — *The Battle Hymn of the Republic, Hail. Hail. The Gang's All Here, The Tennessee Waltz*, anything that would drown the humming in her mind and help her forget the sweats and the aching pain. Just as it seemed the pain could get no worse, Nurse Stitz, or one of her associates, would bring food, which Etta gulped down. Having been a good girl, Etta knew the needle that brought her temporary harmony was on its way.

Afterwards she slept and waited for breakfast.

When David — Jack now, she kept having to remind herself — came to visit, they fought almost from the second the door opened.
"You signed me in here, David —"
"Jack."
"You signed me in here, Jack. You can sign me out."
"It's more complicated than that," he told her. "Anyway, you're not through with your therapy yet."
"If I wasn't a prisoner here, I would be through with it."

"You're not thinking straight," he told her.

"I'm not the one kidnapping people and holding them against their will."

"No, you're the junkie who's drying out. You had your fun; now pay the price."

They were shouting now, screaming at the top of their lungs. Etta paced the room, caged and dangerous, while Jack Fleming, as he was known now, took the center of the living area and held it, slowly spinning to keep his eyes on her.

"Fuck the price." she yelled. "Fuck the goddamn price, you son-of-a-bitch. Now get me out of here."

"No."

"Out."

"No."

"OUT."

"No."

"*OUT!*"

She heard the buzzer at the door sound and turned just in time to see Jack Fleming, FBI Agent, exit. The door closed behind him.

"YOU GET ME OUT OF HERE, YOU SON-OF-A-BITCH."

Her voice echoed in the enclosed room, a loud ringing that stayed in her ears for seconds.

Later, she cried.

Jack's visits slowed to weekly, then less. Two weeks passed, and she didn't see him. He still called, though, and told her about his new friends Wes and Daisy Strong and his new job, what little he could say about it. Sometimes she just listened and said nothing. Sometimes she told him what a shit he was to imprison her like this. Sometimes she was as docile as a lamb with cutlery skills, eyeing the throat of her butcher.

She tempted her orderlies with her body, and they responded enough to look, at the least, and to dream, at the most. They made no move toward her and arranged themselves in her presence so she could make no move on them. They came in twos, sometimes, or left the door open. They retreated when she walked toward them. It was laughable. She screamed at them. A lot.

After four more weeks Dr. Grodin suspended her morning injections altogether, and two weeks later her evening injections were stopped. When the first shot was stopped she expected a tsunami of pain, but it was little more than anxiety, and eventually it passed.

The loss of the second shot was more traumatic. She was placed in the padded room for throwing a coffee table at the door. She screamed and cried, bellowing at anyone wearing white. After a day, she shut up long enough to realize she wasn't in pain. A day later she was allowed back into her room.

The next time she saw Grodin, she asked, "Am I cured?"

"You're no longer addicted to heroin, Mrs. Talbert. The reasons you became addicted to heroin remain, however. That therapy I must leave to someone else. Your sessions with the staff psychiatrist start tomorrow."

That afternoon she returned from her walk to find a man in her room. As was the procedure, the door was closed while she removed the sweatshirt and pants and pulled on her robe. The clothes were off before she realized he was standing there playing with his hat. He was a tall man, Dengler's equal and then some, with a face that possessed cleaner lines, the look of a blue blood. His eyes swept her in without shame, and she allowed him to. Etta had long since learned when it came to men, she gained in influence what she lost in clothing.

"I hope you don't have the wrong room," Etta said easily.

"I know where I am, Miss Warren," he replied.

Etta dropped the clothes on the bed and pulled on her robe, sweeping her hair over the collar. She cinched the robe tight and turned again to face the stranger.

The buzzer beside the door sounded and Etta looked to see orderly Tim Seton looking through the glass window.

"You should give him the clothes," the stranger said. "Everything should be ordinary tonight."

The hair on the back of her neck rose in expectation. He wouldn't say that unless he intended to help her get out. She smiled and carried the sweaty workout clothes to the door. Seton swung the door open and took the clothes without comment.

When he was gone the stranger glanced about the room. "I heard these places were pretty nice. Never had a reason to come here before."

"Who are you?"

"Well," he said with a smile, "if you ever get a chance to describe me to David, he'll probably guess who I am anyway, so, Wesley Strong, at your service."

Etta surveyed him, wondering what this was about. Wes Strong was Jack Fleming's closest associate. "You called him David," Etta said. "I thought his name was Jack now."

"David. Jack. It's the same guy, right?"

"Yes."

"But it brings up an interesting point. To you, he'll always be David, won't he?"

She hesitated, sensing he was leading her somewhere she might not want to go. Finally she said, "Yes, he will," before taking a seat on the couch. He sat down opposite her, on the love seat, opening his jacket for comfort. She saw the weapon dangling in its sling, a revolver.

"'We cannot deny the past.' Do you know who said that? Abraham Lincoln."

"Let me jot that down," she said.

"To us, he will always be Jack Fleming. But to you, he's David Lawrence Dengler. He will always be David Lawrence Dengler, because you grew up with him and went out with him and loved him when he was David Lawrence Dengler. Am I right?"

"Go on."

"Can't change his spots with you, can he?"

"Maybe not."

"Then there's you — Etta Mae Warren. Pretty girl. I just saw how pretty. Real looker. Monroe would have blushed, so pretty."

"Okay. Thanks."

"But Etta Mae became a whore, then a junkie. To him, you'll always be the pretty girl who became a whore. He loves you, I know that. You love him. But he'll never be Jack Fleming with you, and it's the most important thing in the world to him — to be Jack Fleming. And you — you'll always be a whore to him."

"Son-of-a-bitch," she said softly.

Wes merely smiled. The smile said, *I don't mean you any harm. It's true, what I just told you.*

Etta said nothing for several moments. Wesley observed her, obviously interested by what he saw. She wanted out. She wanted as far away from Jack Fleming as she could get. She could love David Dengler — a part of her would always love David Dengler, whatever *love* was — but Jack Fleming had put her in prison. She wouldn't love someone who put her in prison. Finally she said, "I want out."

"I thought you might," Wesley said.

"There are conditions," Etta told him. She was already thinking of the cost of things. There were always costs.

"Of course there are," Wes replied, adjusting his position on the love seat. "What are they?"

"I need some money."

"Okay." He removed an envelope from the inside pocket of his suit jacket and dropped it on the table. The envelope was thick. "Two thousand dollars. Should get you started."

"I need clothes."

"I brought your suitcase. It was left at the cabin."

The cabin. To Etta, that was a million years ago. The cabin. She felt a pang of regret, a momentary yearning to go back to the place where she and David Dengler had made love.

"I'll need it now. They won't let me have anything in here except panties and this robe."

"It's a nice robe," Wes said with a smile as he stood and walked to the door. "I mean, it looks good on you." He rang the buzzer, waited an instant for the door to open, and then leaned out and said something Etta couldn't hear to someone standing outside. A moment later the door was closed.

"How are you going to explain this to David?" Etta said.

"Well, Jack Fleming will be told you escaped. That's what you would do if you could, wouldn't you, escape?"

"Yes."

"Then that's what he'll know. It's just as well, Miss Warren — you don't mind if I call you Etta, do you?"

"No. That's my name."

"It's just as well you leave his life now, Etta, because Jack Fleming is being given a big assignment, and it means you wouldn't be able to see him anyway. You would grow to resent the separation, and he might come to resent your demands on his time."

"I see," she said. Etta didn't believe any of this, of course. She knew how badly David Dengler had it for her and nothing — nothing — would keep him from looking for her. That's why she had to leave the area.

"As for David Dengler, the man Jack Fleming used to be, we've arranged for it to appear he dies. That's happening right now, Etta. You must believe yourself David Dengler is dead and Jack Fleming is an FBI Agent you've never known. Do you understand?"

The buzzer sounded again and Wes went and retrieved a suitcase from someone behind the door Etta didn't see and placed it in front of her. "I had everything cleaned," he said, "just in case you didn't have a chance at the cabin."

"Thanks." Etta took the case and headed for the bathroom.

"About David Dengler," Wes prompted.
"He's dead. I know."
"And Jack Fleming?"
"Never heard of him."

They took her out the back exit after hours. She saw no one. Outside a light snow was falling. There was a Lincoln waiting for them. Wes slipped into the back, with Etta.
"Where are you taking me?" she asked.
"We've rented you a hotel room across town. Nice place. Room service. The works. You'll like it."
"And then what?"
"You fly out tomorrow morning."
"To where?"
"Now that's none of my business, is it?" Strong told her with a hint of a smile. "However, if you're looking for referrals, I might have a few suggestions."

One of the agents carried her bag and Wes signed her in. They took the elevator to the fifteenth floor and then walked a long hall whose walls were papered in a beautiful flowery print, pale yellow and blue. The bellboy opened the suite door and found a light switch. Wes tipped him and sent him on his way.

Etta had never been in such a beautiful place before and spent several minutes admiring the furniture in the bedroom, the bathroom fixtures, and then the paintings in the suite foyer. She turned and was surprised to find herself alone with Wes. He'd removed his overcoat, coat, and tie and was unbuttoning his shirt, his eyes steady and sure and clearly on her.

"How much?" he asked.

Etta hesitated. "I'm expensive," she said finally. "Two hundred."

Wes removed a crisp $50 bill from his wallet and dropped it on the bed. "Now let's be serious," he said.

She began to undress.

- 57 -

May, 1963

David Dengler shifted himself on the pickup seat, moving slightly to readjust his arms and legs and the warmth they generated. It was cold, dark, and miserable. He cursed below his breath and again checked the knit cap to make sure it covered his ears. He never imagined New Orleans could get this cold in spring.

Dengler had been sitting outside this apartment house for four hours. Inside was the man he'd followed for two weeks. Dengler picked him up first at the Marcello mansion several weeks before, a youth who didn't seem to fit any of the stereotypes of gangland associates. He was of average height, no more than five feet eleven inches tall, and lean. The subject had thinning brown hair and a face that would easily fit on the shoulders of a ten-year-old. He never drove, always taking a cab or, more often, walking or catching a bus. He was a former Marine by the name of Lee Oswald.

At various times over the previous several weeks Dengler followed Oswald from the estate of Carlos Marcello to 544 Camp Street, and even inside, where he chanced upon the young man entering the offices of *W. Guy Banister, private investigator*. Banister's office address was actually 531 Lafayette Street. The two addresses were actually for the same building, almost an arm's length apart around the corner from one another, and both entrances led to the same set of offices upstairs.

Two days after Dengler picked Oswald up at the Marcello mansion, Wesley brought him Oswald's FBI file and it reeked of CIA connections. First, there was Oswald's defection to the Soviet Union. Oswald was released from the Marine Corps on a family disability discharge — his mother was supposedly dying of cancer. It wasn't true, and under normal circumstances the Marine Corp. would have taken the time to check it out. Here they didn't, granting him an immediate discharge.

While still in the Marines, Oswald was given a Russian language examination. That they would give an everyday Marine a Russian language test without further objectives in mind stretched reason to its snapping point. To do so with a man alleged to have leftist leanings struck Dengler as unlikely, at best. Oswald was then assigned to a Top Secret job in Japan working as a radar operator covering U-2 long-range reconnaissance flights over the Soviet Union, giving him possession of just the sort of information the Russians might be expected to care about. It was also information the United States might sacrifice in exchange for other goals. Shortly after Oswald defected to the Soviet Union with information about America's spy flights, Major Francis Gary Powers' U-2 spy plane was shot down over Soviet territory.

After spending two years in the Soviet Union, Oswald returned to the United States with his pregnant wife Marina, the daughter of a KGB Colonel. As far as the FBI could determine, the CIA had no interest in Oswald and didn't debrief him, as was customary with returning defectors. Either they had no need to debrief him, or conducted it in secrecy.

Dengler wondered why the FBI hadn't shown an interest in Oswald, at least to the point of questioning him on his return from the Soviet Union.

Now here Oswald was, visiting the mansion of New Orleans Mafia boss Carlos Marcello, as well as the offices of Guy Banister, a former FBI Agent and head of an operation providing guns and supplies to anti-Castro 'Freedom Fighters.'

Dengler met with Wes Strong in the back room of a tire and brake service center on Mission Street, not far from the French Quarter. There was a dirty flat red Coke machine in the room, several calendars on the walls — one the famous Marilyn nude on red silk sheets — and a green leatherette couch with stained chromium armrests and legs. The ashtray on the coffee table was filled to the brim with snubbed-out butts. They were alone.

"He's a mole," Dengler said when he closed Oswald's file.

"So it appears," Wes said. "The question is, for who?"

"Why didn't the FBI pick him up on his return from the Soviet Union?" Dengler asked.

"I'm not sure." Behind Wes Strong's voice there was the sound of air wrenches whining as they unscrewed lug nuts, and beyond that, the sound of traffic out on Mission Boulevard. "But my guess is The Director didn't want to tip his hand about Oswald and let the CIA know we're aware of him."

"They've got to know the FBI's interested. The man defected to the Soviet Union with American state secrets."

"Oswald was old news when he returned," Wes said, staring forward toward the work bays and the street beyond. "The data he gave the Soviets was old stuff. Low echelon, too. Also, the way he got back into the country was a tip-off. The Soviets cleared his exit papers in a matter of days, and the State Department loaned him the money to get back into the country."

"So no one debriefed him when he arrived?"

"Not that I'm aware of," Wes replied. "Like I said, The Director probably didn't want the CIA guys aware of our interest."

Dengler didn't buy that. Something was wrong here. He let it pass. For the moment.

"What about Banister?" Dengler said.

"Former FBI Agent-In-Charge of the Chicago office. He retired and came here. He's a casual friend of the The Director."

"He's CIA now?"

"It happens. People have a right to seek employment wherever they want, you know."

The truth was, the FBI hated the CIA, and the CIA returned the feeling, with interest. *Had Banister been a CIA mole in the FBI?* Dengler wondered.

"So what's Oswald doing with Banister?"

"Banister's got him on the payroll," Wes said. "Under the table, of course. He runs a private detective agency. Divorce cases, mostly. Oswald doesn't work on those, though. He spends a lot of his time circulating *Fair Play For Cuba Committee* flyers. Draws out the leftists and establishes Oswald's 'bona-fides' as a pinko. At least, we think that's what he's doing. It's possible the Russians 'turned' him and he's working for them. Or he's on Marcello's payroll."

"Or he's really working for Banister," Dengler finished. "Not exactly clear, is it?"

"I think that's the idea."

"What's the Marcello Family connection?"

"Oswald's uncle is a soldier in the family. He runs a little book, horse racing, ball games, that kind of thing."

"Does Marcello know Oswald is working for Banister?"

"It's been mentioned on the surveillance wires, but without comment. Someone will say, 'So he's still working for that Banister guy?' and someone else will say, 'Yeah, that's right.' Nothing conclusive there."

"What about Banister?" Dengler said, flipping through the file pages again just in case he missed something.

"Now that's hard to say. We don't have a wire on Banister because The Director hasn't authorized one, but we've walked through the Camp Street place a couple of times. You know, because of the gunrunning business. If Banister knows Oswald is a nephew of one of Marcello's soldiers, we don't know about it. He might know. He might not. He trusts Oswald. Or at least he acts like he trusts him. Oswald has the run of Banister's office, with open file cabinets and all that."

"He thinks Oswald is CIA," Dengler said. It was a statement. *Of course he does*, Dengler thought. *He would have to.*

"Yeah. Can't figure it any other way."

"Which means that's what the CIA is telling him."

"Yeah. That's how it would have to be."

"So Oswald was definitely CIA when he went to Russia." Another statement. *How could it be any other way?* Dengler thought.

"Don't get ahead of yourself," Wesley told him. "Maybe the CIA thought so. Maybe they were wrong."

"There are a lot of maybes."

"Welcome to Spook City," Wes said wryly.

"So what do we do now?"

"You follow Oswald. We wait."

- 58 -

Weeks of following Lee Oswald had led here, at least this day, to a small apartment building in the poorer section of New Orleans.

Four hours. It was beginning to look like a long night. If Oswald's visit went beyond another four hours, Dengler would call a number Wesley gave him and an FBI agent he didn't know would drive up and take his place on the street. Dengler, positioned a block away, would never see the agent's face. Eight or ten hours later, after Dengler had a chance to get some sleep and food, the ritual would reverse, or if Oswald had moved Dengler would call Strong for Oswald's new location. Oswald was never allowed free movement.

Dengler pulled the leather jacket tighter around his shoulders and hunkered down in the seat. Beneath the jacket he felt the grip of the Walther PPK nudge him. *Screw that .38 snub*, he thought of the FBI issued weapon. The Walther didn't take up as much space and provided more firepower.

Dengler found a comfortable position and propped his head on the seat back. His thoughts turned to Etta and what she was doing this moment. Where she was. How she was.

At shortly before 10:30 P.M. the front door of the apartment house opened and Lee Oswald jauntily descended the steps. Standing still, Oswald reminded Dengler of a tree looking for a good spot to fall on, but in motion he was a dynamo whose body parts were oiled and moved in unexpected ways. Dengler had followed a taxi that brought Oswald to this place, but now it seemed the young former Marine was interested in a walk in the night, cold though it was.

Dengler cursed beneath his breath and drummed the steering wheel with his fingers until Oswald disappeared around the corner, then threw open the door and followed.

Oswald was wearing a light cloth jacket and bargain slacks, an outfit not intended to provide warmth, while Dengler at least had a leather jacket, jeans, a knit hat and gloves. Still, Dengler was cold and Oswald didn't appear to be. Oswald didn't shove his hands into his pockets, or pull his arms to his sides to provide warmth. He paced into the cold night air as if embracing it, inhaling it, glorying in it. Dengler thought, *You crazy son-of-a-bitch*.

Dengler gave him some room. He trotted to catch up to within a half block of the smaller man, saw he was too close and slowed down until Oswald had a lead of seventy-five yards. The street was dark but for pools of light shimmying every fifty yards, street lamps suspended by cable writhing with the wind.

The two men paced together for half an hour, Oswald in the lead and setting the tempo, Dengler behind and maintaining his distance. The neighborhoods around them changed as they walked, from the shabby apartment area Oswald had visited, to an industrial section with a number of train spurs, to an older, nicer district where ivy and bushes completely obscured the walls, and houses were large with extensive lawns. Then the neighborhood changed again, to one with smaller houses, still attractive and expensive but not mansions. Dengler found himself incapable of devoting all of his attention to Oswald, who he thought of as a small wire in this huge junction box of cable that might be a conspiracy to kill President John F. Kennedy. His mind drifted to the houses and streets and railroad spurs themselves, drinking in the atmosphere of the moment, this strange time walking in the darkness and the cold. He thought of the conspiracy itself.

He was no closer to an answer about who ordered the murder of Marilyn Monroe now than he was the night he saw Stafford shove a suppository up her anus and watched as her consciousness sank toward death. He'd hoped to hear Stafford's name mentioned in any of the Marcello wire transcripts, but in the months since he transferred to New Orleans nothing even remotely sounding like Stafford's name had been uttered in the Marcello mansion, or at Marcello's olive oil import business located near the port.

During his time in New Orleans Dengler had acted as the odd man out. He wasn't introduced to the FBI team eavesdropping on the Marcello Family, nor to squads assigned to follow Marcello and his major lieutenants. He was, as Wesley liked to call him, the 'unknown factor' and The Director wanted to keep him that way. Dengler knew this meant 'deep penetration' at some point — being placed in contact with Marcello or one of the other people involved in the plot. Until then, he did what he did best — surveil, surveil, surveil. Even here they kept him from potentially exposing his identity as an agent with anyone really important, hence his tail of Oswald. At best Oswald was a double agent who, like himself, was attempting to gain information about what was happening for his superiors, whoever they were. Sheep guarding sheep.

Dengler had asked Wesley for a run-down on what the Bureau found on Stafford since the Monroe murder. The response was disappointing. Stafford made almost a dozen trips to a place called South Viet Nam, which Dengler needed to look up in the library just to find out where it was. Southeast Asia. He'd never heard of

Viet Nam before. Stafford also made trips to Europe, the Soviet Union and Japan. His job as Executive Assistant to the National Security Advisor called him to all hemispheres. Not once in his itinerary was South or Central America mentioned. Or New Orleans.

Dengler still couldn't bring himself to believe John Kennedy would send Stafford to murder Monroe. No matter how much proof he found that Kennedy was a philanderer — and Wes enjoyed bringing Dengler copies of FBI reports about sexual encounters in the White House involving The President and young women — Dengler couldn't make the leap in his mind — lover-of-women to killer-of-women. Still, Stafford was Kennedy's hired gun below cabinet level; Stafford had killed Monroe with the help of two goons from of the Cleveland Mob; and Kennedy was in contact with Carlos Marcello and Sam Giancana, the two most prominent Mafiosi in the country.

Public exposure of Marilyn's diary would have ended the Kennedy presidency.

Dengler snapped out of his reverie when he noticed Oswald wasn't in front of him anymore. He stopped. Instinctively his hand went for the Walther PPK. Without turning his head, Dengler scanned the view directly in front of him, trying to see if Oswald had taken cover nearby but was betraying movement. The scan brought his gaze to the middle of the street where Oswald stood beneath one of the big overhanging street lights, arms crossed at his chest, staring at Dengler.

There was little chance Oswald would be able to identify Dengler later. He was still fifty yards away, and it was dark, but Dengler felt like an idiot allowing this jerk Marine to 'make' him.

Dengler released the Walther and dropped his arms. He stared back.

Moments passed. Did Oswald think Dengler was tailing him for intelligence purposes, or the more likely circumstance — Dengler was going to rob him? Oswald showed no interest in finding out first hand. Like Dengler, he hadn't moved in several minutes. Dengler decided he needed to disengage himself from this impasse. He took a step back.

"That's a good idea," Oswald called. "I've got a gun," he added, his voice high.

Dengler pivoted and ran. He didn't hear Oswald's footsteps behind him. When he reached the corner, he skidded around it on his knees and peeked back. Oswald was gone. *Where?* Dengler wondered. *Forward?* That would mean he had no interest in finding out who followed him. Or did Oswald cut across the block somehow intending to head him off?

Oswald had to consider the possibility he was being followed. If Oswald really was working out of the Office of Naval Intelligence, as Dengler suspected, then at the very least he'd received the same training as Dengler. He couldn't assume Oswald was a deadhead, someone put into place because he knew nothing and was capable of nothing. He couldn't assume that.

Dengler stood finally and stepped back out into the street. The street lamps continued to swing with the wind, and there was a hollow whooshing sound as the gusts bellowed in primal singularity. Oswald was not standing in the street.

Dengler watched the pools of lights writhe to and fro, swinging about to lose this object and gain that object beneath their light. A dog trotted nervously across the street and was lost to the darkness of the far side. A tin can bounced down the pavement landing irregularly, keeping a wind rhythm.

Dengler realized the truth. Oswald had 'shaken' him.

Dengler leapt into a run up the street. It was a guess, but a guess was better than nothing. Dengler took it, turning right. The regular beat of the Walther PPK against his ribs began to hurt in a soft, unyielding, relentless kind of way.

Dengler passed the second block and looked down at the parallel street. No Oswald. He passed the third intersection, then a fourth. No Oswald.

Dengler crossed the seventh block. He was in the middle of the intersection and still running when he saw Oswald standing beside an idling Chevrolet Impala. There was nothing Dengler could do but keep running. He continued across the street and out of sight before slowing to a trot, and then a walk. He limped back to the corner, lungs sucking for breath.

Oswald was still standing in the middle of the street talking with the driver of a 1961 Chevy Impala. The former Marine squatted outside the passenger window. The car was at least a block away. If Oswald or the driver of the car saw Dengler run by, neither showed any interest.

Oswald was listening to something the man in the Impala was saying. Dengler could tell this by the way Oswald occasionally looked around, as if trying to find something to focus his eyes on while he received instructions. He nodded every now and again, gripping the door handle and tugging on it anxiously.

Oswald's handler, Dengler thought. Oswald's version of Wes Strong. Proving Oswald was an agent. Had to be. Who else would meet someone this late at night in a deserted part of the city? Drug dealers, maybe, but Oswald didn't strike Dengler as the drug type.

The driver's foot pressed the brake pedal. Dengler's eyes adjusted to the red glow of the brake lights before realizing Oswald was already gone. The Chevy Impala backed up the middle of the street, transmission whining. For one heart-wrenching moment Dengler thought they might have discovered him and now were coming at him from two sides. His hand went instinctively to the Walther. The Chevy spun around in reverse and quickly accelerated up the street toward Dengler. It was alongside him in an instant, the driver unaware of his presence.

Dengler caught a glimpse of Oswald's handler as he went by.

Gray Stafford.

- 59 -

Dengler sat on the asphalt for a long time. He didn't try to reacquire Oswald. He didn't try to move. He just sat with his back against the brick wall and considered what he'd seen.

Stafford. Jesus God, Stafford. Just thinking about the man opened a sluice of fear. He tried to deny it to himself, but the truth was Dengler feared Stafford in the way a beaten dog fears its master. When Stafford took Dengler's shoe and crushed his genitals against Marilyn Monroe's bathroom counter, something in Dengler snapped. From that moment on he knew he couldn't stand up to torture, that he was less than other men.

Like a beaten dog, he dreamed someday he would kill Gray Stafford.

When Dengler arrived back at his hotel near downtown New Orleans, the desk clerk told him he had a message from Courier. 'Courier' was Wes Strong's current code name, which he changed every month. The message was simple — 'Call me.' Rather than place the call from his room, or from the desk, Dengler found a public phone two blocks away, at a Pure Gasoline station. The line rang three times, then a woman's voice said, "Yes?"

It was Daisy.

Dengler stayed with the protocol. "Is Courier there?"

"Is this Elite?" 'Elite' was Dengler's current code name.

"Yes," Dengler said. He wanted to ask her how she'd been. Their last moments together lingered in his mind like an exotic perfume. *The smell of her. The taste of her.*

"It's been so long," she said. There was something in her voice, something beyond and greater than the forced friendliness of its tone. Dengler wondered, *What's going on here?* She shouldn't answer Wes' business phone. It was against the rules to involve family in the business, and dangerous.

"Yes," Dengler said after a long moment. "A long time."

"Are you going to be home?" she asked.

"It's almost 1:00 A.M.," he said. "Where else would I be?"

"Stay there," she told him. "Courier will be right over."

Dengler found a bottle of rum that he mixed with warm Coca Cola in a twice-used glass. He propped himself up onto the bed and waited. She was coming, but had no idea why, or where Wes was.

Was he coming with her? Had she told Wes about the night they spent together?

He finished the first drink and poured another. It was nearly gone by the time he heard the knock on the door. He asked, "Who is it?" She didn't answer, merely opened the door and pushed it wide. She looked as if she were on her way to brunch. She wore a pale blue skirt and jacket and matching blouse with one of those hats made popular by Jackie Kennedy. She didn't come in until he jumped from the bed and escorted her inside, before anyone could see her. He locked the door behind her.

"Can I get you something to drink?" He asked.

"What have you got?"

"I've got rum. I've got Coke."

"Rum and Coke, then."

He'd saved a clean glass. He poured Coke into it, and then rum. She took it from his hand and downed almost half of it.

Dengler sat on the end of the bed and motioned she could take the room's only seat, a thread-worn wing chair, but she declined with a shake of her head.

"I wondered what happened to you, Jack," she said with a quick sweep of her eyes across the room. "I knew you were going places. You went."

Dengler grinned. "So I did."

"I was down for a visit with Wes. He lives down here now, almost. Anyway, he was called away. Wouldn't say where or why. Said he was expecting a check-in from you and if you called, to say he would be in touch tomorrow, or the next day at the latest. He left your number and the codes."

"He broke ranks," Dengler said softly.

"Yes, he did."

"And you called me. For old times sake."

"In a manner of speaking, yes."

"It's good to see you," Dengler told her. "Really."

Daisy didn't respond. Dengler sensed she was sorting things out. Finally she said, "Could you turn out that light? It's very bright." Dengler opened the door to the bathroom, turned the light on, and then turned off the room light.

"Better?"

"Yes."

She looked lost. Moments passed. Time ticking away was excruciating, the silence crushing. Unable to take it any longer, Dengler strode to the center of the room and wrapped his arms around her. She caught a breath immediately and embraced him. After a moment he heard, "Thank you, thank you. It was awkward, and I didn't know how..."

He kissed her then.

They made love as they had that first night, gently and sweetly. It was difficult for her to find release. He led her to it, sensitively carrying her body to where her mind was hiding. She gasped and stiffened, and then collapsed on top of him. Afterward, they slept side by side.

When he woke she was weeping. "What is it?" he asked, turning so they could look at one another. She resisted the gesture and wrapped his arms around her. After a moment she said, "He's not like with you, Jack. He hits me."

"I know," Dengler said.

"He wasn't like that before we were married. He wasn't like that."

"He owns you now. Anyway, it's the way he thinks."

"He told you that?"

"No. But, the way he talks, the way he acts. Some people think like that. Leave him."

"It's not so easy."

"Yes. It is. Just leave him. He told me you're the one with the money. Just leave him."

"Jesus," she said softly. And then, a few moments later, "I married the wrong son-of-a-bitch, Jack."

"Yeah. I see that."

"No, you don't understand." She pulled out of his arms and turned to look him in the eye. She smelled of sleep now, sleep and warm female skin. She said, "I married the wrong son-of-a-bitch."

"Daisy, I..." He searched for a way to say it, and could find only, "There's someone else."

"Doesn't matter," she said after a long while, easing back into his arms. "Doesn't matter because I married the wrong son-of-a-bitch."

- 60 -

When Dengler woke, the room was bathed with sunlight and it was already growing warm and the air stale. He heard Daisy in the bathroom and rolled out of bed. She was standing at the sink. The Jackie Kennedy suit looked as if it had just come from the cleaners and she was carefully fitting the hat onto her head.

"Morning," he said.

She didn't reply for a moment, and then said, "Hi," with a distant voice.

"Look, I'm sorry about last night," he told her.

"I'm not angry with you," Daisy told him. "Really, it's my fault. I should have known you were spoken for."

"Daisy..."

"No, really. I'm an adult. Didn't I just commit adultery? And really, Jack, you're wonderful in bed, even when it doesn't mean anything to you."

"It meant something to me."

"I'm leaving Wes," Daisy said, stepping back from the mirror and appraising herself. "I'm going straight to the airport. I'll close the house in Georgetown and then fly to be with my parents."

"Okay. Good. That's a good idea."

"I won't see you again, Jack," she told him, turning from the mirror to look at him. "But I want you to know I do... did feel something. I love you, in fact, is what I'm trying to say. So much I can't stand to be around you. So this is it, okay?" Tears were ruining her makeup.

"Yes." Dengler felt cold inside, and adrift. "I never meant to hurt you."

"No, you pitied me."

"I didn't pity you."

"Thank you for loving me, making love to me. I didn't know it could be like that." She placed her hand against his heart, as Etta had done so many times, but he realized it was only to ask him to step aside. He flattened against the wall, and she walked out of the bathroom. Dengler watched Daisy step to the door. She didn't look back. She opened the door and exited.

He didn't hear from Wes Strong for two days. He continued his surveillance of Lee Harvey Oswald, following him from the office at 531 Lafayette Street to the Marcello mansion, and then to a bar where Oswald would sit alone between making telephone calls, nursing a Pabst Blue Ribbon and eating beer nuts.

'Elite' received a call from 'Courier' early that morning, waking Dengler from a deep sleep. When he answered the phone, Wes Strong said merely, "St. Saens, now." It was a bakery near the French quarter. Strong had pointed it out to him weeks before.

Even though Wes said *now*, Dengler arrived half an hour before Strong and was eating a second pastry and nursing a third cup of coffee when Wes stepped through the double doors and took a seat opposite him. Dengler said nothing, but noted his handler looked pale and distraught, even though he was clean-shaven and as well dressed as always.

"I've been out of town," he said. "Daisy said you called."

"Yeah."

"So, what's up?"

"I followed Oswald to his handler."

"Yeah?"

"Gray Stafford."

Strong didn't respond. Instead he looked away, out beyond the glass window at the buildings across the street. The waiter came. Wes ordered espresso. When the waiter was far enough away, Wes said, "How do you know he's Oswald's handler?"

"Deserted street. After eleven o'clock. Oswald didn't even get in the car."

"You sure it was Stafford?"

"Gee, Wes, I think I can remember what Stafford looks like."

"I mean, did you get a close look? Are you sure?" Strong's expression was intense. Dengler's reaction to Stafford was personal and visceral. For Wes and even The Director, Stafford was mostly a name, a player named by Dengler as being involved in the murder of Monroe. Now Oswald appeared to be Stafford's man inside a mob plot to kill the President of the United States. Dengler had better be right, Strong's tone suggested.

Wes downed the espresso as if it were a shot of whisky and motioned for another. "Bring me a pastry, too," he told the waiter. "Something with apples. Do you have anything with apples?"

"Certainly," the waiter said, and was gone, the crinkle of his white uniform diminishing as he moved across the room. "I need something to absorb the acid in my stomach," he told Dengler. "My stomach's been giving me a lot of grief lately."

"I got a good look at Stafford," Dengler told Strong. "He drove right by me."

"Did he see you?"

"No."

"Jesus, are you sure?"

"I'm still alive."

"Wait here," Strong said. There was a phone across the room, near the alcove where the bathrooms were located. Strong slammed several coins into the phone and dialed a long number. He spoke quickly and nervously. Dengler saw the veins sticking out in his neck, even from this distance. Strong returned in two minutes and leaned across the table. "Leave. I'll call you with further instructions."

That night he received a call from 'Courier.' Strong said, "Suspend all activities. I'll be in touch."

Later Dengler went to a movie, ate a hamburger, and drank a Coke at a restaurant where the waitresses wore very short cowgirl skirts and blouses with frills on the arms. He then went back to the hotel and slept, dreaming of Etta and Daisy as if they were the same person.

He also dreamed something about John F. Kennedy, but he couldn't remember what the dream was about the next morning.

The following evening he received a call from 'Courier.' Wes' voice sounded strained. He said simply, "Radio. A-M 790. I think you'd better catch this." Then he hung up.

Dengler turned on the clock radio on the bedside table and lay down to listen. It was a talk-interview show. Too late for the introductions, Dengler guessed by the host's comments that several of the guests, who spoke with Cuban, or at least Spanish accents, had experienced some kind of altercation with Lee Oswald several days before. It was something about Oswald attempting to join their organization by passing himself off as a supporter of the Free Cuba movement. At the urging of one of the Cubans who was alleging Oswald was a communist, the host asked him, "Mr. Oswald, are you a communist?" to which Oswald replied, "No sir, I am a Marxist-Leninist..."

Dengler didn't recognize the car, a beige Chrysler, but he knew the driver immediately. Dengler stood at the curb as if waiting for a bus and the car glided to a stop where busses regularly took on passengers. He slipped inside. The car was in motion before he could close the door. Wes Strong looked grim. Again, Dengler didn't know whether it was because of Daisy or the job. He decided to find out. "How's Daisy?" he asked. Strong looked at him sourly, and then back at the road.

"She's visiting her mother," he said. "Why do you ask?"

"Just making conversation," Dengler lied. "How's she doing?"

"She went home to visit her mother. Just as well. Every time we get together, she drives me nuts. I don't know about marriage, Jack. I mean, what do men really get out of it except a lot of grief? It isn't as if you can't get a piece of ass without a legal document."

"Yeah, that's true," Dengler said, facing forward. "But Daisy's a great girl," he continued. "Lots of personality. Good education. Good looking, too. And she can cook." Dengler said this last as if it were the most important thing in the world. Strong looked at him as if he were a child, and then executed a left turn onto LaFayette Street. They drove past Guy Banister's office building heading for the French Quarter.

They parked the car two blocks from a little outdoor cafe near the center of the French Quarter. The cafe was almost empty. They found a table away from the railing and ordered coffee. The day was glorious, milder, and clearer than it had been in weeks, and the Quarter, never over-populated during the day, was even quieter than normal. Their coffee was brought, and they were left alone. Strong wasn't prepared to speak and Dengler left him to his thoughts for a time, content to think about Daisy and how things might have been different had he never met Etta.

"Your information about the Stafford-Oswald connection surprised us," Strong said finally.

"Why?" It had surprised Dengler, too, but for very personal, not professional reasons.

"Stafford's not CIA anymore. Even if he were, he wouldn't be working at the agent-handling level. He's much higher echelon. Guys like him hire the guys who hire the guys who shovel the crap."

"Okay."

"So if he's working as an agent, then it's a small wheel," Strong told him. "A small group, to keep it ultra-secret."

"You already knew that," Dengler said. "He was at Marilyn's house. Personally shoveling the crap."

Strong's expression tensed. Dengler always knew when Strong was going to say something personally distasteful. "There's something you should know, Jack. Some people in the Bureau believe Kennedy sent Stafford to murder Monroe, to clean up behind him.

They've read the diary and they've read the reports. If this had landed in the hands of the local police, and he wasn't the President of the United States, John Kennedy would have been prosecuted for murder by now."

"I don't think Kennedy's involved," Dengler said, not as sure about it as he sounded.

"Why? Because Kennedy wouldn't have someone killed? He's trying to have Fidel Castro killed right now."

"You don't know that. All you know is there's an envelope, and some mobsters say it's so. Isn't that all there is to it?"

"There's Stafford's man Oswald."

"You've suspected him of being involved with the Cubans all along," Dengler said. It was a debate now, and he was an advocate. *How did I become an advocate?* he wondered. "Now here comes this guy who works for Stafford and who attempts to infiltrate the Cubans, and you're surprised."

"We're surprised because he didn't attempt to infiltrate the Cubans. He already has. He works with the two Cubans you heard on the radio, at Banister's place. They run a military training camp up in the Everglades. They prepare Cubans to go home. With guns, amigo."

Dengler was surprised for only a moment. "Alpha 66. Yeah, so what?" Dengler said evenly. He'd read all about Alpha 66 during the long, boring days spent in the FBI library. "You've suspected he was a mole from day one. He had to be an official mole or he wouldn't have had federal support. The fact Stafford controls him is of less importance than his connection to Banister and those guys."

"No, it isn't," Wes said.

"How do you figure?"

"Oswald is the only link between the Mob and the Cuban counterrevolutionaries. Now we discover Stafford, a representative from the executive branch of government, controls him. What does that suggest to you?"

"Okay, so maybe Kennedy does want Castro dead, and he wants someone on the inside to keep track of things."

"Oswald? Keep track of things?"

"Sure. Why not? He's more capable than he looks."

Strong laughed. "The hell he is." Then, after silence engulfed them both, "Look, maybe the whole thing is a Kennedy ploy, maybe it isn't. But, there is one other possibility you aren't seeing."

"Which is?"

"Why do you think Oswald's public identity has been carefully orchestrated to make him appear to be a communist?"

"Cover," Dengler said, wrapping the word around a bite of a crumbling coffee cake, drowning it a second later with coffee.

"That's not a cover," Wes told him. "It's putting a wolf's coat over a sleeping lamb."

"Okay." Dengler said this in a tone that suggested, *Show it to me.*

"Now they've got him distributing 'Fair Play for Cuba Committee' flyers all over town."

Dengler stopped chewing. "Go on," he said after a moment.

"And when that doesn't attract enough attention, they fabricate a public altercation between two Cuban 'Freedom Fighters,' which they really are, and a 'Marxist-Leninist,' which he isn't, that winds up getting radio and television coverage." Dengler knew nothing about the television footage.

"Yeah, okay, I get that."

"Jesus, Jack, do I have to draw you a picture? Oswald is going to be the patsy. They're going to assassinate the President. And if Stafford is Oswald's handler, that means the plot originates in the White House."

- 61 -

For a long time David Dengler said nothing. If what Wes said was true, then the murder of Marilyn Monroe was merely the first attempt to 'get the Kennedys,' in this case by having the press discover the President was having an affair with the movie star, and discussing with her national security issues she'd recorded in her diary. That having failed, and with a witness to her murder loose who might muddy the waters long enough for the truth to rise to the surface, the allied forces of the CIA, the Mob, and now the Cubans, had moved on to the second plot to remove John F. Kennedy from the White House. By assassination.

"What did The Director say?" Dengler said.

"The Director is in a very precarious position," Wes said carefully. "If the plot is being hatched in the White House, as we suspect, with the aid of the CIA and organized crime, then all manner of retaliation is possible. His life, as well as all of ours, may depend on how he acts in the coming months. For this reason, the FBI must seem to be totally ignorant of the plot."

"The FBI is *the* national law enforcement organization, Wes." Spoken gently, this was nonetheless an indictment.

"I understand that," Strong said, moving forward in his seat. "I understand that better than you do."

"It seems to me, it's the FBI's mission to —"

"Don't tell me what the FBI's goddamn mission is." Wes barked. "That's not what you do. That's not what *your* mission is."

Here for an instant blazed the fire between them. Wes Strong was a Bureau man, and would ever be. Whatever the Bureau said was *Truth*, and nothing would budge him from that position. They both knew Dengler wasn't a Bureau man.

"What is my mission, Wes?" Dengler asked finally.

"You're going in. You're going to contact Oswald. You're going to tell him he's playing a very dangerous game."

"I'm going to do what?" There was no one to look, but had there been, Dengler's bellow would have been heard up and down the block.

After a cursory look around, Wes said, "Keep your voice down."

"Keep my head down is more like it."

"Yeah, that too."

"Are you crazy? Break cover? Just walk in and show my badge and say, 'Jack Fleming, FBI. We're on to the plot, Lee. We know you're really Office of Naval Intelligence on loan to the White House. We know you think you've infiltrated the organization that's planning to assassinate the President, but really, you're just being set up to take the fall.' Just like that?"

"No," Strong said in a near whisper. "Not just like that."

"Explain it to me, then."

"No badge. No Jack Fleming. No FBI." Their eyes locked. Dengler knew it was coming. "You go in as David Dengler." A world of possibilities exploded in Dengler's mind. Possibilities that ended with his death by execution, death by gunfire, death by torture, death by every method known to man, because he would again become David Dengler, murderer of government agents.

"No," he said quietly.

"It's the only way," Wes Strong said.

"No."

"David, consider —" he was already calling him David again — "there's no other way. We don't have time to infiltrate. The President may be assassinated at any moment. We don't know the when, the where, or the how of the assassination. We're blind here. The only way to make up ground quickly is to go in."

"You want me to tell Oswald he's the patsy?"

"Yes."

"The first thing he'll do is report it to his handler. That's what I would do."

"He may," Wes said slowly. "He may not."

"Bullshit. He will."

"No he won't, because he's going to believe you are who you appear to be, and just maybe what you're telling him is the truth — he is the patsy."

"Jesus, Wes."

"Your cover is you've been recruited by the Soviet Union to attempt to stop the assassination," Wes told him evenly.

"Jesus Christ," Dengler whispered again.

"If the President is assassinated, the Russians are going to be blamed for it. They know it and they want to stop the assassination before it gets started. They looked around for someone who could act independently, and nonetheless be controlled. They saw you, an ex-Army Intelligence operative gone bad."

Dengler almost stood up. Strong flinched when he heard Dengler's chair legs scraping on the concrete beneath them. Dengler took no action to leave. He didn't stand up. He didn't walk out.

"Your death was faked by KGB agents as a way of bringing you into the fold," Wes continued. "You will use your real name because the KGB knows Oswald will not believe you unless he can have you checked out independently. Otherwise, he will have to trust Stafford, and an alerted Stafford might lead the FBI to you. Additionally, we have arranged for a Russian intelligence officer to pose as your handler. Oswald knows this KGB man. His name is Kerschov. He's a Major in the KGB assigned to the Soviet Embassy in Washington. He's also an acquaintance of Oswald's wife, Marina, and an associate of her uncle. He was 'turned' five years ago. He will confirm David Dengler is a contract agent of the KGB, should Oswald make inquiries. If Oswald contacts Kerschov personally, or goes through Marina or her uncle to confirm your identity, then we know he doesn't trust Stafford and believes your story. However, if anyone else attempts to confirm your identity through Kerschov, this will mean Oswald has reported you to Stafford, and Stafford will take you out at first opportunity. Kerschov is also our back door into Stafford's office. If Stafford inquires about you through contacts the CIA possesses but we don't know about, Kerschov is in a position to know — all Soviet intelligence originating in the U.S. crosses his desk — and he will inform us. We in turn will warn you, and you will have to get the hell out of there fast. Everything understood so far?"

"Clear," Dengler heard himself say, although the truth was he was 'clear' on none of it. It was all a vision seen through a glass darkly.

"You are to convince Oswald he can't trust Stafford, that Stafford is a major player in the conspiracy, and he should find someone he can trust to bring him in. Don't ever mention the FBI, not by name. He'll come to us by order of elimination."

"You'll have someone else make the contact."

"Well, of course," Wes said, his voice disclosing irritation at having to state the obvious. "You go in to plant the seed of doubt, and to surveil as necessary. We'll get an FBI agent to make contact on another pretext."

Get an FBI agent to make contact... It wasn't lost on Dengler that he didn't say *Get an FBI agent other than Jack Fleming.*

"What happens to me afterward?"

"You become Jack Fleming again."

I'll become Jack Fleming, Dengler thought. *Again.*

- 62 -

For some hours after he left Wes Strong, Dengler walked the streets of New Orleans alone, compressed within a shell of thought. He considered leaving, taking what money he'd stashed away — there wasn't much — and disappearing. It was a comforting idea, but one that was practically impossible unless he left the United States. There was no guarantee he would be able to evade the FBI, whose bureaus were located worldwide and whose contacts included members of most of the world's governments.

His fingerprints would always say *David Dengler*. With what the FBI had on David Dengler, his life would always be on the line.

On the other hand, if they weren't lying to him and he had the opportunity to become Jack Fleming again after the current mission was completed, he would have everything he ever wanted. Maybe even Etta in time. Life as an FBI agent would be challenging, and the pay good.

If he were captured in the guise of *David Dengler*, he doubted he would be valuable enough for The Director to extricate him again. If The Director couldn't extricate him, then David Dengler would have to die, for real this time.

In the early afternoon Dengler caught a bus back to his hotel. He showered as he considered what he was going to do with his life. There was almost nothing he could do. He heard a knock at the door. He wrapped himself in a towel and drew his Walther.

"Who is it?"

"Courier," a voice from beyond the door said. For a moment Dengler thought it was Wes using his code name, but in a second his mind reoriented and he realized it was a real courier.

"Step back," Dengler ordered. He opened the door. A boy of eighteen wearing a green uniform held a package sealed in twine. Dengler signed the clipboard the boy proffered him, then took the package and closed the door. He opened it on the bed.

It was his real identification papers, from before *David Dengler* had become *Jack Fleming*.

There was a second package inside the first. Dengler opened it with trepidation. Inside he found snapshots of his Russian 'handler,' and Gray Stafford. It was something a cautious David Dengler might be expected to do, photograph his Soviet contacts. The Stafford photo was for use if Oswald didn't know his handler's real name, which seemed likely. There was a stack of twenty-dollar bills. There was a list of telephone numbers, marked with such names as *Wash. Sov. Emb.* and *Mexico Sov. Em.* There was a sheath of letters documenting the transactions of a numbered Swiss account. Current balance: $9,388.95. Dengler wondered if it were real. *Of course it was*, he realized; *It would have to be real.*

Dengler plopped onto the bed and covered his eyes with a forearm. After an hour, he told himself that from now on he had to stop thinking of himself as Jack Fleming. He again became David Dengler. Then he slept.

The tapping sound on the door was so light there was no doubt of the tapper's gender. The noise startled Dengler anyway. He rolled from the bed with the Walther ready. After four, then five more gentle taps he approached the door.

"Who is it?"

"Jack," a woman's voice said. Daisy.

Dengler opened the door. Daisy was wearing a skirt and blouse. The full skirt touched her shoes. Embroidered flowers bloomed across the blouse. Her face expressed nothing, not surprise, not happiness, not anger nor pain. Her eyes were clear.

She entered the room, then turned and closed the door for him.

"Daisy, I—"

She touched fingers to his lips. "Sh," she said. "If you talk, I might run away."

Daisy took in the squalid little room with a glance, as much of it as she could see in the darkness, walked to the bed, and began taking off her clothes.

"Please," she said between removing blouse and skirt, "lie down."

Dengler returned to the bed.

Daisy's almond skin reflected light. Dengler saw the small mounds of her breasts, the plane of her stomach, the delta that in this darkness began at a point just below her abdomen.

Dengler didn't move as she lay down beside him. He felt the fall of her hair on his brow, the texture of her skin as her leg brushed against his, the taste of her lips.

They made love.

It seemed an hour later that Dengler rose up on an elbow to look at her. Her skin was pale in this light, her chest rising and falling a beat too fast for sleep, her small breasts lost to gravity.

"Daisy," he said softly, and then could think of nothing else to say.

He just made out her eyes in the darkness. They were on him when she said, "I just wanted you so badly." She rolled close to him so he could enfold her in his arms.

Later, in the eternal darkness of his room, he said, "I have to tell you the truth." She became rigid a moment, and then relaxed. He told her about Etta and how much he loved her, and how his feelings for Etta had somehow come to be directed at Daisy during those dark months while Etta was in the hospital. He also told her about how he came to be in the FBI, the Monroe murder, and his escape — Stafford's name wasn't revealed — everything in fact up to the commencement of his current mission. He said nothing about the suspected plot to assassinate the President or the Lee Harvey Oswald connection.

Daisy seemed to take his confession without rancor. She admitted she'd flirted with him shamelessly from the moment she first met him, even if he didn't know it — he didn't — and there was a part of her, a discrete, uncommunicative part that knew she was going to have this man someday.

When she returned from the bathroom, he asked her, "What are you going to do?"

"Go back to Wes, I suppose." When she gauged his expression, she continued, "I didn't marry him out of hate, you know. That's what my parents think I should do, anyway, give it another chance. Maybe that's what I think I should do, too."

"You didn't tell them Wes beats you?"

"No." She laughed. It was a bitter, experience-weighted laugh. "I don't think my parents could accept that. But, I did tell them I'm not in love with Wes, and I suspect he has affairs. I also told them about our arguments, that they're angry. I couldn't tell them he hits me. I could never tell them that."

"It'll never work out with Wes," Dengler told her. "He'll never change."

"And I could say the same thing about your girl Etta, too. She hates herself too much to hold on to a good thing, you. She'll find some way to screw it up."

"Maybe."

"Better odds with Wes," she said with a smile.

"Yeah, but not much. And Etta has never given me a black eye."

"I'm not going to let him do that anymore. I bought a gun." The brittle sound of her voice made Dengler think she meant it.

After a moment Dengler told her, "I hope you don't have to use it."

In the silence that ensued the one question not asked loomed large. Finally Dengler said, "That leaves us."

"I don't want to lose you, Jack —"

"It's David. David Dengler."

"I don't want to lose you, whatever-the-hell-your-name-is," this last said with a small laugh. "I don't want to stop screwing you or being screwed by you. I won't use the 'L' word again. This isn't an 'L' word thing, I understand that now. I just like the feeling I get when we're together, and I would just as soon not give it up, no matter who I'm married to."

Dengler covered his real thoughts, which was that Daisy could never replace Etta, by saying, "Really, ma'am, I'm yours just as long as you want."

"I want," she said.

She did. Just then.

- 63 -

Dengler had to find a place. He knew location was everything in a situation like this. You didn't just walk up to Lee Oswald and say, "Excuse me. You're the patsy. Let's talk about it." *Well, maybe you do,* Dengler thought. *That's why location is everything.* Confronted with this revelation on a city street, Oswald would certainly turn and walk away. Later he would report the incident to his handler and request extraction. *Cover's blown, it's time to go home.* On the other hand, if Oswald were approached in even a semiprivate place, he might pause to consider what was being said to him. He might even ask questions whose answers would further confirm what was being told to him. Location was everything.

In the ensuing weeks Dengler followed Oswald everywhere, once even to the Soviet Embassy in Mexico. He waited outside the embassy for almost an hour-and-a-half. As he waited, it occurred to him Oswald might be a real Soviet contract agent.

During the time he stood outside the Soviet Embassy he 'made' what he was certain was a CIA observation post opposite the embassy entrance, on the third floor of an office building. It was a little thing, really. Something most people would miss. This particular office window was far cleaner than the windows to either side, or above or below. *Much better to see you with, Little Red Riding Hood. Click.*

Dengler was safe from observation because he stopped half a block down the street where they couldn't photograph him. They must have photographed Oswald, as they must everyone who went into and out of the Soviet Embassy. He would have to report this to Strong.

He followed Oswald back to the United States the following day, riding in the same bus. Even though they were the only two American males of the same age on the bus, Oswald took no notice of him. He was wrapped up in a dilemma of his own, one that made him seem angry and worried.

Two days later Oswald left his rooming house and walked four blocks to a bar called *The Blarney Stone*. Dengler, who had slept that night in the pickup outside Oswald's rooming house, followed him on foot. When Dengler entered the bar, he saw Oswald sitting at a table in the back.

Dengler stepped past Oswald and took one of the bar stools.

Oswald walked to the foyer leading to the bathrooms and public telephone and placed a call. Dengler watched as Oswald spoke a few words, his code name, probably, and then was told something, probably that his handler wasn't immediately available but would be back shortly. Oswald read off the telephone number of the public phone, then hung up and headed for his table.

When the bartender came, Dengler said, "Give me two beers. Forget the glasses." They were *Pabst Blue Ribbons.* Dengler took the long necks between two fingers and a bowl of beer nuts in the other hand and walked to Oswald's table. He sat down with, "Let me buy you a beer. What do you say?"

The look in Oswald's eyes was the same as animals get before they're eaten. He submerged that expression quickly and straightened. "What are you," he said forcefully, "some kind of faggot?"

"Business, Lee. I've come here to talk business."

"What kind of business? And how do you know my name?"

"Remember that night in the middle of the street?" Dengler said gently. "Remember the night when it was so windy and someone was following you?"

"That was you?"

"I've been following you since before that night. Following you everywhere."

Alarms were going off in Oswald's mind, Dengler saw, even as he fought to keep his expression calm and noncommittal. "Why?" Oswald said three seconds after it should have been asked. "I didn't do nothing. Why would you have a reason to follow me?"

"You haven't done anything," Dengler told him between a swallow of beer, "yet."

"What kind of shit is this?" Oswald growled, his high, thin voice pulled down to vibrate off his testicles. He sounded almost tough. He leaned forward across the bar and said, "Who the hell are you, pal?"

"I'm a messenger. I've been sent to tell you something."

"Yeah? Well, what is it?"

"The exact quote is, 'Tell Lee Oswald he is playing a very dangerous game.'"

Lee Oswald sat back against the bench seat and drank short, quick gulps from the beer. He took in Dengler for a moment, and then directed his eyes away, across the bar at the brightly-accented Wurlitzer jukebox. There was no music playing at the moment.

"Who sent you?" Oswald said.

"The Soviet Union."

Oswald snorted. "They don't give a shit about me," he told

Dengler. "They could give a shit less if I live or die. Never did care."

"That was before you joined a conspiracy to assassinate President John F. Kennedy," Dengler said evenly. "That's before you allowed yourself to be set up as the patsy, with the finger pointing directly at the Worker's Paradise."

"Jesus fucking Christ." Oswald blurted. He was out of the booth and heading toward the door before Dengler could stop him. Dengler did the only thing he could think of. "Hope you don't mind, Lee," he called out to him. "I'm going to wait here and take your call."

Oswald pivoted and stared back at Dengler, then past him at the public phone. They could hear the bartender in the adjacent room, loading flats of beers onto a dolly. Oswald returned to the table.

"This is bullshit," he said after a moment, in a voice as strained as it was low. "I don't know what you're talking about."

Dengler laughed. Oswald was an idiot as well as a fool. The disdain he held for the ex-Marine must have shown on his face. Oswald bristled. "Fuck you," he said.

"You got your dick caught in a hinge, Lee," Dengler said. "You think you're working for the CIA, but believe me, you're not."

"Why don't you just lay it all out on the table for me to look at, messenger boy."

"Okay," Dengler told him, and waved to the bartender as he manhandled a dolly laden with crates over the rubber floor mats behind the bar. "Hey, can we have a couple more beers over here?" Dengler paid for them with cash, and waited for the bartender to pace away across the room before he said, "They've set you up, Lee. They told you that *you* were going to infiltrate a plot to assassinate the President. You have. What they didn't tell you is, it's their plot."

"Who the hell are you, anyway?" Oswald asked him. "Who the hell are 'they?'"

"My name is David Dengler. You may have heard of me."

Oswald struggled with the name for a moment. Clearly, he remembered it from somewhere. Then it came to him. "You're dead," Oswald told him. "I saw it on the news." He kept the long-necked beer very close to his chest now, as if it were a weapon held at 'port arms,' and stared at Dengler as if trying to remember something else about him.

Dengler removed an envelope from his jacket pocket, took out several newspaper clippings as well as all of his Dengler ID and dropped them on the table. Oswald glanced at the documents for a long moment as Dengler's eyes rested on him, waiting. Then Oswald moved the documents around with a finger, touching them in a manner not to leave fingerprints. Dengler smiled. *Good,* he thought. *Oswald believes enough to not take chances.*

"How did you get involved in this mess?" Oswald said.

"I saw something I shouldn't have seen. Your handler decided to remove me. I was able to get away, but I had to kill a couple of hoods he contracted from the outside. He turned them into agents on paper in order to justify the public manhunt."

There was no question in Oswald's mind this man sitting before him was David Dengler. Dengler saw recognition in his eyes. The news clippings were the most convincing. While Dengler knew it wouldn't have been hard to forge them and age the paper, Oswald apparently didn't know it could be done. He couldn't know it had been done, because these were real photos of David Dengler, photos that hadn't been printed when the real manhunt for David Dengler was on. The FBI had seen to that.

"Why?" Oswald asked. "What did you see?"

"The murder of Marilyn Monroe," Dengler said evenly. "She was having an affair with the President." He purposely left out Bobby Kennedy and his relationship with the dead movie star. No need to cloud the waters. "Gray Stafford had her killed to implicate the White House."

"Who's Gray Stafford?" Oswald said in what appeared to be seriousness.

Dengler took the Stafford photo from his pocket, dropped it onto the table. "You tell me," he replied.

In spite of himself, Oswald betrayed a flash of recognition. He recovered instantly and shoved the Stafford photo into the pile of other documents. "I don't know who this man is," he said evenly. "I've never seen him before."

"You're full of shit," Dengler said.

"What's your connection with Monroe?"

"Army M.I. graduation assignment out of Fort Lee."

"Don't be an asshole," Oswald said.

"The graduation exercise usually involves placing a known public figure under surveillance for a week. It's always a public figure because as public figures they have no legal right to privacy, and whatever the graduating soldier finds can be verified against previous files."

"So while Gray Stafford was planning to kill Monroe, the Army was sending out trainees to surveil her?"

"Yes."

"You were captured?"

"Yes."

"And they were going to kill you, but you killed two of them first and got away?"

"Yes."

Oswald grinned cynically and shoved the pile of papers back across the table at Dengler. "I was on the run for awhile," Dengler continued. "Then the Soviets brought me in and arranged for my 'death.' They already knew about the plot to assassinate Kennedy and they had to find an independent operative to act in their interests. They knew from the beginning your defection to the Soviet Union was bogus, that you were sent over for some other reason, but they could never figure what that reason was. After you returned to the United States, they had you surveilled until their people were 'made,' and they had to back off. That's when I was brought in."

"You don't know a fucking thing," Oswald said.

"Gray Stafford is a special security advisor to the President," Dengler continued. "If you don't know that, you're stupid or you're being lied to. He's your handler. I saw him the night I followed you and you 'made' me. I don't know, but I suspect he recruited you out of the Marine Corps while you were stationed in Japan. He's the one who arranged for your training in Russian. He's the one who ordered you to defect to the Soviet Union in order to establish a public persona as a communist and a traitor. And now he's the one who's ordered you to infiltrate Guy Banister's organization."

"That doesn't make any sense," Oswald said with a grin that suggested he was dealing with someone who couldn't possibly know the truth. "Everybody knows Mr. Banister's politics, and he isn't a communist sympathizer. My 'public persona' as a communist, as you called it, would be less than worthless with him."

"It will make perfect sense after the assassination," Dengler said, "when Lee Oswald's politics are brought to light. Soviet defector. Communist agitator — *the Fair Play for Cuba Committee*, all that. Let me guess what you've been told. The defection to the Soviet Union was to infiltrate some defense industry of theirs, something like that, but you were never assigned to that area by the Soviets. When Stafford ordered you home, he assigned you to Banister, told you your former cover as a communist could be used by Banister's organization to attract real communist sympathizers so Banister's anti-Castro organization could construct dossiers on them. You would act as a stalking horse. That was a cover, too, because Stafford's 'real' assignment for you," and here Dengler drew quotation marks in the air, "the assignment he told you is real, anyway, is to infiltrate a right-wing plot to assassinate President Kennedy, a plot that involves Guy Banister, the Cuban anti-Castro organization known as Alpha 66, and the CIA."

"Jesus, what a load of crap," Oswald said. "I know Banister. He's this right-wing rah-rah guy who has an office in my building, that's all. I never heard of this Stafford guy. And I am a communist, I have been since high school, and that's the way it is."

"The reality is this, Lee," Dengler said dispassionately. "Stafford and Banister and Alpha 66 and the Carlos Marcello family — you remember them, I've followed you to and from the Marcello mansion a number of times — are united in smuggling guns and operatives into Cuba, and drugs into Miami. The CIA takes its cut from the profits and uses it for its own purposes, training counter-revolutionaries, and the like. Each has its own reasons for killing Kennedy, but they're real reasons. Now the only thing missing from this scenario is a patsy to take the blame for the assassination. That's where you come in. Stafford developed you for this very purpose. There really is a plot to assassinate President Kennedy, except the man you report to is in on it. And you're the fall guy."

"Bullshit."

"Your recent trip to Mexico City and the Soviet Embassy, what was that about?"

"I took a vacation. Period."

"Stafford had you reapply for entry into the Soviet Union. He told you it was needed to confirm your convictions to Cuban communists who were beginning to suspect your reasons for attempting to sign up supporters for the 'Fair Play for Cuba Committee' were other than obvious and straight-forward. This made you angry because the communist part of your cover has already been established, and why should you need to strengthen it? Here's the real reason Stafford sent you to Mexico — so the CIA could photograph you entering and exiting the Soviet Embassy."

Oswald said nothing for a long time and Dengler allowed him the silence. Oswald sipped the last few drops from the long-neck and then dropped it onto the table where it almost tipped over.

"You can confirm everything I've told you," Dengler said, pushing a business card across the table. "Alexei Kerschov, Soviet Attache' for Cultural Affairs — read KGB — the Soviet Embassy in Washington D.C." Dengler watched for some reaction on Oswald's face at the mention of Kerschov, but there was none. "Use the name Collier when you call," Dengler continued. "Collier is a member of the American Communist Party and calls embassy officials through the switchboard all the time. Or you can have someone else check it out, if there's anyone you trust enough."

Oswald merely looked at him. *What a package,* Dengler thought.

The public phone rang. Oswald pocketed the business card, slipped out of the booth and walked to the alcove where the phone was located. He answered it on the fifth ring, said, "Hello," listened for almost a minute, and then hung up. When he passed the table he reached out for his jacket, but said nothing, and moved for the exit.

Dengler followed him.

- 64 -

Dengler followed Oswald to his hotel. Several times Oswald looked back over his shoulder at Dengler, but made no gesture of recognition. He entered his building and Dengler slipped behind the wheel of his pickup. It was almost eleven now and Dengler had been at it for the better part of sixteen hours. He knew Oswald would do nothing about the contact for the moment. He would have to think it out, maybe even take it to Stafford, in which case Dengler would be home free. Wes Strong would yank him from the assignment. At least, that's what Dengler told himself.

Dengler called the 'exchange' and twenty minutes later another agent arrived. Dengler waited down the street until the car previously identified on the phone arrived in front of Oswald's hotel, and then Dengler put the pickup in gear and drove away. He went back to his hotel room — the sixth hotel in as many weeks — showered and fell into bed naked and still wet. He dreamt about Etta and Daisy, and about other, darker subjects he couldn't remember later. When he woke it was almost 10:00 P.M.

Dengler showered again, went down the block to pick up a burger and fries, and a newspaper, returned to his room. He ate the burger hungrily, savored the fries as he read the paper, and allowed the phone to ring the customary four times before picking it up.

"Boston," a male voice said.

"Denver," Dengler replied. He'd never heard this voice before, but knew by the code employed it belonged to one of Wes Strong's men.

"Oswald has packed up and left New Orleans," Boston told him. "We think he's going back to Dallas. He left this morning."

"You're sure it's to Dallas?"

"We're on him."

At this Dengler imagined FBI agents following Oswald's bus across the desert, two white guys wearing thin ties and dark suits driving a Chevy in hot pursuit of the unkempt former Marine riding a Greyhound bus. It made him smile.

"I need to talk to Boulder," Dengler said. "Is he available?"

"Later today, maybe."

"I need to talk to him."

Dengler hung up. The room was very still. The single light bulb hung by a cord from the ceiling was bare and white and ugly. Dengler had lit a fire beneath Oswald, or was ordered back to Dallas and Dengler's involvement was merely incidental. It didn't matter. He got up and began packing.

Strong's call came three hours later, long distance from some place where the wind was blowing so hard Dengler could hear it over the line. He didn't ask Strong where. "Boulder," Strong said, keeping to the protocol.

"Denver," Dengler replied.

"Pack up. Follow him. There's a place called *The Carousel Club*. Get a table there Wednesday night. Someone will make contact." He hung up before Dengler could say goodbye.

The old red truck wasn't ideal for cross-country driving, lacking as it did either a heater or air conditioner, but as he headed west he found that the weather grew milder. The constant whine of the transmission was a lullaby. Dengler fought sleep, keeping the windows opened and the radio blaring, when he was close enough to a town to pick up a radio station.

Dengler thought about Etta, and Daisy. It had been months since he last saw Etta, even longer since their time in the mountains, the last moment he knew peace. Since then he'd met Daisy and made love to her. His feelings for Daisy bothered him — he was being unfaithful to Etta, although she left him and not the other way around. Etta was everything he felt he was — an outsider, someone who was unloved, a person intended by fate to be a loser. Daisy was everything he wasn't, well educated, charming, comfortable inside her skin.

For David Dengler, they were day and night.

Etta the hot nights.

Daisy the cool, free days.

He yearned for each.

Dengler connected with *The Loop* and circled Dallas.

Dallas seemed like a raw city to Dengler, with its wide streets and untended, weed-ensnared lots that reminded him of gaps in teeth. It seemed neglected and negligent, populated by men who wore cowboy hats made of straw, and women who spoke with twangy voices and wore hair glued into submission.

Dengler found a motel in the Oak Park district. It was nearly 8:15 P.M. He called in his location, then showered and then fell into bed and sleep almost simultaneously, the window air conditioner blowing cold air across his body. When he woke, Wes Strong was sitting in the chair opposite his bed, drinking a grape Nehi soda and munching cracker-and-peanut butter wedges he'd bought from the vending machine in the hallway two doors down.

"'Morning,'" Strong said. "Want one?"

"God, no," Dengler said, pulling his naked body up into a sitting position. "How'd you get in?"

"Picked the lock." Strong grinned at his own resourcefulness.

"Next time just knock," Dengler said. "What time is it?"

"After ten."

"What are you doing here?" Dengler said, wrapping the top sheet around him and stumbling toward the toilet. "I thought I was supposed to rendezvous with someone at a place called *The Carousel Club*."

Strong grinned. "We're running a hook-and-back. See if anyone's been paying any attention to you. We'll check for known operatives tonight at the club." Strong raised his voice as Dengler swung the door closed to pee. "It's a big hangout for the locals. Half the Dallas PD is there every night."

Dengler flushed the toilet, threw some tap water into his face and exchanged the sheet for a towel he wrapped around himself with the experience borne of months of motel life. "So you want me to stay away?"

"Hell no," Strong said, tossing the last cracker sandwich into his mouth. "You're the bait. Won't catch anything if there's no bait."

Dengler opened his bag. Everything was wrinkled. He had packed quickly. "So what happens if I'm 'made?'"

"Then we're going to have to yank you out. Jack Fleming will get a foreign assignment for a couple of years. England Station, maybe. But you're not 'made,' David," Strong assured him. "This is a precaution, that's all."

"What about Oswald? Why did they pull him out of New Orleans?"

"Maybe because the President is going to visit Dallas in November."

Dengler said nothing. The silence lingered in the room like a bad taste. Finally, Strong broke it with, "It's going to be announced today."

"Oswald left New Orleans day before yesterday."

Strong smiled. "Apparently he knew about the trip before we did."

Gray Stafford. He knew about the Kennedy trip before them, and they were worried he knew about Dengler, too. Hook-and-back.

"What kind of trip?"

"Political. Speeches. Hand shaking and baby kissing. You know the routine. A motorcade, too."

Dengler dismissed the motorcade immediately. The Secret Service and related agencies would have every building covered so well no one would ever be able to get off a shot at a moving vehicle. Also, the Secret Servicemen assigned to the President would leap over him at the first sign of trouble. The real threat would be at the political gatherings, the pancake breakfasts and rubber chicken lunches, because the public relations people wouldn't want to damage the President's image by placing too much security around him. After all, what did an American President have to worry about when visiting an American city?

"Where's Oswald now?"

"Back with his wife Marina and their child, at least for the present."

- 65 -

September, 1963

The Carousel Club stank of cigarette smoke, beer, sweat, and sex, in equal portions. The smell sex gets when it's sold and served on the half-shell, a day past fresh. Dengler knew the place well, even though he'd never been inside. It was like *The Blue Bell*, the bar his father once frequented. When Dengler entered the club the smell of it was so powerful he almost stepped back.

Dengler took a place at the bar and ordered a Schlitz, then turned with the long neck in hand to survey the room. It was a fat place, almost as wide as it was long, with a bar in one corner and a stage in the other, at opposite corners. There was no curtain on the stage — that would have been too gentile — but a backdrop of a carousel painted in mock modern art style. There were stools in front of the stage, but set up in such an angle as not to block the view to most of the room. Dengler imagined the locals placed their clothed butts there to watch the naked butts perform. He hated the place already and wanted to be somewhere else.

He finished the beer and ordered another. It was early. Wes told him if anyone made contact, it would mean two things. First, Oswald had reported him to Stafford. Second, they expected to turn him. The Carousel Club was a big hangout for cops, and for the small Dallas intelligence community. It was also one of several very popular strip joints and always attracted a large military crowd. It was already half-filled with off-duty cops, cops in plain clothes, servicemen in T-shirts, their cigarettes carried in turned-up sleeves, and men who looked incapable of attracting anything female of the human persuasion.

The band showed up just after seven. It was a five-piece group with a drummer, two guitars, a pianist and a xylophonist. They set up to the left of the stage in an area that was segregated from the rest of the patrons by a small fence, but on the same level as everyone else. Dengler watched them as he nursed the second beer. Then, bored, he turned his gaze on the door and watched as the crowd stringed in, groups of two and three, males for the most part looking dirty around their collars and beneath their nails.

"Don't think I've seen you around here before, mister," the voice said, and Dengler realized he'd been blind-sided. The voice didn't sound like Texas — it was less nasal and sharper, like an east-coast accent, but not exactly that, either. It was also ethnic, Italian, maybe, something urban. When he turned to look at the man he guessed Jewish, although he still wasn't certain.

The man looked to be in his late 40s, a beef roll with marbling at the edges. His hair was thinning on top, short but greased down, more black than gray. His huge hand, which had been extended probably from the moment he arrived, was flinty and callused.

"What?" Dengler said, still too disoriented to say anything even remotely intelligent.

"New around here, right?" the man asked. He was still smiling, but Dengler noted it wasn't a real smile. It was a controlled gesture, probably something he did a hundred times a night.

"Yeah. That's right."

"Jack Ruby," the man said. *Oh*, Dengler thought. *A Jew.* He guessed right.

"David," Dengler said, purposely withholding his last name. He took Ruby's hand and shook it. Ruby's hand was hard, strong, and ugly.

"Welcome to The Carousel Club," Ruby said, still shaking Dengler's hand. It was a moment before Dengler realized Ruby was assessing him. *But for what?*

"Thanks."

"It's my place," Ruby said.

"Oh, well... nice place," Dengler mumbled.

"You like women, David?"

"Sure."

"Beautiful women?"

"Yeah. Yes. Of course."

"Well, that's all we got here. Some of the best-looking exotic dancers west of Chicago and east of Los Angeles. Got more tits and ass than you can shake your stick at."

Dengler didn't quite know how to respond to this. He said nothing. He was vaguely aware he was still smiling, and so was Ruby. His hand was still locked in the beefy man's grasp. Dengler withdrew his hand.

"So you enjoy yourself, you hear?" For a moment Ruby sounded almost Texan.

"Thanks," Dengler said stiffly.

"You need anything — anything at all — you just ask for Jack Ruby. I'll fix you up, and if I can't —" here he gave Dengler a wink and a laugh "— I know someone who can."

The bear of a man wandered out into the burgeoning crowd.

The band played several numbers to an uncaring crowd and then a comic spent the better part of twenty minutes telling lewd jokes that were worse than dirty, they weren't funny. Dengler used the time to watch Ruby as the burly man worked the house. There was more to Ruby than met the eye, Dengler decided, more there than the sourly ingratiating bar owner would ever let anyone see. He was masterful at making everyone in the place, regular and first-time visitor, feel invited.

Ruby moved from table to table, from group to group, greeting each person he found with a hearty handshake and often a bawdy comment. More than once Dengler could read what Ruby was saying from across the room by observing his hand gestures, the thrusting forearm, the finger finding its way into a hole his other hand made. Ruby always laughed and the patrons always laughed, but it wasn't the laughter of amusement. It was the laugh twelve-year-old boys make when they fondle a picture of a naked woman and, ink and paper aside, feel the excitement of intimacy. Dengler had always found this kind of thing repulsive. A part of him wanted to hit Ruby. Instead, he looked away.

Wes Strong entered just after nine but appeared not to notice Dengler. Strong was with two other men who looked like businessmen out for a night of slumming — or like they were FBI agents. Dengler turned when he saw Strong and pretended to check out the liquor stock behind the bar. Dallas was still a dry city, and technically this club was really a speakeasy, but with the liquor as obvious as the cops, the whole statute thing seemed silly.

Dengler turned just as Ruby trotted onto stage to introduce the first of the strippers. Sweat marked Ruby's shirt at armpit and waist. He took the mike and grinned when the first anticipatory applause erupted.

Dengler didn't listen to Ruby's introduction. It didn't matter. Everything he said about the stripper was a lie anyway. Instead, he returned his gaze to the several groups of men who'd drawn his interest repeatedly over the preceding hours, and who now looked in rapt concentration at the stage. In the far corner Wes Strong too stared raptly at the stage, betraying only for an instant a look in Dengler's direction, and a faint, almost invisible smile.

Dengler wondered about this for a moment after the first of the strippers pranced onto the stage. She was a voluptuous girl, a blond very much reminiscent of Marilyn Monroe, wearing a cowboy vest and skirt shorter than most aprons, and little else. She said nothing and moved immediately into a dance that caused her breasts to writhe and threaten to pull the vest apart, but miraculously her nipples remained covered. She wasn't a particularly good dancer — even the music of this band was beyond her skill to accommodate — but the audience loved the performance anyway. They hooted and clapped in animal delight.

He didn't look at her face at first. Her body was so familiar he couldn't take his eyes off of its various lovely parts, this quivering breast, that shaken hip. So perfect were these clues that long before he looked up to see her face he knew who she was.

Etta.

- 66 -

Dengler was aware time was passing, one song succeeding another, his drink shattering against the hardwood floor, moving through groups of men whose dedication to spectacle barely slowed him. Dengler was aware of the anger his passage incited as he pushed men aside. All he had to do was acknowledge one of them to fight. Still, all of this was irrelevant. All of it was secondary to the feelings percolating inside him.

He reached the edge of the stage and stood at its center, ten feet from Etta. She stopped dancing when she saw him. The audience, unaware something momentous was happening, shouted an angry protest. Taking its cue from Etta the band stopped playing and Ruby, halfway across the club, started making his way toward Dengler. "What's he doing?" Ruby said. "What's he doing?"

Etta recognized Dengler, too. A flash of acknowledgment exploded in her expression. Fear, but more than fear too.

Etta stepped away from him, and backed across the stage.

David Dengler wanted to touch her, hold her, talk to her, and make love to her. He was angry, yes, and aware he was inviting a small riot, but he ignored that and jumped up onto the stage. Etta broke and ran. Dengler followed her to the sound of hoots and protests from the crowd.

She made the corner of the stage before his hand found her arm, and behind the stage itself before he was able to spin her around. For crystalline moments they stared at one another, two sets of eyes locked together as if by genetic fusion, before he said, "You bitch," and she smiled bitterly.

A man grabbed his arm, and another man. One of the men was Ruby. "What the fuck are you doing here?" he said. Dengler easily wrenched free from him and moved two steps in Etta's wake before the first blow struck. Dengler turned and dropped the bouncer, a beefy man half again bigger than Ruby, with a short but brutal jab to the gut. Leaning past the falling man, Ruby landed a good one and Dengler felt it before spinning further to confront him. Etta hit him then, from behind, with something that hurt so bad he knew it was hard and long and gripped with two hands. He never saw what it was. The bouncer was back, then, pummeling him with repeated blows which Dengler returned faintly. He went down and found himself looking at her legs, the same ankles that wrapped around him many times as she came and came and came when they were together in the cabin in the mountains. Dengler almost passed out, but he heard, "Get him up. Get him up." Four sets of male hands lifted him up to the level of their shoulders. Etta was turning red now, totally still, and as red as a rose, but he realized it was the blood flowing from a head wound, his head wound, and into his eyes.

The men carried him to the door and opened it. His last glimpse of Etta was as his body angled toward the pavement of the alley outside the back door of *The Carousel Club*. She stood perfectly still and watched him fall, her hands clutched to her vest, mouth half opened as if to say something. He heard no sound after that but felt the burn of the pavement as it scoured his face, the recoil of his body as it butted the earth, and darkness so vast it consumed him.

"Jesus Christ. *Jesus Christ*. Careful. Don't turn him over." It was Wes Strong's voice. It was tinged with worry, but not for him, for something else. Dengler felt no pain. There was no pain, not if that searing brilliance in his mind was something else. He was hurt, certainly, but not in pain. He was a broken thing. "Jesus, look what they did to him," Wes Strong said somewhere off in the distance.

Dengler opened his eyes. Strong was kneeling above him. He was holding Dengler's shoulder, as if to keep him in place, but Dengler wasn't aware of any place he was in. He was in a netherland, an oven of discourteous events. Why was Wes Strong kneeling above him? Where was Etta? Who was that guy who stood above him and kicked the shit out of him for what seemed like hours?

"You're going to be okay," Strong said. "I chased him off. Jesus, he was just kicking you." Dengler had no memory of it. Not directly. He remembered Etta, and the door, and flying through the air, but the rest was meaningless. "Do you know what day it is?" Wes Strong asked him. "Jesus, do you know what year it is?"

"Monday," Dengler responded, but even he knew it wasn't Monday. It was Wednesday. He remembered it was Wednesday. "Wednesday," he said.

"Right. Wednesday."

He felt Strong rifle his clothes. "Didn't get the piece," he heard him say. "Wallet's still here."

"Who," Dengler heard himself ask.

"The bouncer. She had the bouncer come back out and kick the shit out of you."

"She?"

"She was just standing there, looking. Jesus Christ, David, you better stay away from that broad, because she doesn't love you. Not the way she was just standing there looking while you took the beating of your life."

"Etta?" He was beginning to slur his words, or worse, just realizing he'd been slurring them all along. "She wouldn't..."

"Don't you believe it, pal."

"No."

"God, where's the fucking ambulance?"

"No, not Etta."

"Believe it."

He didn't believe it. He never would.

- 67 -

The night Etta spent with Wes Strong, he recommended a job in Dallas, if she wanted to get out of hooking. It was the only true thing she knew about herself, she was attractive to men. She never seriously considered getting out of the trade. Strong suggested there might be another way of selling herself.

"God, you are one sweet piece of ass," he said, again and again, after he'd had her twice, neither time to her satisfaction, of course. He liked to run his hand from her ankle to her womanhood, feeling every curving muscle of her long legs, every minute inlet of skin. "I can see why Dengler's nuts for you. Hell, I can see that plain."

Strong told her about Ruby's operation. "He's got dancers. Some of 'em make a little money on the side, whatever. He's not against his girls turning a buck, but he doesn't take a percentage. Once in awhile he might insist you go out with a cop — Ruby's a big one for keeping cops happy — but mostly you just get up there on stage and shake what God gave you in abundance."

"What's your connection with Ruby?" she asked. Somewhere down the road she might need to know what kept the FBI and Jack Ruby dancing.

"He likes keeping cops happy. I'm a cop."

"You wouldn't tell David?"

"No."

Etta flew to Dallas, Texas the Wednesday after she left the sanitarium. That afternoon she took a cab to Ruby's bar, a real sawdust-on-the-floor kind of place called *The Carousel Club*. She was directed into his office by a bartender. The room was nearly bare except for cheap Apache dancer prints on the walls, a desk, and two chairs.

Etta wore a chic gray suit complete with hat and gloves. She looked class, and she knew it — the outfit was similar to the one worn by Kim Novak in *Vertigo*. She bought it for that very reason. Her hair was pinned up in back, accentuating her eyes and lips.

There were several men with Ruby. He dismissed them, and they left without saying a word. They looked at her as if choosing a thick piece of meat for dinner. When the door closed, Ruby said, "Wes Strong said you're good looking. *You're good looking.* Can you dance?"

Ruby was a rude looking man, fat but not obese, with a slight body odor. She'd slept with less attractive men in her life, but not by choice. Etta sensed he knew she was above him in the normal order of things, and she also knew such men often attempted to prove otherwise, sometimes with painful repercussions.

"Does it matter if I can dance?" She said this with a confident grin. She knew Ruby saw an exquisitely beautiful woman, a Kim Novak, a Marilyn Monroe, confident of her beauty and confident of herself.

"Okay," Ruby said. "Then let's get to what matters. Strip for me."

Etta wanted to ask *Here? Now?* That would have been a break with her facade. That facade was all she possessed at the moment. Instead she said, "What? Just for you? That would be... such a waste."

Ruby looked at her a moment, allowing them both to see she'd taken the upper hand from him. "Okay," he said slowly, anger controlled but obviously there, "Then let's invite a few more people in. In fact, let's move this out to the stage. There's a few people working out there — we're fixing a floor, putting down new floor boards — but you saw that when you came in. You won't mind a couple of carpenters watching, will you?"

Moments later, on stage, Etta stood wearing her Kim Novak suit and waiting for the men to gather. There was no band, of course, this being early afternoon, and the lighting in the club was bright and businesslike.

"Ladies and gentlemen, Etta Warren here," Ruby said to them all, taking one step up onto to the stage and facing the gathering 'audience,' "our new dancer — well, prospective new dancer, shall we say — is going to try out for *The Carousel Club*. I'm sorry, Etta, but we have no musical accompaniment. You're just going to have to wing it."

There were fifteen people. Etta counted them. The two men who had been in Ruby's office when she arrived, carpenters wearing leather pouches filled with nails, bartenders, vendors, one of them wearing a Pepsi Cola insignia on his shirt, two women, one she would later know as the club bookkeeper, and a number of other people she would never identify.

"You can start when you want," Ruby advised, and joined the audience with a big grin on his face that said, *You've just been fucked, baby.*

Etta stood there a while. It felt like eternity. It was fifteen seconds. Then she said, "I can't dance when there isn't any music." Ruby took this as an admission of defeat and made a move for the stage, to let her out of the vice he'd put her into, but she continued, "But as for the rest, yes, let me... *entertain* you."

She might not be a dancer, and she might not even be a stripper, but there was one area Etta had confidence in, her relationship with men. They thought she was special. At least, that's what she told herself as she removed the little jacket that covered her blouse and folded it, carefully laying it across a stool on the stage.

Ruby retreated a step, back to where he stood before, and watched as Etta removed her clothes, one item at a time, slowly, deliberately, with the precise movement of a person who liked clothes, and who protected them. First the shoes, then the blouse revealing the bra, then the skirt revealing the garter belt and stockings, then each stocking, rolling each one carefully and painstakingly so it wouldn't snag. There was nothing salacious about her actions. She might have been in her bedroom removing her clothes at the end of an evening. With the stockings gone she unhooked the garter belt, folded it, then reached back for the clasp of the bra. Her performance was so different from what was normally seen on this stage everyone in the room had become a voyeur, peeping at something that seemed private and shouldn't be seen.

When her fingers found the hook, Etta paused and looked at Ruby. The smirk was gone from his face. He said, "That's okay. Bra and panties are fine. You've got the job." She knew that instant he wanted her and, at least for the moment, didn't want to share her. She despised him. She knew she would be sleeping with him tonight.

"It's okay," he said again.

Etta unsnapped the bra and allowed it to hang from her shoulders for moments, then removed it, holding her left arm across her breasts in a coy pretense of virginity.

"You've got the goddamn job," Ruby barked.

Etta slowly allowed her arm to drop to her side. With both hands at her waist, she pushed the panties off her hips and then to the floor.

"Jesus," one of the vendors said.

Ruby arranged for Etta to have a room in the same hotel he lived in, at least until she could make other arrangements, he said, and then told her he had clients coming in from out of town and would she mind joining them for dinner?

At five Ruby called and told Etta to wear the dress from that afternoon. *Uh-oh*, Etta thought, *here we go.* She attempted to explain to him that particular outfit was a day dress; at night another kind of attire was more appropriate. This wasn't entirely true, of course, although it was true enough to be believable. Ruby insisted on the dress and she finally complied. It was the best outfit she had.

A Ruby associate named Vic picked her up at seven-thirty and drove her, along with two other *girls*, Chrissie and Jasmine, to a supper club in the better section of Dallas, *The Round-Up*.

Etta met Ruby and his two out-of-town clients at a table where they were already sitting. One was a man in his late 50s named Sam Giancana. The other was a subordinate, a man twenty years younger, named Vince but occasionally called Vito by Giancana, as if Giancana forgot he'd changed his name. Etta doubted Giancana ever forgot anything.

Over dinner and small talk it soon became apparent the out-of-town clients were really mobsters from Chicago, Ruby's home town. *How are things with so-and-so*, Ruby would ask, and if they knew something about so-and-so, Giancana or Vince would say something. Chrissie and Jasmine were Sam and Vito's dates, although Sam let it be known he liked Etta very much. He let it slip in conversation he used to date Marilyn Monroe, but Etta didn't believe him. Why would someone who had as much freedom as Marilyn Monroe want to date a man twenty years her senior, and not at all attractive, at that?

"You could be Kim Novak," Chrissie told Etta. She was sincere and sweet, Etta thought.

"Novak," Giancana growled nastily, "she's screwing that nigger, what's his name, Sammy Davis. Beautiful girl like that, screwing a nigger, can you believe it?"

Etta had heard nothing about it, and said so.

"Yeah, they're keeping it quiet, those Jew bastards what run the studios — no offense intended, Jack," he added quickly. It was at this point Etta realized Jack Ruby was a Jew. "If the public was to find out Novak is fucking a nigger, it would be the end of her career, I can tell you. And they'd scrape the balls off that nigger and feed 'em to him, deep fried, for fucking a white girl, and a movie star, too."

A chill passed through Etta. These were the kind of men who just might do such things, she thought.

Later, Sam and Vince took Chrissie and Jasmine to their rooms upstairs leaving Etta and Ruby alone at the table. Ruby just looked at her, smiling in a friendly sort of way, before he asked, "You know who Sam Giancana is?"

"No."

"He's the Boss of Bosses. He calls and even Frank Sinatra comes running. He's a big man."

"He's a mobster," she said flatly.

"Well yeah, I guess he is. What do you think I am?"

"I think you're Jack Ruby. I think you own *The Carousel Club*. Are you a mobster too?"

Ruby continued to smile, but it was clear he was thinking about something. "You want to get a room upstairs?" he said after a long moment.

"Is that a proposition?"

"Strong told me all about you. He said you like smack. I've got some smack. I can cook something up for you, if you want."

Etta hadn't had a fix in months. She never stopped thinking about it, really, never put it completely out of her mind. It no longer pulled on her, asking, pleading, begging her to come back. Some of the best moments of her life were lived high, though. Some of the best. Now she was clean. Because of David Dengler.

"Sure. Why not?"

Ruby got them a room with a view of Dallas at night, the best to be had, as little as it was. She sat in one of the chairs beside the bed while he made the fix in the bathroom. When he entered the room he said, "Lift up your dress. Roll down one of your stockings."

She did as she was told. She hiked up the dress, rolled down the stocking, as Ruby looked at her. He injected her in the inner thigh, and then went back into the bathroom to pack up the kit. Ruby wasn't a drug user. Ruby drank whiskey, which was delivered to the room five minutes later, with a single glass.

Etta sat back and closed her eyes. This was a heavy hit. Her head swirled, and it was like the first time she took heroin, like that first cloud-scraping high. *Oh, thank you, Jack*, she heard her voice say, *Oh thank you thank you thank you...* Soon, too soon, she felt her clothes being tugged off, felt the flow of air conditioned air across her naked nipples, saw the huge, blood-gorged member dangling before her eyes, heard the words, *Take it, baby. Take all of it.* She took all of it, still saying, *Oh, Jack, thank you...* before there was no room in her mouth for the words anymore. Later, she discovered herself draped over the chair and felt the rhythmic pounding of a man's groin at her buttocks. *You want some of this ass?* she heard a voice say, distantly and not right, not Jack's voice at all. *It's good ass*, the voice said. *It's damn good ass. Best ass there ever was, white ass.* She knew it was Giancana whose penis was being pushed into her, Giancana who had turned her into an animal to be mounted.

Then there was another man. The world had become so vague. It didn't matter. All that mattered was the high, the wonderful high, the painless, soaring, swiftness of the high. She didn't care.

When she woke in the morning, she was naked, alone on a bed whose covers had been mussed without being opened. There were several empty bottles of whiskey, and the remains of a room service tray. Some of her clothes were missing, the garter belt, one stocking, her shoes. She was filthy.

She was still high.

Thank you, Jack, she recalled hearing herself say the previous night.

It wasn't until she was off the high, and wishing for another, that she became afraid of these men, these brutal, animalistic men.

- 68 -

A nurse told him he was in ICU and that a doctor would shortly be along to talk with him. That was at 9:00 A.M., but it was after one in the afternoon before he saw a doctor, and then by accident. The doctor was there to see the woman who was in the bed next to him. She was dying. He was checking to make sure the meter was running.

"Doctor," Dengler called when the man turned from the dying woman. "Doctor..."

The doctor might have complained, *Who? Me?* Instead, he walked to Dengler's bedside and retrieved his chart.

"Do you know where you are, Mr. Davidson," the doctor asked him, not looking his way at all, but at the chart. *Davidson. An assumed name. Again.*

"No," Dengler said in a raspy voice. Someone had punched him hard in the voice box. He remembered last night well enough, but not the punch. *But was it last night?*

"You're in Parkland Hospital," the doctor said matter-of-factly. "You're in the ICU, although you don't belong here. Nurse, why is this man here?" He spoke with someone on the far side of the privacy curtain. She didn't respond or Dengler would have heard her. The borrowed doctor returned to say, "I'll contact your doctor," and left.

Later he was moved to a private room, and another doctor arrived to attend to him. Hours passed before a nurse appeared to administer an injection. As she turned to leave Dengler grabbed her wrist. "Wait," He said is a raspy voice. "Has anyone been here to see me?"

"Why yes," she said. "A woman. She's still here, out in the waiting room. But, I was told you didn't want to see anyone."

"Send her in. Please."

Ten minutes passed before his visitor was ushered into the room. Dengler was surprised when it wasn't Etta — somehow he knew it would be Etta, no matter what happened the previous night.

It was Daisy.

She wore a loose brown blouse, and yellow pedal pushers that left her calves partly uncovered. For a time, she stood in the doorway and just looked at him. He understood by her expression how Daisy really felt about him.

"They said you're okay," she told him after awhile. "I just thought I'd stick around and say hello."

"Hello."

"I'm not supposed to be here, you know," she said, entering the room fully but still staying far enough away from the bed to keep from touching him. "I overheard Wes on the phone telling someone about what happened to you, and I just couldn't stay away."

"No," Dengler said.

The bruises and abrasions on his face, hands and arms drew her finally to the bed, and once there she broke down and kissed him, looking back over her shoulder quickly should Wes Strong be standing there, watching.

"I'm sorry," she said finally, and kissed him again, this time more passionately. Dengler didn't return the kiss. It was a conscious act. Daisy deserved better.

"God, you could have been killed," she told him, running her hands over his face and arms. "They could have beaten you to death."

Dengler said nothing.

"Jack?" She still called him Jack, he noted. To her he was Jack, would always be Jack.

"Yes," he said. His eyes were directed at the door, where she still looked from moment to moment.

"Jack, I think he knows."

"Who? Who knows what?"

"Wes. I think he knows about us."

"How?"

"I don't know, but — he knew your old girlfriend was going to be...
"

"I know." Dengler had seen it in Wes' eyes an instant before Etta walked onto the stage, a small, mean little smile that said nothing then but spoke clearly now.

"He was scared, Jack, so goddamn scared," Daisy told him. Her fingers, which had rested gently against his skin, tensed as she spoke. "I've never seen him so scared as last night. I saw it in his eyes. He knew about us. I think this was his revenge, sending you to that nightclub, except it almost went too far."

Dengler didn't know when she left, or in what mood she was in when she did leave. It occurred to him later that maybe he'd passed out — he had, after all, a concussion. It might have been hours he was lost in his thoughts, hours that seemed much longer. His next contact with the real world was a nurse giving him a shot, and afterward, he slept like the dead of old graves.

The next morning, long before first bed call when the nurses made their initial daylight inspection of patients, Dengler rose and stole a pair of pants and a shirt from the room next to his. Barefoot, it was half an hour before he found something more suitable than slippers to wear. He walked out of Emergency looking like hell, but he must have fit in with the clientele because no one stopped him.

Dengler found his motel room as he'd left it. The two bank books, one drawn on a New Orleans bank, the other from a bank in Dallas he'd established the day before, were where he left them, in a hole in the wall near the end of the bathtub. There was some cash, too, in the dresser, and clothes. He changed quickly. Someone had confiscated his piece before he was taken to the hospital, but he still had the Walther PPK that he kept in a pillowcase hung from the back side of the headboard.

He was gone in twenty minutes.

Dengler found another motel room, this one located outside The Loop, and holed up. He bought shelf food at a Piggly Wiggly two blocks away and carried everything back to his room, almost falling twice from dizziness. One passerby thought he was drunk. All dizziness from the injuries was gone in two days, however. The limp disappeared in a week. After that, he started running, and eating hot food.

At night he watched old movies on a local television channel, movies with sound tracks that popped and hissed like burning wood. As the grainy images moved before him like shadows on a wall, he thought about Etta and Ruby, the man he sensed was screwing Etta, and what all of these facts and beliefs meant to him. He recalled the hours and days and weeks he and Etta had spent in the cabin together, making love and loving one another. He thought about the way moonlight reflected from her naked body as she gave herself to him. He thought about killing CIA Agent Jim Keller, watching Marilyn Monroe die, and now trying to stop the assassination of John Kennedy. He was no more clear now about what had happened, and what was happening, than he was the night he met Hoover on the beach and joined in the war against the Agency. Really, all he had was what he believed, and he believed very little.

There was the bouncer, though. He was real. Jack Ruby. Etta.

Dark nights, these, filled with hate and anger and yearning.

- 69 -

A week after he started running Dengler decided he was fully recovered from the beating.

He waited in the alley where he could see people coming and going in front of *The Carousel Club*. The bouncer arrived just before four in the afternoon. He was driving a green 1958 Chevrolet with white sidewall tires. He watched as the bouncer pulled his fat butt out of the driver's seat, saw the car lurch a little, then heard the door slam. The bouncer locked it. The bouncer looked up and down the street but failed to look in the alley where Dengler's pickup was parked. Then he disappeared behind the angle of the building.

Later, after 6:00 P.M., Dengler saw the girls beginning to arrive. He thought he might catch a glimpse of Etta, but he didn't. He waited until past seven, then walked to a phone booth located half a block up the street and placed a call. It was a minute before the phone was answered, and then noise almost overpowered the line. Voices. Music. Laughter.

"Carousel Club."

"Hey, anybody in there own a '58 Chevy?" Dengler asked. "Parked out front?"

"Yeah. Why?"

"Somebody's beating the shit out of it with a baseball bat."

Dengler hung up and casually strolled back down the street toward the parked Chevrolet. He recognized the bouncer the moment the big man rushed into the street. Sweat marked his neck and clothes like half-dried blood and the quiver of his body almost disguised the muscle that supported everything. He ran to the car and circled it, his pace growing progressively slower as he realized he'd been lied to. There was no one here harming his car. By this time Dengler was five paces from him. He rushed the larger man. The bouncer turned and took the first blow fully in the stomach. It didn't hurt him, at least not noticeably, but within seconds Dengler was landing rounds everywhere on the man's body with total impunity. The bouncer lunged at Dengler, but he merely retreated, set himself and landed two punches, then retreated again, this time to the side.

Patrons of *The Carousel Club* pushed outside to see what was going on. Some of them encouraged Dengler, obviously past recipients of the bouncer's attentions, while others turned and reentered the bar. Dengler knew he had no more than several minutes before the police arrived, less if one of the patrons who exited the club was a cop.

Once the giant was humbled, and slowed, Dengler moved in and worked on his face. Dengler was as strong as the bigger man, younger, and much faster. His rounds were accompanied by an *unh* sound as the fat man reacted to each blow. Blood was flowing from the big man now, from his mouth and cuts above his eyes. Dengler's hands were becoming laced with lacerations, the roll of quarters behind each set of knuckles protecting the bones in his hands but doing little for the skin.

"Enough," someone said, which was quickly followed by, "Yeah, let him go." The big man was about to kiss concrete, but Dengler remembered the bouncer kicking him repeatedly when he was down. Dengler strained to make each punch significant and winced as he felt a muscle pull in his mid-back. His left hand useless now, Dengler landed a final right-handed blow and bounced back. The big man dropped to his knees and fell forward onto the concrete.

Dengler was up the street in seconds. He didn't turn to look back. There was a hollowness to his victory, a hunger unsatisfied. He didn't know this guy he'd beaten senseless. He didn't know anything about him except that one night several weeks before he'd stepped in and delivered a beating to David Dengler at the bequest of a bar owner by the name of Jack Ruby, to protect an *exotic dancer*. The fight left him cold. It wasn't the bouncer he really wanted, or even Jack Ruby.

It was Etta.

Dengler cleaned his hands in a gas station men's room, the cuts superficial but bloody, and walked. He returned for his pickup just after midnight. When Dengler arrived at *The Carousel Club*, the bouncer's car was parked where it had been hours before. There was no one on the street, merely the noise of the band as it blared from inside the bar. Dengler glanced at the entrance, wondering if Etta was inside. He instinctively knew Etta wasn't performing at the club, at least not now.

Dengler cut down the alley. His pickup was where he left it. He pulled the driver's door open. A man sat behind the wheel, a lit cigarette dangling from his lips. Dengler froze. In the darkness, he couldn't see whether the man was holding a gun. Thoughts raced through his mind. Was this someone Ruby sent to deliver payback for the bouncer? Or was this simply some drunk who'd wandered out of the bar and found refuge in Dengler's seemingly abandoned pickup?

The figure moved. He took the cigarette from his lips and flicked the ash that fell at Dengler's feet. He leaned forward into the light. It was Agent-In-Charge Robert Lowry, Wes Strong's superior.

"David," he said in a conversational tone, as if he'd just met Dengler again in his grandmother's parlor. "Long time no see."

Lowry's breath reeked of alcohol. His manner was a moment late, an inch off, imprecise in the way of a drunk. He slipped one leg out of the truck, felt for the ground with a toe, found it, and then stepped out. Dengler retreated several paces.

"Haven't seen you since... oh, before the night I arranged for your death. You should have been there that night, David. We lit up the night sky on that one. Big explosion. Nothing left of you."

Nothing left of me, Dengler thought. The truth of that made his spine tingle.

"What are you doing here?" Dengler almost appended a 'Bob,' or 'Agent-In-Charge.' In truth, he'd only talked to Lowry a few times and never got to know him on a first name basis.

"David, it's considered bad form to screw a fellow agent's wife. It works against trust and all that."

Dengler wanted to run. *Jesus, everyone knows.*

"Are you following me so far?"

"Yes." Dengler's voice was raspy. His throat was tight.

"But the one thing we will not tolerate is to let private matters effect the mission. Can't have that, David. Would you like a drink?" Lowry pulled a flask from his jacket pocket and twisted the screw cap off.

"No," Dengler said.

"Because — because," here he swallowed a gulp, "— because nothing else matters. It's the mission. That's what matters, the mission. Q Force needs you, David. The Director, this country, we all need you."

"Yes," Dengler said.

"Now I've talked to Wes. He knows he did wrong in bringing you here to see this woman, what's her name?"

"Etta."

"Right. To see her humiliate herself, and you, by standing up there... Well, he knows he did wrong. It was unprofessional. I'm not saying he doesn't — well, let's be frank here — hate you. I'm not saying he doesn't hate you. I'd hate you too. I'm not saying he does, either, because I don't know. What I am saying is he has given me his word he will conduct himself in a thoroughly professional manner from this point on. Do you understand?"

"He beat her," Dengler said softly.

"What?"

"He beat her. Abused her. Physically."

"Who? The stripper?"

"Daisy. His wife."

Lowry stared at him, surprised Dengler would bring up something like this. He returned the cap to the flask, twisted it several times and pocketed it. "I don't care," he said after a moment. "All I care about is the mission."

For moments both men were silent. Then Lowry said, "You make whatever arrangements with the girl you want, David. Marry her after this is over, I don't care. Or spend time with both women. It doesn't matter to me. Now get in the truck."

Dengler might not have, but he got into the truck.

- 70 -

Dengler took Lowry back to his motel room. Once inside Dengler's room, Lowry asked to use the phone and made a call. A quarter hour later a car pulled into the motel parking lot. Its horn didn't even sound — Lowry recognized the car by the growl of its engine. He stood from the edge of the unmade bed and walked to the door. "Stay in tonight," he told Dengler. "We'll be in touch." Then he left.

Dengler took four aspirin for his pulled back muscle, then turned off the lights and stretched out on the bed. It was nearing 1:00 A.M. He thought about Etta. He thought about nothing but Etta and Ruby's fat, sweaty, naked body lying across her like a stuffed pig. He thought of that fat son-of-a-bitch with his manhood deep inside her, of Etta crying out in pain and pleasure, of Ruby knowing everything Dengler knew about the one woman he ever loved. *Etta. Ruby.*

But did Etta still love him?

She had the bouncer come back out and kick the shit out of you... She was just standing there, looking. Jesus Christ, David, you better stay away from that broad, because she doesn't love you. Not the way she was just standing there looking while you took the beating of your life."

Wes Strong hated him, but Dengler doubted he lied about that night. Dengler had put Etta in a prison. She broke out. Finding her, capturing her again, caging her again, would just make her anger grow hotter.

Etta was gone from his life, Dengler realized, even though she would never be gone from his mind.

Lowry replaced Wes Strong as Dengler's handler. Even though Strong promised to act professionally, someone up the line, Hoover maybe, made the decision to remove him from the detail. Dengler asked about him, but Lowry was reluctant to talk about it. He finally admitted Strong had returned home to Georgetown.

With Daisy.

There was work. It was a rail. He could follow a rail. It led somewhere important.

Dengler watched Oswald for over five minutes as the spindly ex-Marine appeared to be waiting, shifting from foot to foot, looking about. Oswald glanced in Dengler's direction, but Dengler was lost to the shadows in the interior of the parking garage, sitting in the new Ford Dengler had just bought, the reflective angle of the windshield acting as a barrier to view.

Obviously, Oswald was waiting for someone, but who? Now that was an interesting question. Dengler had never followed him to this part of Dallas. He hadn't followed Oswald enough in Dallas to have established any of the ex-Marine's behavior patterns Dengler reminded himself.

Then Oswald was joined by another man. He was stocky, five feet ten or so, with thinning hair combed straight back. *Jesus*, Dengler thought, *Ruby*.

For the several minutes the two men stood at the entrance to the garage and talked, Dengler's mind raced with the possibilities. *Ruby. Oswald. Oswald. Ruby.* Of course, this was the reason Wes Strong had directed him to *The Carousel Club* in the first place. It wasn't just to parade Etta in front of Dengler. Ruby was linked with Sam Giancana, but he also had ties to the Marcello family. *The Carousel Club* was a hub where Dallas mobsters and cops met. If Dengler's presence had aroused suspicion — he hadn't — it would have caused a response.

Oswald took a small manila envelope from Ruby, the kind used as pay envelopes in factories, and shoved it into his belt beneath the T-shirt he was wearing. They exchanged ten words apiece, and then Oswald pivoted, and walked away leaving Ruby staring after him. Dengler waited until Ruby turned and walked in the direction of *The Carousel Club*, and then turned over the Ford's engine. He continued to wait, engine rumbling, for the man following Oswald to walk or drive by, but there was no one. After two minutes he put the car into gear and pulled out.

He was in time to catch Oswald stepping onto a bus three blocks down. He stayed behind the bus and followed it through nine stops. Oswald stepped off the bus then and walked north. Dengler passed him, went around the block, and reacquired him two minutes later.

Oswald. Ruby. Dengler's mind continued to race. If the Marcello family were funneling cash to Oswald, theirs or Alpha 66's, Ruby might be the spigot. They certainly wouldn't wire cash to him, or send him a check, or even cash through the mail. So, was it money in the envelope?

Dengler reacquired Oswald a second time, still walking along the sidewalk, stepping purposefully but seemingly in no hurry. *Where is he going?*

On the third pass he lost Oswald but picked up a shadow. He 'made' the operative immediately, and the operative 'made' him. Their eyes locked. He was driving a Rambler American station wagon. He looked forty-five, slightly overweight, with features that were broad and powerful. He didn't avert his eyes when Dengler looked at him. He returned the stare. Dengler hadn't met this FBI agent, even though he looked vaguely familiar. There were many agents he hadn't met. Obviously, this operative knew him.

Why was Lowry double-booking Oswald, Dengler wondered? The answer was, he wouldn't. The operative must be following someone else. Was Oswald en route to meet a contact? Dengler performed a quick survey of the passersby. It wasn't quick enough. He overshot and had to circle the block. When he returned, Oswald was gone.

Dengler surveyed the storefronts. A JC Penney's, several specialty shops, a bar, *The Four Leaf Clover. The bar, obviously*, he thought. *Oswald slipped into the bar.* Dengler parked a block away.

It took a moment for Dengler's eyes to adjust to the darkness in the bar. There was a line of booths along one wall, tables, then a bar, and then more booths in the back. The bar was half-occupied with lunchtime patrons. Dengler went to the bar first, more to get out of the light of the door than anything else. The bartender approached him. "Coca Cola," Dengler said.

Dengler turned to survey the nearby tables, and then the booths beyond. Oswald wasn't there. Leaving the drink on the counter, Dengler strolled toward the back booths that were located in front of the men's and women's toilet and the telephone kiosk. Oswald was sitting in the back booth talking to a man Dengler didn't recognize. Of course, Oswald knew who Dengler was, but he didn't turn to look at him, didn't acknowledge him in any way, and as Dengler passed he decided Oswald didn't see him. Dengler entered the toilet, urinated, and returned. Oswald was still there with the man whom Dengler saw more clearly this time. He was thirty, lean, professional looking, and Dengler imagined the envelope had already changed hands. *Probably not money, then.*

Dengler returned to his Coke, but found the operative he'd *made* out on the street standing at the bar sipping his drink. "David," he said with a smile, as if they were friends of long standing. "Here, let me buy you a drink. A Coca Cola for my friend here," he said to the bartender. "That was a Coca Cola, wasn't it?"

"Who the hell are you?" Dengler asked in a voice so low he might have slipped it beneath the linoleum. He stopped at the bar, leaned against it. *This guy really looks familiar*, he thought, even as his eyes tracked Oswald across the room.

"Kerschov," the man said. "Alexei Kerschov, KGB."

"What?" Dengler swallowed wrong and coughed. He'd heard Kerschov very well. He remembered him instantly. Wes Strong had sent him a picture of the KGB Major when he reassumed the Dengler identity weeks ago.

"Kerschov," the Russian said again, slapping Dengler on the back as he tried to cough up the soda. "I've been following this geek for the better part of a month," he continued, gesturing toward Oswald, "just trying to locate you, and I must tell you, my friend, trying to make contact with you is very difficult. You are very hard to find, you know, when you don't want to be found."

"KGB?" Dengler said. This one last piece of information was a wrench thrown into the engine of his mind.

"Yes. And I am carrying my ID today. Usually I don't, you understand. Not much use for a KGB ID here. Maybe to pick-up girls with, but really, for American girls, all I need to be is Russian." He was a jokester, this man, a creation of smiles and gestures and friendliness. The performance achieved its goal; Dengler was immediately put at ease. *Kerschov. The KGB. Let's be friends*, his manner suggested.

"You've been following Oswald to contact me?"

"Yes. That's your assignment, isn't it, to follow Oswald?"

Dengler nodded slowly. *Ruby. Oswald. And now the KGB.*

"Why?" Dengler asked.

"Because your President is going to be assassinated, David. The assassins are probably going to blame it on us. And you might be able to stop it." He smiled at this last statement, as if to say he didn't believe it himself, and then continued, "Well, if not stop it, at least point the way to the real killers when the time comes."

"How would I be able to do that?"

"David, you're a bright man. Surely, this must have occurred to you at some point. You suspect Oswald is an operative of American Naval Intelligence, that he thinks he's infiltrating the plot to kill his President, but that he's really the patsy?"

Dengler merely looked at Kerschov. Truly, he hadn't thought of it until just this moment. Truly, not until now. He was already thinking it, a glacier of cold extending the full length of his spine, when Kerschov said, "You, David. *You.* The second gunman. You're the second patsy."

- 71 -

"Consider," Kerschov said a few moments later after they sought refuge in a booth, "Oswald's credentials as a communist are excellent. The CIA has seen to that. They borrowed Oswald from Naval Intelligence, they trained him in our Russian language, they sent him to Russia, they repatriated him back to the U.S., and they gave him pro-Castro leaflets to hand out in New Orleans. They even arranged for him to get press for his activities by concocting a confrontation between his *Fair Play for Cuba Committee* and the Cuban Freedom movement. They made him what he is, what he appears to be. I must say, we in the KGB didn't understand why he was sent to Russia in the first place. He was a nothing, a complete zero, his value to either side so little as to be meaningless. We accepted him for humanitarian reasons — you know he attempted to commit suicide when we turned down his visa request? Well, he did, cutting his wrists, *here, here.*"

Dengler was barely listening to this. *Ruby. Oswald. The KGB.* It was coming too fast, too fast, and he had to think. How had he set himself up to look like an assassin? How?

"I haven't handed out any leaflets," he said in a monotone. "I haven't joined any Fair Play for Cuba Committees."

"You followed Oswald to Mexico several months ago. We have pictures of the two of you together. Is it so hard to believe the CIA did the same thing? There must be dozens of photographs in existence of you in the background and Oswald in the foreground."

"Proving what?"

"After you're both dead, I imagine the photos will be presented as proof you were his bodyguard."

"Bodyguard."

"Or associate in some other fashion. I know from having been contacted regarding your attempt to find out if Oswald trusted his bosses that he does not trust them. No word about you was forthcoming after your contact with Oswald. Still, that leaves..."

"Whose side are you on?" It was crystallizing in his mind now, Alexei Kerschov of the Soviet Embassy, a Major in the KGB, *turned* some years before, Wes had said. The FBI used him as a litmus test. All intelligence generated in the United States passed across his desk at the Soviet Embassy in Washington, and if Oswald reported Dengler contacting him that should have passed before his eyes as well. Or, if Oswald didn't trust his handler Gray Stafford to confirm David Dengler's identity, he might go through Marina's contact in the Soviet Union, her uncle, who was a KGB Major himself, and Kerschov's friend. At least, that's what Wes Strong told him, and David Dengler no longer trusted anything Wes Strong told him. Who was this Kerschov really? Was he an operative of the FBI, a *pocket man* as they were called. Or was he still a Major in the KGB?

"Does it matter whose side I'm on?" Kerschov said with a wan smile. "You're going to go out and confirm everything I tell you anyway. We understand that." When this statement elicited nothing from Dengler, Kerschov continued, "*Turned* is a relative term, isn't it? Sometimes I do what a *turned* agent, a mole, would do; sometimes I do not. I serve the Soviet State, David Dengler, just as you serve the American State. Except I have not been baited into a plan to assassinate my Chairman; I have not been backed into a corner."

"Why are you telling me this?"

The question floated between them for seconds while Kerschov sipped his Coca Cola. Then he said, "My superiors hope once you determine who the major players in the plot are, you will take your weapon and kill them, sacrificing yourself to the cause of justice, of course."

"Really? They think I'll do that?" Dengler said this around a guttural laugh. Cynical, that's how he would have described the laugh. *Ruby. Oswald. The KGB. Yes, very cynical.*

"Well, David, they are bureaucrats, after all, and we board pieces appear as pawns to them, and nothing more. Pawns are to be sacrificed, yes?"

"Why don't they... Why don't you take out the major players?"

"That would involve our becoming players ourselves, and we are not players. Players are too easily made to do what they don't want to. Let us suppose for a moment our active involvement in deterring this conspiracy becomes a matter of public knowledge. How easily this situation could be twisted into proof of our involvement in the actual plot. *Soviet Agents Linked to Assassination Plot.* Oh, the repercussions far exceed our credit. The price is too high."

"It seems like everyone knows about this assassination plot," Dengler said sourly.

"Almost everyone does. Even President Kennedy knows about it. He's placed his best man on the job. You know his best man very well, David. I believe he attempted to have you killed in California."

Gray Stafford.

"If Stafford wanted to use me in this plot, then why did he try to have me killed?"

"I'm not sure," Kerschov said slowly. "I imagine your survival in California made them change their plans about releasing Miss Monroe's diary and ruining Mr. Kennedy politically. Yes, I know about the diary, please don't ask how. When they couldn't reacquire you quickly, I suppose they switched to Plan B, which some players in the conspiracy probably prefer anyway. The ruin of an enemy is sweeter when he bleeds to death from it. In any case, your escape posed new difficulties for them, and new possibilities. Finding someone with an anti-American political background, or at least one that seems anti-American, isn't easy. The two *federal agents* you killed in California qualify you."

"J. Edgar Hoover would never enter into a scheme like this." Dengler said softly. It was unthinkable Hoover, easily the best known and most admired crime fighter in America, could be deterred by a Gray Stafford or, for that matter, by anyone else.

"David, David," Kerschov said, restraining a smile. "I don't know how to tell you this about your Director of the FBI. The truth is, David, he is a pervert with a weakness for photography. The KGB acquired him in the early 1930s, and the CIA in the '50s, by *turning* one of our agents and coming into possession of the full photo portfolio, *full* at least up until that time. I understand the CIA has a special squad whose task it is to secretly acquire photographs of The Director. In any case, there are other photos extant. It is said the Director's unwillingness to *go after* the Mafia is directly related to photos like these, but that remains rumor. What we know for certain is he is a creature of the CIA, David, and does their bidding without hesitation. He recruited you to be the second patsy."

Q Force. The various assignments he'd been given. The clandestine meetings with The Director and his agents. Most important of all, the death of the CIA field team after it had captured Dengler and Etta. All of these events telescoped in Dengler's mind and his ability to accept what Kerschov was saying was finally exceeded. The Director a pervert? He couldn't accept that. "I don't believe you," he said finally.

Kerschov took the photograph from his inside jacket pocket and dropped it on the table, then finished his Coke. He called out to the bartender for another as Dengler looked at the photo upside down, making out the various shapes and textures and what they meant. *Here is.... a man on all fours, and there, a man behind him, up close...* Dengler covered the photograph as the bartender brought two more sodas and placed them on the tabletop. When he left,

Dengler spun the photo around.

"A room at the Algonquin Hotel in New York City, oh, 1932 or thereabouts. Person or persons unknown rigged the room for documenting events. Perfect likeness, wouldn't you say?"

"Jesus." Dengler whispered.

"He likes being dominated, your Director, and humiliation. We have one such person ourselves on the Politburo, but he is a minor figure and will remain so."

"This could be faked," Dengler said, not believing the words as he spoke them.

"Yes, well, they certainly could. The CIA is better at that sort of thing than we are. Still, they could be faked. Except your Director's predilections are known *personally* to certain individuals, some of whom are seen in other photographs — yes, there are more photos, taken at different times, with different people. The Director liked this particular room, it appears. We have those people, too, as does the CIA. There is corroboration, you see, signed statements, promises of secrecy unless certain events make secrecy impossible."

"Why haven't you used it against him? Against the FBI?"

Kerschov laughed. It was a spontaneous laugh and strangely Dengler was almost offended by it. Kerschov saw this and said quickly, "No, no... I laugh because, well... We have almost used it a thousand times. It is so good a weapon, so certain a tactic, we fear misusing it, or perhaps using it at the wrong time, you see? And then wasting it. So we have never used it, and are not really using it now. It is our weakness, David, our bureaucratic thinking. It makes us wait, cautious and fearful, until what we might achieve is lost forever. No, your Director of the FBI will die one morning and free us of this fear, and the file will go unused."

Dengler stared at the photo. It had to be true, and yet it was so awful he hated believing it was true. It occurred to him then. "Wait a minute. If The Director is a creature of the CIA like you say, then who sent me to surveil Marilyn Monroe? It wasn't Gray Stafford, that's for sure."

"It's hard to see these things clearly, David" Kerschov said. "We can't be everywhere and know everything. Consider: When I say Hoover is a creature of the CIA, I do not mean he's willing, only that he's trapped. It's thought the FBI was using all the armed services intelligence schools to surveil Monroe, and other prominent people, too. Using students gives Hoover deniability, and nonetheless leaves open the possibility he will get something on the Agency and free himself. Quid pro quo, I think you call it." Dengler recalled the reason behind the *Q Force* name. "In any case," Kerschov continued, "something happened. What that something was, I don't know. Maybe the CIA found out Hoover was protecting you. There could be another reason." Kerschov placed a stubby forefinger on the photo and spun it around on the bar. "Even as he is unable to stop himself from having these trysts and exposing himself to potential ruin, he is equally unwilling to be damaged by them. He will do anything to crawl out from under CIA control."

Dengler touched the photo. He said, "Can I keep this?"

"Yes," Kerschov replied, observing him closely. "But not today."

"When?"

Kerschov removed an envelope from his jacket pocket. It was similar to the envelope Ruby had given Oswald an hour before. In it was a stack of hundred dollar bills. Later Dengler would count them. *One hundred hundred-dollar bills. Ten thousand dollars.* Kerschov pushed it across the table. Dengler allowed it to remain untouched on the tabletop.

"Ten thousand dollars, David," Kerschov said. "Expenses. We want to hire you to be a contract agent of the KGB, a relationship we will deny of course, unless it is in our interest not to deny it. As compensation for your services we will give you photographs of your Director at the satisfactory completion of your task. It is probably the only currency of real interest to you. If spent correctly, it might buy you your life."

"You want me to kill the players."

"Yes, or eliminate their usefulness. Stop this assassination, David. We do not want your President's blood poured onto the hands of the Soviet People's Republic."

"You could be running a test for Gray Stafford." Dengler said it as if he believed it, but he didn't.

"Yes, I could be. One hell of a test, wouldn't you say?"

After a moment Dengler continued, "I would do what's in the best interests of my country." He fingered the envelope. If he needed to get away quickly, and far, ten thousand dollars would do much.

"Of course. As I do when I pretend to be a creature of the FBI. I serve Russia. Of course." Kerschov removed a card from a worn leather case and placed it on the table. "You may contact me by calling this exchange and leaving a message for the person whose name is printed here. Leave a number at which you may be reached. I will call within the hour, or failing that, when I can."

Dengler lifted the card and looked at it. It was for a used car wholesaler, the last number listed an exchange in Washington.

Oswald walked by just then looking straight ahead. He apparently saw neither of them. He hit the door with both palms extended. The door shut slowly, removing sunlight from the room as if a cloud were passing overhead.

"The other man will wait for awhile," Kerschov said. "It will give Oswald a chance to draw his tail away."

"Do you know who the other man is?" Dengler asked.

"Haven't a clue," Kerschov said with a smile. "Don't care, really. Oswald is your problem; you were mine." He stood. "Well, David, I must say I fear I will not see you again. Alive, anyway. I hope I'm mistaken. You seem to be a decent fellow."

The door opened, light bathed Dengler's face again, and darkness descended. He sat alone in the shadows of the bar for half an hour, the envelope and card in front of him, before he stood, pocketed the items and went out into the light of day.

- 72 -

Dengler left the bar and lost himself for a time, not reawakening until he was behind the wheel of the Ford and miles away. The thought recurred — he might be a dead man. If the FBI and the CIA were working together, then people he'd depended on as allies were not allies. They would stand and watch him die, watch the blood flow from his body, empty their pistols into him.

Friends? None.
Allies? None.
Prospects? None.

Etta. She couldn't be one of them. Etta was too guileless to be one of them. Still, their fingerprints were on her. Wes Strong, or someone else at the Bureau, arranged for Etta to wind up in Dallas in the care of Jack Ruby. She was here for one reason only — to be used as leverage if David Dengler didn't do as he was told. It was pretty clear what that would be. *Second patsy. Yes, Kerschov was right. The second patsy.*

Dengler thought of the CIA field team that he'd assisted in murdering. Stafford wouldn't sacrifice them just to manipulate Dengler, would he? No. Their deaths served a second, greater purpose, one he might never know. Were they traitors of someone who was part of the conspiracy? Were they competitors whose stock was too high, who presented themselves for easy liquidation? He didn't know. When the President of the United States was the ultimate goal, anything was possible, any act justifiable, no matter how bloody, or inhumane. Dengler had fired the bullet that killed Jim Keller. He sacrificed Keller's life, and the lives of his detail, for the greater good and denied the immorality of the act. Dengler dismissed the guilt he felt. He had to focus on the present.

Kennedy was scheduled to visit Dallas in less than four weeks.

First order of business — Lee Oswald.

David Dengler acquired Lee Harvey Oswald Friday morning, November 1st, at his rooming house on Beckley Street. The Ford was parked at the curb a hundred yards down the street and Dengler watched as Oswald paced out of the house and stood at the end of the walk, in front of the curb, and waited for his ride. Dengler had presumed Oswald would take a bus to work — he took a bus almost everywhere he went. This often created problems for Dengler, who had to slow down and in some cases stop the car so as not to pass the bus and lose sight of Oswald, who might exit at any time. Still, here Oswald was, standing and waiting for a ride, which arrived in seven minutes. It was a two-tone 1955 Ford, an earlier version of Dengler's car. Dengler gave the driver a lead of thirty seconds, then put his Ford into gear and followed.

The drive to west Dallas took less than fifteen minutes. Dengler stayed a hundred yards behind Oswald's car, occasionally moving up close enough to see the two men talking, mostly the driver, with Oswald nodding, and looking out on the countryside. These two men were not friends. Whatever it was that cemented their relationship, it wasn't friendship.

The 1955 Ford pulled to the side of the Texas Schoolbook Depository, let Oswald off, and then pulled away. Apparently, the driver didn't work in the building. Dengler found a parking place in the train yard west of the building, pulling up behind a plank fence, and stepped out to survey the Depository. It was of red brick, old, and impressive. West of the building was a plaza made by the junction of four streets, Elm, Main, Commerce and Houston. Elm and Commerce Streets were the sloping angles of an inverted pyramid, with Main dividing the diamond in half, and Houston providing the base at the top. Elm, Main and Commerce all met at the peak of the pyramid, the Stemmons Freeway and its triple underpass and train trestle. A large train yard occupied most of the land to the northwest. In the center were two smaller triangles occupied by grass, and beyond Elm to the north and Commerce to the south, two secondary grassy plazas.

Dengler climbed the plank fence and descended a slight knoll. There was a concrete proscenium to the left, open grass to the right, and beyond the street the plaza. He looked up and saw a number of multi-story buildings, any of which would provide nice sniper locations.

This would be a good place to shoot somebody in a motorcade, Dengler thought. *Cross fire. Traffic slowing because of the turn in the street.* He chose his locations: *One in the Depository on Elm Street, one on the Stemmons Freeway underpass, and one in one of the buildings along Houston Street, or in that big building on Commerce Street. Boom-boom-boom.* The Secret Service would never allow that. First of all, all of the buildings would be checked, windows closed, personnel screened. The 113th Military Intelligence Battalion from Fort Hood would be here now, probably, checking everything out, making sure nothing like that could happen.

Finally, the Secret Service would never allow a motorcade to detour around Dealey Plaza. Clearly, it would be a detour as Main Street was a straight shot to the Stemmons Freeway, and turning right onto Houston Street, and then left onto Elm, would be both unnecessary and dangerous. The opposite direction would be dumber still, a left onto Houston and another left onto Commerce providing an unneeded detour that would place the motorcade in unnecessary peril. Still, to kill Kennedy they would have to get close. The proximity to the patsy's place of work provided a logical association if the other obstacles could be eliminated. Dengler made a mental note: *Check with 113th Intel.*

If I were going to kill Kennedy, how would I go about it? Dengler strolled back up the knoll and sat down beneath a big tree. Above, the limbs and leaves splayed out, green and brown and blue converging to create a pattern, a stationary kaleidoscope. Dengler placed his open palms behind his head as a pillow and felt the cool wind as it drew across him, billowing slightly. The sound of the wind in his ears was singular, lonely, bringing to mind the sound of sheets as they dried on the line in his back yard when he was a boy, before his mother left.

Close up. I would kill him close up. No, that would place the patsy in the hands of the authorities before he could be gotten rid of. So forget the various breakfasts and luncheons and dinners Kennedy would be attending. Security would be even tighter there, he considered.

Dengler again positioned the Ford outside Oswald's house the next morning, this time across the street and facing in the opposite direction. It was Saturday, November 2nd, and Oswald wouldn't be working at the Schoolbook Depository today. Still, he knew Oswald would be out and about sometime. He waited.

Throughout the night Dengler had thought about what he was doing. It seemed everything he'd done in his life, every aspiration he'd possessed, had led to this time and this place. Now here he was, sitting in a car and waiting to follow a man who was going to take the blame for the most infamous assassination since the murder of Julius Caesar, and possibly play the role of the accomplice himself. He didn't know whether he could stop the assassination. He could contact the press, of course, and if he made a positive enough impression someone might run the story. Of course, the immediate repercussions of David Dengler emergence into the light of day would be arrest and imprisonment, and he would be killed, probably by hanging in his own cell. *Suicide. Depression. Mental illness*. All of these would weigh against the message he would deliver. The total result would be his own death and the delay, by a matter of days, weeks, or months, of JFK's assassination.

He might convince Oswald to help him. Was that possible? Oswald acted as if he believed Dengler was a stalking horse, a test to see whether Oswald was remaining loyal. In Oswald's eyes Dengler had probably been sent by Stafford, and so as an extension of Stafford, Dengler scared the hell out of him. Trust was unlikely. If he could somehow convince Oswald he was legitimately who he said he was, he might be able to enlist him in an effort to stop the assassination. Oswald knew the plans of the group, certainly, or knew enough about the plans to be a resource for discovering the true plans. With him, Dengler might be able to position himself at the right place at the right time to stop the assassination as it unfolded. Might. To do that, he would need to know the location of the assassins' nests, if they were going to shoot at the motorcade, or the place of ambush if Kennedy was to be killed entering or exiting a luncheon or breakfast meeting, and the time of the operation. He would need to know their plans.

If Oswald wouldn't cooperate, then he might lead Dengler to the real assassination site and even provide the time. Stafford would have to keep Oswald close to the actual crime in order to blame him later, and probably would feel comfortable involving him on some level with the intention of killing him before he could say anything. The real key wasn't what Oswald knew, although that would have to be constrained too, but what he appeared to know, the places he visited, the actions of his final days. It was Dengler's job to mimic those actions by following Oswald.

Oswald would lead him to the assassination nests. Then Dengler would kill the bastards before the plan could be successfully carried out. That was the sum total of Dengler's plan. Then he would have to get his story to the press before he was killed.

No. They would just kill him anyway and build a stone wall around the entire affair.

Sitting in the Ford parked down the street from Oswald's house, Dengler decided he would have to get his information to Kennedy himself. Certainly, the President would be grateful, presuming he knew Dengler had saved his life rather than threatened it.

Who would Kennedy trust? Stafford. Hoover.

His brother.

Could he get Robert Kennedy on the phone?

No.

Unless he told Kennedy's aide he had photos of Marilyn's diary. Hoover didn't know he kept a copy of Marilyn's diary. Kennedy would at least take his call.

Yes. RFK.

- 73 -

A Dallas PD black-and-white pulled up before Oswald's rooming house. The driver honked three times. Dengler started the engine, pulled into a driveway to turn around and motored past the waiting cruiser as if casually on his way to the market. Dengler looked at the cop out of the corner of his eye. It was the same man he saw several days before, in the bar where Kerschov introduced himself. Oswald was associating with a cop. Why?

Dengler circled the block, coming back onto the street just as the black-and-white pulled away from the curb. Dengler slowed, allowing the police car to make the end of the corner before accelerating again. There were two men in the car. One of them was Oswald.

Dengler caught up and stayed a block behind the black-and-white as it moved out of the Oak Cliff area and toward downtown. Dengler could see the two men talking. Oswald laughed. They were friends. Dengler's mind raced. If you were Oswald, who could you trust? Certainly no one who approached you first. What if what this Dengler guy said is true? Who will be your contact to the outside world if Kennedy is killed and you're the dupe? You need someone who will step forward and speak the truth. But who?

Dengler saw it all, the whole thing, as he drove behind the black-and-white. Oswald could trust no one above himself, so he approached an anonymous person, someone with no personal ax to grind, and yet someone with professional respectability. Oswald had contacted a cop, probably some beat guy, and if things got too sticky he would go to the cop for personal protection. Dengler jotted down the car license number.

Dengler followed the black-and-white through Dallas and beyond, to a shooting range located half a dozen miles out of town. Oswald hopped out of the car carrying what appeared to be a rifle wrapped in a blanket and a pistol in his belt, said several things to the driver, waved, and walked toward the range.

The black-and-white proceeded on.

It nearly took Dengler's breath away.

Dengler returned from the shooting range at approximately 3:00 P.M. He got several dollars in change from an Alcohol Beverage Control Store located not far from his motel, then found a public phone where he could sit down, and called the Justice Department.

"The Attorney General," he told the anonymous female voice on the phone. *One moment please...*

He first talked with an aide who was younger by several years than himself. "No, I must talk with the Attorney General in person."

I'm sorry, but the Attorney General does not take unscreened calls.

"Tell him I have documents which I want to turn over to the government. They involve a certain person in California whose initials were MM. Say it just like that: Initials were MM."

A long pause followed during which Dengler fed the phone with change. Finally, another voice came on the line. *I'm sorry, but what is this call regarding?*

Dengler repeated his message.

And your name, sir?

"I wish to remain anonymous, at least for the present. Just tell the Attorney General I have some documents of a sensitive nature once belonging to a California person whose initials were MM. I procured these documents on 5th Helena Drive, in Los Angeles."

Is this a blackmail attempt?

"Nothing of the kind. I am offering these documents of my own free will, and with no strings attached."

I'm sorry, but it sounded like some kind of blackmail attempt.

"No. However, I will only deal with the Attorney General."

One moment, sir.

Silence for four minutes. More change for the phone. Then a final voice. "This is Todd Carroll. I'm Special Assistant to the Attorney General. I'm afraid he's out of town — out of the country, actually — and isn't expected back for at least a week. Can I be of any assistance to you?"

"No. You have a record of my message?" Carroll read it back to him, verbatim. "This is vitally important for a case the Attorney General is working on," Dengler continued. "Only he knows what it pertains to. I have to talk to him, personally, on my terms. Do you understand?"

"Certainly," Carroll said. "Can I have your phone number?"

"No. I'll call back the day the Attorney General returns. What day is that?"

"November twelfth. That's a Tuesday."

"I'll call him then. Be sure to give him my message."

Dengler hung up.

Dengler returned to his motel room with a burger, fries and a strawberry shake. He plopped down onto the bed and dialed Lowry, to make his report. He told him where Oswald had been that day, and who took him to the range, and the license plate number of the black-and-white. He had to do this because he was sure Lowry's people already knew about the cop, and to not report him would have seemed suspicious.

"Did you push him?" Lowry asked.

"No."

"You've got to make contact again, Dengler," Lowry said forcefully. "You've got to prod him."

"Tomorrow," Dengler responded, and hung up.

Dengler didn't *acquire* Oswald on Sunday, November 3rd, and sat outside his rooming house on Beckley Street for almost three hours. Oswald must have gone home to visit Marina, and he must have left before Dengler arrived on site. Dengler was on the lookout for Lowry's men now, too, because if what Kerschov said was true, they would want to photograph he and Oswald together, although that would present further problems later, after the assassination. *How is it*, Dengler heard some Senator say in his mind, *that you had enough advance warning to follow these two men around Dallas and photograph them, and yet didn't have advance warning of the assassination of our late President itself?* Yet, he saw no one, *made* no one, and he was certain he could spot a tail as well as anyone. Either they weren't on him, or their skills exceeded his ability to detect them.

Dengler became frustrated after three hours and nearly leaped out of the car with anxious energy. He strolled up one street, down another, looking at the houses, which were middle to lower-middle class and dated from the twenties and thirties. Even so, these were better houses than any he'd ever lived in, with space between each one and large yards and lawns that spread like blankets beneath old trees casting old shade. He would have traded every aspiration for adventure he ever dreamed for one of these houses, with Etta inside. That seemed so very distant now, so unlikely.

Dengler returned his mind to the issue at hand. His only real hope would be Kennedy. If he could make Robert Kennedy listen, then perhaps Stafford and Hoover and the others could be brought to justice, or maybe even just brought down. Robert Kennedy could do that. He was the Attorney General, Hoover's boss, and his brother could fire Stafford at a moment's notice.

If he could be made to see the truth.

After twenty minutes Dengler returned to the car and drove back to his motel room.

The next morning Dengler drove directly to the district where the Schoolbook Depository was located, found a restaurant where he could get something to eat, and then arrived at the warehouse at fifteen minutes after ten. He presented himself to the office on the ground floor and asked for Oswald. He told the clerk, and later a manager, he was a relative who was going to be in town for only a few hours and just wanted to say hello to his cousin before he left. He would be no more than five or ten minutes, he promised.

Dengler was directed to the second floor, where there was a lunch room. He bought a Coca Cola out of a machine and sat down at one of the Formica-topped tables and waited. Oswald arrived ten minutes later, entering the room from one of two doors located at each end. Oswald was so surprised to see him he froze in place for a moment, then pushed the door fully open and entered.

When Oswald was almost beside him, he said, "What are you doing here?"

Dengler smiled, took a swig of his soft drink, then placed the circular bottom on the table so it wobbled before it righted itself. His expression didn't change.

"I said..."

"Because I don't think they can shoot photos of us in here, Lee," Dengler said.

"Who?"

"Of course, you never know."

"Listen, you'd better get out of here." He said it as if there were a threat attached to it.

"Why?"

"Because you shouldn't be here, that's why."

"Lee, this is going to come as a complete surprise to you, but the truth is nothing like what you believe it to be."

"And you're going to tell me the truth?"

"Sure," Dengler responded casually. "Why not?"

"You should leave," Oswald said.

"Surely you've begun to suspect the people who recruited you have their own agenda? You must see that."

"I don't know what you're talking about."

"Yes you do, you stupid son-of-a-bitch," Dengler hissed, suddenly leaning close. "You think I work for Gray Stafford, that I'm his cleansing agent, making sure all of his little operatives are good little boys and do what they're told. Well, I've got news for you, pal, and it's this: We are both going to die unless something happens to stop it very soon. We are going to die to cover the tracks of the real assassins. Now me, I've been slipped into this like it was a suit altered to fit. You, on the other hand, are even worse — the suit was custom-made."

Oswald lifted from his seat, but Dengler grabbed his arm, bringing the smaller man back down so they faced one another, almost cheek to cheek.

"Let me go." Oswald almost shouted.

"That's it. That's it. Cause a scene. Get us both ejected out of here. Maybe get yourself fired."

"Stop it." he whispered.

"Tell me what you know, Lee. Maybe I can stop it."

"Let go."

Dengler's grip was tightening around Oswald's biceps. His fingers were digging into the smaller man's flesh. He gripped harder. "We're in this together, Lee. Just you and me. Assassins Number One and Two. That's us. Don't you get it?"

Oswald spun, pulling Dengler with him. Their chairs scraped on the tile floor, their voices constrained but angry. Dengler almost expected someone to come in. No one did.

"But I can get us out, Lee. I can get us out. I've got a direct line to the Attorney General. He's going to meet with me." Oswald attempted to wrench free, but Dengler grabbed the back of his head, directed his eyes around to the front so they were looking at one another again. They were now embraced in a wrestling match, two unevenly paired men.

"Let. Me. Go." Oswald hissed between breaths, struggling.

"He's the President's brother, for christsakes. He's the President's brother. He can't be a party to the plot. We can trust him. Give me something, Lee. Let me inside. Tell me what they're going to do. Then I can get us both out of this."

Oswald burst free and nearly tumbled to the far side of the room. Both men were sweating now, both red-faced and disheveled. "You tell..." Oswald said, sucking for breath, sucking, "... tell Stafford I don't buy it. I'm a rock. I'm a rock, goddamn it, and nobody's going to break me. You tell him that." Then Oswald straightened and exited the room.

Dengler waited to cool off before he went downstairs. He bought another soda and sat at the table they'd shared, he and Oswald, thinking about the fear and paranoia Oswald had to be feeling. Oswald believed Stafford was testing him. He believed Stafford suspected he wasn't capable of completing his mission and was trying to get rid of him before the plot to assassinate the President came to fruition.

Because if Oswald didn't measure up, Stafford would kill him.

Stafford's going to kill you anyway, Dengler thought.

There was doubt, though. There had to be doubt in Oswald's mind, an unrelenting suspicion the pro-Castro leaflets he'd handed out and his defection to Russia and his repeated vocal opposition to his own government, all under orders from Stafford, were to achieve something other than what he was told. Because even Lee Harvey Oswald the patriot was a suspicious man. That's why he'd courted a cop as a friend.

What the hell? Dengler thought, finishing the Coca Cola and placing the empty bottle back in the rack attached to the side of the machine.

He would go to Robert Kennedy with what he had.

- 74 -

Dengler started frequenting movie theaters in the middle of the day. He stopped surveilling Oswald. He turned away from the conservative commentators and pamphleteers and hate mongers who were already beginning to gather at the heart of a city renown for its hatred. The book *None Dare Call It Treason* was on the lips of many Dallas citizens, a book which indicted Kennedy as a traitor who should be recalled — *impeached* was the word, so strange and unused — and prosecuted for handing Cuba over to the Communist Block.

Lowry queried him about Oswald and Dengler answered honestly — the contacts were achieving nothing. Oswald believed Dengler was an operative of Gray Stafford and wouldn't betray even a moment of doubt. "You've got to hit him," Lowry said. "You've got to put the squeeze on him." Dengler agreed, and did nothing. He took care not to present himself to the cameras that he knew were swirling around Oswald. They would be making a case for him now as the principal gunman; they were making a case for Dengler, too, he knew, even though he still couldn't 'make' a tail behind him. He'd decided not to lend himself to that. Film was hard to shoot in the cool, floating darkness of the theaters of downtown Dallas, and a political connection hard to make with a man who appreciated Hollywood movies in the late afternoon.

Lowry provided the name of the police officer Oswald made into a friend: *J. D. Tippett.*

Two weeks passed as he waited for Kennedy's return to the country.

November 12 came. Dengler bought a copy of the *Dallas Times* and read a short piece on Kennedy's coming visit and the rift that existed in the Texas Democratic Party. Beyond 'pressing the flesh' and 'acting Presidential' for the locals, Kennedy as leader of the party was supposed to help cure the feud between Governor Connally and Senator Fred Yarbrough. With Dallas decidedly conservative, the Texas Democratic Party needed a unified front to return its incumbent politicos to office two years hence, and to deliver Texas to Jack Kennedy's reelection campaign.

Dengler bought a roll of quarters at a bank. He tore open the wrapping, slipped two quarters from the roll, dropped them into the public phone located on an anonymous street, and dialed. He was prepared to wind his way through the tunnels of bureaucracy until he finally reached Kennedy, and was surprised when the second voice he heard belonged to the Attorney General.

"Hello?"

"I'm here, Mr. Attorney General."

"You have the better of me, sir," Kennedy said. Dengler thought about the man he saw entering Marilyn Monroe's house, about her claims he wanted her to be his First Lady when he became president. Would this man tell a woman that to gain sexual advantage? He might. He probably had. All's fair in love and war, or so the saying goes. She believed it, and now she was dead. Dengler reminded himself he still didn't know for sure Stafford wasn't sent there that night on the orders of this man. He couldn't be sure.

"You have the better of me, sir," Kennedy repeated, "because you know my name and I don't know yours."

"Are you alone?"

"No. Not entirely."

"Who else is there?"

"I don't think you need to know that, sir," Kennedy said evenly. "And furthermore, unless you tell me what your name is and what it is you want, I intend to hang up."

"Please send everyone else out of the room."

"Why should I do that?"

"Because there is a traitor working for you, Mr. Attorney General."

Dengler imagined Kennedy was exchanging a look with the other people in the room. Moments passed before he said, "Okay, you can go. You too. Close the door on your way out." Fifteen seconds passed. Then, "Very well. I'm alone."

"Thank you, sir."

"Now tell me your name."

"I'm reluctant to do that, Mr. Attorney General."

"Why?"

"Because some lies are attached to it. I don't want you to prejudge me."

"Tell me your name, or I will hang up."

"David Lawrence Dengler," Dengler said slowly, pronouncing each syllable distinctly.

A moment passed before Dengler heard a grunt on the other end of the line, and then, "Well, I am very familiar with the name. I allocated the resources that resulted in a trailer park being blown up. I believe you died in that explosion."

"No," Dengler said, stating the obvious.

"If not you, then who?"

"I don't know, Mr. Attorney General. Ask the FBI."

"Why would the FBI fake your death?"

"To recruit me. For espionage."

"Then you work for the FBI?"

"Technically, I'm an FBI agent."

"With a new identity, I presume?"

"Jack Fleming. You might look into it."

"Yes," Kennedy said. "I might." The change in Kennedy's voice suggested he was jotting something down.

Dengler waited. He saw a Dallas Police cruiser across the street make its way to a stop light, and then cross against the red and speed up. Someone was about to get a ticket. For a moment he lost contact with Kennedy in his mind and became aware of the weather, which was clear and lovely, and the breeze that made the canvas awnings along the street dance, flapping and snapping. Then the voice:

"I was told you had documents belonging to a California personage with the initials MM. Is this some sort of blackmail shakedown?" Worry was hiding in Kennedy's voice.

"No, sir. Not a shakedown. You can have the documents, if you want. Free of charge."

"Why would I be interested in them?"

"The person who owned them... She was killed, Mr. Attorney General. Murdered."

Silence. Then, "Murder isn't in the purview of the Attorney General, or the Department of Justice, except under certain restricted circumstances..."

"She was murdered to expose you," Dengler told him. "She was murdered to expose the President."

Dengler didn't realize he'd been hung up on until he heard the dial tone return. He cursed and redialed. It took two minutes to reach Robert Kennedy again. "I'm sorry," Kennedy told him. "I didn't mean to hang up on you. It was a reflex. I spilled some coffee."

"Okay," Dengler said.

"Now as to this matter of..."

"Murder."

"Yes. Do you know who the murderer was?"

"Yes."

"Can you prove it?"

"Yes."

"How?"

"I was there. I saw them push a suppository into her. I saw them hold her until it took effect. I saw her die, Mr. Attorney General."

There was a long silence. He could hear Kennedy's breath on the receiver, steady but heightened, controlled.

"Were you a part of the kill team?" Kennedy asked.

The phrase 'the kill team' surprised Dengler. It was a strange phrase; one that suggested familiarity with the concept if not the phrase itself, as if he'd used it before, perhaps on more than one occasion. *The Kill Team.*

"No, sir," Dengler said.

"Then how was it you came to witness this?"

"I was captured trying to save her. They were going to kill me elsewhere, but I got away."

"The two 'agents' in Santa Barbara. They were going to kill you, but you killed them instead." It was a statement.

"Yes, sir."

"And the documents you mentioned?"

"Her diary."

"If this is the victim I believe it is, her diary was found at the site," Kennedy said.

"I photographed the diary."

"You took pictures of it?" Rhetorical.

"Yes, sir."

"When?"

"Several nights before her death."

"How did you come to be in a position to take photos of her diary?" Kennedy's tone said he was beginning to doubt all of this, beginning to suspect something else was at work here. Like perhaps an attempt by a news reporter to get him to make the disclosure he'd known Marilyn Monroe, that he was having an affair with her.

"I broke into her house," Dengler said. "I exceeded my orders."

"What orders?"

"To surveil her, sir. I was sent to California to put together a dossier, and I exceeded my orders. I went inside and found the diary."

"Did you read it?"

Dengler froze. Somehow this had never come up in his thinking, the admission of knowledge. He had long since passed the point of no return, however. He was committed, and he knew it.

"Yes, sir," he replied softly. "I read it."

"I've read the diary myself," the voice on the other end of the line said. "Lies. She was a sick woman. Mentally disturbed. There are a number of authorities who can attest to it."

"Yes, sir," Dengler said, thinking of having seen this man enter Marilyn Monroe's house on 5th Helena Drive. He shouldn't bring that up now. No.

"Go on."

"I will turn the photos over to you, free of charge."

"Free of charge?"

"Yes sir."

"You're acting out of the goodness of your heart, is that it?"

The question impacted on Dengler. Of course, he wasn't acting out of the *goodness of his heart*. Far from it. He was acting out of a sense of self-preservation. It had been the *goodness of his heart* that caused his present predicament, the desire to be a patriot and do patriotic things. *To be a hero*, he thought. *That was how I thought I would be paid. By becoming a hero.*

"Sir, it's very likely I will be killed sometime in the next two weeks. You may be able to prevent that. You may not. In any case, you're the best chance I have for survival."

"Someone is going to kill you," Kennedy said, "because you have these photos? They're going to use them in some way?"

"No sir," Dengler replied, "I don't think anybody really cares about the photos anymore. It's gone beyond that."

"How? How has it gone beyond that?"

"I believe the initial plan was to force the President from office," Dengler said. "To use the diary, and other evidence that must exist, photos taken of the President with MM and, frankly, other women, to force the President to resign, or at least acquiesce to the political demands of the blackmailers."

After a moment of noise on the long distance line, hollow hisses and pops, Dengler heard Robert Kennedy formulate the words, "And what happened to the initial plan?"

"I don't know the specifics, sir. Not of this portion of the plot, anyway. But, I imagine there always was a contingent within the conspirators that wanted your brother assassinated. A number of loose strings made the California murder less than perfect as a weapon against you. A witnesses, for one — me. So the objective changed. Assassination of the President, which would also remove you from office."

It seemed like the hisses and pops went on forever. Dengler imagined the Attorney General's young face drawn tight with consideration of the problem just handed him.

"I would like for us to meet, sir," Dengler said softly. "Personally. Face to face."

"Where are you?"

"Dallas."

"Fly to Washington."

"I can't do that, sir."

"Why not?"

"I might not get there alive."

Silence. Then, "I could dispatch someone to meet you and escort you here personally."

"Remember? You've got a traitor in your ranks. I don't trust anyone but you."

"Name the traitor."

"I will. Personally. But only to you. Alone." Dengler knew he couldn't use Stafford's name. Distanced over the phone and unable to be present to defend his position, Dengler knew Stafford would have little trouble discounting the allegation and redirecting it at Dengler.

More silence. Then, "You're making this very difficult, Mr. Dengler, but under the circumstances I have very few options, do I?"

"That's how I feel right about now."

"I can be there tomorrow."

"Check into the Barclay Hotel under the name Field. I'll call with further instructions."

Dengler hung up. For the first time in days he felt like he might live long enough to regret something someday.

- 75 -

The next morning Dengler drove to a parking garage he'd used several times before and left the Ford in the quick turnaround area, then walked two blocks to a public telephone booth, halfway to the Barclay. He called the hotel desk and asked whether Mr. Field had checked in yet.

"There are two Fields listed," the hotel clerk told him. "Which one is your party?"

Dengler cursed under his breath and asked, "What are their first names?"

"Lloyd and Robert."

"Robert," Dengler told him, making the best guess he could.

"Lloyd checked in yesterday," the clerk said in a voice that suggested he was reading something. "We're expecting Robert Field early this afternoon."

Dengler hung up. He checked his watch. It was 11:17. He took a walk.

At 12:20 he called the Barclay desk again, this time getting someone other than the clerk he'd talked with that morning. "I'm sorry, sir, but we're not supposed to give out information over the phone."

"I have an appointment with Robert Field this afternoon," Dengler said.

"When he checks in, I can put you through, of course."

Dengler cursed again. He was four blocks from the hotel. There was a restaurant adjacent to the lobby. He strolled for it.

The restaurant was busy. It was twenty minutes before Dengler was seated at the counter. He ordered coffee. Dengler stood and walked across the restaurant to a bank of public phones. He dialed the desk again. He knew the number from memory. The original clerk answered the phone and recalled him. Field hadn't checked in. Dengler returned to the counter and ordered lunch.

At 1:15, having paid for his lunch, Dengler strolled into the lobby and sat down. There was a used newspaper section beside his seat. He picked it up and began to read. It was the metro section, political stuff, some crime reporting. At least it was a distraction and kept the surface of his mind occupied. After awhile he glanced around the lobby, thinking it unlikely Kennedy would come in through here. He imagined the Attorney General would have a staff member make the necessary arrangements while he entered through the parking garage below and went straight to his room.

Dengler returned his gaze to the newspaper section.

He became aware he was staring at the man some seconds after his gaze drifted off of the printed page. There was something familiar about the man, but Dengler couldn't quite place it. *What is it?* he thought. *Where have I seen this guy before?* The man in question was merely standing in the lobby, looking out into the gray light of day. He was tall, over six feet, with a bald pate rimmed in brown hair, with a long neck, and long fingers. He wore a pinstriped suit, double breasted, very much out of style, with the *John Kennedy/ Rob Petrie/Brooks Brothers* style now in vogue. That bothered Dengler, the suit, and finally he realized why. It was baggy. A loose-fitting suit can hide many things. A gun, maybe.

Dengler felt for his own Walther PPK that hung from a shoulder strap on his left side. The Walther was small and slim enough not to disturb the lines of a good suit. Dengler wasn't wearing a suit, though; he wore a windbreaker and slacks.

The man turned and as his eyes swept across the lobby, Dengler turned to obscure his face, raising the newspaper back into place. He caught the man at the beginning of his move and Dengler's response was in parallel, hiding the fact it was really reactionary. The man didn't notice.

Where? Dengler asked himself. *Where have I seen this guy?*

Dengler thought about the night at the beach when he'd first met Hoover. Had he seen this man there? *No.* He did associate him with his recent experiences.

Maybe school at Fort Lee? *No.*

The man crossed the lobby and waited at the desk, tapping its top impatiently as the clerk dealt with someone else. Dengler watched him closely, curiosity piqued now. He'd never met Kennedy professionally, but he might have met someone with the Bureau who was now detailed to Kennedy. That made sense, didn't it? Yes. So where had he met or seen this man? There were a number of functions he'd attended as Jack Fleming. Was this man one of the agents operating out of Q Force in Washington? *No.*

Dengler shifted on the bench seat and cursed beneath his breath. This was frustrating. He almost convinced himself this man had to be a member of Kennedy's advance party, and he'd seen him somewhere else before. But where?

The man moved into the space previously occupied by the now departing guest and engaged the clerk. He spoke forcefully but soundlessly to the clerk, who checked some paperwork below the level of the counter, and then responded. The man walked back across the lobby to the plate glass windows and looked out.

Then a second man walked in and joined the first and Dengler knew who they both were, and where he'd seen them. The second man's name was Jim Keller. He was a CIA agent. Dengler had killed him. Personally.

CIA Agent Jim Keller appeared quite robust for a man who was shot to death, along with his entire detail, by Wes Strong, David Dengler and their FBI detail a year before. At first, Dengler's mind rejected the entire thing. *How can this be?* his mind raced, *I killed that son-of-a-bitch.* Dengler tried to remember the moment, tried to recall the details and lay them out in his mind for inspection, but he couldn't. It had been so traumatic, the killing of men whose only crime was they worked for the CIA and Gray Stafford. He remembered taking the gun Strong had given him, aiming it, pulling the trigger, watching the blood flow, turning away, sickened by what he'd done.

So sickened, in fact, he hadn't helped with the loading and disposal of the bodies.

Dengler adjusted the paper as Keller's gaze drifted past him. A chill ran up his spine. Even back then, he realized, back in the days when David Dengler was being recruited as *Jack Fleming, FBI Special Agent*, even then they'd known what they wanted to do with him. The entire affair had been a ruse, the apartment, the ID, everything, just to keep him on ice until their plans firmed up. They intended to use his identity as an agent killer to realize his ultimate destiny, second gunman in the murder of the President. In the instant it took for Keller and the unnamed CIA agent to walk to the bank of elevators, press a button, and enter one, Dengler saw the minutiae of his public persona played out. They probably had all sorts of back history planned for him, membership in the Communist Party, contributions to all sorts of left-wing organizations, maybe even documented proof he was a supporter of the Fair Play for Cuba Committee reporting to none other than Lee Harvey Oswald.

That instant Dengler wanted to stand and follow Agent Jim Keller and kill him. *It would be so easy,* he thought. *Merely watch which floor his elevator stopped at, follow it, step out into the hallway and pump eight shells into Keller and his associate, then reenter the elevator before it could leave.* He could reload the Walther PPK on the way down to the lobby, and then stroll casually outside into the dull gray light of day. Keller would be bleeding to death, might even be dead before Dengler reached his Ford parked mere blocks from here. *It would be so easy*, he thought.

They used his aspirations against him, the dream to leave his sleepy little West Virginia town to become an agent for the United States Government, and made a fool of him with it.

On another level, Dengler grasped the true reality of what he'd just seen. *Kennedy told Gray Stafford, or someone who works for Gray Stafford, and this operation is compromised.*

Which meant he was in very serious danger here and should get away as quickly as possible.

Dengler began to stand, but quickly turned the motion into a seat adjustment. He turned the newspaper page. His mind was racing. The question was, *What are those guys doing here?* His eyes quickly took in the rest of the room, reassessing what he'd first assessed minutes before. No one else looked even remotely suspicious. Not that suspicion itself was an issue. The most innocent looking of people might in fact be the exact opposite. No one here looked like a member of Keller's detail that morning in the mountains when Dengler thought he'd committed cold-blooded murder. So what were Keller and his associate doing in this lobby? They weren't checking on the security, that was for sure.

Assumption One: They didn't accompany the Attorney General from Washington. Dengler considered this a given because had they accompanied the Attorney General, and were in the lobby for some official reason, then they would be looking for him, and obviously these guys would have spotted him in an instant. Also, the Attorney General would be traveling as close to incognito as was humanly possible for a high-ranking government official and Dengler doubted Kennedy would allow Stafford, or anyone else, for that matter, to ruin a quiet operation by bringing in the big guns. These guys were definitely *The Big Guns.*

Assumption Two: They're here because Stafford knows about the rendezvous with Kennedy. They're also not here in an official capacity, or more accurately, in any capacity the Attorney General might authorize. Stafford, or someone above, to the side, or below Stafford, had called them in, probably to prevent Dengler from meeting with Kennedy. Which would mean other members of Keller's detail were deployed outside to keep Dengler from entering the hotel. Keller and the other agent had probably gone upstairs to establish security in the vicinity surrounding the Attorney General's room, possibly even place surveillance equipment inside.

Don't get too far ahead on this, Dengler told himself. His mind was racing, placing blocks of logic into a scenario for which there was no substantiation. He had to get that substantiation.

First, are the entrances to the hotel covered?

Dengler stood and strolled to the plate glass front and looked out. He ID'd the agent instantly, recalling him from the escapade in the mountains. He was standing beneath the awning, checking his watch repeatedly as if waiting for his wife, who apparently was late. Only Dengler would notice the man's eyes, too distant here to be made out, but suggested by the turn of his head as he paced. He was a watcher. The pedestrian entrance was covered. That left the dining room and the stairwells. Dengler strolled toward the dining room, acting as if he were waiting for someone himself, not anxiously but with mild annoyance. Obviously, this was a feint that would have convinced no one from Keller's detail if they were close enough to recognize him. From a distance he might have been anybody.

Dengler glanced into the dining room. It was emptying now, the crowd that had clogged it twenty minutes earlier dissipated. There were abandoned spots up and down the counter, with half of the booths vacant. Dengler made out the operative on the far side of the plate glass, outside the hotel, when a truck passed by and cast a shadow that erased the glare on the glass. Dengler didn't recognize the man, but guessed his identity from the way he was observing the exit.

Dengler returned to the couch and sat down. He had to think. There would be a man in the basement, where the parking garage was located. He would be a chauffeur, possibly, or a businessman waiting for an associate. There would be someone on the floor where the Attorney General's suite was located, probably the agent Dengler had first *made* in the lobby. There was no one in the lobby itself because Kennedy's own security staff might *make* him. It didn't matter — this beast could be controlled from its extremities.

Dengler picked up the paper and began to read. He was trapped inside the hotel. He wouldn't be allowed close enough to the Attorney General to give him the information he had, or to receive his protection. He might kill his way out, but that wouldn't allow him a second try at the Attorney General, although it might bring up an interesting situation. If Stafford had to explain how it was one of his agents just happened to be killed in the lobby of the hotel the Attorney General was staying in, other questions would arise. Dengler smiled. *Death: No room for maneuver there.*

Dengler stood and walked to the guest phones, chose the one farthest from the street, and dialed the desk. "Has Robert Field checked in yet?"

"Just a moment," the voice said, and Dengler associated it with the man behind the desk, although his voice was lost to the vastness of the lobby. He watched the man place him on hold, then dial a second number. There was a pause before the clerk said something, nodded, and then hung up. In a moment he returned to Dengler's line. "Is this Mr. Dengler?"

Dengler hung up.

It was twelve paces to the men's room, but it seemed like an eternity to cross. He pushed through the men's room door and steadied himself beside the wall. The clerk mentioning his name had sent a terror worming through Dengler. Would the Attorney General use his real name? *Possibly.* Dengler hadn't given him another name to use. Would Stafford use his real name? *Possibly.* Would either of them use his real name with an intermediary like the front desk of this hotel, creating a record of his existence?

Stafford wouldn't. Unless he intended to kill Dengler in the open, later claiming the FBI had made a mistake about his death in the explosion at the trailer park. Wasn't that what was so sweet about that death, about any death in which there was no corpse to autopsy? It was subject to reversal later.

Dengler checked the stalls and found that he was alone in the men's room. He chose the stall farthest from the door and locked himself in, sitting down to think. Paranoia held him in its grasp, he knew that, and his thinking wasn't as straight as it needed to be. He had to calm himself and think straight.

First of all, he couldn't leave. *Okay,* Dengler thought, *I can't leave.*

Secondly, he couldn't go up to Kennedy's room. Stafford would have it watched. Stafford would intercept him before he got there.

What if he asked for one of Kennedy's men to come down and escort him upstairs to the room?

What if the man Kennedy sent was Gray Stafford, or one of Stafford's men?

Okay, forget that idea.

Can't go upstairs, can't leave. Eventually, Keller would check the lobby. Eventually, they would find him here. *Can't stay here.*

Dengler stood up. That left only one option.

Nothing had changed, Dengler noted, as he crossed the lobby to the front desk. It was nearing 3:00 P.M. and that mid-afternoon malaise that affected public places everywhere had fallen across the lobby. It was sleepy. Beyond the plate glass Dengler could just make out a form he thought was probably one of Keller's detail. The sun had finally come out, blinding all of the glass with a nasty glare.

The clerk took several minutes to wrap up some business at the end of the counter, then came to him.

"I'd like a room, please," Dengler said pleasantly.

- 76 -

Might as well be comfortable, Dengler thought, and rented a suite. The view from the seventh floor was unhindered, providing a view of the city that wasn't truly ugly. Dengler tipped the bellhop, even though there was no luggage, and ushered him out as quickly as he could. He checked the bedroom, which also had a window view, then the bathroom.

Dengler then sat down to think. He would call Kennedy, refuse to talk to anyone but Kennedy, and then arrange a rendezvous in the building. Stafford's men would follow Kennedy, of course, but they could take no action against Dengler with Kennedy there.

Or could they? Dengler cringed with the possibilities. *Let's see,* he thought, *just how dangerous am I to them if Kennedy learns what I know? Would they kill Kennedy to keep him from learning...*

They might. They just might.

Dengler picked up the phone. Would they be watching the hotel switchboard as well? Paranoia was exponential. The rate at which his thoughts were being contaminated with paranoia was incalculable. He was aware his thinking might not be rational, and nonetheless dismissed concerns about rationality as being counterproductive to survival. He needed to be paranoid. It was a survival mechanism. Anything was possible, even if not everything was plausible.

Taking a breath — in his mind he could see one of Keller's detail standing beside the switchboard in some oblong room downstairs, just waiting for this call — Dengler dialed the front desk. "Robert Field's room, please."

"Certainly. Please hold..."

"Wait a minute," Dengler interjected. "What is Field's room number?"

"Presidential Suite," the desk clerk responded. He hadn't heard this voice before and the paranoia whose icy laughter he'd heard repeatedly this last hour sounded again in his mind. "Room Nine Nineteen."

Two floors up, Dengler thought. He waited for the familiar ring, three times repeated, and then a voice that said, "Hello."

"Robert Field," Dengler said.

"May I ask who's calling?"

"No. You may not." Dengler was in no mood for negotiation. One more unexpected variation to this theme and he intended to find some way to steal away from the hotel. Alive.

A moment passed. Then a voice came onto the line. "I'm afraid he's indisposed at the moment. Is this the person he came to Dallas to meet?"

"I think so," Dengler said.

"Are you in the vicinity of the hotel?"

Dengler didn't answer the question, wondering if he'd heard this voice before. Was it familiar? Was it in fact Gray Stafford's voice? Really, he'd only heard Stafford's voice a few times. Once at the graduation ceremony at Lee, once in Marilyn Monroe's house. *What did it sound like anyway?* he wondered, *Gray Stafford's voice?*

"How long will the Attorney General will be indisposed?" Dengler said.

"He went down to the smoke shop," the voice responded carefully. "He was out of cigars."

"Cigars," Dengler repeated, reading into the conversation all that needed to be read into it.

"Yes. He should be back any time. But he just left. Maybe two minutes ago."

Dengler hung up. *He just left. Maybe two minutes ago.* The words resounded in his mind. *Maybe two minutes ago...*

For several minutes Dengler sat on the bed and stared out of the picture window at a sky as gray as Navy paint. This might be the moment he found a way out of the mess he was in, that the country was in, or it might be the moment he died. *Oh, they'll probably kill me somewhere else, but I'll die here, in the Barclay Hotel.*

Stop thinking about it, he told himself. His thoughts had become sinister, his mind infused with paranoia. Robert Kennedy chose a place to meet him, a very public place, a place where they could talk and confer, all in the comforting light of day. All he had to do was go down to the smoke shop and meet with the man.

Dengler made sure the door was locked behind him. He was working on autopilot, because he left nothing in the room and knew he wouldn't return to it. Still, he turned the knob after the door closed to make sure it locked.

The walk to the elevator took a full minute. It was around the corner from his suite, and he was in no hurry. He tried to remember the smoke shop, but couldn't, even though he'd spent more than an hour in the lobby. There was a gift shop on the far side of the lobby, wasn't there? Yes, now he remembered it, a gift shop. Beside that, really no more than a booth, was a smoke shop that also sold candy and newspapers. He tried to recall its specifications, so many feet long to by many feet wide. Was there a false awning that suggested the out-of-doors? He couldn't remember.

Beneath this trivia warred thoughts of survival. How far from the shop was the stairwell, he wondered? How long to cross that expanse of lobby? Could he make a run for one of the front exits, maybe the one that led to the restaurant? Would they chance a public confrontation?

Who is 'they?' Dengler questioned. He couldn't get it out of his mind he had no assurances this was Kennedy he was going to meet and not a paid assassin. *Paranoia, paranoia*, he thought, *I'm dying of paranoia.*

He entered the elevator and pressed the *down* button. There was no one with him. The door shut and he heard the hum of the motor, the *chunk* of the cable telling him it was beginning to move, the knot in his stomach telling him it was moving. The elevator went straight to the lobby, and the doors opened. For a moment he didn't budge, thinking paranoid thoughts. Then he stepped out and looked for the smoke shop where he thought it should be. It wasn't there. The gift shop was there, but there was no smoke shop. The place he remembered as being the smoke shop was a newspaper rack filled with out-of-town papers.

Dengler walked to the front desk. "Is there a smoke shop?" he asked the desk clerk.

"They sell cigarettes in the gift shop," the clerk said. He was busy sorting registration cards and returned his attention to them almost immediately, leaving Dengler alone in the vast room.

Dengler walked across the lobby away from the desk, seeking a position where he could see clearly, without obstruction, through the plate glass to inside the gift shop. There was a clerk, yes, standing behind the counter. He continued on. There was a man standing with his back turned. Was it Robert Kennedy? It might be. He possessed the same build, was roughly the same height, could have been the same age. His hair was brown, Dengler could see that, and there was a lot of it.

Dengler stopped when his angle of observation revealed there were only the two men in the shop. He thought about this. *Two men in the shop.* One might be Kennedy. Otherwise, the lobby was vacant, merely the desk clerk, Dengler, the gift shop clerk, and this man.

Dengler stepped to the plate glass that provided a view of the out-of-doors. He soon recognized the man he'd seen earlier, outside the restaurant. He imagined they had exchanged places, this man and his partner, to minimize exposure, and the agent he'd seen here was now on duty outside the restaurant.

Dengler turned and walked toward the gift shop. He had a plan of action. It wasn't a good plan. It wasn't even a clever plan. It was, however, the only avenue left open to him. He reached inside his jacket and casually lifted the Walther PPK from its home under his left arm and palmed it, bringing the weapon down to the side of his leg. Thirty strides brought him to the entrance to the gift shop. He shoved the door open, walked straight to the man whose back was turned. The clerk looked up when he entered, then returned to what he was doing, restocking cans of roasted peanuts at the opposite end of the small room. Dengler shoved the barrel of the PPK into the man's back.

"Call out and you're dead," he said in a conversational tone.

The man turned.

Gray Stafford.

- 77 -

"You have the instincts of a piranha," Stafford said, grinning with what seemed real admiration. Dengler paid this no attention. His mind was on his hands, one with the PPK, the other around Stafford's right hand, bending it back. It was a moment before he saw the two men from Keller's detail, and a few seconds later Keller himself, standing beyond the plate glass watching him intently. "I said..."

"Shut up." Dengler barked, "Or I'll take my shoe to your balls."

Stafford laughed, but it ignited as a nervous reaction. Obviously, they hadn't planned on Dengler taking such strong and immediate action. They'd planned on taking him while he was still outside the gift shop trying to decide what to do.

"You can let go of my hand," Stafford offered. Dengler's mind was racing. He was in the bowel of the devil now, he knew, already chewed, already swallowed. All that remained was digestion and voiding. The clerk behind the counter was just now beginning to react to the slightly odd behavior of these two men, standing so close to one another, hands gripped together. He was about to comment on this, a smile forming on his lips, when Keller entered the gift shop.

"Get back." Dengler barked again. "Or I'll do something neither of you want."

"Step outside, Jim," Stafford said with a voice that was almost convincingly calm. "We don't want to alarm our friend here."

Keller nodded curtly and stepped back outside.

"You've forgotten to take my piece," Stafford said softly. "I don't want you to misinterpret a gesture I might make and think I'm going for it."

Dengler found the weapon, pulled it from beneath Stafford's coat pocket — it was a .38 special, he noted, much like the one the FBI had issued to him — and slipped it into his own pocket without comment.

Actually, Dengler was trying to think of something to do. He'd already counted the agents he knew from Keller's detail, and their last known locations. Then there were the three standing just outside the gift shop. Where had they been? He hadn't seen any of them. As he considered this, the two agents from outside joined the first three.

"Can I go now?"

The question startled Dengler and pulled him from his thoughts.

It was the clerk and he was standing behind the counter with his fingers steepled on the flat surface, leaning forward on them. It was a nervous reaction, and yet Dengler couldn't stop himself from wondering just how stiff those fingers were, how much weight they were supporting. He saw white replacing pink at the man's knuckles, saw his skin become pasty and reflective with sweat. "Can I go?" he asked again. His face was pale. He was scared to madness.

"Let him go," Stafford urged, playing the humanitarian.

"Shut up," Dengler said, trying to think.

"I won't tell anyone," the clerk offered weakly.

"I said shut up."

"If you're trying to think of a way out of this, forget it. There's no way out." Dengler tightened his grip on Stafford's wrist, continued tightening until Stafford yelped. Stafford got the idea. He swallowed his comments.

"Okay," Dengler told Stafford, bending his wrist in the direction of the door, "we're going out. You tell your boys to back off. Have them bring up a car in the garage."

"Really, David, this is fruitless. Give it up."

"What? So you can put a bullet through my heart? I don't think so."

Stafford attempted a joke. "It didn't hurt Jim Keller, did it?"

They were at the door. Dengler pushed Stafford into it, shoving the door open. He paused once he was fully through the door, Stafford directly ahead of him. Two more of Jim Keller's CIA detail had arrived from places unknown. At this point, no one had pulled a weapon. Except David Dengler.

"Tell them." Dengler snapped.

"Get one of the cars," Stafford told Keller. "Have it brought around downstairs."

Keller gestured assent, sending one of the agents to accomplish the task.

"Okay, I'm moving him to the stairwell," Dengler said. "I don't want anyone closer than twenty feet, or I'll kill the bastard. Don't try me. I would really enjoy killing him."

"Yes, he would," Stafford announced. He was still attempting to appear cool, to those who looked up to him, to himself. He was being pulled along by Dengler's hand-grip, directed like a petulant child toward the door that led to the stairs and the basement parking garage below.

At the stairwell garage exit Dengler gestured for Stafford to open the door, then shoved him through, following and allowing the door to shut behind him. When it was yanked open by Jim Keller a second later, Dengler twisted Stafford's wrist and made him howl. "Stay out." Dengler yelled, and Keller retreated. "Stay out. I don't want anyone in the stairwell. Is that clear?" He didn't wait for an answer and pushed Stafford toward the first step.

"Mistake One," Stafford told him, critiquing his performance between short, quick breaths. "Should have taken the elevator. You can't be sure of retaining control while we go down the stairs."

"Bullshit," Dengler said, pushing him down the steps. "I can't control the power to the elevator. Here all I have to control is you."

"You're really not up to this, Dengler."

"You're wasting your breath."

"You had potential, you know," Stafford said, almost slipping off a step and tumbling down. Dengler held him upright with strength that surprised the older man. The years in the coal mines hadn't been for nothing. "But you really showed what you were made of when your nuts were on the counter," Stafford finished, struggling.

Dengler exploded with energy, driving him down the steps to the halfway-point landing and shoving him up against the wall. Stafford merely smiled at him, and after a moment, laughed. "Here's why you're not going to do anything to me: I'm the only thing keeping you alive, asshole. If you hurt me, Keller's people are going to be all over you and you're going to die in a way unimagined in your little Ozark mind."

Dengler's fists quaked, shook with the power of his anger, one hand holding the PPK, the other gripping Stafford's right palm, twisting — *God, this has got to be painful*, Dengler thought in one part of his mind. When Dengler did nothing, Stafford continued, "You have one chance. Make a deal. Your life for my life. I'm willing to make that trade... but just barely, you hillbilly sack of shit, so don't press me."

Dengler twisted his hand further. Stafford didn't wince. "Break it," he said defiantly. "Go ahead. Break it." Unnerved, Dengler guided him down the last flight of steps to the landing, ordered, "Open the door. You're going first," and then shoved Stafford through.

The garage was empty except for Keller and two agents, who had taken the elevator down. There was no car waiting. "Where's the car?" Dengler asked.

"It takes a few minutes," Keller said. "Hold on."

One of the agents Dengler saw in the lobby drove a Mercury

Comet ragtop up to the curb. "Bullshit!" Dengler bellowed maniacally, firing twice at the car. One round sliced through the fender, the second bullet tore through the right front tire. "No convertibles. I'm not going down to a sniper. Bring up the chase car."

Keller called out, "Bring up the second car." Somewhere in the depths of the garage an engine sounded and, thirty seconds later, a Plymouth Fury hardtop was driven up behind the Mercury.

"Get out." Dengler ordered the driver, the man he'd observed outside the restaurant an hour before. "I want everybody away. Go back into the elevator, take it up to the lobby. All of you."

There were five agents standing before him now, Keller, the two men who had accompanied him from upstairs, and the two men who had driven the Mercury Comet and the Plymouth Fury up to the valet stand. Dengler recognized all of them from the mock mass murder perpetrated by Wes Strong some months before. Keller walked back to the elevator and the other four men followed, at intervals. In a minute all five were in the elevator and the door closed on them.

Dengler opened the passenger door and directed Stafford inside, following him. "You're going to drive," Dengler told him. The keys were dangling from the ignition, the column gear selector set at neutral. "Take us out slow and easy," Dengler told him, looking about anxiously for the sniper he prayed wasn't in place.

Relaxed now, Stafford started the engine. "You know," he said casually, "Chrysler's products are turning to shit."

"Drive the car."

Stafford pulled the gearshift back into low, grinding the gear a little in the process. "Not used to a clutch anymore," he said apologetically. "Well, not one this loose, anyway. Where are we going?"

"Outside. Make a left."

"Right-o."

The Plymouth pulled away from the valet stand, providing as it went the first glimpse of the valets Dengler had seen since his arrival in the basement. They were cowering behind two cars, two red-vested teenagers with greased-back hair and pimple-pocked faces.

"If you're thinking about murdering me, don't," Stafford said.

"Kill an upstanding fellow like you?" Dengler responded with a mock sincerity. "I don't think so."

"Good thinking."

"I left my poison suppositories in my other pants."

The car pulled from the garage into sunlight. The sun had come out now as dusk approached. *Indian sunlight,* Dengler thought. Stafford stopped the car at the hotel stop sign, looked both ways, waited for a Bekins truck to pass, and then executed a left turn in front of the hotel.

"So, where's *Bobby?*"

Stafford smiled. "The Attorney General does not deal with blackmailers. At least, not personally."

"Blackmailer," Dengler said, amazed by the word and resigned to it at the same time.

"I did a little checking and discovered the FBI probably was a bit premature to list you as killed in that explosion. With your record and background, it was obviously not safe for him to make the trip."

"And the Attorney General has nothing to be concerned about, blackmail-wise?" Dengler said, hoping his cynical smile covered the sincere question.

"He screwed Monroe," Stafford replied. "Our President screwed her. Hell, David, everybody screwed her, from Sam Giancana to her houseboy. I'm surprised you didn't screw her, although your time with the woman *was* limited. In the Attorney General's case, he's scared to death his kids will find out he couldn't resist fucking Marilyn Monroe. He's a grown-up alter-boy who's sick with guilt. It's enough to make you want to kill him."

"Let me guess," Dengler said, eyes still taking in the city which was falling behind, "Keller is an FBI agent this trip. He's supposed to bring me back alive. Difficulties will ensue. I go back as a dead *Most Wanted.*"

Stafford said nothing. There was nothing to say.

"Doesn't make my role as the second assassin clear, does it?"

- 78 -

Stafford turned and looked at Dengler with an expression that bordered on awe. In an instant it was controlled. He returned his gaze to the road. "So that's what you wanted to talk to Robert Kennedy about."

"Missed my chance, didn't I?"

"You won't be able to reach him again."

"I didn't think so."

"You see, David, the President, and the Attorney General both know about the plot to assassinate Jack Kennedy. It was set for Miami three weeks ago, and we were in time to shut it down. Robert Kennedy thinks you're really trying to extort money out of him, or gain some other kind of compensation. If you have any real knowledge of a plot to assassinate his brother, it's knowledge of the Miami plot. We convinced him that at best you can't be believed, and at worst you pose a threat to his person."

Neither man said anything for two blocks. Dengler watched for a tail, but found none. Stafford's attention was on the road. Traffic was getting busier.

"Get on the freeway," Dengler told him. "We're going out of town."

Stafford started getting over into the right lane, jumping off point for the upcoming freeway. Dengler, certain now they were not being followed, twisted around in the seat and faced forward.

"This is too bad, David," Stafford said finally. "You and I, we're the same man."

"Now you're insulting me," Dengler hissed.

They drove for an hour, leaving the freeway for two-lane blacktop, then a single lane dusty road, and that for a rut that went west toward the dying sun. When finally they stopped it was in a vast field with the pungent odor of cow manure in the air. Dengler directed Stafford to get out of the car, walked him from the rut into the field, and ordered him, "Turn around."

Stafford turned around. Dengler had taken a position five feet away, Stafford's .38 in hand. He brought the weapon up, aiming it. "On your knees." Dengler barked.

The CIA agent's eyes betrayed no fear. He gestured *no*. "Go on, kill me, David. After what I did to you, maybe I deserve it, I don't know. Shoot me if you must." Here he paused to smile. "But I would consider this, first. By this time Keller has probably already acquired your girlfriend. He knows she leads to you."

The horror crawled from the earth up into Dengler's legs, squeezed his gonads until they were oatmeal, rushed up his spine, and exploded into his brain. *Dear god no.* Stafford watched him, smiling slightly in that way of his. From deep inside, Dengler observed the smug expression that formed on Stafford's face and almost fired. A hard and nasty part of him almost left Etta to her fate and emptied the .38 into Stafford's testicles and chest and brain, to watch in absolute triumph as his blood seeped into the cow manure and sod beneath him.

Finally, Dengler barked, "On the ground."

Stafford lowered himself to one knee, then two and fell sideways, rolling into a prone position. Dengler grabbed the ignition keys out of the Plymouth, and then opened the trunk. He removed the spare tire, rolled it up to the rear driver's side door and shoved it inside. Dengler took out the tire iron, tossed it into the passenger compartment, along with a set of road flares, the jack tower and base. The trunk was empty now except for a small toolbox, and was large enough to take a full-grown man. Dengler opened the toolbox, rummaged through it until he found a roll of duct tape and a small blade.

Dengler ordered Stafford into the trunk and then taped his hands and feet while he was lying in the compartment. Stafford didn't protest — they both remembered what had happened when Dengler hadn't been properly secured in a trunk during a trip to Santa Barbara almost eighteen months before.

Dengler hastily taped Stafford's mouth shut.

It was twenty minutes to the nearest phone. Dengler pulled into a truck stop, the first sign of civilization he'd seen since the field where he intended to kill Stafford. There was a phone booth outside but Dengler didn't have any change. He went inside to get change, and then returned outside to place the call. Crickets were chirping, but it was already too cold for fireflies. The sky was dark but for the horizon, which was red and purple.

Dengler dialed *The Carousel Club*. The phone rang sixteen times before a man answered. It wasn't Ruby. "Is Etta there?" Dengler asked.

"She was here a minute ago. Hold on." Dengler heard the phone being placed on the counter, the conversations of early birds who showed up before the show to drink and socialize with their friends, an occasional bark of laughter. It was four minutes before the man returned. "She left here with some guy," he told Dengler. "I think it's her boyfriend."

"What did he look like?"

"What am I, an encyclopedia? She left with some guy. She's coming right back. She's got a show to do tonight."

"Tell me what he looked like." Dengler said forcefully.

He described Keller.

Dengler bought a long neck beer, and as an afterthought, a second. He walked out into the parking lot in front of the truck stop, his shoes crunching in the gravel. The big overhead lights came on and beyond the gravel yard, where the highway provided two lanes north and two lanes south, the roar of the road was intermittent.

Dengler opened the trunk, yanked the tape from Stafford's mouth, and allowed him a sip of the beer he bought for him, placing it on the fender between swallows.

"They got her," Dengler said.

"Yeah. I was pretty sure they would. That's what I would have done."

"What about this: I trade you for her. We pack up and leave, change our names, and you never hear from us again."

Stafford seemed sincere. "Sure. We can agree on that."

Dengler looked into Stafford's eyes as he spoke. Dengler knew the truth then. Finally, he looked away, far into the distance, which on this dark night was no more than a hundred yards. "No. You have to kill us. You have to kill me, anyway, because I know what you're about to do. And just for good measure, you have to kill anyone I come into real contact with. Isn't that it?"

"You want to cut the tape on my hands?" Stafford asked. "I hate being bottle-fed."

Dengler cut the duct tape.

"I can't tell you anything, can I?" Stafford said. "That's in your profile — you already know it all."

"Okay."

"Let me suggest this: You join us." He swallowed thirstily, upending the beer. "You take part in the deed. You strike a blow for America by smearing this President's brains all over Texas. For the Bay of Pigs. For the Cuban fucking missile crisis. For the war in Vietnam he won't fight. Then you're a part of the whole thing. You're an insider."

Dengler looked past him at the night, listening to the crickets, so late this year, he'd heard said. "Do any of these people know," and here Dengler thought about what he was going to say for a moment, then continued, "that they can't be allowed to live afterward? Can't any of them see that?"

Stafford laughed — it was more of a chortle, soft and inward directed — before emptying the long neck and tossing the bottle, refuse now, out into the gravel parking lot. "Just like your psych profile says — you already know it all."

"It's kept me alive so far."

"Doesn't matter. The truth is, David, there's no one you can get in touch with who will believe you. You're a fugitive, as of this morning on the *Ten Most Wanted* list. If you surface, the cops are just going to fill you with lead and ask questions later."

"What about after the assassination, when Lyndon Johnson is President?" Dengler said.

"Not even then. You'll still be a fugitive, and once you're in custody, you'll die in some fashion that may be a little suspicious but, hell, who cares, right? Weren't you David Dengler, the famous killer and armed robber?"

"So I don't pose a threat?"

"Not in the slightest. Not after today, anyway. Had you met with the Attorney General before we smeared you, well — things might be different now. But they're not."

"No, they're not," Dengler agreed softly.

"So, you trade me for your little tart, you toddle off to some obscure part of the country, change your names and keep from being arrested, and you'll probably be okay. If some law enforcement officer trips over you, your life expectancy will probably drop to forty-eight hours. Procedure, you know. No one will believe your story because it's too fantastic. And anyway, the person telling the story is a wanted criminal, a murderer, a thief, and presumably a liar. I know I wouldn't believe you if I didn't know better."

"So that's the deal."

"That's the deal."

"I'll need a phone number to reach Keller."

Stafford provided him with one.

Dengler forced Stafford down, taped his hands again, and drove east.

- 79 -

They arranged for the exchange at dawn on a dusty road. Dengler didn't like the arrangements particularly — if they double-crossed him he would have to set out across open terrain. On the good side, there was an almost limitless view. The road crested a small rise in what was essentially checkerboard flatlands stretching into infinity. He could see a car for miles, an aircraft tens of miles.

As dawn crept upon them, Dengler removed the tape from Stafford's ankles and wrists and stood him out to one side of the road, alone. Then he crossed the road and stood opposite, beside the Plymouth, and waited.

The Ford wagon took ten minutes to wind up the road, to take the cutoff, and arrive at the junction where Stafford stood. Dengler placed himself behind the Plymouth, the .38 drawn, and waited. As instructed, the driver of the Ford stopped thirty yards from Stafford. Etta was allowed to get out of the car. She looked in good condition, Dengler thought, dressed in jeans and a western blouse and holding a small overnight case. She looked back at the driver of the car, and then cautiously crossed the open space to the Plymouth. She stopped five paces from him and made eye contact. Stafford was friendlier. Dengler turned his attention, and the weapon in his hand, across the abyss at the man behind the wheel of the Ford.

"Get in the car," Dengler told her. Etta slipped into the passenger side. Dengler crossed in front, moved behind the steering wheel, and then started the engine. This was the signal for the Ford to motor past Stafford on the left and Dengler's car on the right. Once the Ford was clear of them, Dengler executed a brisk left turn and accelerated toward the main highway as fast as the Plymouth could take the dirt road.

"Keep watch." Dengler told her. Etta turned in the seat and studied the terrain passing behind her. She emitted an aura of icy rage.

"What did they tell you?"

"You want me this badly?" Etta said. "To kidnap someone to trade for me?"

Dengler laughed. It was crazy. He'd traded nothing for nothing.

"You think it's funny?"

"We have to lay low for a couple of days," he told her. "After that, I'll give you some money and you can go where you want."

"Even back to Dallas?"

No, not back to Dallas. "I have some things to tell to you," Dengler said. "After we get a place to stay."

Stafford and his people would be looking for them at every motel between New Mexico and Kansas, Dengler knew. Instead of renting a room, he drove to a Fort Worth suburb and cruised a neighborhood with houses on one, two and four-acre lots. One house was obscured from the street by poplars. Four newspapers were strewn about its front step. The curtains were drawn. Dengler opened the wire gate, drove the Plymouth back behind the house, and closed the gate behind him.

Dengler jimmied the back door with almost no effort.

Etta sat at the kitchen table while he told her everything. At first, she feigned disinterest, but by the time he got to the part about JFK's assassination, she stood and began to pace. By the time he started telling her about Kerschov informing him that he was the second patsy, a visceral moan erupted from her. When he told her about his last conversation with Stafford, about how he and everyone he knew would have to be killed to keep the conspiracy secret, she stopped pacing and looked at him with an expression half pained, and half terrified. She strode to where he was standing and slapped him. Hard. She drew back to slap him again, but when Dengler didn't attempt to defend himself, her hand stalled midair.

"God damn you," she said and left the kitchen.

Dengler found eggs in the fridge. He made breakfast. Once he stepped to the threshold of the living room and saw Etta sitting in a rocker, staring out the front windows. She'd been crying, but wasn't now.

When the food was ready, he called, "Breakfast," and began to eat, not really expecting her to come, but she did. She sat opposite him. Toast popped up on the counter and Dengler retrieved it for the bread plate. He smeared butter on both pieces and placed them to warm one another, face to face.

"Your friend Wes sprung me from the hospital," she said.

"I know."

"He paid me to have sex with him."

Dengler was going to say, *I know*, but didn't.

"I did it because I knew it would embarrass you."

Dengler nodded, and chewed.

"David," she said, "you made me hate you."

"I know."

"Wes set me up with Jack Ruby."

Dengler knew all of this, of course. He let her tell it anyway.

"When I saw you at the club, I just... wanted to hurt you," she said. "I'm sorry. Jack said you almost died."

Dengler snorted and shook his head, *no*.

"They're really going to kill us?"

"Probably," Dengler said, still chewing. "You and Ruby? A couple?"

Etta dropped her head. "Yes. I thought so, anyway... but when Becker came—"

"Becker?"

"That's what Ruby called him."

"Describe him."

She described Becker.

"His real name is Keller. At least I think Keller is his real name. He's a CIA operative. Go on."

"When Becker... *Keller* came for me, Ruby said, 'Take her.'"

Dengler wanted to laugh, but didn't.

"They're going to kill the president?"

"Yeah, I think they are."

"Isn't there something we can do?"

"I'm open for suggestions."

"We can go to the police."

Dengler explained to her he was a fugitive wanted for murdering two federal agents *for no reason*. In other words, he was crazy. No one would believe him, and he would live no more than a day or two in custody.

"I could tell them."

"Everything you know you learned from me."

"They kidnapped me," Etta said.

"You thought *I* was the kidnapper."

"The news, then. Huntley and Brinkley. Walter Cronkite."

"Same thing."

Etta fell into silence. Dengler finished his meal and went to the sink to wash the dishes. He was a burglar, yes, but he was a neat burglar.

"What can we do?" she said finally.

Dengler took her plate, emptied it into the garbage pail, and then washed it.

"I have a little money. You take it, go somewhere and become a different person. You can do that, right?"

"By myself?"

No, Dengler thought, *Etta isn't real good by herself.*

"I'd say *we* go somewhere, but I know how you feel about me."

Etta was silent for several minutes. Dengler went about tidying up. "Even when I hated you," she said as he emptied the dish drainer, putting everything back into the cupboards, "even then, I still loved you."

Dengler turned and leaned against the counter, crossing his arms in front, dishtowel hanging from one hand. He didn't know what to say. He thought this moment would be triumphant. He felt oddly gray.

Etta stood. "I have to go take a shower," she said. "Freshen up."

She might have said, *Clean the stink of another man off my body.*

Dengler sat on the front porch for an hour and considered the possibilities. They might blend in; they might even fit somewhere, if Etta was off the smack. If Dengler had to supply her with drugs, it was impossible. They would have to go to a big city. He would have to find some way of making enough money to keep her supplied. If he were Stafford, he would key his search for Dengler on drug dealers. They wouldn't last long.

Etta joined him on the porch. She was wearing a cloth robe and nothing else. She squeezed water from her hair with her hands and flung the excess out into the yard. Beads of moisture glistened on her chest. "I'm fresh and clean," she announced. "It feels good."

Dengler nodded. She was beautiful. He tried not to think about the last man she was with, Ruby, or the others she might have serviced. The shower had made her clean and new, her attitude said.

"Etta, are you still using?"

She smiled reassuringly. "I won't lie to you, David. I backslid once, at a party Ruby took me to. But, I realized it's not for me and I've never used it since."

"Good." He told her why. Stafford would use it to anchor his search for them.

"It won't be a problem," she said.

They talked for a while. They made plans, unmade them, and made others. Etta's robe tie worked itself free, the robe fell open a little, top and bottom, exposing her lovely legs and breasts, and skin softer than anything Dengler could think of. She was seducing him, of course.

Dengler put his hand on hers. "Let's not do this," he said.

Tears welled in her eyes. "David, you don't want me?"

"No, I do. That's the point. Everyone wants you. Let's... just take it slow. I don't want to be dazzled just by your beauty." Etta grinned at this. It was the one thing she was certain of, her attractiveness to men. "I want to spend time with the Etta I knew in school."

Etta changed the sheets on the bed as he watched. She was naked. The robe got in the way, she said. She was still trying to seduce him. Watching her reminded him of that first time, in West Virginia, except neither of them was innocent anymore.

They lay together in bed, naked and entwined, Etta's head in the crook of his shoulder. The residue of their lives clung to them, Dengler's anger, Etta's betrayal. After a while all of that fell away. They were just two people lying in one another's arms. "Forgive me, Davey," Etta whispered into his ear. "Please. Forgive me."

Dengler fell into a deep sleep and floated on a vast, quiet sea.

Later, an hour, four hours, he didn't know how much later, he woke with Etta above him. "Davey, I want you," she said, cooing at him. She smelled like wild flowers, her skin as soft as silk, and her breasts full. She was moaning when he opened his eyes, moaning and undulating above him, her eyes closed, her concentration drawn inside for the climax that was sure to come. Dengler realized it wasn't Etta above him, but Marilyn Monroe. The touch of her was different, the smell of her, the taste of her, was different from Etta. When Marilyn opened her eyes, Dengler was surprised she remembered him. She laughed. "Davey, I've thought about this... for so long," she said. Dengler touched her shoulders, pulled her to him, felt the rustle of her blond hair falling past his face, felt her breasts flatten against his chest, touched the rift that ran along her back with his finger tips, held her until she called out in a shrill voice, "Oh. Yes."

He slept again after that, drifting. When he woke, the room was stale and warm. Dengler threw off the covers and realized he'd had a wet dream. Etta wasn't in the room, although the bathroom light was on. Dengler stood and walked stiffly toward the bathroom. "Etta?" he called. Somehow he thought the lovemaking had been real, Etta standing in for Marilyn.

Dengler pushed open the bathroom door. Etta was on the toilet. "Sweetheart," he said, "I..." It took a moment to see something was wrong. She was naked, leaning against the flush-box, her arms lank, and the expression on her face not hers at all. He'd never seen her make a face like that. It was almost a non-expression, a dropping of all human articulation. Her eyes were vague, unfocused, her mouth gaping. Her skin was very, very cold.

Dengler was so stunned he stood beside her for minutes, naked and not understanding, before the truth was processed by his mind, if not his heart. He kneeled in front of her, finding the hypo lying between her feet. He found the rest of the 'kit' between the toilet and the wall. It was the small overnight bag she'd carried when he picked her up earlier.

She'd been dead for hours.

Dengler ran his fingers through her hair. All that was alive of her anymore was that beautiful red hair he treasured. He didn't cry. No, he wouldn't cry.

She was already becoming stiff. He carried her to the bed and laid her out. She was still beautiful, even in death a beautiful human creature. He closed her eyes. He dressed her, placing on her body the outfit she'd worn earlier. He combed her hair but didn't attempt makeup; it was beyond him.

Dengler sat with her until nightfall. He talked to her, telling her everything he ever felt about her. He broke down once and held her cold hand. Then he called the police, reported her death, gathered up his belongings, loaded them into the Plymouth and drove away.

Dengler knew what had happened. They gave her uncut heroin hoping it would kill them both. Stafford's people. Keller.

He knew what had happened.

- 80 -

Wednesday, November 20, 1963

Dengler abandoned the Plymouth on a side street, then took a taxi back to Dallas. The Ford was still in the parking garage where he left it, but it had been moved upstairs to long-term parking, and a special storage fee had accrued. Dengler paid it, and drove out.

Fairly certain they wouldn't look for him, a single man, in Dallas, he rented a room downtown in a hotel with an adjacent parking garage, ordered room service, and sat back onto the bed to think.

Early in the morning of Thursday, November Twenty First, Dengler woke and realized he had been crying in his sleep. He recalled the dream: *Dengler stood in the house of his childhood in West Virginia. The walls were brighter than they became later, after his mother left, when he shared the place with his angry, sullen father. Adam Dengler, face wrenched ugly by stroke but otherwise younger than David recalled him, sat at the kitchen table drawing three half-circles with first one, and then two crosses on top of them. It was the same crude picture Adam Dengler had drawn repeatedly in the weeks before he died, never making his son understand. Dengler noticed different versions of this same drawing were framed and hung on the walls of their old house. Adam looked up at his son with a strange, grisly grin, held up the drawing and pointed at the hills and the crosses on top of them.*

Suddenly Dengler recognized the symbols. He stood on them, the three small hills, one on top of two, in back of their house in West Virginia, as Adam Dengler dug a wide, oval pit into the soil. Adam Dengler's work exposed the body of his mother and her lover, their heads blown away by shotgun blasts, their wounds fresh and slimy red. Adam stopped digging, held up the tablet, poked the top sheet with his good hand and grinned.

David Dengler understood. His mother had not run away. She and her lover were murdered by his father.

Other people joined David and his father on top of the three small hills: Etta and Marilyn, JFK. David Dengler turned to them and said, "My father killed them. My mother. This man. He killed them, see?"

Adam Dengler blew Marilyn's face away with his shotgun.

"No." David Dengler shouted.

Adam Dengler shot Etta. She flew back and into the crude, circu-

lar grave.

David charged his father just as Adam turned the shotgun on Kennedy.

He woke up.

Astonished by the emotions that wrenched him, Dengler barked, "Damn it," and wiped the water from his eyes. "Jesus Christ," he blurted, rolling his legs over the side of the bed and propping his elbows onto his knees. "Damn it to hell, anyway."

Finally, he gave in to it and released himself. At first, he thought the high-pitched wail was a far off siren, but it originated deep from within himself. His mourning grew in intensity until he didn't recognize himself anymore. Bellowing like an orphaned child, which he realized he was, Dengler dropped to the floor, tears and snot and drool running down his face in rivulets. His father killed his mother and her lover, murdered them and buried them in back of the house while he was at school. He must have always known this and denied it, from a very young age. Everyone who ever mattered to him, everyone he loved or whose life he was meant to protect, was dead.

Even Etta, whose life was fresh in his mind, whose warmth and living presence was so real he expected her to enter the room any minute. Gone.

Every one of them.

Except Kennedy.

Dengler found a clothing store within walking distance of his hotel and bought a western-cut linen suit, and Stetson straw hat. Dengler observed himself in the mirror and was struck with just how silly he looked, even though the salesman assured him he looked as *Dallas* as anyone could. He also purchased a pair of new boots with engraved silver toes.

Dengler drove the route the motorcade would take the following day, the map he clipped from the paper unfolded in his lap. It was a lovely Fall day, bright with a blustery wind that billowed the dresses and jackets of pedestrians and made storefront awnings snap. Even though he studied the route from beginning to end, Dengler had already decided where the assassination would be. *Why else get Lee Harvey Oswald a job in the Texas State Schoolbook Depository?*

All along the route, he saw nothing of the advance team that would normally precede a presidential visit. The law enforcement contingent looked lighter than normal, with fewer policemen on the street than he remembered. Then again, Dengler considered, they might be reserving their personnel for the following day. Dengler doubted Stafford's people could control such distant and individual forces as local police departments.

He drove through the Dealey Plaza area, passed beneath the Stemmons Freeway underpass, then doubled back and parked his car several blocks east of the area he was already beginning to think of as the kill zone. Then he walked west at an easy pace. Dengler appeared to be a man with time on his hands enjoying the good weather. He crossed Houston Street, jaywalking to the Plaza from the corner where the County Criminal Courts Building was located. He crossed the grass plaza to Elm Street, and then on to the land fronting the Southern Pacific freight yards. Dengler avoided looking up. He suspected there were people up there looking down. Even if the Army or the Secret Service found it a waste of time to prepare for the President's visit, the conspirators were certainly preparing.

Even so he saw nothing deserving interest.

He sat down on the grass, near the rise and the wood fence, but he was careful not to remove the straw hat, or shift it too far back on his head. They, whoever *They* were, were too far away from him to identify his face, and his clothes clearly placed him as a local and probably not worth much scrutiny. He lit a cigarette (a prop) and crossed his legs, bobbing one booted foot in the air, seeing the new steel toe glisten in the sun.

He looked up at the Schoolbook Depository and imagined what it must look like up there. Big open rooms, he imagined, maybe with shelves for books. Plenty of opportunity not to be seen, even with a rifle.

Stafford's people wouldn't depend solely on a single sniper's nest. There had to be at least one other, and probably two. But where?

If I were doing this where would I put the sniper positions? Dengler asked himself. Well, the Schoolbook Depository, that was certain, but only if the motorcade detoured right on Elm Street. If, on the other hand, the motorcade continued straight for the freeway, the Schoolbook Depository would be out of position for a really easy shot, although it would still be in range.

The map showed the motorcade making a straight run for the freeway from here. If there were a plan to detour, it wasn't being published. It seemed reasonable a detour would occur, if for no other reason than it needed to occur. This was a killing that was going to happen from the inside out, a suicide of a government, so to speak, in which the beast blew its own head off. The beast could change the route of the motorcade if it wanted; indeed, one would expect nothing less.

　Using the natural order of the streets as a guide, Dengler drew a triangle using the Schoolbook Depository as an anchor for one of the points. The first 'leg' of the triangle went south along Houston Street. Any of the buildings on Houston Street, the Dal-Tex Building, the County Records Building, the County Criminal Courts Building and the Old Court House, could provide a platform for a sniper's nest. Dengler dismissed all of them immediately — too many cops coming, going, socializing, and doing police business. A sniper team would draw too much attention setting up. That left the U.S. Post Office Building opposite the Schoolbook Depository across Dealey Plaza. If he was correct and the motorcade diverted right at Houston, and then left at Elm, the Post Office site would be out of position to make a certain shot; if the motorcade continued down Main Street, however, then it would become the primary sniper's nest with the President's motorcade passing below.

　Dengler drew the second 'leg' of the triangle west along Elm, which curved toward the triple underpass. This would be the termination point of the second angle; it provided an anchor for the third 'leg,' drawn from the south. Dengler drew the triangle in his mind. No matter where the motorcade moved inside that triangle, it would come under fire from three sides.

　Dengler stood and strolled toward the Schoolbook Depository. He didn't stop and go inside, though, because he knew that no matter where he was going to be tomorrow, it wouldn't be inside this building. He crossed Houston Street and strolled lazily past the County Records Building, then on to the Criminal Courts Building, then across Main Street to the Old Court House where he stopped. He was a man with time on his hands, so he squatted and looked at something on the ground — it was just a stain in the concrete, but no one looking down from a high spot would know that. In the interim he allowed his peripheral vision to take in the tempo of street activity, to absorb its pattern. Then Dengler stood and strolled across Commerce Street to the front of the Post Office Building, stopping long enough to note that the bottom floor was a dedicated mail processing plant. Dengler turned and looked across Dealey Plaza at the Schoolbook Depository, allowing his eyes to drift west toward the grass, the small rise leading to the board fence, the railroad yard behind it, and then down to the underpass and the Stemmons Freeway.

His opinion hadn't changed since the first time he walked this ground. He would place the first sniper at the underpass, the second in one of the upper windows of the Schoolbook Depository, and the third in the Post Office Building behind him, as insurance, say five or six stories up.

Dengler entered the Post Office Building. To the immediate right was the entrance to the sorting facility, dual glass doors. The racket of conveyor machines was loud, but not overwhelming. There was marble everywhere inside the lobby, grooved marble that reminded him of the flyleaves of old books. There was a bank of elevators at mid-building, three on each side, facing one another. There was a large directory located to the right of two of the elevator doors, repeated on the bank of elevators opposite. Dengler patiently read the directory, removing the Stetson and running his fingers through his sweaty hair. *Now I know where these people get it*, Dengler thought, remembering he'd seen this gesture repeated dozens of times since he came to Dallas. There was nothing extraordinary in the directory, merely an alphabetized list of names and the floors where their offices were located.

The opposite directory was listed by floor, and here there was something odd. *FIFTH FLOOR CLOSED FOR REMODELING*, the sign read. The entire floor was being redone. There would be no access, Dengler thought.

He pressed an *UP* button and waited for an elevator to respond to his call and open its doors. Dengler stepped inside, totally alone in the elevator, and pressed the round button marked *5*. He expected the elevator to be *keyed off*, mechanically restricted from stopping at the fifth floor, but it wasn't. Thirty seconds later the door opened on the fifth floor. Tape crisscrossed the entrance. A sign read, *CLOSED FOR REMODELING — DO NOT ENTER*. Dengler leaned out and saw pink insulation, metal tubing, electrical wire capped off but dangling free from midpoint in the walls. The floor was covered with cardboard and there was dust everywhere.

Dengler stepped through the tape cordon just as the elevator doors began to close. He saw people walking up the hall toward him, blue-collar types wearing dark green work clothes and leather tool-belts. Behind them was open sky.

Dengler retreated quickly, even though the elevator doors had bounced off him and reopened. He pressed the *6* button and heard a voice call out, "Hey, you," just as the doors closed and the elevator took him up. He heard the phrase "restricted area" before the voice fell away.

Dengler exited on the Sixth Floor, then went to the stairwell and began to descend. Unfortunately, not only was the fifth floor stairwell exit locked, all of the stairwell exits were locked. He descended six floors to the street level and exited onto the sidewalk.

Third sniper's nest, Dengler thought.

- 81 -

Dengler spent the rest of the day walking the immediate area surrounding Dealey Plaza. He walked through the railroad yards, then across the underpass, then back around to his car, the entire route taking the better part of two hours. He wanted to seem just another Texan with time on his hands, but in truth he perused every inch of what he knew would be a killing ground, trying to gain an edge on it. There was no edge. The terrain was perfect for an assassination: Close, but not so close as to threaten anonymity or escape.

It had one weakness.

God, I hate this, Dengler thought. He knew they were going to kill him. He was going to die. He thought, *Stafford is going to fire a bullet right through my head.* The site had one weakness. Take control of any of the sniper positions, and an attack on the other two might stop the assassination.

He caught Oswald before he left to spend the night with his family. Dengler just walked up to the front door of the house located on Beckley Street and rang the doorbell. A woman answered the door. "Is Mr. Lee in?" Dengler said. Oswald had taken an alias when he rented the room here. O. H. Lee. *Cute*, Dengler thought on hearing of it. *He likes to play games.*

When Oswald stepped out of his room, he saw Dengler standing at the front door and turned visibly pale. "There's a Mr. Oswald here to see you, Mr. Lee," his landlady told Oswald, and Dengler grinned. *Oswald. I can be cute too*, he thought.

"Thank you, Mrs. Klass," Oswald said, stepping quickly past her and pushing Dengler from the light of the room. The moment the front door closed Oswald's landlady turned on the porch light. Dengler sat down on the porch wall.

"What are you doing here?" Oswald asked.

"I thought I would pay you a little visit," Dengler replied, smiling. "You know, before all the fireworks tomorrow."

"I don't know what you're talking about," Oswald told him. "I haven't got a clue what you're talking about."

"Fine. Have it your way." Dengler said.

"Leave."

"Sure. Actually, I've got things to do, too."

"Fine. Go do them."

"But first..." Dengler smiled again. *Gee, how do you broach the subject of an assassination?* "First I'm going to ask you to be brave tomorrow, Lee."

"I don't know what you're talking about. Fuck you. Now leave."

"I know who you think I am. You think I work for Gray Stafford, but one of these days, if you live long enough, I'll drop a bag with his balls in it right into your hand."

"I'm really impressed."

"There won't be any cavalry tomorrow, Lee," Dengler said softly. "The FBI's not going to pop in at the last moment and arrest the bad guys, no matter what Stafford told you. The shooters Banister or the Mob hired are the real thing. You're the phony. You're the only one the police will catch. Then someone will put you down."

Oswald trembled with the fear that Dengler was right. There was no one the man could trust. No one. *Have you told your cop friend, Tippett?* Dengler thought not. That contingency hadn't played out yet, and probably never would.

"Tomorrow," Dengler said, pushing on, "there will be three sniper positions. I figure, if I'm lucky, I can take out one, then maybe pin down the other. That leaves the Schoolbook Depository."

Oswald didn't reply. His mind was overloaded with possibilities, Dengler saw.

"Now let me guess, each team is divided into a shootist, a spotter, and a lookout, right? Just like we learned in school. You're the lookout, right?"

Oswald said nothing. His eyes burned into Dengler.

"Lee, tomorrow, kill the other two men. Kill them before they can shoot the President."

"Fuck you," Oswald whispered, anger and fear shaking him. Sweat was beading on Oswald's brow, his arms, and the backs of his hands; large beads that seeped from his body like blood though a cut.

"Stop them, Lee. Stop them before they kill an innocent man. I need your help."

"Get out of here." Oswald growled. He took a step toward Dengler, fist balled as if to strike. "Just get out of here."

This last was a shout. The front door opened. Oswald's landlady opened the door and looked out worriedly. "Is everything all right, Mr. Lee?" She studied Dengler, trying to remember him.

Dengler stood, gave Oswald a knowing look, then turned and descended the steps from the porch and trotted to the Ford. In a moment, the engine was started. The last he saw of Lee Oswald that night, the ex-Marine was standing on the porch glaring after him.

- 82 -

Friday, November 22, 1963

There was a light mist that morning. Dengler rose early and went down to the hotel coffee shop instead of ordering in. He sat in a booth rather than at the counter, a change for him, with his back to the street, and read the morning newspaper. The President's motorcade route was printed on the front page. There had been a change. The map showed the motorcade turning right on Houston Street and then left on Elm, taking it directly beneath the Schoolbook Depository.

Dengler ordered coffee and eggs, bacon and toast, which he ate slowly and silently alone. The waitress made small talk when she came to the table, saying, "What about the President? Isn't he a good looking man? And Jackie, she ought to be a Southern girl. She has such good manners." Dengler wouldn't allow himself to be pulled into a discussion and the waitress went away unsatisfied.

After breakfast he called Daisy from the hotel lobby. Dengler half expected Strong to answer the phone, but it was Daisy, on the fifth ring.

"Daisy," he said.

"Jack?" She was happy to hear from him, he realized. "Jack, are you okay?"

"I'm fine," he told her. "I just didn't want to leave it the way—"

"You fell asleep," she said of their last meeting in the hospital. "I had to get back, and then when I went to see you the next day, you were gone. Did they move you? Secretly, I mean?"

"I moved myself." He told her about leaving the hospital, everything that led up to the confrontation with the bouncer outside *The Carousel Club*.

"Did you find Etta?"

Dengler didn't want to tell her about Etta. "That's all in the past," was all he said. "How about you and Wes?"

"I asked him to move out. He says he wants to talk, but so far we can't seem to do it."

"I'm sorry."

"I'm not sure that I am sorry, Jack," she said.

"Daisy, tomorrow you may hear some things about me. I can't go into it now and I may not have a chance to later, so I want you to know the things you'll hear, they're all lies."

"Lies? What are you talking about?"

"Don't tell anyone I called," Dengler continued. "Don't even mention our talking. It's important to me that you know—"

"Know what?" Daisy's voice was rising with concern.

"—know who I am, what I'm capable of, and what I'm not."

Silence strung out along the thousands of miles of telephone lines separating them.

"Jack," she said finally. "*David...* I know who you are."

"Goodbye, Daisy."

Dengler gassed up the Ford, checked out of the hotel and placed all of his belongings, what little there was, in the trunk. Then he drove west toward Dealey Plaza, away from the rising sun that, owing to the drizzle, was partly obscured. This would burn off, he was told over the small transistor radio he'd bought the day before in the hotel gift shop, a *Motorola Wanderer*. It was roughly twice the size of a package of cigarettes and a large sum heavier. He was merely testing it. He turned it off and switched to the Ford radio, learning in a moment the President was having breakfast at a Chamber of Commerce function in Fort Worth and would fly to Dallas shortly.

Dengler listened to man-on-the-street interviews of Dallas citizens about the visit of their President, and most comments were positive. Most people wanted the President to visit their city, wanted him to leave thinking Dallas the young giant of commerce and industry it was. Dallas was perhaps not sophisticated yet, some people said, but it was sure to become so. There were other comments, however, suggesting an undercurrent of anger and resentment directed toward the young President, at his failure to rescue Cuba from communism and his lack of will to face up to the Russians. Dengler wondered how many negative comments the radio station edited out, saving them for airing later, after the President and his staff left the city.

Dengler drove through the Dealey Plaza area and under the triple underpass, parking his car west of the Stemmons Freeway, and then walked back. It was a little after seven-thirty, and the streets were fairly free from the crowds he imagined would fill them later. His last act before checking out of the hotel had been to change into the work clothes bought the previous day after seeing what the men on the fifth floor of the Post Office Building wore. The clothes were new and didn't look worked in, but they were the right color. Now, wearing the work clothes and carrying a lunch-box that might have been holding his lunch, but wasn't, Dengler strolled leisurely toward the building.

Unless his guess was wrong, there would be no workers on the floor this day, but the green suit would at least arouse no interest as he went to what he was already thinking of as *the sniper's nest*. He took the elevator to the fifth floor, stepped past the tape into the hallway. There was one elevator assigned to the reconstruction, and it was usually keyed off, unable to stop at the other floors. With no work scheduled today that elevator had been put back into service and was taped closed at this floor.

Dengler reached back inside and sent the elevator returning to the ground floor, then turned around and visually inspected the site. He didn't expect to find anyone here yet, or at least gambled he wouldn't. He had no idea who the shooters were. If they recognized him, he might find himself in a gun battle before he wanted. Dengler was prepared for that too. His hand was on the .38 taken from Stafford. He would kill, if necessary, and ask questions later. He calculated it would be too dangerous for the shooting team to go in this early. An early placement would increase the possibility of exposure.

There was no one on the site as yet. Dengler walked the floor, memorizing the nascent corridors and rooms. He went to the west face of the building, taking care not to get too close to the open air should a spotter see him, and surveyed the fields of fire, to the underpass, to the Schoolbook Depository, and finally to Elm Street itself, the most difficult shot of all.

He then turned and walked the area in reverse, seeing everything from the opposite angle. Satisfied he'd committed as much of the floor plan to memory as he could, he went to the door leading to the stairwell with the intention of taping the locking mechanism into the open position. A chill ran up his spine when he saw someone had already taped it open.

Here was their entry port.

It would be his, too.

There should have been someone on the roof. Dengler thought of his M.I. training at Fort Lee. This is where all of his former Army siblings should have been, covering Dallas like a blanket prepared to snuff out fire. From this vantage point Dengler could see the top of the Schoolbook Depository, with its Hertz sign and clock. From here he could see Elm Street and Main Street, the triple overpass and Stemmons Freeway.

Dengler pretended to do electrical work. He kept away from the building edge so he couldn't be observed from the ground. He watched as people came to work at the surrounding buildings. Some of them were members of the kill teams, he was sure, but determining just who they were by their appearance was impossible.

Dengler's real concern was the underpass at the Stemmons Freeway. This was the third nest, he was certain. Here, and from the two other nests, the motorcade would be brought under a crucifying triple crossfire. If one of the sharpshooters missed Kennedy, there were two others to get him. In all probability, all three would "get" Kennedy. This was the reason a "conspiracy" was needed, to support the bullet evidence later. More than one assassin had to be offered, and a plot directed logically at a foreign power. If there were only one assassin, the bullet evidence couldn't be explained. Bullets would have to be made to perform all manner of tricks in order to satisfy the evidence of a single gunman, and clearly that wasn't possible. With Dengler as the second assassin, safely dead, of course, the true assassins could walk away, dusting their hands clean of evidence as they went.

The Soviet Union would be blamed indirectly for inspiring the assassins, if not conspiring with them.

Dengler and Oswald would be dead. Their backgrounds would suggest communist tendencies.

A conspiracy.

Now that Dengler was out of the conspiracy, at least as far as being used as a patsy, Stafford's people were probably scrambling to find new assassins to blame.

Periodically Dengler removed the *Motorola Wanderer* from his lunch-box and tuned in a news station to receive the most recent updates regarding the President's progress. After the breakfast meeting in Fort Worth, Dengler learned, the President and his entourage motored to the airport for the six-minute flight to Love Field. They arrived to a massive crowd of well-wishers, a marching band, and hundreds of children intent on seeing the nation's Chief Executive. The motorcade would wind its way through Dallas past Dealey Plaza to the Stemmons Freeway, and then on to the Trade Mart for a luncheon.

Once the motorcade was underway, Dengler pushed the long aerial back into the Wanderer. He placed the radio into his right rear pants pocket, closed the lunch-box, and set it aside. He would never see the lunch-box again. He walked to the edge of the building and looked out. There was no one on the underpass yet, but there seemed to be an older man walking toward it from the north, parallel with the railroad yards. Dengler wondered if the old man was part of the conspiracy, or merely someone looking for a good vantage point from which to watch the world's most powerful man drive by.

There was no way to tell.

Dengler walked toward the stairwell door. He'd taped this door open and didn't need a key to open it and descend.

Dengler waited outside the stairwell entrance to the fifth floor for minutes, trying to listen. *Are they inside? Have they set up already?*

Looking down, he saw his hand on the doorknob and thought of Etta's hand the last time he caressed it, cold as marble. How easily he might be converted into statuary, cold and lifeless, like Etta.

Dengler paused for moments, his hand on the knob.

Then he opened the door and stepped onto the fifth floor.

- 83 -

Wind shot through the building as if it were a tunnel, amplifying gusts to bursts. Due to its total reconstruction, there were no windows to stop the wind, although hanging canvas drapes worked to slow it and caused areas of light and darkness to shift and twist across the construction floor. The peak instant of a gust would stifle all sound but a shout.

Dengler moved laterally to get a view of the most obvious sniper port. He saw nothing due to construction impediments — several stacks of lumber, a bin of finishing nails of various kinds, and the wind-breaking drapes. He continued, one step, two, three, weapon pointed, finger on the trigger, thinking of nothing, flashing on Etta, thinking of nothing.

Dengler saw the first man. He wore a khaki work outfit and a silver hard hat. He was assembling something, kneeling on one leg, and working from a small case. Dengler took two more steps, freezing instantly. He saw a second man standing near a vacant window. *Shooter and Spotter*, Dengler guessed.

The man assembling the weapon said something to the man beside the window and the latter turned. Dengler stepped back, angling out of their line of sight behind a steel beam. *Third man? Where's the third man?* Dengler looked back into the recesses of the floor, but saw no human movement, merely the flutter of the canvas windbreaks and the dance of the sun as it spun light around them, twisting and leaping.

There was no warning except the turn of the doorknob. Dengler stepped wide, fully into the line of sight of the two men forward of him, nearer Dealey Plaza and the motorcade route. Conferring, they didn't turn and look. The door pushed open. The third man, Lookout, entered. He was dressed like the others and carried a sealed cardboard box. Dengler squeezed into the triangular space the opening door made. At that instant Dengler realized his mistake — Lookout would make sure the door was closed and in the process discover him. Dengler lunged for the third man. The cardboard box struck the ground in free fall as Lookout pulled a 9mm automatic from where he'd secured it, in his belt at the small of his back. Dengler stepped past the box and slapped the weapon as it was being brought around, knocking it free. The weapon clattered to the floor as Dengler's hands shoved Lookout.

Dengler intended to push the man back out of sight of his two associates and finish him there, but Lookout had other ideas. He was twenty pounds heavier than Dengler, and more muscular. He shrugged off Dengler's attack and countered simultaneously. Dengler was shoved further into the line of sight of the Shooter and Spotter. Lookout barked a warning to his partners, but the wind swallowed the sound. He advanced on Dengler, whose shoulder slapped the hard plywood flooring, sending Dengler's weapon somersaulting across the floor. Dengler leaped to his feet as Lookout's left hand grabbed his throat. Dengler kicked, then twisted, tightening his neck muscles to compensate for the pressure at his throat as he pulled the larger man from his associates' line of sight. Halfway there Dengler felt the blows land on his stomach and lower chest — three quick bolts — and felt all strength release from his body. He dropped, retaining enough self-possession to roll away from the door and out of sight of the other two killers.

Lookout opted to fall with him rather than release his grip. Now both of Lookout's hands were around Dengler's throat, tightening. The tension Dengler applied to his neck muscles disappeared with the blows to his stomach. He felt blood flow diminish, gasped for air, looked up into Lookout's eyes and saw total commitment to his death written there. Thought was slowly fading — he had to break Lookout's hold on his neck.

Dengler's right fist pounded Lookout's genitals. Dengler's blow was enough to cause Lookout to bellow and release him. Dengler rolled away and coughed.

Lookout drew his legs up and cupped his gonads with both hands. Dengler heard Lookout utter obscenities in what sounded like German. Coughing, Dengler staggered past him to where his weapon lay. Lookout's hands closed around his ankles and Dengler hit the floor. Lookout crawled toward him. Dengler kicked him hard directly in the face. Blood spurted from Lookout's lips and nose, but he continued forward. Dengler kicked him again, and then again, and again, blood leaping from Lookout's face.

Dengler aimed a final blow. The heel of his boot struck Lookout's face. Cartilage twisted and snapped — Dengler felt the man's nose flatten against his face — and his hands went limp. Lookout lay on the floor, blood seeping from his mouth, nose, and eyes. A single tooth was broken. Its shaft protruded from the man's gum.

Dengler massaged his throat. Winded and hurt, soreness already seeping into his muscles, Dengler rose from the floor.

Spotter stood at the end of the hallway, 9mm automatic in his belt, frozen in surprise. Dengler threw all of his strength into a leaping run toward his dislodged weapon before Spotter brought his

9mm up and began firing. The silencer and the wind insured the rounds were soundless. Bullets splintered all around Dengler as he realized his own weapon was too far away. He leaped and landed on Lookout's fallen 9mm and careened behind a pillar, just pulling his legs in as two rounds drilled holes into the plywood floor nearby.

Dengler heard the bark of a voice — Spotter's voice, he was certain, warning Shooter in German they had an intruder. Dengler quickly studied the 9mm automatic — he'd never fired one like this before — saw it was similar to his Walther, made sure the safety was off, and then rolled out, aiming. Spotter was no longer there.

A German voice called out again. The pillars were like an orchard, row upon row of steel trees standing alone and tall. Dengler crouched low and leaped to the next pillar. At the end of one aisle stood the Shooter with his rifle aimed at Dengler. Dengler leaped again as the round sounded — no silencer — and the shell flattened against a steel pillar with a dull pinging sound.

Dengler huddled, pulling his arms and legs into himself, and thought. They had him bracketed. One would advance while the second fired. Dengler would find it very hard to return fire this way. *Think. Think, damn it. What's really going on here?* There had to be a pattern to their movements. The disruption of their mission would certainly mean retreat — the assassins had to presume there were others behind him, others who might not have been warned yet, but men who could be drawn into the fray with overwhelming force. *Retreat. They have to retreat.*

Retreat meant the stairwell behind Dengler.

Retreat meant they would use infantry tactics to flank him and kill him before it would be safe to escape down the stairwell. One would hold him down with covering fire while the second advanced. Dengler knew he had to flank one of them himself in order to survive. Shooter had fired last, and with better accuracy than his pistol-armed associate. Having taken a round from the left, it would be only natural Dengler would move to the right, drawing Spotter's fire and allowing Shooter to advance.

These thoughts buzzed by in the millisecond before Dengler made his decision. With the sound of the last bullet Shooter fired still ringing in his ears, Dengler rolled right, didn't wait to see Spotter taking aim, then spun left and took aim himself. Shooter was advancing when Dengler's rounds caught him mid-step. The noise from Spotter's wayward round should have signaled safety; instead, it signaled the opening of a shooting gallery. Dengler was up immediately and advancing, expending 9mm bullets leading his way, as

Shooter seemed to freeze and float in the air. Then he fell. Dengler dove and rolled past him and behind another pillar, adrenaline racing through his veins like steam through a whistle.

Dengler pulled his limbs in tight and took stock. He was alive. He was unhurt. He had no idea how many rounds he had left in the 9mm automatic. He found the stud that ejected the clip, pressed it, and then counted the rounds. *Two. One in the chamber. That makes three.* He could appropriate Shooter's rifle, but here with naked beams and billowing canvas drapes, a weapon that unwieldy, no matter how accurate, would be a liability. It had certainly proven a liability for Shooter. No, he would stay with the 9mm until it was empty, then retrieve the .38 lost somewhere *over there*, by the door.

As these thoughts railed past his consciousness, Dengler waited for the assault, and realized almost too late there wouldn't be one. Spotter had to be in full retreat now, Dengler realized, heading for the door to the staircase and escape beyond. Dengler peered around the pillar and looked for a sign of movement. There was none. Only the drapes, the prancing sun they danced with, the ghost images the gusting wind made his eyes believe they saw.

Spotter dashed from pillar to pillar toward the stairwell door.

Dengler leapt to his feet and ran flat out toward the door, catching glimpses of Spotter as he emerged from between pillars to Dengler's right. It would have slowed Spotter to turn and look behind him, so he dashed forward unaware Dengler was closing the gap between them.

When Dengler hit Spotter the two men accelerated and flew onto the floor before the staircase exit. Spotter buried an elbow into Dengler's stomach and turned, attempting to bring the 9mm in his right hand to bear. Dengler slapped it away and landed a blow from the base of his own 9mm that jerked Spotter's chin to one side and scraped away skin and blood. The advantage was momentary. Spotter grabbed Dengler's gun barrel with both hands, directing the weapon toward its owner. Now angled badly to one side, Dengler found himself unable to land a good blow with his free hand and watched as the weapon in his right hand was slowly turned against him.

Dengler kicked at the man's groin, found himself out of range, attempted to strike his stomach, found it hard as a washboard, and then bit Spotter's right ear. Spotter bellowed and fell back, freeing Dengler, who kicked away with the 9mm still in his control, spitting out the lobe of the killer's ear.

Spotter counterattacked an instant later with a claw hammer he found at the base of an unfinished interior wall. Two bullets fired from Dengler's 9mm found Spotter's brow and exploded through it.

Dengler fell back against a metal abutment and searched for his breath. He couldn't breathe, and suddenly his head hurt. Blood pounded through him, shaking his body, his arms, his legs. It took half a minute to compose himself, before he could pull his legs up beneath him, lean forward into a squatting stance, then stand. He found his own .38 near the door, scooped it up, then grabbed Spotter's body by his belt and dragged it away from the stairwell door.

Dengler found Shooter's rifle fifteen yards closer to the street side of the building and moved for the sniper's nest.

- 84 -

Zero Minus 10:00

Dengler placed the Wanderer radio on the sill and extended the aerial which was crimped but still worked. The news reporter said the motorcade was in route and was expected at the Trade Mart in less than ten minutes. Kennedy was receiving a magnificent welcome, the reporter said. Dallas was out in force today to welcome its President.

Dengler examined the rifle, then the attached scope. He'd never fired one like this before. He was an expert shot, however, and would adapt. Reloading the weapon with a six-shot magazine, Dengler positioned himself beside the open-air window. He wiped away sweat that was still cascading down his brow, controlled his still-surging breathing, and sighted.

The underpass fell beneath the view of the scope. Dengler followed the center strut of the freeway up to the bridge level. The old man he'd seen earlier was gone. Apparently, he'd been en route somewhere else. Instead, three other men stood on the underpass. *Three men. Shooter, Spotter, Lookout*, just like the nest he'd just destroyed. *Yes, possibly*, Dengler thought, adjusting himself to the feel of the trigger, which was grooved like the serrated edge of a fish-gutting knife. Still, no one was in place. The Spotter should have been down five or ten feet, the Lookout posted at one end of the underpass. In fact, this position called for two Lookouts.

Dengler swung the sight down to the bottom, southern end of the underpass, and then up to the northern end. No one at either position. He returned his sight to the three men. They were middle-aged, plump, all wearing Stetsons. *Something wrong here*, Dengler thought. Assassination was a young man's game. People over 30 would be rare. *Families. Responsibilities. Good sense.* These men were in their late 40s, and even that would be giving them the benefit of the doubt.

Dengler swung the scope east, along the path that wormed along the fence behind the grass, the railroad yard area. He followed the fence east, toward the Book Depository and Dealey Plaza itself. A crowd had gathered since morning, people standing in the plaza, some of them on the north side opposite the plaza, all waiting for a look at the President. His scope view continued east. He saw people standing on the west corners of Main and Houston Streets become animated and realized they had just seen the first car in the motorcade.

Jesus. Dengler thought. *Where is it?* Was he wrong? Had he chosen the wrong spot for the third nest? He had to find it. Dengler swung the scope west again, quickly moving past the areas he'd just covered. There was a cop behind the fence. *Cop? No.* He continued on. He saw a railroad service worker walking casually, halfway between the underpass and the fence. Could this be the Spotter, or the Lookout? Somehow he thought he would just look at them and instantly *know.* Then he would send bullets rocketing through their brains. He would save Kennedy and expose Stafford and pay him back for what he did to Etta. He would pay the bastard back.

His gun sight was back on the underpass again. One of the men removed his Stetson and wiped the sweatband with a kerchief. Another pushed back the brim of his hat and was lighting a cigar. *No. NO. Not these people.* Dengler swung the weapon east again, the sight trailing along the fence. The railroad worker was standing beside the cop now. They were looking out toward Elm Street, exchanging a word or two. The railroad worker was smiling.

The scope view moved east. There was a man standing on the concrete memorial, a woman standing behind him with her arms around his waist. He held what looked like a small movie camera.

The sight moved east. There was a woman wearing a red bandanna over her hair with what appeared to be a still camera in her hands. She was looking anxiously back toward Main Street, waiting for the motorcade.

The sight moved east. A man and boy. The man was lifting the boy up onto his shoulders so he could see the President.

The scope moved east. The Schoolbook Depository. Dengler adjusted his view of the entrance upward, rising to the higher floors. The nest could be anywhere, Dengler knew, anywhere on the upper floors. He checked each window. Some were open. Some had people sticking out of them. No one had a gun in his hands. None was Oswald.

The sight moved south. The motorcade turned right from Main Street onto Houston. Dengler saw the President's car, a Lincoln, leading the motorcade. He yanked the sight across the expanse below him back to the underpass. The three men at the underpass were still standing where they had before, casually talking to one another. One man twisted to his left, spat on the concrete, and Dengler knew for sure these men were not killers. He abandoned them forever.

The scope moved east again, stopping on the cop and the railroad worker who was wearing a hard hat. They had separated a little now, maybe five feet, and were no longer talking. Dengler observed them for some moments. The separation would be right. The Spotter would keep the Shooter informed of what was happening around the target, because the Shooter would know nothing but what was in the small, circular image of his gunsight. Where was the Lookout? It would be his job to keep the Spotter informed, and to direct people away from the vicinity. Dengler took the sight up, looking into the parking lot behind the fence. Now here was a sweet deal, Dengler considered. The parking lot would provide instant retreat. A waiting car, guns stored in a trunk, destinations in opposite directions. If he were doing this, this parking lot would look very inviting.

There was no one standing in the parking lot.

Then he caught the man in the suit. He'd been lost to the trees behind the picket fence, swallowed by the shadows until an old man, the one Dengler saw earlier, was intercepted by the suited man. They exchanged words; the suited man took out an ID, showed it to the old man and told him, apparently, to move along. *Something wrong here*, Dengler thought. First, no one else was controlling the area. Why would this one agent control this one small part of the area? Then there was the suit. It didn't look right. It didn't fit right. This was a man who normally didn't wear suits. He looked uncomfortable in it.

Dengler jerked the sight back to the fence. The railroad worker had moved again, this time closer in. The cop was doing no policing at all. He was merely looking, waiting.

The assassins.

Dengler cocked a round into the weapon. The rifle hadn't been zeroed for his eye, meaning his personal body tendencies and size hadn't been factored into the adjustment of the sight. It would mean he probably wouldn't be a crack shot with this weapon. He thought, *maybe I won't have to be.* He brought the bead down onto the cop. The cop's brow centered the scope. Dengler lowered it. His neck. Lowered it yet again. Upper chest, lower throat. The bullet would destroy this man. If it went true, the assassin would never speak again, if he were lucky — never breathe again, if he wasn't.

Dengler's finger massaged the grooved trigger. *What if he's a real cop?* The thought played in his mind, repeating itself. What if he were about to kill a real cop? What if this man were as innocent as the man riding in the limo? Dengler guessed the limo was turning left from Houston onto Elm Street now, moving through the blind space directly beneath the Schoolbook Depository before it reappeared again heading for the Stemmons Freeway.

Dengler gave up his bead and drew the sight east again, to the President's limo, which was making the curve that took it directly below the Schoolbook Depository. He took the sight up, floor by floor, searching for Oswald's doppelgänger. Dengler didn't find him. The sniper was waiting until the last minute to expose his position.

Come on, Lee, Dengler pleaded. *Do it. Kill them.*

Dengler imagined what Oswald was doing this exact moment. He'd probably been dispatched to watch the stairwell, or maybe the elevator, and would now be looking at the two men across the room from him, near the window. Oswald would be armed with a hand weapon, one of the 9mm automatics, probably. One of the two men would have the model rifle Dengler now held in his hands, the other assassin a 9mm as well. Oswald could simply attack the two men from the rear, killing them both, and then retreat outside. He could call his chosen contact, Dallas Police Officer J. D. Tippett, the one man he could be sure hadn't been sent to surveil him, and arrange to be *brought in*, after which he would report everything to the Secret Service. Stafford could do nothing then. Stafford would be the fugitive, then.

Come on, Lee, Dengler pleaded. *Do it!*

An instant had transpired. Dengler snapped from this dark reverie and pulled the sight west again toward the police officer. He was gone. The railroad worker was still there, but he was looking down to his right, as if saying something to someone who was out of sight. Dengler knew then. He knew for certain. This was the second kill team.

Dengler assumed a relaxed firing position, getting comfortable, looking for the *sweet spot* that would allow him to shoot clean and sure. The cop stood back up from behind the fence then, holding something oblong in his hand, a rifle that was probably a duplicate of the one now in Dengler's hands.

Dengler's aim took seconds to secure. This wasn't his weapon, the sighting not his. He had to be absolutely sure. The cop brought his rifle up and sought his *own sweet spot*. Dengler's finger gently caressed the serrated trigger.

He heard the noise behind him and knew he wasn't alone.

Dengler ignored the noise. *Doesn't matter*, he told himself. The noise was getting closer. Dengler centered his mind and body on the small, circular image of the cop beside the fence, aiming at his torso just below his neck. He slowly squeezed the trigger. The recoil surprised him. The sound of the explosion matched another sound almost like it, distant and echoing slightly. Two rounds, one on top of the other. Dengler's heart jumped. He was late. He relocated his target. The cop was still aiming, but The Spotter, the railroad worker, was now looking across the great expanse of Dealey Plaza at Dengler. The bullet must have whizzed past them, inches off.

The sound behind Dengler was very close now.

Dengler cocked the weapon again, brought it back to bear. For what seemed like months the image of the cop wavered and steadied, wavered and steadied, in Dengler's sight.

Then Dengler fired an instant after the cop. Dengler regained his target in a tenth of a second. The cop was holding his head, feeling his ear, while the railroad worker was tugging on him, dragging him away from the fence.

Dengler slammed another round into the breach just as what felt like a rope cinched around his neck and yanked him back. Dengler was pulled erect fighting for breath, his hands digging at a belt looped around his neck. Dengler heard himself gag, felt the slap of his hands on unidentified objects as the stranger tightened the cinch. Then, seeking strength from deep within, Dengler snapped his elbows back. They struck flesh. Dengler's attacker didn't react. He heard the man's labored, guttural breathing. Dengler felt his consciousness begin to ebb, slipping from the real world into an almost dream state. Moments passed as the edges of reality softened.

The sound of the explosion startled Dengler. The body of Lookout was thrown back from the open-air window and into shadows. Dengler became aware of the rifle in his hands only as its steel flesh seemed to reemerge from dreamland. He realized he must have reached for it and killed.

Dengler coughed and threw himself back into sunlight. He brought the rifle up, re-aimed, searching for the cop and the railroad worker for seconds within the tight, circular boundary of the scope sight, but they were gone, lost behind the fence, lost under the darkness of the trees, lost.

Dengler spun the sight around and aimed it at the upper floors of the Schoolbook Depository. One window that had been previously closed was open, and vacant.

He pulled the sight down to the Lincoln, which was already accelerating away. Someone, a woman wearing a pink suit, was on the trunk lid trying to gather something up while a Secret Service agent leaped onto the car, spread-eagling across her.

Dengler lowered the rifle.

It was done.

- 85 -

Dengler stumbled out into Dealey Plaza less than two minutes later. He felt as if someone had hit him in the solar plexus. He had trouble breathing.

It was all David Dengler could do, he did all he could, and it wasn't enough.

In his hands was the box Lookout had carried into the nest when Dengler first found him. It was sealed, taped shut. Dengler pulled it open. Inside was a pile of playing cards. Dengler recognized the playing cards immediately. The deck was a cheap brand he'd bought at a truck stop in Louisiana back when he first began surveilling Oswald. The symbol on the back of the cards was a medieval rendering of *Death* riding a bicycle. He'd left the cards at a hotel months before. *Fingerprints*, he realized. *My fingerprints. All over them.*

The second patsy.

Prior to leaving the nest Dengler had wiped every weapon clean. No fingerprints. He turned the box upside down, allowed the cards to flutter to the sidewalk, and then dropped the box.

Dengler stumbled across Houston Street into the Plaza. People were milling about as the police returned from a surge into what would be called *The Grassy Knoll*. Dengler knew it well. He'd fired into it minutes before.

Some of the people were crying. *Why are they crying?* Dengler questioned. *Maybe the President is okay*. Dengler could tell by their expressions, these people knew. They saw more clearly than he what was done to the President. They knew who the woman in the pink suit was, and what she was trying to retrieve from the top of the Lincoln's trunk.

Lee Oswald slipped out the front door of the Texas Schoolbook Depository. The two men met, eye-to-eye, twenty feet from one another, before Oswald averted his eyes, turned and moved away.

Dengler almost went after him, but stopped himself.

It's done.

Dengler found a place on the knoll across from Dealey Plaza, the place where he'd sat the previous day wearing a Stetson, and sat down. There was no energy left in him. He allowed his mind to wander, releasing it from this place and this time. He thought of Marilyn Monroe. The young President entered his thoughts, the speeches he gave, the way he excited people and motivated them to change things, lost now. Eventually he thought of Etta. He'd kept her at arm's distance since the crying incident the day before. After a time his eyes filled with tears.

That night Dengler retrieved his Ford and drove west. He sold the car for cash in Lubbock, then bought a two-year-old Plymouth Fury and drove on into New Mexico, Arizona, and finally into California. He took short naps beside the road instead of stopping at motels, ate at drive-in restaurants, and used gas station restrooms when needed.

As the hours passed into days, and his car radio lost A.M. stations to the east and gained them to the west, he heard about Tippett's murder and Oswald's arrest. He knew somehow Oswald had eluded Stafford's plans, even though his police contact Tippett had been killed and his murder blamed on Oswald. Stafford couldn't take the chance Oswald might confess to the police, Dengler knew. Tippett's murder was inevitable.

As Dengler approached California he heard about Oswald's murder and Jack Ruby's arrest. It was truly done then. Finished. Already the facts were becoming clouded. Soon they would be history.

Outside the small desert town of Needles, California, a man driving an old, green, dented Desoto almost ran Dengler off the road. He passed Dengler's Plymouth at breakneck speed, honking and waving wildly. His car careened off a dirt embankment ahead. He stepped out of the car, leaving its door gaping, and walked back toward Dengler, who was slowly reaching for his Walther PPK. The man reached inside his ill-fitting suit jacket, withdrew a manila envelope and handed it to Dengler. He returned to his car without saying a word and drove back the way he came, dust swirling after.

Dengler opened the envelope. Inside was a photograph of The Director of the Federal Bureau of Investigation, and a friend. A note clipped to the photo read, *'Crazy Gunman Theory' replaced 'Conspiracy Theory' almost immediately. Thought Special Agent Jack Fleming might like to have this.*

Kerschov.

Dengler slipped the photo back into the envelope. *Really*, he mused, *Director Hoover should be more circumspect.*

Dengler rented an apartment in Malibu, made a dozen copies of the photo, secreted them in as many places, and contacted The Director, suggesting Special Agent Jack Fleming might enjoy working out of the L.A. office.

After consultation, The Director agreed, with a stipulation.

To fulfill that stipulation, Dengler flew to Washington D.C. in February and waited for a jogger on the Capitol Mall at 6:15 in the morning. There was a mist in the air, early morning fog caressing trees and bushes. The jogger approached slowly, pacing himself, and Dengler, standing within a copse of trees, spent the moments observing the runner thinking about the weather, and how it reminded him of that night north of Santa Barbara. *Yes, it's very similar, really.*

When the runner approached Dengler stepped into the clear and fired once with his Walther PPK, knocking the man to the ground. A red spot widened across the man's *Washington & Lee University* sweatshirt. The jogger was unarmed, of course, or he would have already put his weapon into action. Dengler walked the ten yards separating them and kneeled.

Stafford's eyes became ovals of fear. His staccato breathing sent puffs of body steam shooting out into the cold morning air. Stafford's eyes reminded him of Marilyn's so many months ago.

"Give my regards to the President," Dengler said, finally.

"No!" Stafford uttered. Dengler placed the barrel of the Walther PPK against the front of Stafford's brow, not far from the area where Kennedy's brain had been expunged from his body, and pulled the trigger.

Red mist.

Later, The Director informed Dengler of the tragic death of Jim Keller and his entire CIA detail in Turkey when their C-47 crashed en route from Greece. Coincidentally, Special Agent Jack Fleming checked into the L.A. office of the FBI the following day. These events reminded Dengler of the conversation he'd had with Stafford in Texas before the assassination. *"Do any of these people know,"* David Dengler had asked, *"they can't be allowed to live afterward? Can't any of them see that?"*

The answer was no.

Daisy moved out to California in April, after she and Dengler exchanged letters, first, then phone calls, and finally weekends. She was estranged from Wes now and divorcing him.

Daisy's love for David was true and deep. She held him when nightmare's fingers caught him. She made love to him and taught him many things. She reminded him the world was full of goodness, too.

Daisy was solace in the night.
For the night was long.

THE END

Printed by Amazon Italia Logistica S.r.l.
Torrazza Piemonte (TO), Italy